RAPTUROUS

RAPTUROUS

A Work of Fiction

Brent Buell

AUTHOR'S NOTE

Rapturous is a work of fiction. I made it up.

But in a nation where we are asked to believe that abortion is murder; where we are asked to believe that drone attacks on civilians abroad is a beneficent gesture to impart American freedom to the survivors; when we are asked to accept that corporations are people; when we are asked to believe that towers in downtown Manhattan were destroyed at the behest of a lone man with bad kidneys sitting in a cave in the Middle East—and that those towers imploded perfectly because of structural weakness; when we are asked to believe that a 747 jet could fly through the Pentagon, the world's most intensely video-protected building, leave no visual record and a hole too small for its fuselage; when we are asked to believe that incarcerating millions is justice; when we are asked to believe that being given the choice of two capitalists for President constitutes democracy; when we are asked to believe that racism is a thing of the past because there is a Black President; when we are asked to believe that the measure of one's social expertise arises from the size of one's bank account; when we are asked to believe that teachers deserve vilification while CEOs deserve deification; when we are asked to believe that the loving God of the Universe is going to take a small number of *Bible* believers to heaven while He tortures the rest of us—it seemed perfectly natural to write this book.

In fact, compared to the whoppers that we're supposed to swallow from the Government and religious leaders, this book hardly seems like fiction at all.

Except, it is fiction. I made it up.

—Brent Buell

DAY ONE

Wednesday

October 30, 2008

CHAPTER 1

"Mom and Dad have been downstairs with those mu'fuckin' born-agains all day praying that *Jesus* will make sure that Tim Michaeljohn wins this election and follows Dubya as the next president of the United Fascist States of America." Eighteen-year old Lyla Edwards played with the ball in her tongue for a moment, moved the cell to her other ear and continued. "They did the same thing in 2004—and back then, frickin' Jesus said, 'yes.'"

"Jesus had nothing to do with it," came the voice at the other end. "Remember the Ohio vote? That election and the one before it—the whole Florida thing and the Supreme Court—nothing supernatural. It was a stolen election, clear and simple."

"True. But they just make me so fuckin' angry."

"You know I agree with you, dear. I just wish you could say it another way without the language. I feel like washing your mouth with soap. You know, 'Michaeljohn' and 'Bush'—that's language I can't tolerate."

Lyla laughed. "Geez, Grandma, you're okay. How did *you* ever end up having my mom?"

"Life is cruel sometimes, honey. But your mom may be okay when she grows up. So will this country. All it needs is some adult supervision. It just hasn't gotten any lately."

"You got that right." Lyla paused. "And Grandma, you're cool with my being an anarchist? I could really get into breaking some corporate windows."

"Don't get yourself killed, and you're fine with me. I'll still go ahead and vote for Obama, because I have no other choice. But never forget what *I* really stand for. Anarchy seems tame compared to what I want."

Lyla loved her Grandma Cattel. Marie Victoria Cattel, 65 years old, retired sociology and community development professor. In the late 90's she took on Mayor Rudolph Giuliani's get tough policing policy and condemned its source, the ultra conservative Manhattan Institute think tank.

She gained notoriety when she labeled the mayor's tactics as "basic fascism," and became vocal at demonstrations protesting the murder of Amadou Diallo by NYPD detectives. She took every opportunity to say that for cops to shoot an unarmed man 41 times while standing in his own doorway was outrageous no matter how cleverly the little mayor tried to spin it. Marie continued her high-profile protests when Giuliani undercover officers shot and killed another unarmed man—Patrick Dorismond—because he wouldn't participate in a drug sting. By the time all the officers in both cases had been found innocent on all charges and had been praised again and again by Giuliani for their heroic work, Marie Cattel was a household name. Photographs of her with Reverend Al Sharpton being dragged off in handcuffs filled tabloid covers. Even the newspaper of record, *The New York Times,* had deigned to quote her scathing rebukes of Giuliani and his "Gestapo," accompanied by a photo of her carrying one of Robert Lederman's satirical drawings of Giuliani as Hitler.

Lyla always asked her grandmother how it was possible that she had spawned her mother, Anna. An active Republican, Anna served as a local campaign director for Giuliani and later worked with equal vigor for the election of George W. Bush. A stay-at-home Staten Island mother, Anna spoke frequently and long about her current candidate's born again religious status, and frequently gushed, "Tim Michaeljohn is such a lovely, Christian gentleman."

This naturally put Anna on a collision course with Marie and Lyla. At the moment, the godly woman was on her knees downstairs in the living room with her husband, Julian Edwards, and three other couples from her church. Whispers of "Yes Jesus, sweet Jesus" escaped her lips. Julian was praying fervently. His face was upturned as he raised his hands above his head in praise.

"As your humble servant, Lord," he said in his rich baritone, "I beg Thee to hear our prayers seven days before the most crucial day in history. We are poised to hasten the blessed coming of your Son or to move disastrously away from it. We come before Thee asking Thy intervention to stop those who foolishly cry 'peace, peace' for we know there will be no peace. Thou hast appointed thy servant Tim Michaeljohn as thy child. He wants to bring about the glorious day, the return of Thy dear son, Jesus!"

On the word "Jesus," there were cries of "Yes Jesus, oh yes, Lord, sweet Jesus," from the seven others kneeling on Anna's new rug from Levitz.

Marked nearly three hundred dollars originally, Anna got it on closeout for $59.95. She called it her Answered Prayer rug.

Julian's voice raised again, "Oh Lord," he began. "Lord, Precious Lord, we know that the coming of Thy Son to take the righteous home can only happen when the fullness of days has come. Only when Thy prophecies have been fulfilled can our Savior take us home."

There was another round of "Hallelujahs" and "Yes Lord."

"Armageddon, Armageddon, Armageddon!" Julian shouted the word like it was the name of his favorite football team. "Blessed Lord, Thy servant Tim Michaeljohn is not afraid of Armageddon! He will not shrink from the fulfillment of Thy word. He is ready for Thy Final War. Thou hast given this country, these precious United States, the power of weapons that can be used in Thy behalf to destroy those who would attack our Christian way of life. Thou hast given us the power to turn to ash them that worship false gods and who are so full of Allah this and Allah that."

Thinking himself clever, Julian gave what he called a "holy laugh"—sort of "Ah-Ha-Ha!" He'd used that laugh several times in church when delivering the main prayer and even gotten praise from a number of parishioners who marveled that he was so comfortable in his relationship with the Lord that he was able to laugh in His presence.

Anna poked him with her elbow when he began the second laugh for effect.

"Lord, touch the fingers of those using the Diebold voting machines next week. Point those fingers in the right direction. Place them on the column, which holds the name of Thy servant Tim Michaeljohn. And should those fingers be willful, should those fingers stray from the tender guidance of Thy hand… then Lord take ahold of those microchips and confound Thine enemies! Let the Democrats, the Independents, the Greens, the Communists, the Socialists and those godless New World Order Progressive Reformers feel Thy power. Let them watch Thee turn their votes from Satanic liberal votes into pure conservative Republican votes for Tim Michaeljohn, the chosen successor to Thy servant George W. Bush!"

In that moment of ecstasy and devotion, Julian outstretched his arms to embrace the ruler of the universe and then was silent.

* * * *

"Bye Grandma," Lyla said, and hung up the phone. There was a welcome quiet in the house. She listened for a moment at her door to make sure the prayer circle had disbanded. Hearing nothing she figured it was safe to go to the kitchen for a snack. She would later remember humming "Sympathy for the Devil," on the stairs just before blurting, "Holy Shit!"

CHAPTER 2

The police had Grandma Cattel cornered on one side of the room and Lyla on the other.

"I was on the phone with my granddaughter right before she hung up and went downstairs. It wasn't more than five minutes before she called to tell me about *this*."

Lyla, tired of her inquisitor's disbelief, repeated her story slowly in less difficult words hoping someone would comprehend. "I hung up the phone from talking to Grandma. The house was quiet, so I came downstairs to get some food in the kitchen. Are you with me so far?"

"Don't get smart. Just tell your story." Detective Darcy O'Neil was twenty-seven years on the job and certain no new case could be more than a rearrangement of old ones.

"So I'm about *there* on the stairs," she gestured to the midpoint of the stairway, "when I look down here where they had been kneeling and praying all day… and at first I just thought they had gone, but then I saw those." She gestured again.

"We're taking this down lady, describe what you saw."

"*Those!* Eight wedding rings, four dresses, four men's shirts and expand-a-pants, eight pairs of shoes, and *those*, uh, all that… underwear."

"And where were they—the clothes—how were they situated?" O'Neil pretended to take notes.

"Just the way they are now, in a circle—a man's clothes, then a woman's—right around the circle. Mom's clothes are right there next to Dad's—and their wedding rings are with them. Is this fuckin' weird or what?"

"You don't need to curse, young lady."

"Well what would you do if your crazy-assed parents had been praying all day that Tim Michaeljohn would become our next president—strike that—*THEIR* next president, and then you frickin' come down the stairs and all they've left you are some sorry assed clothes and some tighty whities?"

"And where do you think they have gone?"

"I dunno, a nudist colony?"

"Don't get smart," the cop was tiring of his pierced witness.

"Then don't ask stupid questions. How should I know where they went? My parents didn't go outside naked. Hell, since they got into that born again shit, I don't think they even *showered* naked."

Marie was straining to hear what Lyla was being asked. "For heaven's sake," she said to the cop standing in front of her. "Get out of my way. My granddaughter has just lost her parents—or whatever has happened— and they are badgering her." She stood, pushed past the officer and tapped O'Neil on the shoulder, "Excuse me young man," she said. "I think my granddaughter has been through quite enough for one day."

The burly detective was about to speak when his cell rang. "One minute," he said, raising a finger to Marie in the universal "I've got a call" sign.

Marie had just put her arm around Lyla when O'Neil snapped, "Turn on your TV."

"Dad got rid of the TV down here," Lyla said—her anger at her missing father evident in her tone. "He got rid of mine, the one in the great room, the one in mom's bedroom, and the one in the kitchen. The only one left is the one in his bedroom where he watched the *144,000 Club* and shit like that."

"Then let's go there." Signaling an officer to finish photographing the circle of clothes, O'Neil followed Marie and Lyla upstairs.

"This is my father's cell," Lyla said, pushing the door open. Julian Edward's bedroom had been the small guest room until the day nine years before when he and Marie had agreed that sexual relations after the possibil- ity of conception were tantamount to fornication. The decision gave each of them a sense of righteousness, even though they were equally aware that very little was begin given up. Julian moved his clothes, religious books, television and overstuffed Berkline recliner into the room. He bought heavy drapes which obscured all light, and that done, declared the room home.

"He spent most of his time in here—and in his bathroom," Lyla said, adding, "You don't want to go in there unless you want to read *Bible* verses printed on toilet paper."

O'Neil was fumbling with the TV remote.

"How do you get it on CNN?" he was evidently frustrated.

"He's got it blocked. You can only watch CBN on there."

"CBN?"

Lyla sighed. "Yeah, Christ's Broadcasting Network. Twenty-four hours a day of preaching to the choir. You know, Robinson Patrick…"

"The guy who was calling for assassinations of foreign presidents?"

"That one."

The TV flickered on. A special news bulletin splashed across the lower third of the screen. Above it three very white Christians with good hair—two men and a woman—sat on an expensive couch in an elaborate living room set. Their eyes were squeezed shut so tightly that even the woman's surgically stretched skin had wrinkles.

"Oh Lord," the man ossified with Aqua Net prayed, "Oh Lord, is this the sign we have waited for? Is this the outpouring of the Holy Spirit? Is this the coming of the thief in the night?"

Apparently the man's musings were interrupted by a message through his earpiece. "Oh, we have to cut away for a moment; we have a news feed from City Hall. Mayor Ari Barken is speaking."

"We will track down and kill every one of these terrorists," the diminutive mayor shouted. "We'll show them that you kidnap New Yorkers at your own risk!"

The news feed ended abruptly and the man with the pretty hair thumped the very comfy couch he was sitting on. "There!" he said, emphasizing the word again with another thump, "you see? The mayor of New York who is of a different persuasion than we—he is unprepared to see the meaning of what is happening because he is not rooted in *The Word*!"

"Who's that nut?" O'Neil demanded. "And what's he talking about?"

"That's Robinson Butthole Patrick," Lyla said, "and I don't have a clue."

A news crawl began right to left at the bottom of the screen: *Rash of disappearances reported in neighborhoods on Staten Island, NY. Police baffled, but Evangelical Christians prepared to rejoice.*

"What the . . ?" It was O'Neil. "What are they . . ?"

"Good Lord." A horrified Marie looked like she'd just seen Dick Cheney. O'Neil turned to her.

"I think I know what they're talking about." She pointed at the screen. "If there are other people missing in the same way as Julian and Anna—these people aren't thinking crime, they're thinking it's The Rapture."

"The what?"

"The Rapture, the Secret Rapture. It's a thing with some born-again Christians who say that at the end of time, right before the so-called 'Time of Trouble,' Jesus their Christ is going to come like a 'thief in the night' and take the righteous to heaven. They're expecting millions of their kind just to disappear—poof."

O'Neil looked at Lyla, prepared to ask if her grandmother was crazy.

Lyla shook her head. "Naw, no shit. Grandma's right. That's what my parents believed. They talked about it all the time. They had this whole set of books—didn't you hear about them on *60 Minutes*—called the *Left Behind* series? Two guys—terrible writers—and they sold like 100 million copies of that shit."

Reverend Robinson Patrick was working himself into a sweat. "It's the righteous born aloft. Hallelujah!"

The news crawl continued. An estimated 100 people had simply vanished. Four car wrecks were reported. At each wreck, the police found nothing but the personal items of the disappeared. Along with clothes and jewelry, several weapons had been found—a Brazos Pro sX, a Ceska Zbrojovka 75B, several Glock 17's, and two AK 47's. God's special children apparently had a taste for exotic weaponry.

O'Neil was back on his cellphone. "Listen, Captain, I've got eight more missing here. Exactly like the others. Religious nuts, y'know. You watching CBN?" There was a short pause. "CBN—you know, Christ's Broadcasting Network?" Another pause. "No, I'm not watching MSNBC or CNN or ABC or CBS or NBC or FOX. I'm watching CBN." Another pause. "Because it's the only fucking channel that this nut case allows on his TV—that's why."

A closeup of a second man with purple-rinsed hair filled the screen. O'Neil signaled Lyla to turn up the volume.

"Thou hast heard our cry, oh Lord God," the man said, tears very effectively streaking his cheeks. "But we ache to know Thy will, Thy plan. Answer us, oh Savior, oh Lord, oh Ruler of the Universe."

Lyla rolled her eyes. "Grandma, this is fuckin' weird. Julian and Anna weren't raptured anywhere. That's for sure. But where'd they go?"

It seemed the people on TV had the same question. Prayers finished, they began a roundtable discussion.

The Reverend Robinson Patrick, who sounded like a deputy sheriff from Alabama, was perplexed. "If this is the Rapture that we have so longed for, then *why* is it happenin' only there on Staten Island, New York? Why are we, who have so anticipated being with our Lord and Savior still sittin' here in a television studio? I wish that all you were seein' on the screen was three sets of clothes and Pearl Millicent's jewelry."

The woman with the stretched face smiled politely at the mention of her name and somewhat distractedly pawed at her considerable assemblage of rhinestones.

O'Neil snapped his cellphone shut with a whispered curse. "Damn if I know what's going on. NYPD is all over this. They've got Homeland Security coming in to see if this is some terrorist operation. Seems one of the things the Pentagon has been sitting on is an ultrasonic device that can vaporize people. Now they're worried it got into the wrong hands."

The surgically enhanced woman on TV, identified onscreen as *Reverend* Pearl Millicent, was addressing the issue. "Aren't all us righteous supposed to be taken at once? I just can't imagine that the only righteous people on the face of this earth are on Staten Island. I haven't even *been* there!"

"Had enough?" Lyla looked at O'Neil wearily.

"Yeah. Let's go back downstairs to the crime scene."

"Crime scene?" Marie made a face. "From the way my daughter and son-in-law have been acting, I wouldn't be surprised if this is some kind of elaborate hoax—all part of them 'witnessing' their faith or something. I don't think you should go calling it a crime until you come up with some bodies. My guess is that butt naked or not, they're going to come home after a few days and tell us that they were waiting on some mountaintop for Jesus, and that he stood them up. Want some coffee?"

Moments after the three left the room, "Breaking News" flashed across the screen. The governor of Texas was missing.

DAY TWO

Thursday

October 31, 2008

CHAPTER 3

Governor Duke Wexler always wore a Smith and Wesson .38 in a shoulder holster. During his election campaign he'd said it was a sign that he was going to return Texas to its glory days. In some people's minds he'd kept his promise, already executing more prisoners in Huntsville during his first year than his predecessor G. Dubya Bush.

A hard drinking man, Wexler had just been served a double Jack Daniels straight up when he vanished. Along with his BVD's, fringe-trimmed designer suit and cowboy boots—his six-shooter, holster and a *Bible* were all that was left behind.

According to CNN, the bartender, Bobby Ray Hatchett, was arrested by local sheriffs and held on suspicion of murder. The Sheriff, Billy Buck Worley, a connoisseur of pulp fiction, conjectured that after the murder, Hatchett, who weighed nearly four hundred pounds, had consumed the body. The handcuffed bartender was rushed to the nearest hospital for X-rays and stomach pumping.

The story headlined national media and dominated local news. It was repeating while Duke's wife Daisy-Ann had her make up applied for a TV interview.

"Go easy, honey," she said, "I'm a grievin' *maybe* widow and I don't wanna look like I'm gettin' ready to go out dancin'. Be a doll and get my hair a little higher… praise the Lord, I'm not gonna be wearin' no little black hat."

In the background, technicians readied lighting equipment. Although local stations flocked to the governor's mansion anticipating a statement by the widow, Daisy-Ann stayed inside, preferring to grant an exclusive to Babs Waller of *40/40*. Waller, famous for landing high-profile interviews, called Daisy-Ann's office three minutes after the disappearance story broke and said, "Don't talk to anyone else." She flew to San Antonio on a chartered jet and simply announced her arrival. Now she was conferring with her cameraman about flattering angles.

When the interview began, Daisy-Ann looked the part of a grieving widow. Her usual fever blue eyeshadow was now a muted brown, her arched, pencil-thin eyebrows now soft and feathered. Only her hair—once complimented by Dolly Parton—retained its steel-like rigidity.

"I am here in San Antonio with the first lady of Texas, Mrs. Duke Wexler," Babs Waller began, "honored that she has granted me the first exclusive interview about her husband's tragic disappearance."

"Please call me Daisy-Ann," the first lady responded, sounding like a harsh imitation of Laura Bush. "Ah cain't tell you what a comfort it is to me that ah can be here in ma house—*our* house, Duke's and mine's—and tawk to y'all." She blotted her left eye gently with a hanky. The move, which gave the impression that she was removing tears, was actually prompted by a pesky chunk of mascara dangling from an eyelash.

Babs leaned forward. "I can tell you that in this moment of sorrow, the entire nation is consumed with a vast sympathy for you."

"Really? How very sweet of y'all."

"Can we just speak candidly, woman to woman?"

"You betcha."

"Now Daisy-Ann, I have to ask you, what do you think really has happened to your husband?"

Daisy-Ann was tempted to speak honestly. "Babs, that son of a bitch has taken off with one of the little whores he's been bangin' behind my back. I think he's in cahoots with the bartender down there who's one of the people who makes sure my no-good husband always has a ready supply of Tex-ass pussy. But I have to admit that I'm glad their little plan backfired and that the liquor slinger is in jail. I'd be sittin' here ballin' my eyes out for Duke if I wasn't so glad to get rid of him."

But honesty was not always, in Daisy-Ann's estimation, the best policy. And in this case it *definitely* was not the best policy because she already planned to run for her husband's vacant seat. Texas had a long history of elevating crusty ladies to high office, and now it was time to prove that neither alcohol, poor taste, nor scandal would stand in her way. After all, Laura Bush had risen to power after rolling her car over her boyfriend. To the best of her recollection, Daisy-Ann at least had never actually *killed* anybody.

"Babs, ah'm so glad that you asked me that very question." She stopped, because for a moment she couldn't remember what the question was. "Ah believe yew want to know how ah feel."

Waller looked down at her notes. The interview would be edited—thank God it wasn't live. Rumors had swirled for years that the erratic public behavior often exhibited by the Duke was because of his fondness for cocaine. When asked about it by reporters, Duke would always smile and say, "Hold on fellas, I think you've got me confused with a *former* governor of Texas." And he would laugh and flash all 32 of his teeth at the cameras. Now Babs was wondering what had gone up the nostrils of Duke's wife.

Waller tried to bring the interview back on subject. "Of course I want to know what you feel, Daisy-Ann, but what I was asking…"

"Well ah am just heart-broken. Can you imagine? Ah've been with that man—that *same* man—for something like 36 years! Ah have cooked for him, warshed those clothes he wears—includin' the BVD's they found in the bar there. Ah've born him three beautiful children—all of whom would have been here tonight to comfort me if they weren't off on various vacations. Ah feel like somethin' has been ripped right from my bosom, my *bosom*."

Since Daisy-Ann considered the referenced area of her anatomy one of the top reasons she would be elected to replace her husband, she thought it best to mention *them* as an *it*. Had she not been in grief mode, she would have referred to the singular bosom as the plural, "my titties." But overcome as she was, decorum was in order.

"How can one evah describe what they feel when they have lawst the love of their ly-if?"

Here Daisy-Ann stopped long enough for Babs to intervene and try to salvage the raw meat of the interview.

"Daisy-Ann, I know your heart is breaking. The whole world is seeing it right now on their television screens—as you know *40/40* has been the highest rated nighttime network show for the last 32 weeks—and we are with you, *we are with you*." She reached out and grabbed Daisy-Ann's forearm with such graceful vengeance that viewers assumed it was a merciful show of support. It wasn't. Babs was determined that the most important question on her list was going to be answered, answered clearly, and if it took pain to keep her interviewee on subject, so be it.

"Ow," the first lady grimaced.

"I know, I know," Babs spoke through clenched teeth, "You are in such pain. But before we say another word…"

Daisy-Ann looked like she was about to speak so Babs applied even more pressure before she continued. "Let me ask you the question that America wants me to ask you: *What do you think really has happened to your husband?*"

Had God himself been on the receiving end of Babs' pain-assisted questioning, *He* couldn't have refused to answer.

Now sporting real tears, Daisy-Ann became clear headed and lost some of her southern accent. She pried her arm free and began to speak. "Ah think there are two possibilities," she said, circling her right hand around the throbbing area of her left arm. "I think it may be true that ma dear husband was mercilessly cut down by a very odd man. Maybe he had some perversion or other that drove him to undress my husband and eat him *after* he killed him. I *hope* it was after he killed him anyway. I have to believe it, 'cause Billy Buck said it was one of the possibilities. But!" She used the word like the pointed end of a crowbar, "there is another possibility."

Babs put on her listening face and made sure that camera two was catching it close up. "Well, go on dear," she said.

"You know my husband was a godly man," Daisy-Ann began. "Ah've seen him studyin' his *Bible*, readin' the scriptures, and lookin' for God's guidance as he walked this path called life."

"Thou shalt not lie." The voice was quite impressive, quite loud, and apparently inside Daisy-Ann's head.

"Go on dear," Babs prodded.

"Oh, uh," the first lady struggled to regain her composure. "I was saying that my husband literally walked with God. Yes he did. He did. He did. He wanted to do God's will. He wanted God's guiding hand to lead him. Do you know what? More than once I saw him just thumbin' through a lot of papers for more than fifteen minutes before he put his signature on 'em. Fifteen minutes without a break! That's how much time he was givin' God the chance to speak directly to him and tell him what to do."

Babs did her head tip, eye blink, mouth curl and then said, "My! And what were these papers over which he struggled for such a long time seeking God's divine guidance?"

"Oh, death orders—y'know the execution thing. Duke once told me that every time he signed one of those things—and he never ever *didn't* sign 'em—that God just whispered to him in this real deep voice, 'That nigger'—oh, can I say that on TV? Well, you just cut it out if it's one of those little words that's a no, no. God would say, 'That nigger is guilty as sin.' Apparently God said that even the time the criminal was white, 'cause Duke just signed those things and then slept like a baby. Isn't it wonderful the peace that comes from walkin' with the Lord God Jesus Christ, the Almighty Savior of the World?"

"Cut!" Marty Devine, Babs' director called. "John is having a coughing fit. Let's take a break for five until he calms down."

John Solomon the cameraman had filmed people talking in behalf of capital punishment many times and although he was a fierce opponent, he had never gotten apoplectic.

The director approached him. "John, John, don't be so sensitive. We all know that you're a *good* African American. It's not like she was referring to you or something. Don't be so sensitive."

Marty returned moments later—rather red—and announced that the interview would resume with a different cameraman. John Solomon had tendered his resignation upon learning that the director thought Daisy-Ann was a "card" and that the interview was a "slam-dunk."

"Now Daisy-Ann," Babs was back at it slightly ruffled, "perhaps you'll tell us *what do you think happened to your husband?*"

"Well, I have been thinkin' about that a lot—dealin' with my grief and all—and just while I was waitin' to talk to you I heard on the radio that somethin' like this is happenin' in Staten Island, New York! Staten Island is Republican, so it could be happenin' there. Well, since Duke was so godly I think it's possible that this is the Rapture. I mean we have been learnin' about it in scripture all our lives as we sit in church every Sunday."

In reality, Daisy-Ann hadn't been to a church in a very long while, but she had caught many hours of Christ's Broadcasting Network while she was having her nails done by Wing Yee, a devoted Chinese Baptist.

The first lady was prepared to give far more detail about her husband and her supposition when the director yelled "Cut" again. He came and whispered in Babs Waller's ear and then retreated into the darkness behind the lights.

"You'll have to excuse me, Daisy-Ann. I thank you for your time and your insight, but I have to leave immediately for Denver. It seems that Reverend Teddy Dobbin and his entire Jesus Dome staff have disappeared."

CHAPTER 4

Reverend Teddy Dobbin was America's publishing sensation. His inspirational book, *The Goal Guided Life,* had sold nearly 80 million copies in hardback. Whatever critics might say about Dobbin's literary abilities, there was no arguing with his success. Gray haired ladies and Rodeo Drive jet setters alike were carrying the volume in their purses. Men's *Bible* study groups were devoted to discussing the book chapter by chapter. It was rumored in the press that at least one murder was prevented when a prostitute read the book to a man who was threatening to kill her rather than pay her.

Dobbin headquarters was the 40,000 seat Jesus Dome in Denver—a former indoor football stadium transformed into the world's largest church. His congregation poured $375 million into the sanctified project, which included the "Savior's Mall" featuring retailers like "No-Gap (Between Christ 'n Me) Jeans," and "Wall of the Heavenly CityMart." There was a "John the Baptist Water Park," "Bowling for Jesus" family recreation center, "Heaven Bound Hamburgers," and a fitness center called "The Temple of God." The Dome boasted its own cantilevered heliport. Critics were appalled by Dobbin's sheer commercialization of religion, but the faithful trumpeted exploding profits as a sign of God's blessing.

Dobbin was credited with creating a smiling, happy Jesus. He was unperturbed by cartoons showing him rubbing the stomach of a "fat, laughing Jesus." When more avuncular preachers railed against him from their pulpits, Dobbin would summon his biggest smile—the one that showed his sparkling teeth, highlighted his eyes and somehow drew attention to his carefully arranged dark locks of gently curling hair on his forehead and say, "Praise Jesus for that. He is my rock, He is my shield, and I rejoice in Him."

His willingness to smile through any attack infuriated his opponents and transported his followers with bliss.

"He is Jesus' vessel," was a phrase frequently heard from passionate followers and often repeated by Dobbin himself.

His was not an overnight success. Before turning to religion, Dobbin had narrowly escaped indictment on fraud charges after the bankruptcy of his fledgling fast food franchise operation. Proclaiming exoneration and epiphany, Dobbin became a self-ordained preacher. There had been several failed attempts at establishing congregations based on Dobbin's unique vision of Christianity as a deified financial project—with heaven being the payoff for faithful investors. It was during that period of monetary struggle that Dobbin penned *The Goal Guided Life,* which at first achieved negligible sales.

It was not until Reverend Robinson Patrick invited Dobbin to appear with Reverend Tommy Piersen on his nationally televised *144,000 Club* that Dobbin established himself fully and became what many derisively called the "Sam Walton of preachers."

The stated purpose of the broadcast was to kick off the 40-city continental Tommy Piersen Christian Crusade. Piersen, the 80-year-old king of American evangelism was, in Dobbin's mind, an unwelcome rival in the struggle to procure born again Christian dollars. God's Old Giant, as he was affectionately known, had just announced that the theme of his revival services would be "God's Fury Unleashed," an apocalyptic series on sin, terrorists, and the American way of life.

Although Dobbin privately hated Piersen, he saw Piersen's upcoming crusade as a possible chance to ride his rival's coattails to great heights. Dobbin's was a gentler, more pleasing message, and in meetings with his advisers he had come to the opinion that he might be able to influence Piersen to invite him along on the tour speaking about *The Goal Guided Life*. Early in the broadcast, he held up his book, referring to its title while avoiding the appearance of hawking sales.

"My friends in Jesus," he began, stopping long enough to flash a wide smile while slowly batting his eyes, *The Goal Guided Life* happens to be the title of my new book from Sanctification Press. In it you will find that no matter how difficult your situation, no matter how stingy your boss or how long you've been unemployed, Jesus has dollars stored up just for you. All He is asking is that you step out in faith, place what you have in His hands, and let him do the investing for you." He had the foresight not to mention his current *Heavenly Homes* pyramid fundraising venture, which was under investigation by federal authorities.

"Praise God," Piersen responded, sensing a chance to segue to an offering appeal. "Praise His blessed name. Yes, praise It. You raise a crucial point my brother," he said, stroking his pompadour as though it might have moved. "Your book can guide millions into a closer walk with the Almighty through your profound three-point program for sanctification: '1) grasp the faith of old; 2) accept God's plan for you; and 3) carry the sword of justice.' Profound, profound indeed."

Off the record, Piersen dubbed Dobbin's book "Ponzi Protestantism," but now he furrowed his brow and repeated a third time, "Profound." Once again he paused, seeming to search for a heavenly teleprompter. "Your message has great merit, my brother. And yet, I am going to have to abide by the dictates of God's Spirit as it weighs upon me. I have been instructed," and here a cynic could have discerned a note of smugness, "by *God Himself*, that I must begin my national 'God's Fury Unleashed,' 40-city crusade on the subject of the sanctity of life."

At this point, the Piersen Crusaders broke into applause and Dobbin, who knew the American people just wanted to feel good while being told they could get rich, looked a little nervous.

When the applause died down, Piersen grasped his podium with both hands, glared into the camera and screamed, "God hates baby killers! He hates the doctors who destroy human life, and he hates the fallen women who willfully bring the little lambs to the slaughterhouse. I have spent years fighting this country's immoral laws born of Sodom and Gomorrah that were instituted by shameless liberals rather than by God's word! And the Lord Jesus Christ has layed it upon my heart to deliver this as the opening message of my crusade. Each night I will attack a different sin—abortion, homosexuality, and socialism—to impress upon the heart of America that God loves each an every soul that accepts Him through His son Jesus, but He HATES sinners."

Dobbin was stunned by Piersen's bad marketing. Hatred of sinners never filled pews. Dobbin condemned the same issues Piersen had mentioned, but he did it with a smile and an assurance that God was smiling too. He might be a struggling preacher, but his methods were paying off. His nascent church was growing. He realized that a rebuke from Piersen on national television could be the kiss of death—or an opportunity.

"My brother," Dobbin began, "let us pray together on this matter."

"I have prayed," Piersen countered.

"Jesus wants us to talk to Him. I can't believe that He wants to turn away any of his children or that hatred ever enters His heart. He *loves* sinners…"

Piersen interrupted. "GOD *hates* sinners. He smites them. He burns them. He eviscerates them. He is going to wipe them from the face of the earth through His holiness, which the wicked will not be able to stand."

Armed with his own sword of faith, Dobbin parried, "It is through Christ's sacrifice alone, His wonderful sacrifice on the cross, that we are going to be ushered into earthly prosperity, happiness, and be welcomed into His eternal kingdom, his heavenly home. Can I get an amen?" Dobbin was emboldened when the studio audience yelled, "Amen!"

"Armageddon," Piersen was more intense, "Armageddon will separate the putrid, sex-crazed deviants from those compliant with God's divinity. The power of the atom will be unleashed on their perverted souls and they will be cast into utter darkness."

Dobbin scanned the live audience. Piersen's message clearly terrified them. Besides, Piersen had steered the subject away from Dobbin's book and was using scare tactics that current research showed was a contributing factor in lower tithing rates. It was time to thrust a sword through his opponent's vital organs. He was certain that Christ, with the assistance of a discrete private detective, had prepared him for this moment.

"I am reminded," he began in his most charming, utterly defenseless tone, "of a morning two years ago when a young man—a sinful young man came into my office. He was sick, penniless and remorseful. For several tearful hours he poured forth the story of his life—a life ravaged by Satan's allures: drugs, alcohol, and sexual excess. His honesty was extreme. And I praise God that I was able to assure him of the forgiving nature of Jesus, and to tell him to put aside his memories of the negative past and just sing and smile in the happiness of sure financial future."

"My crusade will address the sins you have mentioned and ROOT THEM OUT!" Piersen shouted.

"That may be," Dobbin continued, "but the young man's tale was so heartfelt, so detailed, that the spirit of the Lord has impressed upon me that I must share it with our viewers. You see," and here he lowered his eyes and gave his head a grave shake before continuing, "this young man had been *selling his body* in order to survive. How terrible a burden that must have been for him to carry." Dobbin, head still down looked slyly up at Piersen, who at the moment, seemed unsuspecting that he was facing a turning point in his life.

"He repeated over and over to me that he hated Jesus. *Hated* Him. And yet I assured him again and again that his hatred was met with nothing but a smile and love and an offer of the life abundant. After several hours—hours filled with such grief that his entire body was shaking—this young man confessed that his professed hatred arose from the fact that his downfall in life, his first step into a degraded life came when a famous preacher…"

Piersen was no longer unsuspecting. He looked as though sin—that big chunk of iniquity he so loved to point at *over there*—had just clomped squarely on his head. When he began making strange guttural sounds, Reverend Robinson Patrick quickly announced that the *144,000 Club* was going to take a short commercial break—this, despite the fact that the show had no sponsors.

Piersen's tour was cancelled, but not before he made an impassioned confession on live television, and with tears streaming down his face intoned again and again, "I have sinned, I have sinned the sin of Sodom." Like the God of Piersen's sermons, thousands of faithful viewers were outraged and withdrew their financial support. Piersen made an attempt at a comeback endorsing a retail store/church franchise business called "Holy Malls." But when a cartoonist dubbed them "Homo Malls," depicting the esteemed preacher in the doorway beckoning a Little League team to come and "shop," the enterprise quickly failed.

Dobbin, on the other hand, acted the compassionate, forgiving role, ever pointing to the fact that—as said in his book—one must look, not to the negative agonies of the past, but rejoice in the irrepressible joy that God provides his children every day. Within a week his book hit the *New York Times* bestseller list and remained there for over three years. Despite accusations from the Piersen camp that Dobbin had knowingly destroyed their leader, Dobbin maintained that he had no knowledge that the fornicating preacher was Piersen, and that he was simply illustrating God's mercy to the best of his ability. And a remarkable ability it was. Within a month after the Piersen confrontation, Dobbin's private detective retired to a large home in Miami. The Jesus Dome, the Savior's Mall, and "Jesus Wants You in Real Estate" seminars followed shortly after.

Dobbin shrewdly positioned himself politically. His ability to influence votes was not lost on Washington. When the Supreme Court placed G.W. Bush in office, the new President received an effusive letter of introduction to Dobbin from none other than Judge Clarence Thomas. Soon Dobbin began what would become weekly visits with the Commander in Chief. On Sundays, a large cardboard cutout of George Bush commanded a spot on the Jesus Dome stage—and Dobbin encouraged members of the audience to come up and put their "hands of blessing" on *God's President.* This ritual reached a fever pitch when Dobbin threw his considerable influence behind a new Bush wedge issue: the criminalization of unwed motherhood.

Karl Rove hit upon the idea almost as a joke during a cabinet meeting where Cheney was bellyaching about the fact that there "weren't enough wedges between our people and theirs." There were guffaws over the suggestion, but the laughter faded when Condoleeza Rice extolled the idea as "brilliant" and explained how easily the prosecution phase would be. "We simply threaten the permanent removal of the baby to a state facility," she said in her demure executioner's manner. "Those mothers will cave. They'll gladly take a felony conviction if their sentence is reduced to six months and they get to keep the kid. It's win-win. Ninety percent of them are Democrats so we get them off the voting lists for life, and we'll probably foster a black market marriage-for-hire business, which can be criminalized and prosecuted later. Like I said, it's win-win in my book."

George loved the idea, proclaiming it a "10 to 1 advantage" in favor of his white constituents. "They've got the money to take care of their little 'problems' before it ever gets to the criminal stage."

Cheney, smirking as he spoke said, "But we've nearly made abortion illegal, George. I mean, for *those people*, not ours."

With that catch-22 clarified, the idea passed unanimously, even though everyone knew one more Supreme Court justice would have to die and be replaced with an obedient hack for it to become the law of the land.

The Reverend Teddy Dobbin, lover of the gentle Jesus, found the draconian idea delightful. "I can preach on the goodness of that one forever," he told his writing staff the morning after the President called to tell him the new idea. "I can preach and the coffers will jing, jing, jingle. I'll put a smiley face on it, of course, but I can get way out in front on this one."

So it was in just such a climate, a month before the disappearances, that Dobbin was sitting with the President in the Oval Office. He had offered a fervent prayer for God's guidance as the President weighed one of the most pressing issues he had ever initiated: the ending of inheritance taxes for the nation's ultra-rich.

"Oh Lord," Dobbin intoned with his familiar dose of perky enthusiasm, "we know you love those you have blessed with your riches. We now ask that you will guide the Congress of these United States—your beloved country—to follow the lead of your divinely appointed ruler, uh, leader who wants to end the highway robbery going on in the name of death taxation. In your Son's Holy name. Amen."

Neither Dobbin nor Bush had kneeled. Each of them thought it demeaning to their station in life, so they simply sat in two chairs, legs sprawled, as they "talked with God."

"Now Teddy Boy," George began before the "Amen" had reached the far wall, "there's another issha I wanna talk to you 'bout."

"Of course, brother."

"Ah truly believe that we're livin' in the very end of time. Ah believe that the Lord Jesus Christ is about to return with power and great glory."

"Hallelujah, brother, you have interpreted scripture correctly."

"But Brother Dobbin," George looked like he was thinking, "Ah'm troubled by somethin'. Ah jest don't think that we're gonna be able to make every person in the world accept the Lawrd Jesus Christ. Ah mean you've got all those Jews, a whole bunch of them Buddistish people, those Moslem/Muslim whatever people—most of 'em terrorists… and I've been thinking…"

"You are the Lord's servant, brother."

"Yes, I know," George sounded a little annoyed at the interruption. "Well, we're never gonna corral all these people into the blessed faith of our Lord—not even reach 'em all with the message. So where does that leave us? I'm not much interested in jus' doin' all the things a President has got to do, and I sure as heck don't want to do the things that an ex-Pres gets stuck with. Can you see me cutting the ribbon at a library or feedin' poor kids? I mean… *bor-ing*."

Taking his cue from the last interruption, Dobbin just nodded his head and furrowed his brow.

"So Teddy Boy, here's what I think. I know that somewhere there in the scriptures it says that there's gotta be a war, a final war, the war of Armagideon or something…"

"Armageddon, Mr. Bush."

"Whatever. I jest think that the thing for us to do is to kinda hurry that up a little. I thought we had it taken care of back in 2006 when we had it look like the Lebanish people had attacked the Jews. I was pushin' for blamin' it all on the Iran folk—but oh no, that fella there in Russia he just wasn't havin' it and calmed the whole thing down. And where does all the peace, peace and negotiate stuff leave us? Well it leaves us right here where we are with no lovin' Jesus in no clouds. So seems to me we've gotta do somethin' really big to jes' goose everbody up and get 'em fightin' and blowin' things up, and then Jesus can come back in power and great glory. Did Ah get that right?"

"Amen, brother," Dobbin said, thinking privately that the chief exccutive was crazier than any Kennedy had ever implied.

"Do ya think we can do it? I've got all 'em nukulars jest waitin', doin' absolutely nothin', so why not pop a few off and see what happens? I'd just need you to soften up the Americun people so's they'd like the idea."

"I'll have to pray on that, George."

"You'll have FOX network on your side."

"I figured that. But still, you're asking a lot."

"I can give you a whole lotta power."

Dobbin bowed his head and wiggled his lips in mock prayer. He was far from talking to God; he was making quick calculations in his head. He knew the stakes were high. The afterlife was not a proven entity and Dobbin generally liked banking on the bankable. He saw the move as sacrificial since Armageddon could cost him the bulk of the earthly blessings the Lord had bestowed on him. If Armageddon should begin, the Jesus Dome and the Teddy Dobbin Christian Crusade would never realize their full financial glory. On the other hand it was an opportunity to extract every pound of flesh he could in exchange for his loyalty. If his mortal kingdom was to be cut short, he would at least make sure that whatever time he had was guaranteed to be extremely comfortable. What was bankable was the promise of almost unimaginable power. Ka-Ching!

"Amen," he whispered, raising his head and looking directly into the eyes of the waiting President. "I'll do it."

While Dubya worked in secret, it was Dobbin's job to act in public and make Armageddon seem user friendly.

The morning of his disappearance, Dobbin called his "flock" together for prayer. The flock included some 1,400 minimum wage employees who worked at the Jesus Dome, none of whom received benefits. "Benefits would be like stealing directly from the Lord to take extras that you don't earn," Dobbin wrote in the employee manual, "—extras that show you lack faith in the Lord. For instance, health insurance is a way of telling God that you doubt His goodness and His personal love for you. Pensions are a way of telling God you think He will abandon you just because you are old, just as Social Security and Medicare are an insult to faith in the Most High." That part of the flock—the hourly staff—sat in a first-come first-served section of the Jesus Dome. Another part of the flock—the highly paid, highly insured, golden parachuted business partners, —sat in an upholstered reserved seat section.

"Blessed Lord and Savior," Dobbin said, shaking his head just a little so his hair would jiggle, "we are so happy to be here today in our very own Jesus Dome to talk to you, to pray to you, to praise you and lift you up." He raised his arms high in the air, as did the entire flock. "We are here, gathered together to seek your blessing as we go forward to hasten the day of Jesus' return. Hallelujah!"

In the non-insured staff section sat Hogan Cafferty, head of security for the Teddy Dobbin Christian Crusades. He and the entire staff echoed, "Hallelujah."

"Oh Lord God, we have studied your Word. We have looked into the pages of the Holy *Bible* and seen that you are the Alpha and Omega."

Even at this sacred moment, Hogan smiled. The first time he had heard Dobbin talking about "Alpha and Omega," he thought it was a supermarket chain. He pushed that thought out so he could concentrate on the message.

"Oh Lord, God, Ruler of the Universe, we ask you to guide us now as we face a great and looming challenge." Dobbin stopped and peeked one eye open to make sure his audience was with him. "We are about to embark on a terrible mission, a crusade for Thee, Oh Lord, for we know that Thy Blessed Son can return only after the Great Battle of Armageddon! Armageddon! Armageddon! Can I get a witness?"

The staff of the Jesus Dome began a rhythmic chant of "Armageddon! Armageddon! Armageddon!"

Above the din, aided by his powerful sound reinforcement system, Dobbin cried, "And we shall hasten that day Oh Lord God Ruler of the Uni…" And then he and the entire Teddy Dobbin Christian Crusade staff simply vanished from the Jesus Dome—except for Hogan Cafferty who sat alone in the vast building, hearing nothing but the echoes of rings and small change dropping to the floor.

CHAPTER 5

On Staten Island, Marie Cattel and Lyla Edwards ate their lunch, while watching CNN accounts of growing disappearances. The absence of grief at the disappearance of their loved ones—something duly noted by the police—continued.

"This is so totally fucked," Lyla said, holding a hot cup of coffee to her upper chest like a water bottle.

"You can say that again, dear." Marie patted her granddaughter's knee. "I have no idea what this is about, but you can bet your bippie on the fact that this is no Divine Rapture, and that these aren't people that God—assuming there is one—could stomach. That idiot Governor Wexler in Texas and that baby-faced Dobbin preacher—if they went to heaven just now… makes hell look mighty attractive." She couldn't help but laugh at the notion. "And then there's your mother. She may have been my own daughter, but your mother—and of course your father—aren't the neighbors you'd hope to have for eternity. There was no reasoning with them."

"Well if reason had anything to do with it, they wouldn't have been spouting that shit in the first place. They'd have been doing something useful."

"Well said. You'd think after all these years, your mother would have at least stopped talking long enough to listen to me when it was clear that she was going off the deep end."

"Her crazed-assed minister convinced her that tuning everyone out and yelling 'Jaeysus' every time she opened her mouth was a sign of her sanctifuckation, grandma. You know that."

"I know it, but I just don't get it. Your mom was *not* a nut job when she was a kid. I've got some good memories. Hell, we could smoke a reefer together and talk like girlfriends."

"Yeah, that's one of the sins my father was forever bringing up—and another reason mom wasn't supposed to have anything to do with you.

You're just a sort of wrinkly Satan."

Marie was about to laugh when her eye caught a "Breaking News" graphic on the TV.

In Huntsville, Texas, death row was missing 88 of its 412 condemned prisoners.

CHAPTER 6

When Babs Waller heard about the disappearance of Reverend Teddy Dobbin and his entire staff, she abruptly left Daisy-Ann Wexler and hired a private jet to Denver. She knew there was one "survivor" named Hogan Cafferty, chief of security for the Dobbin Christian Crusades and the Jesus Dome. She was determined to scoop the competition and interview him. But when she arrived, cameras in tow, Cafferty was curled in fetal position and had barricaded himself in the corner of one of Dobbin's celebrity sky boxes. He could do nothing more than repeat over and over, "Holy Shit— oh forgive me Jesus. Holy Shit—oh forgive me Jesus." Since the family amusement giant, Biznee, owned the network that paid her bills, Waller knew Cafferty would be bleeped more than he was heard. Her contacts in New York located a therapist in Denver who specialized in trauma cases and Dr. Erich von Schlessin was rushed to the Jesus Dome.

Despite her advanced age and the toll repeated epidermal surgery had taken on her system, Babs was rarely lacking energy. She produced and hosted the newsmagazine *40/40*, a daytime girl-talk show and had enough endorsement deals in her portfolio to keep her homes and staff well paid. Yet sitting in the vast Jesus Dome, Babs was suddenly more tired than she could remember. Angry that she was being made to wait, she channeled a portable TV sampling the news bulletins that were coming nonstop.

Dr. von Schlessin was plying his trade on the incoherent Cafferty when Babs learned of the Huntsville story.

"Come here!" she shouted to her make-up man, Danny LaFogg, who was applying a coat of clear polish to his newly buffed nails. "That stupid Little Perky Miss Morning Show is on—and she's got a big story. Just because she's anchoring nighttime news she thinks she's hot."

The reporter in question was at the Huntsville death house interviewing Superintendent Lester Merles.

The burly, I've-seen-it-all Merles assured Miss Perky, "Listen to me, this has nuttin' to do with all the other stuff goin' on. We've got a passel of desperate men in this place, and this so-called disappearance is nothing but a clever ploy by them to exploit a national tragedy as cover for an escape." It would have helped his credibility if Merles wasn't sweating so profusely. He mopped his brow with a sopping handkerchief and continued, "Nobody needs to fear. By nightfall, these dangerous condemned inmates will be captured and confined again."

Miss Perky seemed truly and genuinely and absurdly pleased by his assurance. She didn't ask a single follow-up question, didn't inquire as to how each prisoner's clothes and shoes had ended up in little piles in their cells, nor did she ask how the men could have escaped when the prison's 24 hour video surveillance tapes showed there had been no lapses in security.

Babs turned to Danny LaFogg, "Did you see the interview?"

"Of course," he said in his droll way. "You commanded my presence."

"Well, it was a travesty," Babs snapped. "I could have reduced that fat warden to a quivering vat of mia culpas. He knows damn well they aren't going to find those convicts by tonight. Hell, Miss Perky didn't even ask him about the other disappearances! Why is that shrink taking so long? Hogan Cafferty—our *survivor*—should have been chirping ten minutes ago. Hasn't anyone heard of *drugs*?"

"Obviously *you* have Babsy—what are we chewing today? Ex? A little Crystal?"

"Shut up! You're here to do make up."

"Treat me nice or the little droop from your stroke will show on TV."

Babs looked like she was going to kill Danny for a moment, then patted his face and said, "I love these little bitch to bitches we have, don't you?" She headed off toward the therapist and her prey.

CHAPTER 7

President George Walker Bush used a rubber band to shoot a spit wad at Condoleeza Rice. The imperturbable one brushed the offending object out of her hair with militaristic precision. George snorted with glee. His frat boy enthusiasm was matched by Karl Rove who sat to his left.

After his much-ballyhooed "resignation," Rove assumed even more power in the White House—in effect unofficially joining Dick Cheney in running the nation. His office was moved to the same sub-basement level of the White House that Michaeljohn's command center used. There was a constant jockeying for space as Rove's operation expanded. A television studio, complete with backdrops and green screen flats, allowed Rove to do television interviews that had him appear to be in Texas or anywhere else his "retirement" supposedly took him. In truth, he was very much a resident of the White House.

The Vice President called the meeting to order. He aimed a remote and switched the flat panel TV on the east wall from FOX News to a live feed from Israel with General Moishi Schravetz, the rabidly right wing rogue commander operating within the Mossad. He didn't look happy.

"General." It was Cheney who began the conversation.

"What is going on here?" Schravetz demanded. "We are losing people here, important people, people on our side."

Cheney stopped a drool from the low side of his mouth by placing his fist against his chin—a move millions of Americans would have gladly, quickly, and *forcefully* made for him. "A minor glitch," he snarled.

"We are not happy about this," the General seemed to think that Dick was solely responsible.

"Like I told you, a minor glitch. Now we have business to conduct."

The General coughed, but it seemed to all in the room that during the expulsion of air he distinctly said, "Christians!" as a curse. Cheney, whose notion of worship focused somewhere between chemical and nuclear, ignored him. "Let's get to work. We've got a lot to coordinate." He turned to the commander in chief who was preparing another missile of well-chewed paper. "George?"

"What?"

"It's time to read that order you want to give."

"What order?"

"That one." Cheney pointed to the paper in front of George that already had three chunks torn from it. "I believe you're about to shoot part of it at Karl."

"Oh, that one." Some presidents, coming to the realization that they had been making spit wads from a classified document, might have said, "Sorry." But not George. He was too strong, too powerful, too unbending to admit an error. "Should I read it loud, Dick?"

"Yes, George. Loud."

"Okay." The Decider picked up what was left of the paper. "Op Secret," he proclaimed.

"That's Top Secret, George. You musta torn off the 'T'."

"Okay. Should I start again?"

"Just read the order that you wrote."

"I didn't write it. I don't even know…"

"Read it!" Dick looked like he wanted to take George out hunting.

"These words have a lot of dashes in them, Dick."

The Vice-President leaned over and whispered a spittle-laden message in George's ear. "That's phonetic spelling so you won't sound like an idiot. Now for God's sake, read that shit."

George, taking on his inimitable cousin-of-a-deer expression said, "Okay, General. I'm going to read this shit now." He stared at the page. "Uh, just a minute. I got to get my speculums on."

Condoleeza groaned as the President put on his reading glasses. She mouthed, "Just say 'specs' George," but knew it was useless.

Prepared as he was for a matter of world importance, George cleared his throat. "This order is to clarify the operation sub-SE-kwent…" He looked at Dick and shrugged.

"You got it right. Go on."

"The operation sub-SE-kwent to *Operation Divine Shield*. It shall be known as *Operation Om-nish-ent Scepter*. It shall be employed upon orders from the Commander in Chief of the United States of America. — That's me," George beamed, searching the room for approving affirmation of his power of deduction. Finding none, he returned to his order. "Be it hereby understood that upon this directive, the Israeli Air Force will conduct a series of surgical strikes against Iran. These strikes will specifically target schools, hospitals, mosques and water purification plants sime-ul-tAn-E-us-ly and will maximize civilian casualties."

"Shock and awe for the collaterals, shock and awe for the collaterals," Cheney actually broke into what some observers would call a "grim"—a frightening combination of a grimace and a happy sneer.

"These strikes will trigger rE-tal-E-uh-tory attacks from Iran, at which time the United States will be justified in utilizing tactical nuclear devices against that country and Russia."

"Russia?" It was the Israeli general who voiced the shock felt by some others in the room.

"Yes Russia." Condoleeza made sure that she displayed absolute control over her facial muscles. "Russia has been the problem for years and this will be a prime opportunity…"

"But Russia won't have anything to do with this!" Even the radical general sensed a disconnect.

Ms. Rice shot back, "So bomb Russia yourself then, General. I don't really care who does it just so long as it gets done."

"Did I write this?" George was lost in the morass.

"Just read it!" Dick was edgy because he was missing a pit bull fight being held on his property. The no-fly zone over Dick's house—what the US military thought was a top-priority security measure—was actually in place to prevent the PETA-minded of the nation from discovering the wagering on animal combat conducted for Washington's elite by Dick's wife, Lynne.

"That's where it ends, Dick."

"Uh, oh… yes, that's where it ends." The VP's concentration, broken as it was by his delight in imagining the yelps and howls of wounded dogs mingled with the groans of dying Arab civilians, was caught up short. "General Schravetz, that brings you up to date with *Om-nish-ent Scepter*."

"But you haven't…"

"Thank you very much." Dick picked up the remote. "So long Heeb." The VP waved at the screen as the Israeli General disappeared.

Immediately the General's face was replaced by FOX's own pit bull, Bill O'Reilly screaming about "towel heads from Mexico who are bringing their hoobie doobie African religions to destroy our way of life."

George was bewildered. "Is that all I've got to read, Dick?"

"No. There's more. I'll give it to you in a minute. We just needed to get rid of the General."

He handed another document to George who exclaimed, "This one is Top Secret too!"

"Yes, isn't that exciting…"

"You don't have to get sarcaustic…"

"Read, George."

"Okay. This says, sub-sE-kwent to the tactical nukular strikes, the final operation will begin. In order for this to be effective, there will be a change in nukular protocol. The 'football' briefcase that contains the authorization codes for nukular missile strikes will no longer be kept with a military aide. It will be kept in the study of the President of the United States of America." Again, George stopped. "That's me."

"George."

"The Vice President will no longer have to enter any codes or utilize any keys to begin a war. The President alone will have the power for such an in-ish-ill-I-zA-shun."

Relying on his protege's impetuosity, Uncle Dick gave the key to George so he wouldn't need permission to play with the world's ultimate toy. Thus, the Connecticut Texan was once again able to make an end run around checks and balances, a maneuver he had practiced well when AWOL from the National Guard.

There was shock on every face in the room except those of Karl Rove, Dick Cheney, and Condoleeza Rice. Observing the disquiet of the cabinet's majority, Dick quickly said, "I believe the room should be cleared at this time of everyone but me, Karl, Condi, and George."

There was a murmur of discontent as the President's cabinet left the room. Once they were gone, Dick uttered a self-congratulatory, "That went pretty well. Now you can read the rest of it, George."

"Okay. This says in big print: 'Details of *Operation Om-nish-ent Scepter: Armageddon.*"

Cheney nodded. "Good boy. Now we get to the fun stuff." His face was stuck in that eternal deranged sneer, but inside, his metallic heart was leaping with joy. Others in the room thought they heard the happy ping of stainless steel beating in accelerated rhythm.

CHAPTER 8

Somewhere in the bowels of the White House, NSA agents were feverishly monitoring wiretaps and email surveillance, while others sat stone-faced assessing all network and cable news. Even though the Office of Total Information—the department charged with putting out false news stories favorable to the United States—had been officially outlawed, through the machinations of the reigning George Bush, all functions of the office had been maintained, buried as they were beneath the house George lived in. Government "journalists" sat in their cubicles composing reassuring stories for the American public.

Jeff Tollsen, brought to the office personally by Dick Cheney, was reading portions of his latest release to the AP:

Sources close to the White House downplayed reports of certain disappearances in remote areas of Staten Island, Texas, Colorado and elsewhere. President Bush is devoted to the principles of the Holy Bible, *an ardent student of its prophecies, and is being briefed constantly. He is confident that there is nothing occurring which should cause anyone alarm.*

Since the *New York Times'* morning edition had carried a story about the disappearances' possible link to the military's vaporizer technology, the President was quoted with an adamant:

That is just blather being circulated by liberal press people who hate the democratic principles upon which this Christian nation was established.

Another story led,

The President is spending these hours in communication with his God and is eager to assure everyone, particularly Wall Street, that with God in control of the White House and his beloved nation America, no one should have one moment of concern. "Enjoy your God-given lifestyle," the President advises, "Go out and shop."

Despite the reassuring words being electronically dispatched to the nation's news outlets, despite the instructions for those outlets to stop spreading panic by their endless focus on the disappearances, the mood in the Total Information office was hardly "Let's go to the mall." A phone call from Dick Cheney had seriously eroded morale.

Agent Ken Durgan was repeating the VP's words to underlings who had been unable to hear the call directly. "He said our asses were grass unless we could come up with a logical explanation for this disappearance thing in 30 minutes. He's pissed as hell that we let one word get out that would encourage the Christian Crazies to get going on this Rapture frenzy. He said the White House has been flooded with calls threatening the entire Administration because they blame Bush and Cheney for the fact that so few people have been raptured when we are a Christian nation with a Christian born-again president. He said Robinson Patrick and that whole gang is threatening to withdraw support from Michaeljohn unless the Administration can provide a plausible explanation for the disappearances that completely rules out the possibility of a *pathetically small Rapture*."

"Cheney said all that?" It was Tollsen who responded.

"He said a lot more. That old asshole has the ugliest vocabulary of anyone who's ever entered this building."

"Worse than Nixon?"

"Nixon was a choirboy."

"They *are* both dicks."

"Funny boy. Careful what you say."

"Hoo ha."

"Listen, only thing he was happy about was that FOX News is clearly on message."

"FOX? I've been monitoring print services, I haven't heard a thing about FOX." Tollsen felt less like joking.

"Check this out." Durgan grabbed the remote for his TIVO. A FOX editorial brightened the screen.

* * * *

We at FOX News maintain a vigilant watch on the health of America. We provide absolute balance in our coverage of all events, and uphold our undying belief in the intelligence and perspicacity of our viewing audience. Perspicacity means the ability to catch on good and fast. And we know you can. That is why we feel that it is our duty to present a fair analysis of all news stories that come to us, and to interpret them for you in a way which appeals to that perspicacity which is so uniquely yours—our FOX viewers. We know that you have been hearing these here and there reports about some folks being missing on Staten Island and such, and just a little while ago there was an unconfirmed report about some of Reverend Teddy Dobbin's folks having been misplaced. Now, if any of this is true we need to ask who would be doing it? And the answer comes back to us loud and clear: those people who hate our American way of freedom and liberty. The left wingers right here in the United States and their terrorist cohorts everywhere else, would just love to have everybody here take their minds off what is important. They'd just love to have you worrying about things that don't much matter. They don't want you to think about serious issues. For instance, you know our President is working to end the curse of unwed motherhood in this country, and that vote is coming up in Congress real soon. They don't want you to think about that. There are homosexuals right now who are being united in what some states are actually calling "holy matrimony" the very same way normal people would be joined. But the leftist terrorist sympathizers don't want you thinking about that. We here at FOX have to keep it on the front burner and remind you how this perversion is a threat to our nation. It is the opinion of this reporter and the entire news staff that supports me that this smoke screen about the end of the world and all is nothing more than a post-Communist totalitarian terrorist bunch of hooligan propaganda. It should be treated like the filth that it is. We are calling upon the Department of Homeland Security to take action against anyone who is in any way cooperating with this subversive hoax. Thank you for listening to this special edition of FOX News, Fact Without Opinion.

"That's clever, '*Fact Without Opinion.*' Maybe we need to get a slogan," Tollsen ventured. "Something like 'Not From the Bowels of the White House.' After all, we started the Iraq war with imaginary facts from the 'Colin' of the White House."

"Enough with the jokes. Michaeljohn will be arriving any minute. We'd better be ready to snow him too."

CHAPTER 9

In Tel Aviv, General Moishi Schravetz was huddled with his fifteen most trusted colleagues in secret police headquarters as he laid out the essential details of *Operation Omniscient Scepter*. Among those present were Generals Yitzhak Scherman, Nosson Twerski, and Menashe Ungarischer who nodded approvingly as they learned of the plan to attack Iran, thus precipitating an attack on Israel, which would be defended by the United States.

"The civilian casualties in those countries will be so great," Schravetz proclaimed, "their spirit will be broken and their counter attacks minimal."

Again everyone, including the three generals nodded their agreement.

"Any questions?" Schravetz scanned the room. "If not, take your printed orders and be prepared to move with fifteen minutes' notice. You may go."

In a show of unanimous approval, the military men stood, applauded Schravetz and left the room. Generals Scherman, Twerski, and Ungarischer made their way to a nearby house.

Once safely inside, Gen. Scherman tossed the classified orders on the table. "Like the American he follows, he is out of his mind. He's talking the way that idiot Donald Rumsfeld talked before his invasion of Iraq—like it's going to be simple and clean."

Gen. Nosson gesticulated wildly. "Did you hear him talk about civilian casualties as if that was a happy goal?"

"He is a madman."

"He is a madman, Yitzhak."

Gen. Ungarischer sank onto the old leather couch. "What are we to do? This is coming from the Americans—that filthy George Bush." He spit on the floor. "What is he up to? I don't trust him. He doesn't care about Jews."

"We must leak this information."

"Yitzhak, they will destroy us."

"If it's God's will… if not. One way or the other Israel is in the crosshairs."

Gen. Nosson grabbed the manila folder with his orders. "My friend, Sammie Akbar, he writes for the *New York Times*. We'll get this to him."

"You are brave, my friend. Well, so long as it isn't Judith Miller… I'm with you." Scherman moved towards the back door.

Ungarischer could not hide his surprise. "So soon," he asked, "you're going so soon?"

"We have no time to waste. Come, my friends."

The three generals quietly moved around the back of the house and got into Gen. Nosson's late model Mercedes. "To the *New York Times*," he said.

They headed out of the narrow alley and turned left onto Yerushalyim Street, following it for four blocks before signaling a right turn onto Jabotinsky Street. It was the right turn signal, which triggered the explosion.

A sorrowful General Moishi Schravetz mourned openly on television that evening. He wept as he said, "I have lost my three beloved and trusted friends—heroes all—who died today at the hands of inhuman Iranian terrorists."

It was not until later that he was able to privately thank a member of his own explosives division for his excellent work.

CHAPTER 10

When Senator Tim Michaeljohn was summoned by Vice President Cheney to return to Washington from a campaign appearance in Salt Lake City, he was oblivious to the seriousness with which the White House was taking the disappearances and unaware of the threat they posed to his campaign. He was in a jovial mood as he flew across the country in his chartered jet.

"Never loved Dick Cheney more," he said to Elizabeth Garvin, his chief of staff. "Miserable bastard that he is, he at least showed enough love for me to save me from the Mormons. Talk about scary. Do you know that they're officially *against* polygamy now?"

"Duh…"

"Well, can you imagine how much cheating must be going on as a result?" Michaeljohn laughed and made the sign of the cross. "I was a little worried, y'know," he continued, "It wasn't until about 1978 that they got their 'message from God' saying that it was now actually possible for Black people to go to heaven. Before that they believed that everyone Black was condemned."

"Careful, Fritz," she countered. "They're still the Christian Right and if this plane is bugged, you just lost a few million votes."

"Yeah, yeah," Fitz was on a roll. "I mean these people will believe anything they're told comes from on high! But the rest of America seemed to think there was something wrong with eternal damnation based on skin color. Isn't it wonderful, Elizabeth, how public pressure can change God's mind?"

"Hmm, look how it's changed Dubya's mind… he conceded yesterday that it's been hotter in El Paso lately than usual. Can his pro-Kyoto address be far behind?"

Michaeljohn was stuffing an artificially worn *Book of Mormon* into his briefcase, a prop he wouldn't be needing. "Yep, Uncle Dick saved me by calling me back to DC. He sure does get worked up about stupid little stuff. So there are some people unaccounted for—we've been making people disappear for years. Latin America would be a commie stronghold by now if we hadn't."

"Check your watch, Tim. We've driven them far left very effectively."

"Have another drink, Liz. And ask Santa for a sense of humor."

That was on the plane. Now, in the sub-sub basement of the White House, two stories below the Presidential Emergency Operations Center (PEOC), Michaeljohn was no longer jovial. Santa or no Santa, Elizabeth Garvin wasn't either. They were huddled with former presidential "brain" Karl Rove. In his unofficial role as ruler of the country, Rove was also chief adviser to Michaeljohn's campaign.

"Look, Fitz," it was Rove speaking, "you're in deep shit. Your entire Christian base is eroding as we speak. You've got to take a new strategy."

"Like what?" Michaeljohn didn't appreciate being told what to do. "What? You want me to go out there and say that I'm getting instructions from God?"

"Exactly."

"Fuck you."

"God's appointed messenger should never talk like that."

"And what is God telling me?"

"He's telling you that every American had better listen very closely to their President. *Very* closely. Have you got that, Tim?"

"Is that some kind of threat?"

The rather chubby former Presidential adviser looked positively cherubic. "Why Tim Michaeljohn," he chided in a motherly way, "whatever do you mean?"

This friendly conversation was interrupted by Jeff Tollsen. "I think you'd better come and see this report running on ABC," he said, turning on a monitor.

A breathless Diane Sawyer, standing in the middle of Times Square was addressing the camera: "We aren't sure what is happening, but there are unconfirmed reports that there are no children missing—even in areas where many people seemingly cannot be found. And just minutes ago, Times Square police alerted us to the fact that there are several hundred small children wandering through the theater district without their parents.

In fact I see some right over there."

And the indefatigable Ms. Sawyer moved across 7th Avenue and Broadway heading for 45th Street where there stood about a hundred little children all stupefied by the lights and billboards of the Disney-promo-slathered Crossroads of the World.

"Hello children. And where are your mommies and daddies?"

At this the children began to tell where they thought their parents were. To a child they said either "jail" or "Hell." Ms. Sawyer was taken aback.

"What are you saying? Surely you don't think…"

And in a chorus the children cried, "Yes we do!"

Ms. Sawyer turned to the cameraman, gesticulating wildly that he should pan away from the children who now had begun happily to dance in Times Square. Running her fingers through her famous hair, the anchorwoman and former Nixon confidante began a torturous attempt at explanation.

"As should be evident to everyone watching this broadcast, these children have been deeply, deeply traumatized. The degree of their despair, the heartwrenching display of their grief…"—she was momentarily drowned out by the sound of the children's laughter and singing—"cannot adequately be described. Perhaps this is what the terrorists have wanted. Perhaps this is the carnage they hoped to cause. All I can say as a compassionate human being is that I want to scoop each and every one of these little ones into my arms and take them home. This is Diane Sawyer reporting from Times Square in New York."

Ms. Sawyer, her sign-off face frozen and staring into the camera remained in place expecting that the network would cut to a commercial or station identification. Unfortunately, the producer in charge had just disappeared, leaving some worn khaki pants, a slightly moist T-shirt and a pair of jogging shoes. No commercial appeared, no station break interrupted the blonde's stare.

Assuming that she must at last be off the air, Ms. Sawyer blurted, "What the hell was that? What? These kids have got no more respect for their parents than that? I'm ready to believe the nut cases who say this is the end of the world!"

It is said that ABC officials would have fired her the next day, except for the fact that she disappeared in her sleep that night.

CHAPTER 11

Superintendent Lester Merles crammed another five Tums into his mouth and chewed. TV interview completed, he returned to his office alone. He was pleased that his staff had managed to plug the information leak. Death Row wasn't the only part of Huntsville missing prisoners. Panicked corrections officers in the other cellblocks were reporting the all too familiar description of clothes and personal effects left behind in little piles. Merles knew he had to account for the 88 missing condemned men by nightfall or there would be no way to stem the tide of negative press.

There was a knock at the door. It was Assistant Deputy Superintendent Harold Druckle, head of security. His opening remark stunned Merles.

"Damndest thing, Lester," he said, "There's no trouble in the blocks. We're missing 20 percent of our prisoners in Texas, and there's no trouble. There's a lot of confusion, but no real trouble. That Markus fella—you know the one that calls himself 'Divine X,' the one that smuggles out his own radio show and has got so much press saying he's innocent? . . Well, wouldn't you know he's out there getting people organized and helping to keep things calm. We've got frickin' murderers out there doin' what the CO's are supposed to be doing except we're missing about 70% of our CO's!

Merles' head snapped up. "Can't be!"

"It's true. You're in charge of a facility that's currently being run by goddam inmates."

Merles' intercom interrupted the conversation.

"A call from New York, Superintendent. Line two."

Merles picked up.

"Yeah? How many? . . Same thing here… What? . . I don't know. I'll have that checked out. Thanks… Let me know if I can be of any help… What? . . Sorry it's just an expression, I know I can't be."

Druckle knew better than to press Merles about the phone call. He went to the window and stared through the bars.

"That was Corrick, Superintendent of Sing Sing," Merles began. "Same thing happening there—right on the banks of the Hudson River in New York."

"I wonder if…"

"If what?"

"Well I wonder if it's really the same thing there."

Merles wasn't in the mood for riddles. "Out with it. What are you talking about?"

"It's… it's *who's* missing that has got me baffled."

"If you know something Druckle…"

"Well, we did a quick check. It's almost like someone knew cases. We're missing child rapists, the serial killers, that guy who confessed to multiple cop executions—that kind of people. I mean everybody is on death row, but the ones left… well, y'know, they're ones we've had no trouble with—no tickets, no time in ICU—the ones we sometimes wonder if they're really guilty…"

"Yeah, innocent like Divine X Marcus, the original 'I didn't do it.' They're all guilty as sin and you know it Druckle."

"Well still… I'd better get back to the blocks." Druckle hesitated for a moment and then let himself out.

Merles, sweating heavily again, sat down at his computer and began looking up the records of the missing.

In the mess hall, Divine X Marcus was going over callout sheets left behind by the disappeared corrections officers.

Officer Daryl Young stood next to him, pointing to various names. "That Omar Ferguson there, that's Dawoo," he said, connecting a missing prisoner's government name with his prison moniker.

"Dawoo's gone, huh? That's a good thing." Divine X smiled at the realization. "I guess that accounts for everybody. Let's get all the fellas in here so we can get organized and keep the chow flowin'."

Officer Young radioed for a gate to be opened so men could get to the mess hall. A confirmation crackled, and soon the first men in white jump suits began to come through the door. They were quiet, orderly, and formed neat rows facing Divine X. When everyone was assembled, he spoke.

"Fellas, we got a situation here and I want to begin by thanking you in the name of Allah the Merciful and in the name of his prophet Mohammed for your cooperation. We are setting an example for the whole nation. I don't know any more than you do what's happened, but I do know that if we all work together, we'll get through this."

Within five minutes, Divine X outlined committees, assigned jobs, and dismissed the meeting. Thirty minutes later the men were enjoying chow, and for the first time in memory were being given more than ten minutes to eat it.

CHAPTER 12

From the moment he crawled into the skybox, Hogan Cafferty felt the air inside his head getting hot. He could feel it moving through the little curves and furrows of his brain. It had started on the right side about an hour ago, squeezing little by little inward. The air was moving from his right ear toward the center of his brain. While it was happening, he felt the constant need to curse. He realized, much to his amazement, that there was a direct link between air pressure points in his brain and cursing mechanisms in his mouth. A loud "shit," "hell" or "fuck" provided immediate relief to painful bloating in his head. But there was the problem--the seemingly insurmountable, agonizing irony of the situation he was in. He was a *Christian*, and even a "darn" or "frick" was never supposed to escape his lips. He could hear his own voice as though it was coming from across the room—except the room ended inside the left side of his skull.

"You are failing God's test." The echoing voice was his own. "God is giving you the hot air test and you are failing."

He clamped his lips tightly. It was about that time Dr. von Schlessin first squatted in front of him and asked if he could speak. That's when the air got hotter and started its journey back to the right side of his head. The need to dispel the air became more intense and only long streams of vulgarities and curses brought beginning relief. His sense of sin rose in direct proportion to the number and vileness of the curses, and so every time there was pressure relief, he asked forgiveness from Jesus.

Dr. von Schlessin was unaware of the strictly physical nature of the problem. Cafferty would have laughed at him if he weren't in so much pain. The earnestness with which the therapist approached him was absurd.

"Mr. Cafferty," von Schlessin began, "how are you doing?"

Cafferty assessed the incompetence with digital speed. "What do they teach these guys in therapy school?" he wondered. "How am I doing? How am I supposed to be doing? I was in the middle of the morning prayer service with Reverend Dobbin and my Christian brothers and sisters, and all of a sudden I was standing there looking at piles of pants, shirts, dresses and underwear. And this asshole is asking me how I'm doing? Forgive me Jesus."

There was a sudden shift of hot air and Cafferty gasped.

"Mr. Cafferty?" Dr. von Schlessin was genuinely alarmed.

"Oh fuck. It's the hot air," Cafferty snapped. "It was in the center, now it's moving left."

"Yes, yes, I understand, Mr. Cafferty. Now can you tell me…"

"You understand? The hell you do—hell, shit, fuck, damn. Forgive me Jesus."

"If you could just avoid the profanity, Mr. Cafferty. I'm a born again Christian myself."

"How fucking nice. Forgive me Jesus."

"I'm here to help you."

"Pick up the fucking wedding rings. They're everywhere. Hock 'em. Give me the money. Shit! Forgive me Jesus."

"Mr. Cafferty, if you're going to take the Lord's name with such vain abandon…"

"Whoo, whoo, who the fuck are you talking to about abandon. I'm the one who's fucking abandoned here—the only fucker in the room—and all my Christian brothers and sisters are fucking gone. Forgive me Jesus."

An impatient Babs Waller and her smirking cosmatologist waited for Dr. von Schlessin to work a mental miracle so the interview could begin.

To say that his behavior was uncustomary would not do justice to the person of Hogan Cafferty. His involvement with Reverend Dobbin and the Jesus Dome came from a deep and sincere wish to better the plight of people he saw every day. In 2006 he reached his breaking point. Even though he'd voted for him twice, it didn't look like George Bush was going to make things right. He'd believed that the President was a dedicated, born again Christian man, but it bothered him to learn that after the public speeches there were secretive presidential "findings" that hurt people. On a cool spring day he stepped up onto a milk carton at the corner of 15th and Cheyenne in Denver and began to beg people in Civic Center Park to help change the direction of America. He asked that economic selfishness be replaced with fairness, he asked that the pursuit of war with its oil bounty be stopped and replaced with health care and adequate food for all Americans.

He was, of course, considered part of the lunatic fringe. Anyone who'd crawl up onto a plastic box and shout about justice had to be unhinged, unstable, or playing an angle. But he wasn't. Hogan Cafferty's heart was breaking. The bloated posturing of politicians made him shake. The callous disregard for humanity and the world's environment made him sick. He ached with the desire to do something to rectify the human condition.

That is when he met Adam Brigante, a 23-year-old Iraq War veteran left without legs after an IED attack. Brigante, a Colorado native, joined the National Guard in peacetime, hoping to pay for college. Then came 9/11, the Iraq War and his injuries. He returned home filled with a conviction that wars could be waged forever without a conclusion, never achieving betterment for any side. He also returned home with a terrible, deadly secret.

On the day of their meeting, Brigante had ridden his wheelchair downtown on his way to an AIDS rally. There he saw a man in his mid forties standing on a milk carton talking about justice. He wasn't preaching, he wasn't condemning, he was imploring people to wake up and see that their country was on the wrong course. He had never seen or heard anything like it. It wasn't fancy, it was sincere. He rolled up and was Cafferty's first respectful audience.

For the next two weeks they met daily in a small coffee shop and talked about the state of the world and what could be done about it.

It was during one of those conversations that Adam said something Hogan Cafferty would never forget. They had been talking about solutions to world problems—global warming, economic turmoil, and war.

"It's too big," Hogan said. "It's all too big. We can't ever tackle it. Look what happens when I talk in the park—I get one guy in a wheelchair to stop and listen to me." He smiled at his friend. "And I sure am lucky he did."

"Me too. Listen, Hogan…"

"Yeah?"

"There's something you ought to know… about me, that is."

Hogan faked a shocked look. "You a bank robber or something?"

"I'm serious."

"Listen, there's nothing could shake my trust of you."

"It's not that. It's…" Adam looked around as if he was afraid someone might be listening. "It's that… this may sound paranoid… but you might be in danger being around me."

"What? You go psycho from time to time?" Hogan still thought Adam was joking.

"Not danger from me. Danger from… others."

"Others?"

"The government. I can't really talk about it, but just watch your back. I don't want to scare you off or anything, I just wouldn't want anything happening."

"Hey Adam, you've heard me talking in the park. You don't think I know the government could be upset with me? You talk about trying to do something to change the world and that gets a lot of people mad."

"You don't know what I know."

The waitress brought their food just then and the conversation drifted to other things. The subject never came up again.

A week later, Adam saw his friend enter the coffee shop grinning widely.

"Look at this book," Hogan said as he sat down across from Adam. This is amazing."

"*The Goal Guided Life*. What's it about?" Adam turned the book over to check the notes on the back jacket.

"It's the book that could change the world."

"It's religion."

"Yeah. And that can change the world."

Adam shook his head. "I'm not buying it, Hogan. You know what I think of religion."

"But this is different. This guy is on to something."

"Maybe *on* something. These guys are all alike. Which one is he? Oh yeah, now I remember. He's the guy with the Jesus Dome."

"Exactly."

"Jesus hot dogs or something."

"Not exactly."

"Well, count me out."

"Your choice, but I'm gonna go there and see what's happening. Maybe with that mall and stuff I could get a job and really start making a difference."

"You'll be barefoot, selling flowers at the airport before long."

Hogan liked Adam's humor, even about religion. Still, he was a little irked that his friend gave no credence to what had him so excited. After lunch, he went to the Jesus Dome, applied for and got a job as a security guard. He threw himself into his work with a zeal the Jesus Dome had seldom encountered. Within two years he was named head of security for the entire Dobbin enterprise. Now he had an income and something he saw as a means of changing the world.

Adam Brigante went his own way. He saw a notice of an "Impeach Bush/Cheney" rally, and soon was working to change the world in his way.

Hogan Cafferty had hoped that his part in world change might be somewhat more direct. He enjoyed his work, but the security offices were on the lower level of the Jesus Dome, and since a computer controlled the immense operation, there rarely was a need for him to leave and meet people. He learned from the daily prayer sessions that God was working in powerful ways through Dobbin to transform the world for Christ. Dark thoughts occasionally came to him in the form of wishing that Dobbin would not always withhold specifics—but he delighted in the assurance that God had something huge afoot in Denver. Sunday mornings with 34,000 worshipers swaying to the music and holding their hands aloft and crying, "Jaeysus, Jaeysus, Hallelujah," he could not help but feel he had been led to the place he belonged.

"I tell you, Adam, this thing here is bigger than we could have ever dreamed," he emailed Brigante. "I never was much of a religion man. We talked enough that you know that. I've generally thought there was a God… or something, but I mean, I have this sense of right and wrong, justice and injustice, and it just burns inside me. I knew I needed a place where I could put everything—my whole self, my whole life, all my energy—into helping people have better lives. Man, I saw a woman this afternoon. She had a baby and was standing outside the welfare office. She wasn't asking for money or anything. She was just standing there. But the look on her face—the totally helpless look on her face while her baby cried—man, I couldn't stand it. We're the richest country in the world. We've got practically everything. But we don't have a heart. That's the problem. We just don't have a heart. I don't understand Bush, man. I know he's a good man, a man who wants to be righteous, but no matter how much support we give him (did I tell you that Dobbin says he personally turned out over two million votes for Bush?), it just seems like things get worse. Well, I don't mean to get into politics here, but sometimes you just can't help it. Anyway, Dobbin says that we're on our way to a better world for everyone and that we can just all rejoice in the spirit and know that God is at the helm of the Jesus Dome. I didn't know it, but last week someone told me that there's a stock on the stock exchange called JDE which actually stands for Jesus Dome Enterprises, and it's going through the roof. I'll bet Dobbin will announce that on Sunday and show us how much God is blessing this church. Well, buddy, I better sign off. I hope you're doing okay there. I'm working on finding a place for you in this church, I just know they would love you if you were here working with them."

Adam Brigante responded by mailing Cafferty a copy of *Newsweek* with Dobbin on the cover. The headline read, "God's Entrepreneur—Godly or Greedy?" Stapled to it was a post card: "Impeach the Bastards Now."

The following Sunday, Reverend Dobbin advised his church not to read the *Newsweek* article saying that it had been inspired by "Satanic influences within the liberal media." Cafferty wrote a sweet email to Adam encouraging him to stay away from *Newsweek* so he wouldn't be led astray. Adam smiled when he got the warning, thinking it was a little late, since he was the one who had sent the magazine in the first place.

Every Sunday at the Jesus Dome and on his nationally televised "Jesus' Dominion" show, Dobbin preached with increasing fervor about The Rapture, promising that soon God's saints would be swept up in a Divine gesture of Grace and taken to meet their Maker. Left behind, in a chaotic morass of sin, degradation and radiation would be those who had rejected God's promised forgiveness and redemption through Jesus Christ. He said that for seven years they would be forced to endure the worst carnage and suffering the world had known.

Perhaps, unfortunately for Dobbin, on the fateful day that he had intended to comply with the President's wishes and advocate the rush to Armageddon, he and over fifteen hundred of the faithful simply disappeared.

Now, sitting on the floor of the emptied Jesus Dome, poor Hogan Cafferty was convinced that his uncontrollable cursing proved he was an irredeemable sinner. The Rapture had come and gone and he had been left behind.

With the hot air pushing its way through his brain, Cafferty thought of his friend—legless—sitting in a wheelchair. It had been three months since they'd had any communication. Cafferty couldn't bring himself to believe that such a good person had become a pawn of the Devil, so while staring at the therapist, he assumed that perhaps his friend had been raptured too.

An hour into his therapeutic endeavors Dr. von Schlessin had the frantic look of an engineer who'd lost control of his train.

"You talk to him," he said when Babs approached. "I'm out of here. I've had enough."

Always ready to demonstrate that she was wise beyond all competition, Babs stretched out her hand, "Mr. Cafferty, I'm Babs Waller of ABC."

"I know who you are, but where the fuck is God?" Cafferty snarled. "Forgive me Jesus."

"Excuse me?"

"You fucking heard me. Where's God? Forgive me Jesus."

Babs signaled her cameraman to start rolling. Assuming her most compassionate voice she began, "Mr. Cafferty, what are you feeling at this moment? You have suffered the sudden disappearance of everyone that you have worked with and communed with in this lovely church family."

"What the hell am I supposed to feel? Forgive me Jesus. Do you have any idea of what our so-called God is up to? Forgive me Jesus."

Babs could see her cameraman, shaking his head, knowing that there was nothing airable. He got a piercing look of disapproval from his anchorwoman.

"I know, I know," she said, reaching out to give Cafferty's hand a comforting touch—a touch that was famous for evoking copious tears from her guests.

"Don't touch me! Forgive me Jesus."

Hand withdrawn, Babs continued. "I'm sorry."

"You should be."

Babs gave a "keep rolling" sign and pressed on. "What was happening at the time of the disappearance, Mr. Cafferty? Was there anything usual?"

"Unusual? What the—do you think fifteen hundred staff members and Christian supporters vanishing into thin air was usual? Shit! Forgive me Jesus."

The woman with a peculiarly taut face tried once more to touch Hogan's hand for visual effect. He cursed again, but the pressure wouldn't release. The woman was repeating her questions with a voice so strident it was changing the patterns of the hot air inside his head. He had to do something to stop the pain. That's how Babs Waller got her black eye.

CHAPTER 13

Daisy-Ann Wexler was not pleased. Sipping an Irish coffee, she complained to her chief of staff, Judy Seymour, "Jes' a little while after Babs Waller left, my doorbell rang and it was that abysmally serious Black fellow, John Solomon—the camerman who quit. He was here tryin' to explain how offensive Ah was tawkin' about the executions and all. Ah towld him there wasn't a grain of prejudice in ma whole body—an' that I was jes speakin' fact. It's not ma fawlt that it jest happened to be niggers that was fried by Duke. Well, he was all uppity and wasn't hearin' none of it and really jes' about ruined ma day. Is it ma fawlt if they's the ones gets 'emselves the lousy lawyers? He was pretendin' to be awl nice and polite, but I knew what he was doin'. Duke awlways tawked about those rabble rousers who's constantly tryin' to get what they don't deserve. Ah was about to suggest that if he didn't like it here he awt to go and check out Africa and see what we folks here saved him from. But he got real heated an' not so nice an' took off on another tirade about reparations. Can you 'magine? Duke not dead more'n hours and he's complaining to me like it's my fawlt the bridges are fallin' apart. And he was tawkin' like those repairs were jest comin' to Black folks! Honestly!"

Daisy-Ann stopped a moment to let Judy Seymour absorb the full impact of Solomon's insult. Seymour did nothing but shake her head and mutter, "I don't know why I work for you."

Daisy-Ann resumed. "He was there tawkin' away and practically sayin' that this country ain't the land of opportunity! Made me suspec' he had some ties to them terrorist fellas like bin Muhammad or whoever it was dropped the towers."

Solomon's words had a larger effect on Daisy-Ann than she let on. In fact, they had repeated themselves so often in her mind that they somewhat frightened her.

She thought there was something sneaky about the way Babs Waller talked to her and certainly something detrimental to her political destiny in the way Waller had corralled her into talking about the Rapture. She hadn't meant to go anywhere near that subject, but Waller's grip on her arm was so painful that she'd blurted out the whole thing on national television. It was humiliating. Daisy-Ann hadn't believed a word she heard in church since the day the preacher launched into a sermon about the evil of vanity. That was when she was fifteen. Now she'd gone on record as being part of the lunatic fringe.

The strange thing was that by the next morning her poll numbers were up significantly. Emails and phone messages flooded into her husband's office saying that she should run for Duke's seat because she was a lady who wasn't afraid to "speak God's truth." Many of those responding begged her to explain why they might have been left behind, what they could do about it, and how she planned to proceed in trying to get a "second chance with Lord God Almighty."

Daisy-Ann decided immediately—with a conviction that she surmised would convert Satan himself—that the Rapture would be central to her campaign. She'd bill herself as "Second Chance Wexler" and planned to spice her stump speeches with messages of redemption and salvation, seeing as how she was the second Godly Wexler to run for the governor's seat.

"Haven't got a clue how to pull it off, Judy," she said. "But I just gotta. Why I'd want to end up in the same office as Duke, I'll never know, but I *am* sure I want to be governor. You don't think they'll find him, do ya?"

At that moment she glanced up at her muted plasma TV.

"Oh ma gawd! Looky what it says!" She grabbed the remote and restored the volume.

CNN reporter Cynthia Miles was standing in front of the White House. Her face was contorted and her voice trembling as she announced the message Daisy-Ann had seen crawl across the screen moments earlier.

"Sources close to the White House have… disclosed… on assurance of anonymity, that Vice President Dick Cheney… has disappeared."

"Ah didn't even know that Dick was a born again and *could* be saved," Daisy-Ann said turning to Judy.

"Maybe total organ replacement with bionic parts qualifies as being born again."

"Don't you be sacrilegious, young lady. If he got raptured, it's becawse he deserved it. And I guess that sweet wiaff of his is left behind. You cain't possibly think anything other than that she deserved to go be with Sweet Jesus now can you? Just think back to the way she does her hair and how nice she always dresses herself."

Judy Semour looked at her boss with a cynical eye. "Jesus isn't Mr. Blackwell. He doesn't choose people for their outfits. If that Cheney woman could've, she'd have stuffed every abortion back into the mothers. She'd want them to bear those babies and feel that pain. She thinks people choose termination because they don't want to get 'emselves stretch marks. So much for the love of Christ."

"I'm telling you not to be sacrilegious, Judy. It's a dangerous time to do anything that is steppin' on Gawd's feet. Now you just stop talking. They really don't know where Dick is! Listen to this report."

"I don't need to."

"Why not?"

Judy flashed a wry smile and said, "Because Dick's *always* in some 'undisclosed location.'"

Daisy-Ann sighed and turned the volume up on the TV. Cynthia Miles was interviewing a visibly shaken male staff member whose face was obscured.

"I walked back into his office—I had only been gone for a couple of minutes—and so I walked back in sort of ready to continue taking down the notes Vice President Cheney was dictating to me, and at first I thought his seat was just empty."

"You saw nothing but an empty seat? What did you think?"

"Well, I thought maybe he'd gotten up to go to the bathroom. He had a prostate they couldn't replace and it just caused him all kinds of problems, you know—so he was always getting up and going to the bathroom. And so I just went back to take my seat—I'd been sitting right across the desk from him—and I saw all this metal stuff lying in his chair."

"Metal stuff?"

"Well, yes. Nothing I recognized at first—just a little pile of metal stuff. And then I saw his shirt sort of draped over the arm of the chair. I couldn't figure it out until I recognized one of the metal things. It looked like one of those old Chinese Finger Traps we used to play with when we were kids, except that it was real little and..." The staffer was shaking now. "And I realized that it was an arterial stent, and there were others, and there was a pace maker, and a heart valve and a bunch of tubes and then I leaned over and looked down at the floor and there were his pants, his shoes, and that horrible metal knee. I couldn't believe it. I thought someone was playing a sick joke on me because right there in the middle of it all… well… do you really think the Vice President of the United States should have been wearing a thong?"

Daisy-Ann's private line was ringing. Without muting the TV she picked up.

"Yes, of course, ah've heard the news. Lynn's own Dick gone to glory and me sittin' here. What do you mean that's the old news? What? *Who* is missing?"

She dropped the phone.

"Judy," she said, "they cain't find the Pope."

CHAPTER 14

Cardinal Alberto Marchese, Prefect of the Congregation of the Doctrine of Faith and confidant to Pope Maximilian IV, stood by the window of the Aposentos Papales high above St. Peter's Square. The sun was rising, casting long shadows across the multitude of despondent faithful gathered below—all peering anxiously upward toward the small balcony in front of them. Through the din he heard the sound of agonized prayers. Marchese marveled at the speed news traveled when the highest church authorities had wanted *no* news to travel. Since his discovery of the Pope's empty bed three hours earlier, it seemed the gates of hell had swung open. Now the entire world's attention was focused on the Vatican.

In the course of his duties Cardinal Marchese awakened the pontiff each morning, brought him his coffee, dressed him, and insured that the leader of the One True Church had sufficiently overcome his hangover to conduct morning mass. The task had never been easy. Often, the stupefied successor of Saint Peter was so thoroughly toxified by his excessive intake of alcohol that he appeared dead. Marchese had become used to a momentary panic, thinking he'd discovered the corpse of God on Earth.

But the events of this particular morning had been substantially different. Armed with a silver tray, Papal coffee mug and morning vestments, Marchese made his way through the Papal chambers to the pontiff's bedroom door. When there was no answer to his knock—an all too familiar occurrence—Marchese entered quietly and placed the tray on a side table and then hung the vestments on a golden hook next to the full-length mirror where God's representative fretted daily about his weight, his unruly hair, and consoled himself by admiring his frequently new red Gucci shoes.

Since Maximilian's metabolism was unusually slow, even in warm months he required layers of heavy bedding to keep him from shivering. Years of careful observation had enabled Marchese to detect the difference between a shiver and delirium tremens. Papal bedsheets, required by canonic law to be made of the finest linens, were heavy in themselves. When at least four down quilts were added, each encased in a heavily embroidered brocade duvet and topped by assorted sacred pillows, the elderly Marchese was dealing with an assemblage so massive that finding the Pontiff often resembled a kind of treasure hunt.

On the morning in question, Marchese approached the Papal bed and cleared his throat saying, "Good morning, Your Holiness." As had become his custom, he repeated the cheery message three times, increasing the volume with each repetition. When there was no response, he began, layer by layer to remove the heavy comforters by folding them downward—with perfect symmetry—to the foot of the bed.

When he reached the Papal sheets, he later remembered thinking fleetingly that his boss was getting painfully thin. He reached for the highest point of the rumpled sheets, intending to give the Pontiff a gentle shake. To his amazement his hand went straight to the Holy mattress. He seized the corner of the linen and with a mighty tug revealed a bed empty save for a frilly pink Papal nightshirt—an exact replica of the one worn by the cross-dressing Pope Joan, who ruled as Pope John VIII in the ninth century.

Thinking at first that perhaps his charge had crawled out of bed and could be at that very moment wandering the halls of the Vatican stark naked, Marchese refrained from ringing the emergency bell, but instead went in search of the leader of 900 million Catholics. When a ten-minute hunt showed absolutely no sign of the Holy One, Marchese returned to the bed. He moved the nightshirt, and there, in plain sight, was the Papal Ring. Marchese hit the bell signaling highest emergency.

A Swiss Guardsman was the first to answer the call. Marchese suspected it was he who inadvertently mentioned the missing Pontiff within earshot of a Vatican employee, and the worldwide news panic ensued.

As with any political machine, the Vatican was not interested in having millions of faithful believe that its leader had vanished into thin air. It could not attribute the disappearance to the Divine Rapture because that religious belief was held only by the kind of Christians the Church had proclaimed destined for hell. It could not attribute the disappearance to kidnapping, because the faithful would literally attack and devour those responsible for the lapse in security. A rapidly convened Council toyed with the idea of claiming that the Holy Father had been taken to Heaven in a golden chariot like Elijah of old. That story, however, gave too much credence to the Old Testament of the *Bible* and thus to Jewish theology.

But then, the Council perceived Divine Inspiration. Three hours later *Operation Holy See* was in place. Vatican operatives had long recognized that a low level janitor assigned to the Sistine Chapel, Giuseppe Fognolio, bore a striking resemblance to Maximilian IV. The elderly gentleman was a deaf mute and had a pronounced limp, but otherwise—feature for feature—could have been the Pope's identical twin. The poor old fellow was now standing on the Pope's dressing platform having finishing touches put on a wig with the curlicues the Pontiff was so fond of. He was wrapped in an enormous gold and white ceremonial robe. Once the Papal hairdresser pronounced the curls complete, the heavy Triple Crown was placed upon Giuseppe's head. The bewildered man—still wearing his work boots—was uncomprehending of the situation due to the fact that he was deaf and because the Bishops, Archbishops, Cardinals and Vatican staff tended not to move their lips as they spoke. When the Swiss Guard arrived at his tiny room to escort him to the Pope's chambers, he was terrified thinking he had committed some unpardonable breach of Vatican law. His terror grew when Church officials—none of whom in the past would have allowed themselves eye contact with this most inferior mortal—suddenly greeted him with tearful jubilation.

Giuseppe had long ago established the ability to concoct credible scenarios about any life experience without the aid of auditory input. He could watch an Italian soap opera on TV and regale anyone who understood sign language with his version of the story line. Frequently his interpretation of visual images was far more interesting and far more perverse than anything allowed on Italian television, and thus the young people of his family were often his willing audience.

Now he was in the Holy Father's apartment wearing the Holy Father's clothes—the fine undergarments felt good—and being treated like Divine Royalty. He was devising a theory that he was in the midst of being thrown an extravagant retirement party when someone approached from behind and put the crushingly heavy crown on his head. He could, perhaps, have managed to fit the idea of a gold watch into the retirement fantasy, but the crown perplexed him no end. He signed, "What? What? What goes on here?" But no one answered.

A young boy in white vestments who for some reason made great show of avoiding one of the Bishops approached Giuseppe with a cane that looked like a giant hook. He'd seen the Pontiff standing on his balcony holding a cane amazingly similar to the one he now clutched in his hands.

Instantly thereafter, Cardinal Alberto Marchese stepped directly in front of him and with exaggerated lip movement meant to assist in communication began to speak to Giuseppe.

"You are now going to step to the window," Marchese intoned. "You are then going to bestow a Papal blessing on the crowd. Do not be afraid. They will be jubilant. You are going to restore faith to hundreds of millions."

Giuseppe blanched. His inability to hear and Marchese's peculiar lip movements scrambled the message. It seemed that he, a humble janitor, was about to be thrown out of the window to crowds below, and for this his family would be paid millions. He tried to protest, but the Papal attendants were already propelling him towards the fateful arch.

In the square far below, nearly half a million concerned souls strained their eyes upward. Suddenly, the familiar window of the Pope's residence flung open. A deafening cry went up from the crowd. Thousands surged forward to improve their view of the Holy Father. The tip of a crown appeared and then, screaming at the top of his lungs, the Pontiff lurched forward clinging to draperies, windowsills—anything stationary. The crowd exhaled a collective gasp. Securing the hooked end of his staff to a massive curtain rod, the Pope came to a stop. A Bishop stood beside him obviously distressed and gesticulating at rapid speed. The Pontiff shook his head. The Bishop remonstrated further. The Pontiff shook his head again, this time so vigorously that the crown shifted to a precarious angle. The crowd—agape—witnessed the spectacle. There was rejoicing that the Holy Father was alive, but utter astonishment at his erratic behavior. As quickly as he had appeared in the window, the Pope disappeared—propelled backwards as if jettisoned by unseen hands. With that, the window slammed shut.

Despite questions by sundry reporters about the Pope's unusual benediction, word spread internationally within minutes that the rumor was false and that the leader of the Roman Catholic Church was indeed alive, well, and safely within the confines of Vatican City.

That story dominated the news for nearly thirty minutes until all hell broke loose.

CHAPTER 15

Just before the tumult, just before what some would call "the beginning of the end," the national mood was surprisingly quiet. The disappearance of Dick Cheney made little stir. The populace was so accustomed to the disagreeable Vice President being squirreled away whenever there was a threat—real, perceived, or contrived—that the news was met with indifference rather than despair. There were some humorous headlines. *The Onion* led with, "Bush's Most Vital Organ Disappears," and a less prudent website asked, "Can George Still Screw America Without His Dick?"

At the White House, the ever playful President began referring to a large bronze bust of Cheney as the "Dickhead."

Inside Edition and a few other quasi news programs broadcast lurid pictures of the VP's remains, spending a considerable amount of time in conjecture on the colorful thong. But there was far more stir about the vanishing of Reverend Teddy Dobbin and his Jesus dome staff. Since it was sweeps week, the networks, with the assistance of the Office of Total Information, had decided to broadcast their best sitcoms and reality shows while keeping hard news to a minimum. Cute stories prevailed. A cat, stuck in a Missouri drainpipe occupied five networks for at least six hours. Since the disappearances were localized, the American populace was no more disturbed by them than they were by the nightly accounts of the military war dead whose names they didn't recognize. Besides, the reappearance of the Pope had calmed millions.

It was 9 PM Eastern time. Americans coast to coast were settling in for a night of beer, popcorn, and television. On the West coast, the network newscasts were a half hour away. In the central states, the family friendly sitcoms were beginning. On the East Coast the highly rated dramadies were running their one-minute opening teases.

Lyla Edwards and Grandma Cattel had moved the TV downstairs from

Julian's Edward's bedroom into the living room, managed to remove the channel blocker and were enjoying non-religious programming. Despite the unusual events taking place internationally, having the house to themselves without the censorious monitoring of their every move was such a luxury that grandmother and granddaughter were in high spirits.

Sixteen hundred miles to the west at Huntsville, Divine X had so organized the population of death row, that the prison was running itself. "Damndest thing I ever saw," was all Superintendent Lester Merles had been able to say.

In Texas, Daisy-Ann Wexler was tired of everything—television, phone calls, politics. Instructing Judy Seymour to make sure she wasn't disturbed, she crawled into bed with a copy of a romance novel titled *Sweet Savage Fire*.

In Rome, Giuseppe Fognolio—stripped of all papal vestments—was sound asleep, unaware of the noisy crowd beneath his window.

In the sub-sub basement of the White House, Tim Michaeljohn was huddled with his advisers, developing a strategy explaining why, as a born again candidate he had not been raptured, and why, given the religious fervor that swept the nation during the Bush years, the Rapture was, thus far, so pathetically small. Grant Millican, Michaeljohn's speechwriter—a lifelong member of Opus Dai and the person who perhaps had been the most militant voice against *The DaVinci Code*, sat cradling a Douay-Rheims Version of the New Testament—the only translation of the *Bible* sanctioned by the Roman Catholic Church and the only version to which he would refer.

"I mean, you are George's chosen successor. You'd think the bastard'd come down here himself and give us a hand. He's up there having late dinner with Laura and that guy who's established himself emperor for life of Whatchamacallit over there near Burma. We've got people disappearing, and all he can do is sit up there and make squid and booze disappear."

"And a truckload of cocaine for dessert…" It was Michaeljohn's wife, Helen who spoke.

"Shut up, Helen." Millican spit the words at her.

Helen hated Washington, hated everything it had come to stand for. She'd met Tim Michaeljohn thirty years before when he was a struggling labor lawyer representing the rights of coal miners in Kentucky. Her father, Rainey McDermott, was the president of the local UMW, and was leading a strike supported by the miners in ten local counties. After six weeks of strife that had torn towns and families apart, the national union backed out. McDermott was advised to settle and get his men back to work. With no support from the national, the local union was foundering. Two miners were shot and killed by company goons when they tried to put up signs along a highway. Another miner died of a heart attack when he came home to find his wife and newborn baby frozen to death. It was at that point that Tim Michaeljohn, just 26 years old, arrived in town and offered his services pro bono. Acting as lawyer, investigator, and journalist he uncovered the unholy alliance between the company and the national union brass. Calling on broadcast media, he managed to produce documents and stock transactions that resulted in the indictment of both national union leaders and the mine owners. Within weeks Tim Michaeljohn, the crusading lawyer for the little guy, was a household name.

Helen McDermott, then a twenty-year old college student, returned home to help her family during the strike. She spent countless hours on the picket line, suffered frostbite, and was beaten during a riot near the mine entrance when scab workers attacked the striking miners. The arrival of Tim Michaeljohn was to her the single most thrilling and encouraging moment of her life. Michaeljohn was tall, and despite his slender build, looked and acted rugged. When he wore his black knit cap, his hair fell out over his collar in a way she thought irresistible. But it was his courage, his unflagging devotion to the impoverished miners and their families that had her fall in love with him. Two weeks before he got the story of union/corporate corruption onto the national scene, she married him.

The wedding was a small affair with neither party able to spend a dime for new clothes, decorations or food. Still, Helen always remembered it as the happiest day of her life. Tim looked dashing in his clean faded jeans and a white shirt borrowed from the local pastor. Helen wore a wedding dress — short, slightly torn — which had been handed down through three generations of miner's wives. She had daisies in her hair—a gift from miner's children. And the reception—held in an open field—was rich in dancing and laughter even though it was modest in food and drink.

Tim Michaeljohn stayed with the miners until they could hold out no longer. In the end, they were forced to settle for the draconian package they had been offered before the strike. Tim went on to represent other unions, but Helen was aware of a change in him. It wasn't a dramatic shift, most people wouldn't have noticed it—but occasionally he would make a comment about "we're not where the power is," and have a tone of bitterness which she often concluded had a touch of envy.

On a night five years later, a time that coincided with another union loss, Tim and Helen were finishing dinner. Tim was swirling the last of his Gallo wine in a cheap tumbler.

"We need to talk," he said. He got up and went to the couch that was just a foot or two from the table in their cramped apartment. "Please sit here," he patted the cushion next to him.

Helen sat down and looked into the eyes of the man she so admired.

"I can't go on like this." He sighed and looked down at the remaining wine. It seemed like he was going to continue, but then he drank the last drops slowly and remained quiet.

Helen put her hand on his arm. "Just talk to me," she whispered.

As though he was lifting a heavy weight with his chest, Tim took in a breath, turned to her and said, "I'm in a losing battle. Life is short. I can see where the power, the comfort, the success lies. It isn't here struggling with people who will always be poor, always be on the desperate side of the fence. I can't do this anymore." He looked down—ashamed, she thought—and then continued. "These people don't even know when you're helping them. They don't even know when you're sacrificing everything good that life has to offer, trying to give them a break. They turn on you. Carney Russell— my right hand man—accused me of being a sellout because I said that a strike in the Garbey Mine would be suicide."

There was a long silence. Helen could feel her heart pounding from fear. She had dreaded this day, but long suspected it was coming.

"I'm resigning from the union," Tim said at last. "Old man Garbey wants me to run for state representative."

"Garbey!" Helen practically spit the word. "That bastard has been responsible for more misery among the people here than…"

"I've already resigned and told Garbey that I'll run as the Republican candidate. It's simple pragmatism. I can do more good working within the system."

That is the moment from which Helen's hatred of Tim Michaeljohn began to grow like an unstoppable cancer. She vowed silently over and over that she would leave him, campaign against him, expose him for the fraud he had become. But she had never found the right moment to do it. She was packing her bags just before his election to the Kentucky State Senate where he won by championing strict identification laws for voters that disenfranchised thousands of the poor. She had prepared her farewell speech just days before he was elected to the United States House of Representatives where he won on a platform of corporate deregulation. She intended to walk out right before he was elected to the United States Senate with support from Strom Thurmond and Jesse Helms in exchange for his denunciation of people calling for reparations for African Americans. And she had written a letter asking for a divorce the week Tim announced his bid for the Presidency, with the promise that he would complete George Bush's vision of a "perfect" Supreme Court. Helen knew right from wrong, decency from ruthless selfishness, but she also had a sense of her rightful position in life. It was so strong that she was unable to break from the Michaeljohn ego train.

Now she was far beneath the White House with her husband, the hand-picked successor to George W. Bush, facing the reality that the man she slept with could become the completion of the fascist revolution begun by the crazies of *The Project for the New American Century*.

"You've got to get out in front on this issue and, in effect, be the spokesperson for Jesus." It was Grant Millican again. "I'll start crafting your message—a new interpretation of scripture which shows that there will be an Early Rapture and a Latter Rapture… the early one simply being Jesus' warning shot across the bow to let people know he means business."

"Beautiful. You can find a passage like that in the *Bible*?"

"You can find anything you want in the *Bible*. It's all there for the taking."

It was during that conversation that Helen slipped from the room.

Across America, the flickering lull of television sets had the populace right where they were wanted. They were where they were wanted, that is, until 9:50 Eastern Standard Time. On the east coast, anchors were preparing for the 11 o'clock local news. The central zone was preparing for the 10 o'clock local news. On the west coast, reality was represented by contestants swallowing live worms.

Helen had just reached the Michaeljohn limousine and told the driver to take her home, when the first report came as "Breaking News" on the radio. Minutes before noon, all traders on the floor of the Tokyo stock exchange had simply disappeared.

CHAPTER 16

Once the financial markets were affected, the story took on a life of its own.

REPORTER IN TOKYO: *There was panic in the streets of Tokyo today. Here in the Nihombashi district, over 200 people apparently vanished as they stampeded towards the stock market on news of the disappearances. The Nikkei average dropped 46%, futures have plummeted in all markets. We have received word that warnings are being issued for employees of the New York Stock Exchange, American Stock Exchange and NASDAQ. They have been ordered, under threats of termination, to be present for work when the exchanges open in New York. This is Gayu Nikagami reporting from Tokyo.*

CHAPTER 17

Federal Reserve Chairman Norman Graham was summoned to the White House where, in an extraordinary after dinner move, George Bush was staying up with the adults. The President was fretful because it had been nearly 18 hours since Dick Cheney had told him what to do.

Electric companies across the country reported record demand as neighbors called neighbors and vast numbers of people turned on their television sets to watch the Japanese stock market spectacle.

The first video from Tokyo was stunning. The trading floor was littered with clothing while unattended computer monitors flickered from every desk. Clearly in shock, low level employees and cleaning staff wandered around the periphery as Tokyo police searched the premises.

Watching events on three monitors, Babs Waller sat in the control trailer the network had provided for her in Denver. Since the Jesus Dome situation had been the single largest disappearance to date, she'd hedged her bets and stayed to follow the story. Now she was cursing herself and everyone around her because she was stuck in a hick town when she should be on the East coast, ready to cover the opening of the New York Stock Exchange. All flights from the Denver airport were suspended after an American Airlines jet crashed when both its pilot and co-pilot disappeared. The private jet she'd chartered to get into town had already left to rescue the family of computer magnate, Winslow Boolean, who'd disappeared at the wheel of his Hummer H2. His wife, Chandra, narrowly escaped death. Some reports said that a miracle had taken place and stopped the behemoth of a car before it plunged over a cliff.

That idea was quickly pooh-pooed by Reverend Robinson Patrick on the *144,000 Club*. Eyeing a Colorado newspaper headline he said with an odd glint in his eye, "God does not save miraculously those who bring shame to his name. As you know, Winslow Boolean was a righteous man who contributed millions upon millions of dollars to God's causes. It would be no wonder if he has been Raptured. Why just think, in one instance he gave 100 million dollars to provide particular medicines for dark people in Africa to cure a disease that resulted from a lifestyle that Winslow abhorred. But!" The trollish little man held up his hand like he was stopping traffic, "Winslow Boolean's selfish little shrew of a wife, Chandra, has done everything she could to stop his generosity. She's even tried to undercut the spectacular goodness of his medical gestures. I do not think that God would want to spare such a wife when she has shown such callous disregard for the savage dark people of that big country, Africa."

Like his President, Reverend Patrick thought Africa was a country. He had little use for its descendants except when they provided a fundraising opportunity for his empire or cleaned his bathrooms.

The good Reverend then did his trademark scrunching of the eyes that indicated fervent prayer. "Good Lord, Merciful Lord, Gentle Lord—we come before Thee today to rejoice in Thy ultimate wisdom and grace. Thou hast taken home—we presume—one of Thy children, and left behind those that would have dragged him down, stifled his good works, and squandered the fortune he wanted to leave to Thy service, including, I might say, to the *144,000 Club* and our new *Claiming America for Christ* campaign."

To the casual observer the good Reverend's demeanor and pronouncements might have seemed either unhinged or fully hateful. To the believers and sycophants of the *144,000 Club*, they appeared inspired by God. To anyone who had read a newspaper in the last two years, they seemed patently absurd.

Winslow Boolean's multi-billion dollar empire, MacroGent, was built on a succession of clever, marginally legal takeovers of small software companies. No new ideas had emerged from Boolean or his root company. All innovation arose from outside individuals who then had the unfortunate experience of being approached by Boolean, told that they could either sell their company to him for a firesale price, or that he would reverse engineer their invention, integrate it into his mega-software, and put them out of business within a year. Because of the size of MacroGent, no one could refuse Boolean's offers.

The philanthropic African adventure alluded to by the good Reverend Robinson Patrick, was particularly clever. When George Bush announced a plan to wipe out AIDS in Africa—conveniently omitting a plan for funding it—Winslow Boolean, whose personal popularity was practically non-existent, saw an opportunity for a public relations clean sweep. He arranged a visit to the White House and with Bush at his side in the Rose Garden, pledged 100 million dollars for AIDS medications to the "people of the Dark Continent." Boolean beamed. Cameras flashed. Bush smirked.

What on the surface appeared to be a magnanimous gesture was in fact a desperate but clever attempt to prop up certain pharmaceutical companies in the United States. The three companies, one of which was owned by Boolean, all manufactured anti-HIV medications. The exclusive patents on these medications was scheduled to expire in four months, and already pharmaceutical giants in Argentina and Germany had announced that they would be producing generic versions at less than 1/20th the price of the original brands. They also announced that in a cooperative effort, they would be making massive donations of the generics to African countries. Boolean and the CEOs of the two other companies had taken every possible legal step to block the Argentines and Germans. Boolean knew if the generic products were allowed on the market his stranglehold on millions of desperately ill people would be broken. It would *cost* him—and so, the pledge of $100 million in donated pharmaceuticals. The glory was to him. $70 million of the donation was coming from the other two U.S. companies but that wasn't mentioned in the Rose Garden.

And there was one other thing. The countries accepting the contributed medications to save the lives of their citizens had to sign a little agreement. It was short. It simply stated that by accepting the noblesse oblige of the American companies, recipient countries agreed to refuse generic drugs in perpetuity. Of course the language was far more dense and difficult to understand than that. In fact, most legal analysts were later to say that no one could have understood the ramifications of the document no matter what their level of legal expertise.

As a favorite of the White House, Boolean basked in the glow of his "generosity" and locked in his profits knowing that each dollar was bought with the suffering and death of thousands. An ardent Evangelical Christian, Boolean gloried in his state of salvation each Sunday and crafted more avaricious schemes Monday through Saturday.

And so, Reverend Robinson Patrick bestowed saintly status to Winslow Boolean because he was gone and demon status to Chandra Boolean because she wasn't. However, the holy man's accusation that Chandra had "stood in the way of Winslow's generosity" wasn't exactly true. What Chandra Boolean *had* done was try to block her husband's stranglehold on Africa by leaking his plan to the press. Winslow would have divorced her for the action, but he wisely realized that the timing of the divorce would counter the effect of his denials.

When Chandra Boolean married Winslow, the great entrepreneur required her to sign a prenuptial agreement crafted by his lawyers, which in language as dense as the African contracts, stated that if there were a divorce, Chandra would relinquish custody of "any and all children from the marriage." When she first mentioned a divorce, Winslow's lawyers informed her of the relinquishment clause. She could not bear the idea of such a separation from her young son and daughter, and thus was reduced to the role of Winslow's defacto nanny.

Babs Waller, fretting in Denver, knew all the facts of the Boolean story. She had done what she could to right what in her mind was a terrible wrong done to Winslow by his wife, and had given him an entire hour's special broadcast to explain his side. Chandra Boolean was not allowed comment on the program, while Winslow was led step by step through prearranged questions to vindicate himself and restore his image of philanthropic largesse. In a trademark move Babs had even gotten water from a stone. She called upon the memory of Winslow's saintly grandmother and a toy truck of long ago to evoke a tearful response from the corporate giant.

"She gave me that little red truck," Winslow said, his lip quivering in a manner Babs had approved before the show. "She gave it to me and said, Winnie—she always called me Winnie—this little truck is my gift to you. It is going to get you out of poverty and shame and bring you success." He wiped a tear from his eye and wished the ammonia fumes that induced it didn't burn his nose so badly. "Granny was right. I rode the dream of that little red truck to this point in life where I'm actually able to… to…" He seemed overcome. ". . . actually save lives."

Here Babs patted the shoulder of the man who now was overcome with his own humility and largesse.

While the segment was good theater, it couldn't have been further from the truth. Boolean was not raised in poverty. He was raised *by* poverty. His father owned over 70 slum buildings; managed a for-profit welfare corporation that fed off of Medicare; owned 12 supermarkets that serviced the poorest areas of the New York City by providing substandard food at superstandard prices. So Winslow Boolean was no stranger to poverty, he *lived* off it. His grandmother, long since banished to a state senior home, was hardly his favorite. And the little red truck never existed. Other than that, Babs' report was 100% factual.

But now, stuck in Denver, Babs wasn't worrying about how many Black people were being buried in Africa, she wasn't worried about the future of the pharmaceutical branch of Boolean Industries or about the future of the *whole financial world*. What sickened and tormented Babs Waller was the fact that she had missed a scoop.

"The Tokyo Stock Exchange decimated—God knows how many people missing. Well, I suppose *He* does know…" Babs chuckled at her own joke. "And I'm stuck in this God-forsaken airport with my crew and no place to go."

But Babs was resourceful. If the airports were closed, charters were unavailable and major stories were elsewhere—she would create her own story. Cupping her cellphone to her ear, she began to lay out her plan.

DAY THREE

Friday

October 31, 2008

CHAPTER 18

Wall Street was impassable. Cordons of police and massive cement barricades blocked the Broadway and Broad Street entrances. The American and New York Stock Exchanges were surrounded by masses of hastily installed surveillance equipment and phalanxes of security personnel.

Further uptown, Times Square was shut off to motor traffic. NASDAQ headquarters was protected in the same manner as the downtown exchanges. The FBI, NSA, and CIA operated from the ABC television building just north of NASDAQ. "Good Morning America" was forced to broadcast from ABC's uptown studios even though they vociferously protested that their proximity to NASDAQ would provide a huge public service. After all, they argued, having their cameras aimed out onto Times Square and into the NASDAQ windows might provide spectacular disappearance footage.

Jerrod Parker, a 32-year-old broker, rushed from his apartment on East 82nd Street. He was slightly hung over, the result of some generous self-medication the night before. He'd needed it. All the news about disappearances and speculation about the Rapture had shaken Jerrod to his core. There are times when a man is forced to question even his most strongly held beliefs and this was such a time for Jerrod. When his friends carried him out of the taxi at 3 AM Jerrod was still repeating the phrase he'd been slurring all evening, "Maybe I *should* have been a Christian."

The irony of the statement was not lost on his companions, but they were also concerned about the despair of their otherwise very sensible friend. They were aware of the incredible stress he had been under for the past five years and had just begun to think that he was emerging from his ordeal stronger than ever. But then with the disappearances and endless talk of Rapture, Jerrod buckled.

Six years earlier the picture was very different. Jerrod and his wife, Nancy, inspired envy in many circles. Equally beautiful as Jerrod was handsome,

Nancy had achieved considerable commercial success in the fashion world. During the boom of the 90's, she started a clothing line called "Naughty." For a few thousand dollars, rich, cultured, refined and otherwise repressed women could look like the Hollywood version of a hooker. There were enough cultured/repressed women with a few thousands dollars to make Nancy Parker very rich. But two things happened when the 90's boom came to a screeching halt: 1) Nancy's business dropped by 87%, and 2) she bought a book called *The Goal Guided Life* by Reverend Teddy Dobbin. She earnestly memorized the three-point plan for sanctification, which Dobbin asserted, would also restore any reader's financial health. As more than 60 million Americans recited over and over, Dobbin's plan was: 1) grasp the faith of old; 2) accept God's plan for you; and 3) carry the sword of justice.

Nancy seized the points with a literal zeal no one could have anticipated. While Jerrod struggled to save his client's portfolios, Nancy set out on a quest of her own. In order to "grasp the faith of old," she searched the Yellow Pages for a church that proclaimed itself absolutely Biblically fundamental. Through a process of elimination—one church eschewed the Old Testament, another condoned dancing, and yet another questioned the existence of a literal hell—Nancy found three churches, albeit obscure ones, which were sufficiently primitive in their approach to Biblical teaching to merit her consideration.

It was in this "three church phase" that Jerrod noticed a distinct change in his wife. Gone was the biting humor, the sassy demeanor and the laugh he had fallen in love with. Also gone were Nancy's fashion touches that had always drawn a following. On a particular Wednesday night, Jerrod arrived home by eight, rather than his usual 10, to find Nancy leaving the house wearing a housedress which fell some six inches below her knees, a pair of old hiking boots, and what can only be described as a cowboy scarf over her head, tied modestly under her chin.

"Happy Halloween," he cried when he saw her, thinking she would charm him with a crusty retort.

Instead, she brushed past him saying, "I'm sorry, I didn't think you would be home yet. I'm late." She blew a kiss in his direction—he thought it missed—and ran out the door.

Eighteen months later he would remember the incident as the beginning of the end. At the time, he dismissed it as a new phase in his wife's adventure with life.

It was on that night—dressed in her simple schemata—that Nancy narrowed her choice to a single church. Reverend Arnold Purdey was a nervous but brilliant student of the Holy Writ. He found endless delight in parsing phrases in English, Hebrew, Latin and Greek, particularly when those phrases—all of which he was sure had been spoken by God Himself—provided new ways to curtail, restrict or otherwise monitor the actions of his parishioners. Hell was real. It was a flaming living creature just orgasmic with the anticipation of roasting its next visitor. Death was a portal, an irreversible fork in the road that led either up the steep stairs to heaven or plummeted unstoppably into Satan's kingdom below. Infractions of God's law were stains upon the soul that only the blood of Jesus could remove. Purdey was fond of calling that blood "Super Fantastic," naming it after the Dow Chemical all-purpose cleaner upon which God clearly had smiled, blessing it with financial success. According to Purdey, that particular blessing—the blessing of financial success—was God's favorite means of showing approval to his children.

"The kingdom of God," Purdey declared from the pulpit the night that Nancy sat in the third row wearing her uncomfortable hiking boots and her cowboy headwrap, "is not made up of failures, of people who have stupidly avoided the riches that God wants to provide. It is not filled with lazy, good-for-nothing welfare mammas who want a free ride on the labor of God's saints. No! God's kingdom is for those who have seized upon His promises and pole-vaulted themselves into *Divine Prosperity*."

Divine Prosperity, a state of righteousness available only to members of Purdey's congregation, was something that Nancy desperately wanted. She had yet to learn that when God blesses one with Divine Prosperity, those riches are not to stay in one's own hands, but are to be turned over to the single entity on earth sanctioned by the Creator Himself: The Church of Divine Prosperity. But Nancy didn't know that one little catch, which would later—in her cell—have her consider that perhaps she had made some tiny errors of judgement. Instead, she marveled in the fact that out of the thousands of religions, all the denominations that had divided and fought and regrouped, all the preachers and all the bands of disciples in the world, all the deceivers Reverend Purdey had named like Reverend Teddy Dobbin, she had managed, right in the middle of New York City to find the *one and only* church that met God's demanding approval. The thought was so pleasing, so overwhelmingly astonishing, so rapturously soothing to her ego, that she wondered how she had ever existed in her previous shallow, meaningless, Beelzebub-inspired life and marriage. And then and there, she seized the second of the Dobbin commandments and "accepted God's plan" for her.

"I want you to come with me to The Church of Divine Prosperity tonight," she said as she put a bowl of tossed salad on the dining table. "Jerrod, it's the most wonderful thing. You have got to experience it for yourself."

The evening in question was just two weeks after Nancy had submitted her request to be baptized into the aforementioned church. It was also the first time that Jerrod had heard about The Church of Divine Prosperity.

"The what?" He asked innocently, not sarcastically, because he hadn't clearly heard Nancy's words.

"You see?" She said, nearly hurling the salad at him, "If it matters to me, if *I* discover it, it means nothing to you!"

"I just didn't hear what you said."

"You never do. I would think, with only the biggest thing in the whole world happening to me right under your nose that you would notice *something*. But no. You don't even hear me when I tell you that I have discovered the *truth*. Let me rephrase that: *THE TRUTH*."

Jerrod was reaching for the salad when Nancy jerked it away from him. "I heard you say something the other night about finding the truth, but we'd just been talking about 9/11 and so I thought you were talking about that movie *Loose Change*."

"Isn't that just like you, Jerrod Parker? You thought. You *thought*. Well you thought wrong."

"Well tell me what this is truth about."

"It happens to be the truth about *everything*. Is that enough for you? The truth about *ev-rey-thing*. Haven't you seen the change in me? Haven't you seen the new peace that has flooded my soul?"

Jerrod had seen a change in his wife, but he'd thought that since the hooker line of clothing had failed, perhaps she was experimenting in another extreme direction. She'd always had late evening meetings, mysterious forays into the fashion world which had neither interested nor troubled him, so it had never occurred to him that her new out-six-night-a-week schedule was anything other than a new business plan. By the time he got home he was too exhausted, too agonizingly frayed by the losses his clients were enduring to think of anything but setting the alarm and taking a sleeping pill.

"I'm sorry that I've missed something here, Nancy. Really," he said, trying to direct the conversation in a more constructive vein. "I would really like to know what it is that you've found and what it is you would like me to do."

"It probably isn't your cup of tea, Mr. Stockbroker, so don't even trouble yourself."

"What's gotten into you? You were never like this before."

"Finally you notice you big jerk. Now that I'm furious you finally notice that I am filled with the Holy Spirit and his love? That I am *filled with the Spirit of God and His righteousness in a way that brings peace, prosperity, tranquility, and the assurance of eternal life into my heart?*"

The list had not been on the tip of Jerrod's tongue.

"You said you want me to go somewhere with you. Where was it?"

"The Church of Divine Prosperity—and you are formally disinvited. If you can't embrace TRUTH when you hear it, you not only don't deserve it, you are an enemy to it." Nancy shoved the salad towards him and left the room. Jerrod ate damp lettuce in silence.

The market slump continued. Jerrod quickly lost track of everything but the misery of his clients and his own mounting debt. Nancy's absence from his house and his life had little effect in relation to the much larger crises he was enduring.

It was quite the opposite with Nancy. Members of The Church of Divine Prosperity were abundantly aware that the new member, the woman who had been snatched from Satan's grasp, was on an ever-so-very-lonely spiritual journey. By her own confession, her husband, someone they had never met, refused to be persuaded by his wife's sweet, Christlike call and was pursuing a headlong path to perdition.

"I have begged him to turn to the Lord," she said during a marathon prayer vigil. "I have done everything that I possibly could to turn his heart towards heaven. But the Devil has a grip on him that I am powerless to break. I feel so terribly, terribly, terribly alone." And she gave a long, slow, sideways glance towards Marcus DuChamps, a lawyer who, despite his having been saved by Reverend Purdey, still was rumored to have considerable ties to the mob. Corruption or not, DuChamps had God's blessing written all over his astonishingly handsome face, his gym-sculpted body, his celebrity salon groomed hair, and his $3000 suits.

Seeing the beseeching look from this damsel in distress, DuChamps had what the Reverend often referred to as a "stirring in his loins." He nodded to Nancy and made a mental note to nail her as soon as possible.

Such an ungodly mental note was, of course, something unconditionally forbidden in The Church of Divine Prosperity—even between married partners. But DuChamps was no ordinary member of the church. He was, in fact, a very special member. Currently facing indictment on charges that could carry 25 to life, his lawyers recommended he adopt the appearance of sanctification. He had, of course, failed to mention the external pressure that had brought him to the little congregation and Reverend Arnold Purdey was not one to delve much into the backgrounds of people who came to him with checkbooks already out of their pockets.

Four hours later, Nancy was banging towards nirvana in a new way—directly under the tutelage of Marcus DuChamps. She marveled that a Thermapedic mattress made no giveaway squeaks despite the pounding it was receiving. Far away, oh how far away were thoughts of her irreligious husband—and of Jesus for that matter. She did manage a kind of religious outburst as she screamed again and again, *"OH MY GOD!"*

With DuChamps as her own personal Christian Soldier, Nancy was about to embrace the third Dobbin commandment and "carry the sword of justice."

Jerrod frequently asked his car service to drop him off on the East Side near the 59th Street tramway so he could walk the twenty-some blocks up the parkway to his house. That is exactly what he did on a night several months later. The crisp air and the fresh salt smell of the East River estuary invigorated him and prepared him mentally for the increasingly unpleasant welcome he would receive upon his arrival at home. There was an area next to an old hospital that was covered by scaffolding where the otherwise wide and well-lighted jogging path narrowed and darkened. About half way through the plywood-encased tunnel, Jerrod thought he saw a motion in the darkness to his left. He was turning to get a look when a baseball bat hit him squarely across the bridge of his nose. Both eye sockets shattered instantly. He was propelled backwards by the impact, but stopped abruptly when another bat found its mark against his occipital lobe. That contact mercifully ended his awareness of pain as successive blows hit his genitals, knees, rib cage and, perhaps as a little insurance, another 25 times on his skull and face.

"You are lucky to be alive," a disembodied voice said to him three weeks later when he regained consciousness in Mt. Sinai Hospital. He would have argued with the voice had his jaw not been wired shut, had his eyes not failed to open, and had the pain not robbed him of awareness at that moment.

He didn't hear about the arrests for another a month. It was during a particularly grueling physical therapy session that he overheard a nurse whispering, "And to think it was his own *wife*."

"I heard what you said," Jerrod mumbled through the wires and the enormous stainless steel cage that was bolted to his skull. "What are you talking about?"

He had thought it strange that Nancy never came to see him and that when he would enquire about her his friends made nervous excuses about her fragile state and her inability to endure seeing him suffer further. But now he was about to learn the truth.

The nurse, who feared losing her job as a result of slipping the forbidden information, ran to her supervisor and asked what to do. Within the hour Jerrod's attending physician was in his room with a seven-week-old copy of *The Daily News*. "I think you should see this," he said, handing him the paper with a three-inch high headline, *Born Again Lovers Arrested in Kill Plot*.

It was to Jerrod as if earth itself had changed course. He wept through what was left of his eye sockets, screamed with what was left of his larynx, and beat against the sheets with what was left of his right hand. Only a shot from a fast thinking nurse stopped him from ripping at the apparatus that was keeping him alive.

The trial of Nancy Parker and Marcus DuChamps was headline news for days. DuChamps received 15 to life for conspiracy to commit murder, assault, and attempted murder. His consecutive 25 to life sentence for mob activities nearly guaranteed his absence from Purdey's church services for some time.

Nancy, who had rediscovered her fashion sense, appealed for leniency from the jury. Against the advice of her attorney she took the stand in her own defense.

The courtroom was a tightly packed box of silence and curiosity. "What do you wish to say in your own defense?" Judge Sven Tonkelsen asked.

"Your honor, members of the jury, I am a seeker after God's will. I thought I had found it. My marriage was a loveless marriage and in the person of DuChamps I found someone who was united in my quest for perfect truth."

There was a ripple of laughter in the crowd because jaded New Yorkers were aware that there was no "truth," let alone a murderous partnership based on the search for it.

"You see, your honor, there came a time when I realized that I could not go on with my marriage to Jerrod Parker and that God was calling me to unite body and soul with Marcus DuChamps. We were fulfilling the mission Christ in his mercy made abundantly clear to us—to serve Him and God the Father with every fiber of our being." On the word "fiber," Nancy made a motion—not unlike an orgasmic shiver—that was noticed with interest by every red-blooded man in the room.

Judge Tonkelsen was not amused. "Ms. Parker, you and your partner Mr. DuChamps mercilessly beat Mr. Parker about the head, neck, chest, genitals, knees and lower legs until he by all reasonable accounts should have been dead. Then you smashed his hands until they were pulp, and for good measure returned to his head for what the doctors believe was another 25 blows. Is this a partnership sanctioned by Christ and God the Father? If you were in love with Mr. DuChamps, there are legal means by which you could end your marriage to Mr. Parker and live your life with Mr. DuChamps! I am appalled and disgusted by your presentation."

Upon this declaration by the judge, Nancy's attorney, Virgil Gallet, was on his feet screaming his objections.

Tonkelsen banged his gavel and shouted, "Sit down. Motion denied." He turned back to Nancy. "I ask you once again, Ms. Parker, do you have something to say in your defense?"

Nancy took a deep breath and released it slowly as a prolonged and heartbreaking sigh. "As I have been trying to explain, your Honor, I have been on a search—a long and arduous search for truth. I found that truth in the teachings of Reverend Arnold Purdey and The Church of Divine Prosperity. And within that blessed place, those hallowed halls I met the man with whom I could share utterly my love of truth and goodness and love."

"Then why did you attempt to brutally murder your husband?"

"Your honor! There was no way out, no way for our lives to proceed while I was still married to a man who shunned truth and was led by Satanic desires for poverty and an uncomfortable life."

"Ms. Parker, have you ever heard of divorce?" The judge leaned forward and stared at Nancy with the hope he would stop her heart.

The defendant slowly uncrossed her legs, adjusted her creeping skirt and recrossed in the opposite direction. Her new position attained, she concentrated her efforts on a look of horror.

"Your Honor! How can you even suggest that? We who love the Lord, who follow his principles and are on the path to an eternity with Him—we are forbidden by the Holy Word and the teachings of Reverend Arnold Purdey to *divorce*! It is immoral!"

With that the chambers erupted into a sustained pandemonium. Buried beneath the overwhelming laughter which reached ear-damaging decibels, could be heard the cries of Nancy's church friends screaming, "Jaesus, Jaesus! Thank you Jaesus!"

Nancy got fifteen to life.

Now on this day, five years later, Jerrod Parker with his considerable emotional baggage, was entering the New York Stock Exchange, fully expecting it to be the day he would either be swept away or left behind. Had he been asked, he would not have been able to answer which alternative he hoped for. Little did he know he was going to have a third choice.

CHAPTER 19

Her plan in motion, Babs Waller was undergoing make up.

"It's going to be a fabulous interview—the interview of the century, Danny," she said—trying to move her face enough to show an expression despite the surgical tension and Botox.

"I don't doubt that it will. Honey, you got that Hogan Cafferty born again Christian who can't do much more than curse and you bring him together with Chandra Boolean, the richest widow in the world who everybody thinks is the Bitch of Satan—girl you've got yourself a show!" Danny punctuated the last words with three little pokes of the blush brush.

"I'm going to get them both to cry. I'm going to get them to compare notes about what it means to lose those close to you. I'll hit Hogan Cafferty with questions about financial irregularities in the Jesus Dome and I'll make sure that Chandra Boolean makes a fool of herself acting like God saved her from destruction while everyone is saying that she was just Left Behind."

"I notice *you're* still here."

"That's different."

"Speaking of different—have you noticed that your left behind is a little lower than your right?"

"Danny, your claws are showing."

"I'll shut up, Mamma Lion."

Bab's excitement arose from the fact that she was the first to learn that Chandra Boolean had been successfully rescued and was returning to Denver. In what could be the coup of the entire disappearance saga, Babs got the Boolean/Hogan double interview. Hogan Cafferty had agreed to appear simply because he seemed incapable of refusing. He had tried saying "no" a number of times, but all that would escape his lips was a string of curses and "forgive me Jesus." Babs reached Chandra Boolean in the emergency room of the University of Denver Hospital.

"Ms. Boolean, this is Babs Waller of *40/40*."

"I'm not interested in being interviewed, Miss Waller." Chandra was firm but polite.

Babs had planned the entire conversation before the call, so Chandra's statement was irrelevant. "I assure you, Ms. Boolean that I believe in you as a good woman, and I don't for a minute believe what everyone is saying—that you have been left behind as a form of punishment."

"My husband was planning to kill me, Ms. Waller. The accident in which Winslow disappeared was intended for me, not him."

The response was not part of the intended conversation, so Babs ignored and pressed on. "After all, you have saved many, many of those primitive Black African types of people from certain death."

"I've said what I have to say."

"You could clear your name after all the things your husband said about you in his interview with me."

"The one you barred me from?"

Again, not part of the planned chat.

"You will be given ample time to correct anything he said, and it will be a wonderful opportunity to express your thanks to God for sparing you."

Chandra was grateful she'd been spared death. She didn't imagine God had much to do with it. She hesitated.

Babs burrowed into the opening. "So is that a yes, Ms. Boolean?"

"If this can be done quickly. I want to get to California to join my mother and children."

"It can be immediately. I'll switch you to my producer to make final arrangements," and before anything further could be said, Babs transferred the call.

Babs was elated. Now it was time to throw the two lambs into the Mix Master.

From the emergency room, Chandra called her mother's home in Van Nuys, California. After several rings, her nanny, Felice, picked up. "Felice, oh, it's so good to hear your voice."

"Oh Miss Boo… uh, Chandra!"

"That's more like it, Felice."

"I have been so worried!"

"I'm okay. I'll tell you everything when I get to California. Is mother there?"

"No, she just went to church to thank God that you are alive."

Even though Chandra wasn't religious, she was moved to think of her mother in church expressing her thanks. "That's sweet," she said. "Are Santee and Vertaine there?"

"Of course. I'll put them on speakerphone."

"Hello my darlings."

Seven-year-old Santee called out, "Hello Mommy. I miss you." In the background, five-year-old Vertaine could be heard saying, "Mommy, Mommy."

"I miss you too. Mommy's just fine. I'm going to come to Grandma's house very soon to be with you."

"Okay, Mommy. I love you," Santee repeated.

Vertaine joined repeating, "I love you, I love you."

"Are they really okay, Felice? I mean—they don't…"

Felice said, "Just a moment." Chandra heard her telling the children to go back and play in their room. A moment later she returned to the phone. "They don't know anything," she said. Your mother has been wonderful. The children have never even seen her cry. Are you sure you're all right?"

"I really am, Felice. You'll see when I get there."

"Was this one of those disappearances, Miss Chandra?"

"I don't know. I really don't. I know that one moment Winslow was driving terribly fast towards a cliff and the next moment he was gone. I'll tell you about it there. I shouldn't stay so long on the phone. I have to give an interview, Felice. It's very important. The children can stay there with Mother. I can't wait to see them. Tell mother I love her. I'll be there as soon as possible. Kiss the children for me."

She had no idea how long that kiss would have to last.

CHAPTER 20

Despite all she'd been through, Chandra Boolean had maintained 100% of her beauty. Arriving at the Jesus Dome television studio she was immediately the center of male attention and female comparison. The tears Babs expected to elicit fell easily as Chandra told crewmembers how close she had come to death. "It was a matter of a few feet between the chasm and me" she said. "I was afraid to move in the car for fear that any motion would send me over the edge. I know that people are saying that Winslow was Raptured and that I was left behind, but frankly, I think that whatever happened to him, it wasn't the Rapture, and I was simply protected."

"Tell them to get away from her," Babs seethed. "They're going to use her up and there will be nothing left for my interview."

Danny LaFogg was heading towards the weeping widow just as Hogan Cafferty entered the room. Chandra looked up and for one astonishing moment was staring into the eyes of the most exquisitely sad man she had ever seen. He was looking back and seeing the eyes of someone who had been left behind despite her obviously pure soul.

Neither spoke.

Danny spun on his heels and returned to Babs. "Did you see that? The breeders have met like a deodorant commercial. I think I'm gonna barf."

"Get your nelly ass over there and make sure nothing more happens before the cameras are rolling."

"Oui oui your pissiness." And Danny headed back for the two interview subjects who were now blushing and looking anywhere but one another's eyes.

Babs removed the paper bib she wore to protect her dress and walked briskly towards her prey. "Good afternoon," she said extending her hand to Chandra, "I'm Babs Waller. Mr. Cafferty and I have already met. I see that the two of you have already… *met.*"

Chandra's blush deepened and Hogan mumbled something inaudibly followed by "forgive me Jesus."

"Shall we get seated and begin?" Babs was bright and upbeat. "We don't want to tire you since I know you two have been through so much, so if you'll just come over here and take a seat, they can get the lights adjusted and we'll begin."

"Who is this gentleman?" Chandra asked, following Babs.

"Oh! Hogan Cafferty, the head of security for Reverend Teddy Dobbin. He seems to have done a remarkable job of protection, don't you think?" And with that sarcastic response, Babs led the way to the set.

There were three red upholstered seats. The center seat was slightly higher than the other two—an intentional nod to the queen of television who was to sit in it. But instinctively, Chandra and Hogan sat next to each other—Hogan in the center seat—leaving Babs in a snit because she didn't want to upset her guests by rearranging them. A quick conference with the set decorator resulted in the third chair being raised even higher than the first two, so much so that when Babs hopped into it, her feet were dangling a full three inches above the floor. Still, she had achieved supreme height and was quite pleased with herself.

Of course, with Babs on the seat to the far right, lighting had to be readjusted. Babs feared the wasted minutes would diffuse the spontaneity of her guests, so she kept up a constant prattle intended to keep everyone's mind off their current events.

When she was satisfied that the lighting flattered her, Babs nodded to her producer and director—local affiliate employees who were more than thrilled to be involved with a Babs Waller exclusive.

It would have been quite an interview had something not happened at that very moment which so distracted the crew and interviewees that it was impossible to proceed. Just as Babs was raising her 4 x 6 question cards to begin the interview, someone in the control room called over the intercom, "Hold it. We need all creative personnel in the control room. We're suspending all other programming. Something has happened. We're supposed to get a live feed from New York."

The producer, director and makeup man scrambled away, leaving Babs, Chandra, Hogan, and a lone cameraman on the empty set. And then, there was pandemonium in the control room.

CHAPTER 21

Babs, Hogan and Chandra were left in the studio. When no one returned to explain why there was such panic in the control room, Babs began to mutter to herself. Then over the squawk box: "Miss Waller, we will not be able to proceed. You're needed up here immediately."

In a rage, Babs screamed at her guests, "This interview was a *shonda*. I never wanted to do it in the first place. I hate you! You interfered with Winslow's good works. And *you*!" She glowered at Hogan, "You're nothing but a babbling idiot. If I ever get stuck with a minor story like this again, I'm going to sue the network—just like Dan Rather." She stomped off to the control room.

After some moments of awkward silence, Hogan asked, "Would you like to get something to eat?" He stopped, shocked that he hadn't cursed. Chandra was just saying "I'd like that," when Hogan blurted, "The hot air's gone!"

"What?"

"The hot air. There's been this hot air in my head—it's been moving around and the only thing that made it stop hurting was to curse. . . You think I'm crazy, don't you?"

"I don't know enough to think that. Let's go outside. We can talk while we look for a coffee shop." They left the Jesus Dome together. "I don't think you're crazy. I think something crazy is going on around us, but you and I are remarkably fine."

Hogan hesitated, fearful that the air and cursing would return. "I… think… you're right!" He smiled at his success.

"I'm sorry for what happened to you in there."

"It's just that being the only one left does make me feel like I'm a terrible person."

"I'm not so sure." Chandra took his arm gently. "I'm not so sure that being the one left here means that you are necessarily bad."

"You don't?"

"No. I was left behind—it was my husband who disappeared."

"But wasn't he that person who was always giving away huge amounts of money to help people?"

"That was the story for the press. I actually thought of him as a very evil person."

"Wow." Hogan stopped walking and turned to Chandra. "I have to tell you something," he whispered.

"Go ahead."

"You see, I've had doubts."

"Doubts? About what?"

"Uh, you're going to think this is horrible."

"Try me."

"Well, recently, I've wondered from time to time if Teddy Dobbin really gets his instructions from God. Forgive me Jesus."

Chandra raised an eyebrow, "Careful."

Hogan didn't understand.

"You said, 'Forgive me Jesus,' just like this afternoon."

"Oh. I'm sorry."

"No, don't be sorry, just be aware. And don't be sorry doubting Reverend Teddy Dobbin. You'd be very wrong if you didn't." Chandra pointed across the street to a small diner. "Let's go in there."

They found a booth near a window. Hogan was not aware that Chandra hadn't been in a diner for nearly twenty years.

"Everything looks so good," she said of the brightly colored pictures of the meals in the menu. "I can't believe I'm hungry after what's happened."

"I'm afraid you're not going to get to eat."

"Why not?"

"Look out the window." Hogan nodded in its direction.

There, amassed in the parking lot were television news trucks, reporters and cameramen who had been locked out of the Jesus Dome at Babs Waller's command. A quick count put the number at eleven different stations. One of the reporters was furiously gesturing towards the diner and within moments there was a stampede of people with cameras and microphones.

"Quick. Someone's spotted us." Chandra grabbed Hogan's hand and headed for the kitchen door. She led the way past a surprised cook and an indifferent dishwasher, finally locating the back door. "My car is in the mul-tistory garage across the street. When I count to three, run."

Chandra kicked off her high heels and began to count. When she reached "three," both she and Hogan bolted across the street and into the parking garage. They were nearly inside when they heard a reporter shout, "There they are over there!"

Hogan looked around and saw an army of press running towards them.

"Are you up for a sprint?" Chandra gave Hogan a funny smile and headed up the curved incline. "I'm on the third level," she called over her shoulder. She was surprised when Hogan sprinted past her.

"I do the charity marathons," he said on his way by.

Chandra already had her keys out when they reached the car. She had started it remotely from the level below.

Hogan was impressed. "That's a neat trick," he said, climbing into the passenger's seat. The BMW left a black track of rubber when Chandra gunned it toward the exit. She got down to the second level and was circling to ground when ahead of them came the reporters.

"Hold on," she said. She blasted her horn—holding it steady and con-tinuing towards the reporters who scattered to the railings on both sides of the ramp. One more turn and they were on the street.

"I need to get back to my house," she said. "I haven't been back there since the accident. Do you need to be somewhere?"

"I just want to make one phone call."

"You can do it from my place. We can be there in an hour and a half."

Considering the kind of day it had been, Hogan felt pretty good.

CHAPTER 22

At the same time that Chandra Boolean and Hogan Cafferty were with Babs Waller in the Jesus Dome in Denver waiting to be interviewed, Jerrod Parker traveled through three layers of security and stood at last on the trading floor of the New York Stock Exchange. Tension was a norm in that vast room with its television monitors, its runners in blue jackets and representative scions of America's financial royalty. But this day was different. Television cameras lined the balconies poised like hungry vultures to capture the possible bloodless carnage about to take place. New York policemen, the stoic, implacable men in blue, now looked apprehensive and unsure. A runner knocked into a television monitor and it fell to the floor with a loud shatter. Three hundred people ducked for cover. It was *not* a normal day.

Jerrod went to his station and began to study the numbers on the screen. He blanched. The market was poised for a historic tumble. He had done his best to protect his clients. He'd shifted vast amounts of capital out of stocks predicted to be affected by the disappearances, but now it seemed that every stock on the board was ready to crash.

High above the floor was the imposing podium with the famous bell. Today's honorary bell ringers were the Senate Chaplain Most Reverend Bartholomew Oppenheimer of the Presbyterian faith; Archbishop Antonio Irrelevencio of St. Patricks Cathedral; Rabbi Yissocher Tatz of Temple Emmanuel in Manhattan; Imam Omar Al-Farir of the 96th Street Mosque; Shinto Priest Nisshutsu; Erlik Subramuniya a Hindu shaman; Priestess Eve-Michele Boisette a practitioner of Santa Ria; and for good measure, Madam Ola, a Gypsy fortune teller whose establishment on Canal Street was trafficked by many a Wall Street investor. It was the somewhat puerile thinking of the Exchange president, that having a high-placed minister of the protestant Gospel, a Catholic Archbishop, a Rabbi, an Imam, a Buddhist priest, a Hindu shaman, a voodoo priestess and a Gypsy fortune teller would be the best insurance for the titans of industry assembled in his building. For good measure he also had Szandrada DeVreek, a priest from the Church of Satan; a coven of witches; and vampire Lord Zimula performing rituals in the basement.

Moments before the floor was to commence trading, the eight clergy who professed communication with the higher world stepped forward to ring the bell.

Jerrod, who had turned away from his monitor to watch the proceedings, was immediately distracted by some motion to his left. It was as if a sea of people was being rapidly parted, forming a path leading precisely in his direction. The eight defenders of otherworldly control stopped short of ringing the bell because they too had seen the motion on the floor.

One would have expected the crowd to be making a great deal of noise given the high state of nerves in the room. Instead there was silence as masses of exchange employees fell back to allow one lone man to proceed to the center of the floor.

Photographers jockeyed for position in the balcony. Television cameras panned back and forth hoping to be aimed at the right spot at the right time.

Jerrod, his heart pumping in an oddly irregular but forceful pattern, found himself pressed tightly against the pillar next to his station, his head rigidly pulled back as though he was expecting a sudden impact.

The motion on the floor was nearly upon him, and then he heard a cry from the balcony, "Oh my god, it's *JESUS*."

And there standing directly in front of him was a handsome Black man with waist-length locks wearing a long crimson robe. He stopped and looked at Jerrod with a depth of kindness the young trader had never experienced. "Hello," the man in the crimson robe said, looking directly at Jerrod. "My name is Jesus. Would you mind helping me to get up there to the podium? I'd like to make an announcement."

From high in the visitor's gallery a voice boomed, "Hold it right there, or we open fire." At least two dozen marksmen had their rifles trained on the stranger and two more were aiming at Jerrod as a bit of insurance.

Jesus raised his right hand and pointed skyward with one finger. At that moment, empty clothing began to flutter to the floor, rings went rolling one direction and another and the monitors went dark. Jerrod would later remember his amusement at seeing a pair of dentures on the floor near him settled neatly on top of a blue trader's jacket and black pants.

CHAPTER 23

NEW YORK, NY—9:05 AM EST

In whatever religious tutelage Jerrod had endured, Jesus had been presented as a tall, pale man with curly blond hair. In every painting he'd seen, Jesus had blue eyes, thin arms, and essentially looked a lot like Percy McDermott, a kid Jerrod knew in sixth grade who had weak bones and said he planned to be a girl when he grew up. Now he was facing a six-foot four-inch Black man who looked like the photos on the front of *Muscle and Fitness* magazine. His eyes were black, his hair was black, his skin was black and had that satin glow Jerrod thought possible only in the movies. The man was still gazing at him with an intensity that had nothing but kindness. It did seem that he had just cleared much of the room of its human occupancy, but the gaze was incredibly kind. The right hand that was still pointed upward was attached to an arm that looked like it was made of twisted steel; a Gaugin sculpture pulsing with life. Now the arm was lowering and extending towards him.

"Take my hand," Jesus said.

Jerrod grasped the outstretched hand. It was at that moment he realized there were still several guns pointed directly at him and his new partner.

"We'll have to hurry," Jesus whispered. "Trust me."

There was an eruption of gunfire. Jerrod considered himself dead. Dead, that is, until he realized that he and Jesus were standing behind the desk where the opening and closing bell was rung.

"Brothers and sisters." It was Jesus speaking. His voice was strong and deep. It penetrated to the farthest corners of the room. "I have come to bring…"

"Make one more move and you're dead." Standing among the piles of clothes on the trading floor was a lone man in a dark suit. It was Detective Darcy O'Neil, the same detective who'd been sent to question Lyla and Grandma Cattell. Just that morning, Mayor Ari Barkin had appointed him

Chief of Investigations on the disappearances for the NYPD. He gestured to the sharpshooters stationed around the room and said, "Step out from behind the podium with your hands up."

"I don't think you want me to do that," Jesus said, somehow managing to look merciful even as he was clearly serious.

"Just do what I say—both of you."

Jesus tipped his head toward Jerrod. "Listen, Jerrod, I know this is all a big surprise to you and that you've been through a whole lot of crap recently. But I know I can trust you. I'll be with you always—you can count on that. Right now I've got to obey their orders for your protection, even though these New York cops really are dumber than I thought."

With that, Jesus raised his hands above his head. As he did so, every remaining gun in the room fell to the floor accompanied by the clothes, jewelry and artificial body parts of the marksmen who'd been holding them.

In the confusion Jesus disappeared and Jerrod found himself facing a small but very angry group of people.

O'Neil was still in place. His terror was masked by fury. "Enough!" he screamed. "Obey my command."

Jerrod thought it was funny that a policeman would practically be quoting Jesus under these circumstances, but decided he should comply. He raised his hands above his head. As he did so he realized that the remaining people in the room ducked in a reflex motion fearing that they would be the next to disappear. He backed away from the podium just as four burly cops tackled him from behind.

"Please," he cried, "I don't know what happened. I have a plate in my head. My cheekbones are fragile because my wife and her boyfriend…"

"Shut up," a cop growled as he slammed Jerrod's head against the floor. Jarrod's cheek made an odd cracking sound.

"Don't move, mu'fucker." The cops handcuffed him and strapped his ankles with plastic. Once jerked to his feet, Jerrod was directly facing O'Neil.

"You're under arrest," he snarled. "I don't know what the fuck you and your boyfriend think you're doing, but you're not going to do it in my city. What was this, one of those instant Internet happenings? You plan this whole thing with your big Black boyfriend? You the one behind everything that's been going on? You think you got some neat little trick?"

The pain in Jerrod's face likely saved him further injury at the moment because contrary to his impulse to answer the questions and explain that he was just as astonished by recent events as his captors, he found he could say nothing.

"Go ahead, stonewall me, you fucking piece of shit. We've got all the time in the world to get the truth out of you. Somebody read him his rights and then drag him to the wagon." O'Neil turned away in disgust and surveyed the room. On the trading floor terrified runners in blue jackets cowered near their computer terminals. In the balconies men and women were holding one another and weeping. Amidst the random piles of clothing and weapons there was a prosthetic leg. In all his years on the force he'd never been faced with a more staggering sight and yet something told him that it was all a farce, a computer-age illusion of immense proportion. He'd been on the force when the hoaxes happened in the 80's. He'd personally investigated the mass fainting hoax on Phil Donahue's TV show and tried to arrest it's organizer, Alan Abel. But this was different. How could anyone, no matter how clever, have gotten his sharpshooters to participate in a hoax? There was no denying that there were guns of every description—9mm Luger Parabellums to Beretta UGB25 Xcels and XM8 assault rifles—scattered like debris among the crumpled piles of uniforms. And there was no denying that everything happened with split-second precision.

O'Neil had once taken his daughter to see David Copperfield's magic show. He'd always prided himself on his ability to take in a situation, memorize every detail, and miss nothing. But as Copperfield made people come and go, get ripped apart and put back together again, O'Neil was baffled. He didn't like the emotion and refused to go to another Copperfield show. But now he was experiencing those emotions again on the floor of the New York Stock Exchange.

Even in his semi-dazed state, his experienced detective eyes automatically searched the room for clues—anything out of the ordinary. What was he thinking? *Everything* was out of the ordinary. But there was something beyond the extraordinary. What was it? He tried to shake off the overload fog and surveyed the room again. Of the nearly two thousand people present before the disappearance, perhaps sixty remained. Clearly in shock, they were either sitting where they had been, calming one another, or moving towards the exits. Missing people and survivors—at least that had precedent—but there was something else. His trained gaze circumnavigated the room again. The television cameras! There were fifty or so TV cameras set up around the balcony ready to capture with vulturous excitement the anticipated trouble on the trading floor. Some cameramen had escaped the disappearance and were still standing by their equipment. O'Neil couldn't spot a single reporter and assumed that they had left the building. But the cameras themselves—every camera—had a shattered lens. The actual moment of the disappearance had probably been lost to the TV audience.

O'Neil's radio squawked. "O'Neil here."

"Detective… are you okay?" It was Murphy at One Police Plaza.

"Fine."

"What happened in there?"

"You don't know?"

"No sir. Television reception went down from there. There's something going on, Sir."

"No kidding."

"*There* too?"

"What do you mean 'there too?'" O'Neil barked. "We've got hundreds of people missing here. Haven't you got any reports?"

"No sir, there's something else."

CHAPTER 24

Eight cops dragged Jerrod down through the labyrinthine corridors beneath the exchange. One cop read him his Miranda rights, while others kept saying things like, "You're in deep shit, asshole." Then they grabbed him by his aching arms and shuttled him forward. They hoped to escape the attention of reporters and thousands of curious onlookers outside. A police wagon was parked at the Nassau Street entrance ready for its prisoner.

Jerrod's face felt like fire where it had been slammed against the floor. He was sure the impact had undone his last three surgeries. His tethered ankles made it impossible for him to do anything but drag along with the cops. Hurtling down a final corridor towards a double door, he could hear the sounds of a crowd outside. As the doors opened, surprisingly there was mingled sound of sobbing and cheers. Listening intently, he realized the cheering was much stronger than the sobbing. Was this about him? Was there a crowd waiting to tear him limb from limb? He distinctly heard music. Jerrod lifted his head to survey the scene. Crowds of people milled in the street. An impromptu dance broke out at the Wall Street corner. Some men in expensive suits were looking very sad or crying, but a group of janitors were merrily high-fiving twenty feet from where he stood. Police were everywhere. Next to the patrol wagon he saw O'Neil, seemingly frozen in place. He held his police radio like it was a body part contaminated by an unknown virus. Just moments before the disembodied voice of Murphy had given him the news: President George W. Bush was missing.

CHAPTER 25

A chain of events unfolded in Washington D.C. concurrent with the events in New York. The President had just finished his morning run, ridden his bicycle, taken his shower, eaten his breakfast, and was about to wade through his one page daily briefing, when Laura heard a strange noise from his study. It was different than George's usual flatulence or the sound of him sniffing whatever it was that he removed from the table each morning with his nose. She knocked at the door and said in that sweet, sweet way of hers, "Geowrge?" There was no answer. She knocked again. For some reason George had instructed her never to open the study door unexpectedly. It wasn't that he was concerned about privacy. He said it had to do with the fact that if there was a draft, something valuable would blow off his desk. Laura was always impressed that there was anything that meant that much to George—his being somewhat detached from the rest of reality. In any event, upon the third try at the door, she became alarmed. She would have become very alarmed, but her Xanex prevented those extremes. "Geowrge?" she ventured again. There was no answer. She started towards his desk, but stopped suddenly and let out a muted scream. The desk was covered with baking soda, or so she thought, and George's chair was covered with his little jogging shorts, a T-shirt, and a rolled-up hundred-dollar bill.

Laura stood there a moment and then in a flurry of medicinally suppressed panic ran into the hall and said loudly, "Ah think there is something wrong with Geowrge. If you wouldn't mind—can anyone hear me—if you wouldn't mind comin' to the nap room, I think that George has maybe gowan and run away." And with that she smoothed her dress and returned to the study trying to arrange her thoughts for the inevitable photo op.

Martin Danson, a tall, broad-shouldered Secret Service agent entered the room. "Where is the President?" he demanded of the now serenely composed Laura.

"Ah towld yew I believe he has gowan and run away," she said again, turning to a mirror to make sure that her hair still looked liked perfectly arranged vinyl.

Martin had a momentary vision of the Commander in Chief trudging down the driveway with his belongings packed into a red bandana suspended from a stick over his shoulder.

"Well, dew somethin'," the First Lady implored. "We have gawt enough problems in this country without having Geowrge goin' and runnin' away, now don't we?"

Her tone, what one would have expected if a dog failed to perform a favorite trick, did not alarm Martin the way she believed it should.

"Mrs. Bush," he began with heavy overtones of patronization, "I'm sure the President is nearby. You know that when there are certain alterations of his 'state' he tends to wander away."

"What on earth are yew tawking about?"

"Well, I don't want to detail certain things, Mrs. Bush, but…"

"Well, Mr. Smartypants, look'y here," and the First Lady gave a grand gesture towards the desk with its remnants of presidential pleasures.

"Now he snorts in the nude," Martin muttered.

"What was that?"

"Nothing, Mrs. Bush. I was just noticing that the President left some things behind that perhaps it would be best if we cleaned up—before any word gets out."

"Left behind? Yew aren't really implyin' that whatever George is doin' has something to do with him and those crazy whacko Christians who think everybody is being raptured, now are you?"

"Mrs. Bush, you're one of those people."

"Oh. Well, I don't wear it on my sleeve like some snot I've wiped off my nose, now do I?"

"No, Mrs. Bush, you certainly do not. You are very discrete about the depths of your beliefs." Martin suppressed a smile.

Laura gestured again towards the white powder and undies. "Are you going to do something or not?"

Martin went into the adjoining bathroom and returned with a wet towel. "For starters, Mrs. Bush, I'm going to wipe this white powder off the President's desk. Then I'm going to call security and get everyone looking for him. I'm sure he hasn't gone far. They'll be able to spot him on the locator box."

"Yew don't really think that he could have disappeared like those people in Denver or Texas or Staten Island do yew?"

"No, and I don't think he disappeared like the people from the New York Stock Exchange." Martin liked being the one to bring bad news to Madame Laura. There were many in-house bets about who could get her agitated despite the chemicals. While there had been no television coverage from inside the Exchange, Martin had been watching as reporters outside were able to describe the disappearances. Then Laura called him to the study.

"The New York Stock Exchange?" He'd awakened Laura's interest.

"Yes ma'am, they lost their staff today."

"Oh ma gawd. That's just truly awful. Will that affect ma investments in any way, Martin?"

"Yes ma'am, I should supposed it might."

"Ah think, Martin, that in light of the upsettin' news you're tellin' me, ah had better attend to job number one."

"Yes ma'am, finding the President."

"No Martin, callin' my broker."

CHAPTER 26

For an hour, White House staff and security searched for the missing President without success. There was no signal picked up by the locator box, a satellite driven GPS device that normally could track the President anywhere in the world. The usual corners, closets and gutters had been carefully surveyed, and still no signs of the Commander in Chief. Agent Martin Danson placed a call to Karl Rove's office far below the White House. With both George and his Dick missing, Karl delightedly accepted the fact that the country was his to rule.

"Look Martin, keep this entirely hush hush. Nobody's to know that George has wandered off. We don't know if this is just his usual disorientation or if it's that other disappearance stuff going on. I don't want to get the Christian Crazies in an uproar. Oh, and Martin, don't let the Speaker of the House know I'm running things. She'd kill."

Although there were White House threats of federal prosecution against any employee who leaked information, Martin could not resist calling one person on the press—a columnist loyal to the Bush Administration who had once outed an undercover CIA operative at the behest of the Vice President. He went by the code name *Novicane*.

"Novi," Martin used a familiar abbreviation of the columnist's name to let him know it was a friend calling. "Martin at the White House. A quick tip for you. Bush is missing. Left behind his skivvies, a t-shirt, and enough cocaine to put a smile on a Senator's face. Don't know where he wandered off to. We don't think it's related to the other disappearances, but hey, you never know."

The leak worked quickly. "George AWOL *AGAIN*," ripped across front pages of special editions in four-inch type. All four media companies that controlled the news lead their broadcasts with "George MIA." In Los Angeles and New York, writers got to work on jokes for Leno and Letterman. With all the sad news of the last days, the country was ready for a lift.

CHAPTER 27

By the time Jerrod was delivered to Central Booking, New York City was on red alert. He was taken down two flights of stairs and into what was known as the "tank"—a central desk that looked like a hospital's nursing stand flanked by two rows of cells—ten cells on each side. Jerrod was thrown into a cell alone. The officer who turned the key in the lock muttered, "Fucking towelhead."

Jerrod was astute enough to know that the disappearance of a few hundred stock brokers couldn't possibly have caused the amount of drama he was witnessing, any more than the disappearance of a few hundred lawyers would have caused. There were police everywhere—seeming multitudes of them—guarding his cell. And then there were the men in suits. They swarmed into the tank wearing their little American flag lapel pins and adjusting the curlicue wires that ran to their ears from under their collars. Feds. Had to be. Jerrod strained to hear their hushed conversations in vain. He thought he heard the word "President" once, but he wasn't sure.

He studied his cell. Clearly it was made to hold ten or more men. There were stainless steel benches around the periphery and to one side a toilet attached to the wall. He needed to use it, but couldn't imagine exposing himself to the dozens of men and women who kept glancing in his direction. After a long hour, three men in suits approached his cell. An officer opened the door and they entered.

"Jerrod Parker?" a squat man with a pencil-thin mustache was the first to address him.

"Yes."

The squat man pulled out a wallet and flashed a badge at Jerrod. "Flagman, Homeland Security," he said, putting the badge back in his coat pocket.

"Homeland Security?"

"You're in very big trouble, son."

"I didn't even know that guy."

"I think you should remember that anything you say at this point can and will be used against you. You are under arrest for violation of The Patriot Act."

"What for?"

"We don't have to tell you squat."

Jerrod smiled. He thought it was funny that the squat man had said "squat."

"You think that's funny, asshole?"

"No sir, I just don't…"

"Shut up."

"But why did you arrest me? I've never seen the guy with locks before and…"

"Mr. Parker, you are being considered an Enemy Combatant and you will be remanded to an undisclosed location."

Jerrod smiled again, suppressing the desire to ask if in an undisclosed location he would be with Vice President Cheney.

"Go ahead and smile, asshole. It will likely be the last time that you smile for the rest of your sorry-assed life."

"I need a doctor," Jerrod said, pointing to the left side of his face.

A humorless suit with patchy blond hair and no eyebrows stepped forward and shoved his face inches from Jerrod's eyes. "You should have thought of that before you decided to be a terrorist, you stinking turdball."

The suits left.

Alone in his cell, Jerrod was getting desperate. The pain in his face was increasing and he feared that his headache could be a sign of intracranial bleeding.

"Officer," he called, "please, I need to see a doctor. Officer!"

The guy with the patchy blonde hair returned. "What asshole?"

"Sir, I need a doctor. I have recently had a serious head injury and I'm afraid that…"

"You should have thought of that before you got involved in kidnaping hundreds of people and murdering the President of the United States, you piece of shit."

"What are you talking about?"

The patchy one walked away.

"I want a lawyer! I want to call a lawyer!"

The patchy one turned to face him again. "A lawyer? Have you read that little legal document called *The Patriot Act*? Practically every dumbfuck Senator and Representative voted it in and now it's law forever—you hear that last word, *forever?* That means that you don't need to be charged with anything, you don't deserve a lawyer, and we can just keep you in a hole in the ground for… *forever*. Now shut the fuck up."

The patchy one headed for a box of donuts. Even though his head was throbbing, Jerrod smiled again. Maybe people were dancing in the streets because George W. Bush was gone.

CHAPTER 28

On Staten Island, Marie Cattel and her granddaughter were playing cards. They'd seen the news about the Tokyo stock exchange the night before, and had both agreed they'd keep the TV off and enjoy the luxury of a quiet day at home.

"Lyla, honey, it's amazing how calm you've become since your mom and daddy decided to… well, you know."

"I hope they're okay and everything, but it is nice being able to run my own life and not to be hearing about how much Jesus hates me, grandma."

"Gin!"

"You want a drink?"

"No, I just won the game." Marie leaned back and smiled.

"What?"

"Oh, I was just thinking that with all these disappearances… well, have you noticed just *who's* disappearing?"

Lyla was about to answer when there was a knock at the door.

"Who can that be? I hope it's not another reporter. If it is, don't let them in, Lyla."

"No problem. I'm interviewed out." She peeked through the viewer in the door. "Awesome."

"What?"

"There's a totally hot dude out there. He's definitely not a reporter—unless he's from *Rolling Stone* or something."

Marie laughed. "If he's here to kidnap your parents, he's a little late."

"Maybe he's the guy I've been writing to on Facebook."

"I'm in a gambling mood. Let him in. Young he's yours, old he's mine—in the middle, you're in for one hell of a catfight."

Lyla opened the door. "Hello," she said. "And you're?"

"Jesus Christ," the man in the Phat Farm jeans said. "May I come in?"

Lyla took one look at his hair and said, "Sure." As soon as the guest passed her she looked at her grandmother and shook at her hand indicating "hot."

"Grandma, this is Jesus Christ, Jesus, this is my grandmother… holy Christ!"

"Yes?"

"No, I mean—I'm sorry, I thought you said your name was…"

"It is."

"You mean you're?"

"Uh, like yeah." Jesus was doing Valley Girl.

Lyla rolled her eyes. "Look, you're cute, that's why I let you in. But we've been through a lot of shit—so please don't mess with us. This is my grandma. Now level with the name."

The extraordinary man walked to Marie, took her hand and said, "I have been looking for you."

"I thought you'd be a little older, but I've been looking for you too!" she said.

"We don't have much time."

"I'm not *that* old," Marie countered.

Jesus looked disappointed. "I'm not here for romance, Ms. Cattel. My Dad has sent me on a mission, and it's turning out to be more difficult than I thought."

"Your Dad?"

"Yes. I don't have time to explain everything now. But I need your assistance."

"Whoa, dude," Lyla stepped between Jesus and Marie. "Slow down. You come in here saying you're Jesus Christ. Well, we're atheists and we don't have time for bullshit."

There was a long sigh from the Christ. "Oh boy. I really didn't think it was going to be this hard," he said. "It's easy for me to forget that there's this 'is there or isn't there a god' stuff that goes on down here. What a waste of time. You've *all* got it wrong anyway. Like this whole idea about the Big Happy Giant in the sky who's supposed to be *GOD--ridiculous*. Everybody is trying to give him a name or claim he's this or that or him or her. They want to say he demands this or that." He sighed again. "The big problem is that everybody just thinks too small, too literal, too… ugh, *human*."

"So exactly what are you saying?" Marie's hackles were up.

"What I'm saying is that when I'm here and you're looking at me, it's what it is. It's me here as me now. But that doesn't mean that in another resonance…"

"Resonance?"

"Look. When I talk about my Dad, and you get all tight about saying you don't believe in 'him'—you're just falling into the oldest trap there is. Think big. Think forces of nature, think of infinity, think of resonances beyond your imagination."

Lyla moved closer to Marie, perhaps to reinforce their combined strength in opposing whatever it was their visitor was getting at. "Okay, we're thinking big. Make your point. Too much shit has gone on here to have a conversation that's not making a lot of sense."

Jesus smiled nicely. "I know these last hours have been very weird for you. I'd just hoped that you'd be glad."

"You mean Mom and Dad disappearing? Yeah, that's okay. I mean, I don't miss them if that's what you're getting at."

"Not exactly. See, I thought after I did a little cleaning up, the really interesting people would just be happy and welcome me."

"Cleaning up?"

"We don't have time for all of this. There's this good guy—he's been picked up by the Feds. God knows what they're going to do to him."

"Well, if God knows, why don't you ask him?" Lyla felt like being a smart ass.

"Dad holds out on me. He says it strengthens my character. He wants me to sleuth things out for myself."

"Look," it was Marie taking over, "I don't know who you are—but Lyla thinks you're cute and so do I. What do you really want?"

"Okay, just to speed things up—my name is Jesus, I was born in Bethlehem on May 27th. I lived on earth for about 30 years, tried to do a good job educating people, but what I said made them mad so they killed me. Speaking truth to power isn't a piece of cake, as I believe you'd say."

Marie folded her arms. "That's a cliche. I wouldn't say it that way. But go ahead."

"Then, like anyone else who dies, I traveled to the other resonance. Simple."

"And?"

"Well, fifty years later they start writing about me, concocting all kinds of stories, and making it hard for anyone with a rational mind to trust anything I said. And then this guy Paul—Mr. Apostle. Now there was a piece of work—he comes and takes just about everything I stood for and flips it for his own purposes. I mean, the guy was a sadist and a bigot!"

Marie turned towards the kitchen, "You want something to drink? I'm liking you better."

"A beer would be nice, but I shouldn't take the time. I've had a rough day—close call at the Stock Exchange. Trust me, that place is a whole lot worse than the temple in Jerusalem. I mean, could you see me on *Wall Street* making people run scared with just a piece of rope? Give me a break."

If Lyla had been watching her grandmother in action at a lesbian bar, she couldn't have been more staggered. The girl who prided herself on having seen everything and being impressed by nothing was shaken. She ricocheted between thinking her grandmother was crazy for listening to some gorgeous hunk who was clearly mad, to thinking she was right to like the guy.

"Hey," she said. "What're you about? Straight up. We've got major problems here—it's been stressful."

"You were just playing cards."

"Stick it. We're coping, OK? Now what do you really want?"

"Okay. I've got this list from Dad. There are a few people he said I could totally trust to help me—and you and your grandma were on the list. It's not like I sit around watching everything you do… that was Paul's idea too—total power trip. Wish he'd never written that stuff. It's just that you're on Dad's list. Now are you going to help me or not? We've got to get to the poor guy that was with me at the Stock Exchange this morning—he's on Dad's list too."

"Oh yeah? What's his name?"

"Jerrod Parker, 32 years old. He's a stock broker whose heart isn't in it. Got a nasty break from his wife and her jerk of a lover. He was hit everywhere with baseball bats—with an additional 25 hits to his skull. He had to wear a stainless steel cage on his head."

"That the guy you talked about, grandma?"

Marie shook her head. "I never heard about the stainless steel."

"Look, Mrs. Cattel, that never made the press. But it's right here on Dad's list."

"You have it with you?"

"Of course."

"Let's see it."

Jesus reached into his pocket and pulled out a piece of polished white stone inscribed in gold with five names. The first three: Jerrod Parker, Marie Cattel, Lyla Edwards.

Lyla whistled. "Jesus Christ!"

"Yes?"

"No, no I meant like *wow*."

"Please, let's not waste any more time."

Marie shook her head. "We don't even believe in you."

"You don't have to. That's the insanity of all this 'Jesus' stuff. You don't have to *believe* in me. You already believe in what I was trying to teach."

Lyla backed away, "You got that wrong. I don't want any part of all that hell shit. Besides, I've got what you would call a potty mouth—a mufuckin' potty mouth."

"You're one funny lady. I like you. Now get over all that stuff. Let's go do something good for a guy who's on my list and who's already gotten a bum rap." Jesus started to move towards the door as he slipped the stone into his pocket.

"What should we do, grandma?"

"Well, unless you're dying to play another hand of gin, I'd say let's go for the adventure."

"Fuckin' A," Lyla said giving Marie dap.

Jesus was standing near the front door which was still closed. "Hold my hands," he said, stretching them out and looking for all the world like the picture of Jesus that nobody ever paints.

Lyla and Marie put out their hands and took his.

"We're going to Brooklyn," he said.

CHAPTER 29
CNN SPECIAL REPORT—1:35 PM EST

WOLF BLIZZARD: The White House is denying reports today that thousands of children have been rounded up and taken to juvenile detention centers across the nation. But Red Cross officials say that they have been able to confirm the stories as true.

We take you now to a location just outside of Los Angeles, where our correspondent Tyson Briggs is standing by. Tyson?

TYSON BRIGGS: Thank you Charles. I'm not able to disclose my exact location, but I am up on the Ridge Route above Los Angeles not far off I-5 near Mt. Potrero. In the distance—there, on the right side of your screen—we can see a corner of what is reported to be a massive detention center exclusively for children. While we have been stationed here, we have seen a caravan of busses turning off I-5 and heading towards those buildings. According to our sources, children of the disappeared are being apprehended by local and state police and processed over there in what we've thought was the newest Los Angeles mega football stadium. We've reported on the controversy about the billions of city and state funds being spent on its construction. But from our vantage point it's clear that what has been built is a kind of massive jail. If we could just pan our cameras around here, you'll see… Wait! What are you doing? Hey! Leave my cameraman alone! Don't touch…

WOLF BLIZZARD: We seem to have lost signal from Tyson. We'll continue his very troubling report as soon as we can reestablish contact.

CHAPTER 30

Hogan Cafferty had never seen a home like Chandra Boolean's. Set on a rock bluff in Summerwood overlooking pristine Lake Dillon, the $45 million home was sheer perfection in its blend of modernity and rustic mountain lodge.

"There's a phone, Hogan," Chandra said tossing her keys on a small table. "Make yourself at home. I'll get some coffee going. Would you like some?"

"Sounds great."

"Come on out to the kitchen and help yourself in a few minutes. I'm just going to try to reach my mother. She was in church last time I called."

"She live nearby?"

"No. My children are with her in California. Wow, this place seems awfully quiet…" She stopped and looked around.

"You okay?"

"Yeah. It's just the first time I've been here since the accident."

"What do you feel?"

"Not sad. I honestly don't feel sad. Winslow had become so evil—I felt I was part of protracted horror just being with him—like I was agreeing to his rape of the world simply by living in this house."

"Why didn't you leave?"

"Because he had total control over the children and I would have lost them. I couldn't stand that."

"How are the kids doing with his disappearance?"

"They don't know yet."

"How do you think they'll be?"

"Oh, shocked at first—scared by the accident and what nearly happened to me. I think they'll be okay. To tell you the truth, Winslow hadn't really been a father for a very long time. It was like they knew who he was, but they knew some of his company's products better than they knew him. I'm sorry. Go ahead and make your call."

Chandra went into the kitchen and Hogan punched in Adam's familiar number. The phone rang seven times. He was about to hang up when someone picked up.

"Hello?"

The voice was familiar, welcome, and for a moment Hogan thought he would cry. Adam Brigante, a vet with no legs, bound to a wheelchair. His friend.

"Adam, this is Hogan."

"Oh man, brother, you're okay? I heard about the Jesus Dome and thought that everyone was gone."

"I was the only person left behind. I guess I wasn't able to get to the kind of sanctification that… when I was in shock earlier I couldn't do much but swear and ask for forgiveness. I hardly think the Lord would take someone like that in the Rapture."

"The Rapture? Is that what you think happened?"

"Well, yes. I guess. I mean how else would you explain it?"

"I don't know, but brah, this is the weirdest rapture I ever saw. I mean they're even saying that that guy Boolean got raptured. If that's true, everybody has been reading the wrong *Bible*."

Hogan was silent.

"Hogan? You there?"

"Yeah. I… funny you should mention him. I'm in Winslow Boolean's house right now. It's a long story."

"Are you kidding?"

"No. I'm here in his house. I met his wife when we were supposed to do an interview and she's letting me use her phone."

"Uh huh. You had to go to her house to use a phone. You ever hear of cellphones, man? Uh, did you think to use yours?"

"Actually, I forgot that I had it. This is embarrassing."

"Right. Listen, man. I know we had sort of a parting of the ways, but let me tell you, you're not some sinner who's been left behind in a rapture. You have your head on straighter than practically anybody I know."

"You wouldn't have said that if you'd seen me this morning."

"I saw you on a soapbox in the park. That's all I need."

Chandra placed a creamer on a coaster.

"I'm talking to my best friend," Hogan whispered.

"He from here?"

"Not far away."

"Invite him here."

Hogan smiled. "Adam, how are you fixed for wheels?"

"Let's see, I'm either sitting in my chair facing north, or sitting in my chair facing south."

"I meant, do you have a car?"

"Man, I got the finest ride—all manual controls."

"How'd you like to drive up here? I've got a million things to tell you."

"How far? How do you get there?"

Hogan gave quick instructions. "See you here in two hours, man. It's been too long. I'm so sorry…"

"Hey, no sorries, Hogan. You've tried to be true to what you believe."

"But maybe I was very wrong."

"We'll talk."

Hogan hung up. He didn't want Chandra to see his tears.

"Good friend?" Chandra put a hand on his shoulder.

"The very best—and… I've failed him. To tell you about him is to tell you my worst. You reach your mom?"

"No, it's odd. She was supposed to be there with the kids and their nanny. I guess they went out to eat. No answer on our nanny's cellphone either. I do wish my mom would let me get her a cell. She's so funny. I offered and she said, 'I'd rather carry a toilet around my neck.' That's exactly what she said!"

Hogan laughed and then said, "I guess I better tell you some of my story. I don't want you to hear it from anyone but me. There's stuff I'm not proud of."

By the time Adam rang at the security gate, Chandra had heard enough to be convinced that the disappearance of Dobbin and his "picture perfect" church was definitely not a secret redemption of the righteous.

"Look Hogan," she said, "you were swept along with something that you *thought* was right and it had you forget what you *knew* was right. I have a feeling that Adam understood that all along."

When Adam's van pulled under the portico, Hogan was there to meet him. Seeing his friend made the events of the last twenty-four hours vivid in a way that was overwhelming. As Adam's wheelchair lowered to the ground, Hogan's remorse flowed as he threw his arms around his friend's neck. Adam wasn't going to have a sob session.

"Look, brah," he finally said, "I'm here. Let's get inside, I've got a million questions.

Chandra was waiting at the front door and fell in love with Adam the moment she saw him. It wasn't pity. It was admiration of strength.

"I'm glad you're here, Adam," she said. "I've fixed some sandwiches, come on in the kitchen."

The three friends relaxed, thinking with what they'd survived, that they were ready for anything. They weren't.

CHAPTER 31

"There's still no answer at my mother's." Chandra hung up the phone. "They were all there just a little while ago when I called. Maybe she took them to a movie or something. It just seems weird."

FOX News was broadcasting another special bulletin. Chandra turned up the volume.

Ever mindful of ratings no matter what the situation, FOX network outdid its competition by broadcasting the grisliest photographs of the incident. Parents were warned not to let their children watch—a technique that had been proven to boost viewership by nearly 7%.

The story of the moment—the one which caught Chandra, Hogan and Adam by complete surprise—was promoted by FOX as "Disgrace Ultimately Claims the Life of Great American." The network was apparently unaware of the contradiction in the statement.

The FOX reporter, working very hard at looking tragic, described the situation that was accompanied by bloody photographs:

"Retired Secretary of Defense Donald Rumsfeld has died today. Police are saying that it was by his own hand. Mr. Rumsfeld's little round glasses still sit on the high desk where he stands to do his work. Some of his clothing remains nearby. But this is no disappearance through Divine Rapture. This is the tragic end of a great American.... an American who disgraced himself so badly he could no longer bear to live."

The report cut to a pudgy-faced Karl Rove who looked like he was working overtime not to burst into laughter. "What a day this is," Rove mused. "People are very sad, very sad indeed. We have lost someone. We have lost someone." It was impossible to parse his words and come to any conclusion other than that something had happened and it probably mattered to someone, somewhere far away.

The truth was that there had never been any love lost between Rumsfeld and Rove. It was clear to the latter that the former was a sociopath—occasionally charming, inventive, and completely without a moral compass. Those, to Rove, were Rumsfeld's strengths. But with those qualities came an almost imbecilic simplification of life and world situations that irritated Rove no end. Even Rove was aware that Rumsfeld considered world politics in much the same way a sane person would consider a game of Monopoly. It was true that Rumsfeld had been obedient to a fault in matters of neo-conservative philosophy, but once he was bestowed the reigns of power, his madness became a distinct problem.

Shortly before the 2002 invasion of Iraq, he summoned Rove to the Pentagon.

"Karlie," he began, using an appellation he knew sent memories of an abusive mother racing through Rove's brain, "Karlie, I want to show you something majestic. Sit down by this table, my boy. What do you see?"

"I see toy soldiers and M&M's," Rove answered.

"And what else?"

"A Barbie doll."

"Yes. Now what do you suppose I intend to show you?"

Since Rove rarely understood Rumsfeld even *after* a demonstration, he was unable to answer the question.

Undeterred by Rove's puzzled silence, Rumsfeld proceeded enthusiastically. "You see, Karlie, these brave green soldiers—I'm using plastic soldiers because my good ones were accidentally packed away—these green soldiers represent our brave American forces. Each soldier represents one thousand men. I'll save you counting time—there are 150 of them. Now you know, we are not a unilateral force, we are a Coalition of the Willing, and so what do you suppose that pink soldier, that green soldier, and that yellow soldier represent? Humm?"

"I couldn't guess."

Missing the sarcasm, Rumsfeld's face lit up like a pre-teen plucking wings off a bee. "They are *the Coalition of the Willing!* Don't you see? And so—here we go with our troops right into Baghdad. . ."

Rove gave a disgusted humph and said, "CENTCOM and the Generals on the ground say that we will need at least 350,000 troops to stabilize the country."

"Poppycock! We'll already have had the biggest bombardment in history! Those little towelheads will be running around holding their ears and seeing nothing but flashing lights. And even though they'll have a lot of mess and bodies to clear up, they'll be chanting, 'American, American come save us!' You should see them dance when they get excited. I saw it once when I was a guest of Saddam's—big palace y'know—great food and girls and everything. Well, those fellows can really dance. I haven't seen a jigaboo here in this country who could do anything wilder, trust me."

"Donald."

"Oh yes. Well, so here come our troops. Now, what do you think the M&M's are?"

"Again, no idea."

"Karl, you don't play enough board games. Those are Saddam's little army. And look!" With his thumb Rumsfeld began squashing M&M's into the tabletop—they apparently had been warmed before Rove's appearance. "See? See? Just squish, squish, squish. And here we are!"

"Where?"

"Why, in the middle of Baghdad and everyone is just jumping around like this." Rumsfeld began playing with the tiny soldiers in a way that foreshadowed the scandals that would follow Rumsfeld to the grave.

"What's the Barbie doing there?"

"Nothing. That's my Barbie doll. She just likes to be there to watch. Kind of like my 'happy spot.'"

"Is that it?"

"Well, I could show you how they are going to throw flowers, but you'll have to wait a little while, the florist hasn't delivered them yet."

"I have to go. . ," Rove said rising from the chair, and then added soto voce, "and throw up."

From that day on, there had been little personal communication between Rove and Rumsfeld other than, "I told you so." Rove was a star witness testifying against Rumsfeld at his treason trial. Now carefully documenting the ex-secretary's suicide, Rove chose words that carried no regret. He had none. An enemy was gone, and he had found and destroyed the note Rumsfeld had intended for the State Department, fingering Rove and Cheney as the architects of America's undoing.

CHAPTER 32

"You ever been to Brooklyn you frickin' white towelhead?" A federal agent was standing over Jerrod.

Jerrod's face was swollen to twice its natural size and his head ached the way it had those days in the stainless cage.

"I said…"

"I heard you, Sir. Yes, I've been to Brooklyn."

"Have you seen the nicest part of Brooklyn?"

"What? You mean Park Slope? Prospect Park?"

"Funny-assed terrorist. No, I'm talking about the Brooklyn Federal House of Detention. The pretty building with the green siding where people like you go so we can find out what you know."

"I haven't been there."

"Funny, I could'a sworn I saw someone who looked just like you there. Oh no, it wasn't there. It was on a 'wanted dead or alive' poster. Your last name bin Laden?" The Fed laughed in a nasty way and Jerrod tried to turn his head in the opposite direction.

"I'm talking to you, boy."

"Yes sir."

"Well…"

"Well?"

"Well answer my question."

"I'm afraid I don't know what the question was."

The Fed reached down and slapped the damaged side of Jerrod's face and left the cell, slamming the bars behind him.

The pain from the blow knocked Jerrod out. He wasn't sure how much time had passed when he felt himself being roughly raised to his feet. Big hands were under his arms and propelled him along. The men with him were talking.

"Where's he going, Sir?"

"Where do you think people like him go? They go to the Brooklyn Federal House of Detention, that's where they go."

"Yep, Brooklyn Federal House of Detention is the place for assholes like this that decide they are going to hook up with the towelheads and kidnap people."

"He's kind of like the David Copperfield of terrorism, right sir?"

"Something like that."

They had reached a large bus that had a windshield and side windows for the driver and a row of small windows running along the top of the rear compartment. It was a bus used for transporting prisoners to and from Riker's Island on their way to court. Jerrod was shoved up the steps and pushed into a seat where he was manacled to large rings on the side of the bus.

"That isn't necessary," he said weakly, hoping that he would be allowed enough freedom of movement so he could lie down. He was seeing flashing lights, but wasn't sure if they were coming through the window or happening inside his head.

"Shut the fuck up. You aren't the one who decides what's necessary, you stinking piece of garbage."

It crossed Jerrod's mind to comment on the lack of originality in the vocabularies of the law enforcement agents, but he decided silence was indeed valor.

The cage-like door to the compartment was bolted shut. Jerrod could see two armed federal officers standing watch right behind the driver. He was the only occupant in the rear. After much starting and stopping the bus gained speed. The motion and the pain lulled the prisoner and soon he was close to sleep. It wasn't until he heard the sound of an airplane flying dangerously low that he came to. There was another plane. And yet another. He knew the Federal House of Detention was just off the BQE near the Brooklyn Costco. Planes didn't fly low there. He tried to see something out the window above him. Nothing. Just sky. The bus came to a halt. Another Federal officer accompanied by an Army Captain in uniform got on the bus. They exchanged a few words with the agents, who then unbolted the door.

"Jerrod Parker?"

"Yes."

"I'm Captain Marshall Briggs. I'm here to inform you that you are charged as an enemy combatant and that my facility now owns you.”

"*Owns* me? Where are we? What is your facility?”

"You'll know that soon enough. Gentlemen, be so kind as to escort Mr. Parker to the waiting plane.”

"Where are you taking me?” Jerrod could hear the panic in his own voice.

Briggs exited the bus and the two feds detached Jerrod's shackles from the rings and jerked him to his feet.

"Please, where am I going?”

The Feds were silent. They forced Jerrod down the steps and out into the blazing sunlight. For a moment, he couldn't see anything, but then saw a small private jet on the tarmac ahead of him. There was a logo on the side that said, "North Woods Airlines.”

Standing by the plane were two military police. The Feds shoved Jerrod towards them. His head felt like it was going to explode. His heart was racing. Jerrod tried to make eye contact with one of the MP's.

"Please, tell me. Where am I going?”

The MP had a strange smirk on his face as he said in an exaggerated and mocking Spanish accent, "The reeel Cuba Libre.”

CHAPTER 33

As Jerrod was hearing those words, Lyla, Marie, and Jesus were walking towards the Brooklyn Federal House of Detention. The subway trip had taken nearly an hour. Jesus, sporting a short 'fro with his Phat Pharms looked very unlike the New York Stock Exchange culprit of the morning.

"Why'd we have to come here on the frickin' subway, that's what I want to know." It was an irritated Lyla talking. "I mean you're supposed to be *Jesus*. Why didn't you just go 'poof' and get us here?"

"Long story."

"I'm off the clock."

"Well, Dad doesn't want me doing miracles—no more than I did when I was here 2,000 years ago. He didn't give me the power to move other people. I mean you never hear of the disciples suddenly being transported somewhere far away did you? So, I can move around—appear and disappear—pretty easily, but mostly can't transport others."

"Yeah right. What about the people in the stock exchange?"

"That was a different kind of moving. I'll explain later. Right now we've got to get someone out of this place."

"How you going to get in there?" Lyla asked.

"It's complicated," Jesus said, holding his hands above his head. "I'm only allowed a few tricks." With that he dropped his hands and was standing there in a Brooks Brothers suit and a fade so short it was nearly a baldy.

"Jesus!" Lyla couldn't help herself.

"Yes?"

"No, I'm mean that was awesome. Could you do a little Prada for me? I mean, normally, I wouldn't ask, but like if it doesn't *cost* anything."

Jesus was already walking briskly across the street. "Wait here," he said turning back, "I'll be back in a minute."

"What's he doing, you suppose?" Marie was enjoying watching Jesus walk. "That is one fine hunk of man, Lyla. No wonder he's got so many followers. And I thought that the nuns marrying him were crazy!"

"You're gonna get hit by lightning, Grandma."

"Do you think if you just called me *Marie* around him it would better my chances?"

"Geesh, *Marie*…"

They stood looking at the massive building. From inside they could hear the voices of men calling out messages to no one.

"It's full of people, isn't it grandma?"

"Yes."

"That makes me sick. How come we lock one another up like that?"

"Because we've decided that some people are 'good' and some people are 'bad.' That gives the 'good' ones the right to throw the bad ones away, forget them without feeling lousy for a minute. Wonderful, isn't it? We have human garbage disposals and they're legal."

"I wish I had the *big key*."

"Look, some people likely belong in there. But nobody deserves to be forgotten."

They stopped talking. After a while a prisoner transport bus pulled up to the side of the building and entered through a steel gate which rose, then fell once the bus was inside. They were intent on the process and didn't see Jesus running towards them.

"He's not here!" he cried, clearly distressed and on the verge of tears. "Bastards! They lied. They've messed up the plan. *Patriot Act!* You ever hear anything so sick? A patriot is a person who loves his country, who protects what the country is about, who would lay down his life for those principles when they are good. And what have you got here? You've got a bunch of economic hogs who've tailored the law to make sure that their trough is full of slop. That's what you've got!"

"Amen, brother. You got that right," Marie came back. "They used 9/11 to turn this country 180 degrees to the donkey's tail. Where have they taken him?"

"They just laughed when I asked."

"Don't you know everything?" Lyla inquired.

"No more than you do! I'm just trying to do what Dad asked and sometimes, trust me, he gives instructions that are nearly impossible to follow. In this case I'd say that he was dead wrong. That really pisses him off because he likes to be right, but nobody can be right all the time. I'm always telling him, Dad, it's okay, so you messed up. You'll get it right next time. I mean, you can't imagine what he's gone through for not having diddled with the natural progression of DNA to prevent Dick Cheney's birth. He's burdened with guilt. I mean, talk about seeing a grown man cry!"

"God hates Dick Cheney? Cool." Lyla was beginning to think Jesus was hot, but that his Dad might be okay too. "So where did they take this Jericho guy?"

"Jerrod. He's been through so much. I mean when I tell you what this guy has endured… well, it will just break your heart. And to think all this has come down on his head just because I found him at the Stock Exchange and asked him to stand with me! I feel terrible."

"Well, it wasn't your fault."

"Who am I supposed to blame? Dad? My instructions said I should come to the New York Stock Exchange, find Jerrod Parker and ask him to stand with me during my announcement."

"What announcement?"

"Well, I was supposed to stand there and tell everyone—since the TV cameras were all going—about the purpose behind the disappearances, and that everything was under control and that it was all for the good, yada, yada, yada."

"You like Seinfeld?"

"Love him. Dad thinks George is the funniest guy on earth next to Dave Chappelle. He can't stand Dane Cook, by the way. Anyway, I was supposed to stand up there and make this announcement with Jerrod by my side and then I was supposed to take him with me and go and find you!"

"So why didn't you?" Lyla was really getting into being an interrogator.

"Because. Because the minute I began talking to him and said he should take me up to the podium, we got rushed and I just sort of had this moment of panic. I mean, it wasn't that I did anything that I wasn't supposed to do. I was *supposed* to make all those people disappear. But I was supposed to do it *after* I made my statement and the whole thing had been broadcast. But instead, I was totally premature and not only made them disappear—I cracked the lenses on all the TV cameras. I mean, there is no photographic record of what happened. Trust me."

Marie stepped forward. "We do trust you. And that is coming from someone who has taken your name in vain, used you in curses, and who has led a campaign to take churches by eminent domain and turn them all into theaters."

"What a good idea."

"We'll talk about it later."

"Dad just hates those places. Wouldn't go near them. They give him the creeps. I mean, can you imagine? He stays away from all of them—churches, synagogues, mosques, temples—he has claustrophobia for one thing. And about taking my 'name in vain?' Boy have they twisted that one. All it means is, don't call yourself a follower of Yaweh, Allah, Buddah, Muhammad, God, or even Christ if you are a fuck-up. Don't give us a bad name because you're a selfish bastard who thinks you should be on top of the human heap. You can "use our names" all you want goddamn it! Just don't bring shame on us by claiming us and then shitting on people."

"You are so rad," Lyla said. She slapped Jesus on the back and then gave an embarrassed laugh as she pulled her hand away.

"Thanks, Lyla," Jesus said.

Marie was impatient. "So how do we find this Jerrod Parker? Did they tell you anything inside?"

"Nothing. They were laughing at me. One of the guys was looking at me—maybe he recognized me from the descriptions. I figured I'd better beat it out of there. The cameras at the Stock Exchange weren't working, but I'll bet there are some eyewitnesses with big mouths."

"So what do we do?"

"Well, Dad always says, 'When in doubt, consult the universe.'"

"I can deal with that."

Lyla looked puzzled. "You mean you don't *pray?*"

"Well, not the way it's done now. You ever seen that Robinson Patrick guy?" Jesus pantomimed gagging. "Dad can't stand him. He was watching him do all his squishy eye stuff and going 'Oh Lord God' and all that—and Dad just looked over at me shook his head and quoted Jack Nicholson from that movie *Terms of Endearment* saying, 'I'd rather stick needles in my eyes.'"

That made Lyla laugh. "So what *do* you do?"

"I do what Dad does—just talk to the universe. We're here to enjoy it and take care of it—so talk to it."

"But don't you get to do miracles for people and stuff?"

"You've been reading way too much *Bible*," he said. "You know, I'd do something nice for people and they just had to make it extraordinary. Of course, like I've said, they didn't write about it until fifty or seventy years later, so it was pretty much like playing *telephone*—you know where you whisper in someone's ear at a party and then they whisper in the next person's ear and by the end the story is completely different? Well, that's what happened. They weren't *miracles*, they were just nice things I did for people. But that pissed some folks off. It made them feel like *they* should be doing nice things for people. So, what did they do? They turned them all into *miracles* so they had an excuse for being selfish and greedy and sitting on their asses and doing nothing for no one."

"So feeding the five thousand…"

"Hardest day of my life. It wasn't it a miracle. It was the biggest barbeque in history. It's just that when my old friends got to writing about it, it made them look a whole lot more important to have been part of a miracle rather than that they were doing filet of fish for 5,000 people. So, you were asking?"

"I asked you if you pray?"

"And I said that I just talk to the universe. It's taken care of us—more or less—for billions of years, and if it doesn't get blown up by something that's been invented down here, we should do okay."

"So how are we going to find this guy?"

"Dad doesn't tell me everything."

Lyla, who preferred action to theory, pressed, "Can't you sorta ask him so we can rescue the dude?"

"It's not that easy. See, I've got a few tricks, but that's just what they are. They're just natural. They're right here and anyone can do them. But *information*, that's a whole lot harder—unless you're my Dad. Have you got an iPod in your purse?"

"Huh? Yeah… and…"

"Let me have the earpiece."

Lyla handed him the dual earpiece. Jesus stripped the second bud back. "Hey!"

"I'll get you another one." He stuck the single bud in his right ear and fed the cord up over his ear and down inside his collar. "I'll be back in a minute."

Lyla rolled her eyes. "Does he think anyone is going to believe he's a fed with that earpiece?"

"Well," Marie said, "Some people have believed George is the President despite that *brain*."

Lyla laughed.

Jesus disappeared around the side of the building where the prison bus had been admitted.

There was an Army MP stationed by the steel retractable door. Jesus walked up swiftly. "Bartle, Homeland Security. You got Parker, the perp from the Stock Exchange incoming?"

"Naw, he's not coming here. You didn't get the message?"

"Guess not. Where is he?"

"Gitmo, man. The dude is goin' to Gitmo."

CHAPTER 34

The news leak from the White House was out of control. Every newspaper in the country—The *New York Post* , *New York Times, Los Angeles Times, Chicago Tribune, Cincinnati Inquirer, Miami Herald, New York Daily News,* and the *Sacramento Bee*—followed with sensational banners. Television commentators were busy. The most invited guest was Dan Rather. Everyone wanted him to appear and gloat while having a moment to reflect on George W. Bush's disappearance.

"The way I figure it," the once beleaguered ex-anchor said, "with poll numbers in the single digits, George simply opted to walk away much as he did during military service. I'm willing to bet the $70 million I won from CBS that he'll be found partying somewhere."

Other commentators, particularly those on the left, were much more ominous. They were sure that Bush had gone into seclusion with advisers to find a way to suspend elections and remain in power. They noted his lack of recent campaign appearances with Senator Tim Michaeljohn.

In squares and parks across the country, jubilant crowds of the poor and middle class celebrated the apparent removal of George Bush. It was like the 4th of July without having to endure explosive patriotism. The disappearances of the morning, while sobering to some, did little to dampen the spirits of millions.

Religious commentators were, naturally, furthering the doctrine of the Rapture. Chief among them was Reverend Robinson Patrick. His little eyes were squished tightly shut and his little head was shaking back and forth as he talked to "his lord" on television. "We know sweet Jesus, ah, that you have taken your chosen son, ah, because he was a man who walked with yew, ah, he was a Christ-tian, ah, a follower of the Lord of Lords, ah, and yew has taken him, ah, to live with you and your saints forever. Praise Jesus. Yes, praise Jesus, Hallelujah."

Robinson preferred to stay in prayer through much of the broadcast. That way he could keep talking about those taken in the Rapture and the righteousness of G.W. Bush, leading capitalists and real estate developers who had seemingly gone to their reward, without having to address the nagging question of why he had been left behind. Over 150,000 emails had come into the CBN studios with exactly that question. And Reverend Patrick feared that 150,000 pieces of snail mail would follow with no checks.

It came as something of a relief to the Good Reverend when CNN announced that the President George Walker Bush had indeed been located. The reports were oddly short on detail seeing as how they were about the discovery of a missing President of the United States. It was not until bloggers revealed the location of the discovery that it was clear why the major news outlets had been extremely circumspect. The President had been found hiding under Condoleeza Rice's bed.

DAY FOUR

Saturday

November 1, 2008

CHAPTER 35

Cardinal Alberto Marchese decided that for the ruse to be complete, Giuseppe Fognolio had to become, in every respect, the Pope. The poor janitor still did not comprehend what was happening to him. The first evening, when a group of Vatican staff came to strip him of his vestments he feared the worst. The priest entrusted to remove the Pope's undergarments received the most vociferous of his defense mechanisms. The priest however, was well versed in removing the undergarments of innocent little protestors, so he was able to subdue Fognolio and render him naked. To his credit, the faux pope put up a credible fight—and to the end had his hand firmly planted between his two rather thin "cheeks," so the "gate to the papal city" was never unguarded.

At first the crushing weight of the holy bedclothes rather terrified him, but the 1,000 count sheets of Egyptian cotton and the comforters which were plump with the down of holy geese soon had him drifting into a more peaceful state of semi-existence.

Morning brought a resumption of his fears. He was facing another appearance before the Vatican Square crowd. Little did he know that it would also bring him the beginning of an important friendship.

Giuseppe Fognolio, although a simple man, was by no means a stupid man. Many on the Vatican staff assumed that he was mentally deficient and treated him that way. The truth was, Fognolio's deafness actually enhanced his ability to focus. He had been so frightened the day before that he momentarily lost his inquisitive nature, but by morning it returned to him.

Just as he had the day before, Cardinal Alberto Marchese arrived and oversaw the donning of the Papal vestments. And as before, Fognolio was propelled towards the papal window so the crowds could see him and rejoice in the fact that their leader—their literal God on earth—was in prime condition. But on this occasion, there was no reluctance on the part of the pontiff, no hooking of the staff, and no rapid departure. When the papal windows were closed, Fognolio's vestments were removed, and wearing nothing but his Holy Father boxers and wifebeater, the janitor was left alone in the vast Holy bedroom. Moments after Cardinal Marchese and his fellow holy men left the suite, an elderly Cardinal knocked and entered. He looked at Fognolio for a moment and then raised his hands and signed, "I am a friend."

After all he had been through at the hands of the Vatican's righteous men, this gesture brought infinite joy to the poor janitor's heart.

"I am grateful to God," he signed back.

"Yes. But what you have been seeing is not the work of God," the elderly cleric signed. "What you have been witnessing is the desire of power hungry men to circumvent the will of God. I am Cardinal Vonsecco. I will not intrude now, but if you need me, I will never be far away."

"What are they doing with me?" Fognolio beseeched.

"Pope Maxmillian IV is one of the *disappeared*. You have heard of them?"

"Read about them, yes."

"Vanished into thin air. Cardinal Marchese is using you to deceive the people into thinking that the Pontiff is still here—and will attempt to use you to fulfill the intentions of that selfish bastard of a Pope."

Poor Fognolio nearly fainted with the concentration of news, the awareness of his central involvement, and the old Cardinal's blasphemous reference to the Pope.

"You have spoken ill of the Holy Father, Cardinal. May God have mercy upon your soul."

"Your life is in danger Giuseppe Fognolio. The man of whom I have spoken ill is neither holy nor a father. I come to you as a friend." Despite his advanced age, Vonsecco had great agility. He signed rapidly and accurately. "There is a terrible secret you must know, my friend. While you are alone here in the Papal quarters you have what may be the only opportunity to save the earth from a terrible fate."

Although he was a loyal and devoted Catholic, Fognolio had been troubled by the election of the most recent pope. He just didn't like him. In the course of a day's work he could observe many things and what he had observed since the arrival of Pope Maxmillian IV disturbed him. There were subtle changes taking place in the Vatican. Nothing blatant, just something stiff, something less simpatico. And then there were the papers he'd found in the trash. He'd hidden them, and continued to observe and disapprove. Now a Cardinal was speaking to him, confirming his observations.

"You must keep everything I am about to tell you to yourself until you have obtained all the evidence. Then you must contact me and together we will find a way to warn the world."

"You have my word, Cardinal."

In the next three minutes of rapid signing, Cardinal Vonsecco outlined a secret so vast and terrible that Fognolio shook with fear. It was fear for what might happen, and fear because the mantel of responsibility lay so heavily on his shoulders.

As quickly and quietly as he had arrived, Cardinal Vonsecco left, closing and locking the door behind him. Fognolio was alone in the grand suite that Pope Maxmillian occupied. Maxmillian was missing, but his personal effects weren't.

Facing the windows to Vatican Square, he looked around the room. Vonsecco's instructions had been clear: look everywhere. He knelt down and looked under the massive Papal bed. There, in a neat row were a pair of Papal slippers, a copy of *The Goal Guided Life* by Reverend Teddy Dobbin, *Mein Kampf* by Adolph Hitler, and two recent issues of *Playboy*. The items were in keeping with Vonsecco's words, but provided none of the evidence he sought.

Getting up, he went to the bookcases on the far side of the room. Thinking there might be a secret passage or a moving panel, he carefully tapped his way along until he was satisfied that there was none.

He checked beneath the carpets, behind the Holy dresser, and in the Papal closet. Nothing.

Returning to the main room, he walked to the pontiff's desk. It was a massive thing made of carved hardwoods inlaid with copper, brass, mother of pearl and gold. An enormous *Bible* occupied the center of the highly polished desktop. Fognolio noted that despite its age the *Bible* looked quite unused. To the left of the Holy Book was a small ivory box that contained five rosaries. To the right of the desk was a pen and a pad of paper bearing the Papal insignia. There were only two drawers in the desk—large draw-ers side by side, which took up the entire width of the Holy furniture. Fognolio opened the left drawer and looked through the contents. There were additional writing tools, a papal seal for envelopes, a box of sealing wax, some matches and a box of paper clips. He moved to the right drawer which refused to open. He bent down to see if the drawer had a lock, but it didn't. Then, remembering a similar desk in the office at the Sistine Chapel, Fognolio reached down and felt the indentations on the ornate wood leg that undulated its way to the floor. Directly beneath what appeared to be a large lotus blossom he felt a slight give. A quick press and the drawer opened.

Inside there was an assemblage of letters, several very old notebooks, and a fancy little wooden box. Since he could not rely on his hearing, he moved the Papal chair so he could watch the door and make sure it remained shut. That done, Fognolio sat down for some investigative work.

He started by methodically reading the letters. He observed the order of the envelopes and made sure that he preserved that order. Yet occasionally after reading, he put a letter on the desk. There were 17 letters in all, each of them short. When he completed the letters, he began with the notebooks. Again, his work was methodical. When he was done, there was one notebook on the desk. Finally, he removed the wooden box and examined its contents. The entire box remained on the desk.

Fognolio went to the closet and removed the bag of cleaning materials he had been using when he was first rushed into the Papal suite. He removed several layers of rags, then placed the box, the notebook and the letters inside and covered them up. It was as Vonsecco had revealed. Now he had only to tell the world.

CHAPTER 36

At first, corporate America pretty much wrote off the Staten Island, Denver and Texas disappearances as an aberration and continued business as usual. That all changed with the spectacular events at the Tokyo Stock Exchange and when Jesus hit Wall Street. Then there was a huge selloff. The Dow Jones fell sixty percent overnight.

Sensing a national emergency, the president of Exxon/Mobil, Arbet Portent, took to the morning airwaves and with a straight face, almost a concerned face said, "As a major supplier of America's energy resources, we at Exxon/Mobil take the current succession of events on our shores with great seriousness. We realize that we have a grave and awesome responsibility to the American people. We must protect our most precious national resources and strive to protect you. Therefore, we have made the painful decision to raise the price of our refined petroleum product, gasoline, from $3 to $10.35 a gallon. God bless America."

By noon, Exxon/Mobil stocks, which had declined 35%, rose 42%.

With the rise in the price of gas the national mood turned somber. Earlier disappearances, even though thousands were missing, had not touched the pocketbooks of the average citizen. Now there was a general sense of panic. Opinion Polls showed that the populace blamed George W. Bush for everything. He was rated in the single digits in general approval, and in fractions on specific topics such as protecting national interests, international policy and managing the economy.

Since elections were barely a week away, Bush was a lame duck extraordinaire, and Tim Michaeljohn was poised to seize the "gold ring" easily. His election was practically guaranteed. All he had to do was distance himself from the faltering President and present a calming voice amidst the fury. Paperless voting machines would do the rest. Barack Hussein Obama didn't stand a chance.

Hunkered down with his strategists in the White House sub-basement, Michaeljohn began writing a national address. His campaign planned to purchase a half hour of primetime television on all five major networks. He intended to outline a strategy for national defense—a strategy that called on a revitalized nuclear arsenal, the development of a new weapon with a technology far too destructive to divulge, and a fervent dedication of the nation to God and the sanctify of life. His staff agreed that those three points "covered the bases." The nuclear capacity of the nation would scare off known enemies, the threat of a secret weapon would scare off future enemies, and the promise of God's protection would take care of the rest. For months before Obama's nomination, he'd felt smugly assured of victory—even if there wasn't ballot fraud—because of the "Good Morning America" appearance of the person who seemed to be the undisputed Democratic presidential candidate, Senator Hillary Rodham Clinton.

Ms. Clinton, dressed in an appropriately vague color of blue, sat down with Diane Sawyer who, applying concerned expression #3, posed questions of blistering depth to the former First Lady.

"Senator Clinton, so good to have you here at this most difficult time in our nation."

"I am always pleased to be here, Diane. Of course, I'm not entirely pleased as you know, because I am also very saddened by recent events."

"Yes, and speaking of those events, do you believe that the disappearances on Staten Island, in Texas, the disappearance of the Vice-President, and yesterday's occurrences on Wall Street and in Tokyo—do you believe that these are all related?"

"Well, Diane, as you know, there have been a number of occurrences in the last days. I say 'last days' not in the sense of *the* last days, but in the sense of the last few days. Do you understand?

"Yes, I understand your direction."

"Well, Diane, these occurrences have had a striking similarity, one to the other. It would seem that they are deeply, deeply related. If not in causation, certainly in appearance."

"So you believe that they are related."

"If you so choose to see them that way, yes. On the other hand, they may not be related at all. They may be unrelated."

"Well, which do you believe?"

"I believe that the relation or non-relation of these events will prove to be a very important matter to the American people."

"If elected, what would be your strategy to stop these disappearances, and if possible, to locate the people who have vanished?"

"I am so glad that you asked that, Diane. I have a plan which the Republicans would be unable to attempt and which they are completely ill-equipped to undertake."

"And that would be…"

"As a former member of the board of directors of the Coca-Cola Corporation, I am very familiar with allegations of so-called 'disappearances.' We had allegations like that made all the time against us—as a corporation—regarding certain union revolutionaries who attempted to disrupt our operations in South and Central America. People disappeared and suddenly it was *our fault*. There were attempts, even by people right here in our own country calling themselves *Killer Coke* to establish a link between some rogue bands of private militia and our corporation! Can you imagine? A few very unpleasant people—enemies of democracy and free enterprise—disappear in a foreign country, and suddenly we were accused of having something to do with it!"

"Why would that happen?"

"Well, just because the actions of these militias in some ways reduced the population of our enemies—that is, just because they seemed to target personages who were opposed to our corporation's operations and expansion—there were those who wanted to portray us as complicit."

"And this has to do with recent events in what way?"

"I think the answer is obvious, Diane, and I will be happy to explain it to you. We at Coca-Cola have always denied, not only complicity with the disappearances, but we have seriously questioned whether they took place at all!"

"And?"

"Well, don't you see? If I were President, I would not only strongly disagree with those who said one thing or another, but I would be in complete agreement with those who said something else. I think that decisive leadership is the key and I hope that the American people will see that my firm stands on all issues will bring us whatever it is that we need to face the crisis that lies before us—a crisis which may or may not actually exist."

"We are deeply honored to have you here today," said the slightly dazed Diane.

"Well, Diane, God bless America if you believe in him, and for those who are agnostics and atheists, I offer a statement of non-religious sentiment as well."

Michaeljohn knew he could attack from all sides and had decided to use the phrase, "to waffle is awful." His speech writer Grant Millican thought the phrase nauseating, but Michaeljohn said he was certain that used against Hillary the way "flip-flop" was used against John Kerry, the phrase was his key to success. Millican reluctantly complied and peppered the evening's script with many "waffles" and "awfuls." Unfortunately for Michaeljohn, Millican stayed focused on those words and not on an underdog candidate, Barack Obama.

It was approaching noon, and upstairs at the White House the President had had his bath and was about to partake of lunch. When he entered his study, Karl Rove was waiting for him.

"We've got to get on the air tonight, George," he said.

"Aw, tonight's the playoffs."

"George, listen to me. Paul, Richard and even Jeb feel it's crucial for you go on tonight and read a speech I've written for you. We don't need to try to explain it now. Just go on the air—we'll secure all networks and pressure PBS. All you've got to do is read what I've written. When what it's all about dawns on you, I think you'll really like it."

"Can Condi be there?"

"For God's sake, George, tone down the thing with Condi. We got worldwide coverage yesterday with you hiding under her bed and two weeks ago from that photo with your hand on her ass."

"Nice ass."

"George! Listen to me. We've got to do this tonight. You have got to pay attention and keep your hands off Condi."

"Can she at least *be* there. I like looking."

"She can be there *after* you give the speech."

"What's the speech about?"

"You know that a lot of people have just disappeared into thin air, right?"

"Yeah, I miss Dick."

"I'm sure he misses you. Now listen. Yesterday, a fella who claims to be Jesus Christ got into the New York Stock exchange somehow and…"

"Why didn't somebody tell me about this?"

"You don't know about it?"

"Hell no. You think if Jesus was going to be down there on Wall Street, I wouldn't of made sure I was there for the photos and stuff?"

"George, hundreds of people disappeared, markets are crashing around the world."

"That's bad, right?"

"Yes, that's bad." Rove took George by the shoulder. "Look, George, try to concentrate!"

"Concentrate! We've got Jesus running around and you didn't get me even one autographed picture." The President was clearly not happy.

"Listen! This guy's an imposter. All hell is going to break loose if you don't get out there tonight."

The President got a strangely intelligent look on his face. "How are my family's interests doing?"

"They are tanking, George. Well, Exxon/Mobil is doing OK, but the Saudi family is worried."

"I'm not talking about the oil. I'm talking about the, you know…"

"Cocaine imports haven't been affected that we can tell."

"And…"

"And nothing has slowed either crack or meth labs…yet. Heroin is through the roof."

"So what's the problem? You're all upset because people are stressed out over these disappearances?" The President seemed downright wiley.

"Yes. The national mood is approaching panic."

"Doesn't that usually increase sales?"

"George!" Rove stamped his little foot. "Will you listen to me? If you want to hold onto what we've worked so hard to get, you'll forget your play-offs and go on TV tonight."

"Can I TiVo the game?"

"Yes."

"Okay. I'll do it. When do I get to read the script?"

"I think it's best that you wait until tonight. It's a big speech, George. I'd just as soon that you didn't understand it until *after* you've given it."

"Okay, Karl. Can I eat now?"

Within ten minutes promos hit the networks and PBS that the President would address the nation at 9 PM.

CHAPTER 37

"Stay out of her way, she's breathing fire again," one of Babs Waller's assistants whispered to another employee just entering the office. "She just hit Danny in the face because she said he purposely did her lips so you could see the droop."

Danny LaFogg came out of Babs' office, his left cheek noticeably brighter pink than the right. "She's fucking crazy," he said, tears ruining his autumn-brown mascara. "I don't know why I put up with that bitch. Is it my fault that she has lousy surgery and massive strokes? It's going to take a crane to lift that side of her face!"

The two assistants watched him exit down the hallway and then followed him. Neither looked back.

Inside her office Waller was studying her face in a mirror. For 75, she looked remarkably good. Her skin was taught, her hair was her own. Her brows, recently lifted, gave an expression of eternal surprise—very good, she thought for a interviewer who got the top stories. At seven million a year, she could afford the best money could buy. She preferred Chanel for her suits and Jimmy Choo for her shoes. Her bags were Prada. It was all perfection… except. The "except" was a slight droop to her lip on the right side. She'd experienced TMI's—a number of small strokes—the first of which had seemed quite chic because it occurred close to the time Ed Koch, then Mayor of New York had his. But the third time she had one, it left a noticeable weakness in the muscles around her mouth. She rushed to corrective surgery, but there was further nerve damage. She won a lawsuit against the surgeon, but the droop remained. Despite his considerable skill, Danny was unable to completely disguise the problem when it was viewed from multiple angles, and multiple angles were what Babs checked constantly. Danny had suggested a Botox injection for the other side to create a matching droop. That's when Babs hit him.

Forcing a theatrical smile—her trademark expression—Babs looked directly into the mirror. "Babs Waller," she said, "You may have been scooped, you may have been stranded, but there is greatness in you yet." And there she stopped and took a deep breath. She changed her expression to one of determination—the look she had used when interviewing Bill Clinton about Monica Lewinsky—the look that said, "What I have decided to get out of you, I *will* get out of you no matter how long it takes." That expression established, she stared into her own eyes and stamped out the following words, "You Babs Waller are going to track down and get an exclusive with the crazy Black dreadlocked prick behind all the disappearances. And you are going to get him to talk and talk and talk and *cry*. And then you're going to stand back and let the massacre begin."

If the right side of her mouth had popped back into place, Babs Waller could not have been a happier woman. Her mission was clear and once she began she never stopped until she could quote her beloved President as he spoke on the deck of the aircraft carrier in his little jumpsuit with the genital lift saying, "Mission accomplished."

CHAPTER 38

To Jerrod Parker, it felt like it was 120 degrees. Unbearable heat rose from the red dust beneath his shackled feet. He was being forced to do something halfway between and shuffle and a trot. The heavy steel manacles cut into his ankles and his legs ached from the repeated jolts from the short chains. A thick black hood over his head prevented him from seeing where he was going. He could feel terror rising like a dry sponge stuck in his throat.

Why had a trip to Brooklyn required an airplane? Where was he? Who were the people torturing him while they asked him questions? Had he actually heard the word Miami during the night?

He was suffocating under the hood. He'd seen these hoods on television in reports about Abu Ghraib some years before. Now he was wearing one.

Shortly after he was dragged off the plane, his captors tore off his pants and underwear. In his fear he urinated on himself. One of his captors kicked his genitals yelling, "You are all pigs."

Jerrod groaned. Since his hands were tied behind him, he remained on his side and raised his knees towards his face in an attempt at self protection.

"I cain't for the liaf of me figger you people out."

The voice reminded Jerrod of characters in *Deliverance,* a film he had once thought exaggerated the density of the white American underbelly. Now he realized that he'd been wrong. His very life was in ignorant hands.

"Yew all has got the same stewpid way of layin' on the floor." The speaker seemed to think that statement was terribly funny. His laugh was backwards. It happened by sucking air *in,* not out.

Jerrod determined to discover the man's identity, but in vain. After what seemed hours, four men grabbed him and forced him into his present shackle trot.

Even naked, Jerrod was hot to the point of fainting. Maybe it was the black sack over his head. He'd read somewhere that 25% of body heat is radiated through the head. That was it. The heat couldn't radiate. His body temperature was quickly rising. Breathing became nearly impossible. He could run no further. That's when he was knocked down and dragged. And then—nothing.

The water felt good until it kept coming when he was trying to take in a breath. He gagged and coughed. He realized that there was no bag over his head. He was sitting in a chair, his arms tied high above him. And the water kept coming. It had a force that made it impossible for him to open his eyes. But he could hear the laughter. It was sucking in, not out.

"Yew better'n swim, yew better'n swim else yews gonna drowned!" And the laughter again.

"Cut the hose, Frinkle."

"Yessir, Cap'n Reilly."

"That is all. You can go."

"Yessir, Cap'n. He's a live one, that'n."

"Frinkle!"

"Yessir."

The man left. He had an odd shuffle. A door closed.

"Jerrod Parker. I am Captain Marshall Briggs. We met yesterday after your arrest. Welcome to Gitmo."

The word hit Jerrod like a spinning razor.

"Gitmo?"

"Guantanamo, Cuba. You ever heard of it?"

"Yes."

"It's going to be your home for a long time."

"Cuba?"

"You stupid or something? I'm trying to be nice and give you a chance here, but you're just acting stupid."

"No, I just…"

"You've been arrested under the Patriot Act. No charges have been filed against you, therefore you have no need to see a lawyer. You'll be talking to some of our people since they intend to find out what you and your friend are up to. By the way, they found the President. Apparently you failed to kill him. Have a nice day."

Briggs left the room and Jerrod heard the door close. He slowly tried to open his eyes. At first he could see nothing. His shoulders ached even though his hands were numb. He expected the cretin to return with his hose, but there was no sound. As his eyes adjusted, he could see that the water that had hit him had loosened the blood on his face and a sickly pink trickle was running down his naked body. The room was ten by ten feet—cement block walls painted black—with a double florescent fixture about three feet in front of him. Above him were hooks and pulleys, some of which were employed to keep his arms aloft. Ahead of him was a steel door which hinged inward. He was on a simple, heavy wooden chair. He thought it was not unlike the old electric chair he'd once seen at the Sing Sing Museum.

There was a noise in the hall and two soldiers entered, followed by a man in civilian dress.

"Jerrod Parker?"

"Hmmm."

"Who is your friend?"

"What?"

"Who is your friend? I think that question was asked in appropriate English. Who is your friend?"

"What friend?" Jerrod felt dissociated from his surroundings, like the night he was attacked.

The civilian nodded and one of the soldiers stepped forward and pointed a stun gun at Jerrod's naked penis.

"Jesus!" Jerrod exclaimed.

"And that was your friend?" the civilian smirked.

"What?"

"You said the friend was Jesus."

"No, I meant that thing."

"Your best friend is your penis?"

The soldier pulled the trigger to let Jerrod see the sparks between contact points.

Involuntarily reacting, Jerrod again exclaimed, "Jesus!"

"What a friend you have in Jesus, Mr. Parker. You see, if you want to play these little games we're perfectly capable of playing little games back."

The sparking object made contact this time and Jerrod fainted.

"Mr. Parker! Mr. Parker!" a hand hit its mark on Jerrod's damaged face.

Jerrod opened his eyes.

"That's better, Mr. Parker. We were just beginning a conversation. Now, who was your friend?"

"He wasn't my friend."

"So Jesus isn't your friend."

"He only said he was. I don't know."

"And how long have you and 'Jesus' been planning your little adventure at the NYSE? You do work there, do you not?"

"Yes I work there. I never saw him before today."

This time when the sparks flew and he passed out, nobody slapped him. He came to some time later in another empty room. Again, noises in the hall. Two female soldiers entered. Jerrod was acutely aware of his nakedness. One of the females approached him and placed a dog collar around his neck. It was one of the collars used on pit bulls and rottweilers, the kind made of chain with blunt spikes that turn inward and a loop that allows one end of the chain to slide and thus tighten the spikes to the skin. The other female, at least it seemed female, stepped forward with a long leash. She clipped it to the collar while the other female lowered Jerrod's arms.

"Say 'thank you,'" she whispered in his ear.

"Thank you," he said.

She patted his head. "Good doggy."

And with that the other female jerked the leash with astonishing force. The spikes in the collar ripped into Jerrod's neck and he fell face forward onto the floor.

"Stay like that," the androgynous soldier commanded. "Now crawl. We don't have far to go."

Even though Jerrod's ankles were shackled and his hands bound together, he was forced to approximate a crawl across the room, through the door and into a short hallways lined with cells. His captors shoved him into one. The leash had just been disconnected when a steel-toed boot rammed his rib cage and knocked him over. The two soldiers laughed, shut the cell door and left.

He had never felt more alone. He pulled his knees up to his chest and cried.

"Jerrod?"

He must have dozed off because the voice came through the fog of sleep.

"Jerrod! Wake up!" The voice, even though of recent acquaintance was unmistakable. "Jerrod, it's me. I'm here."

The suffering man slowly studied the figure in front of him: Army boots, camouflage pants, camouflage shirt, an olive-Black face, a tiny Bob Marley lapel pin and thick locks falling all the way to the soldier's knees. The soldier smiled.

Jerrod's eyes widened. "You're the guy from the stock exch. . ."

"Yeah. Sorry about all… this." Jesus gestured at the bars surrounding them.

"But how did you get here?"

"I've got a great frequent flier plan."

"What happened yesterday—was it yesterday?"

"I'll explain later, right now we've got to get our game plan."

"They're going to hear us."

"They can't… a little gift from Dad."

"Can you get me out of here?" Jerrod felt a moment of hope.

"I was coming to get you out of here."

"*Was?*"

"I talked to Dad. We need you here right now. He hadn't told me this was going to happen. But there's something you've got to find out—see with your own eyes. We're going to need you to be able to tell things that you've witnessed first hand."

"I can't deal with this."

"Yes you can. We'll never make you carry more than you can bear."

"Are you the one who said that?"

"Well, that was from Oprah, but I have said things like that. Point is, I mean it."

Jerrod tried to rise up on his elbow. "What do you need me to find out?"

"Just observe everything. Talk to people. Dad said you'll be able to communicate—language won't be a barrier. Just ask questions and remember everything."

"Ask questions about what?"

"You'll know when the time comes. I have to go now. You've got more friends than you're aware of. I left two of them on a street corner."

The soldier saluted and disappeared, leaving Jerrod to wonder if he was hallucinating. He was on the verge of that conclusion when he saw the tiny Bob Marley pin on his pillow. "I guess I'm on a mission from God," he whispered. Even though it hurt, the line from *The Blues Brothers* was funny, and he couldn't help laughing.

CHAPTER 39

The Brooklyn sun was hot. Lyla and Marie moved to a spot behind a dilapidated garage where there was a little shade.

"Hello."

The voice was familiar. Standing there was a soldier with extremely long locks.

Lyla was laughing. "You freak me out, Dude. What's with the military thing?"

"Long story." Jesus lifted his arms. When they came back down he had the fade again and was wearing jeans and a simple Woodstock '69 T-shirt.

Marie tapped his chest. "Now that's my type of T-shirt," she said. "I was *there*."

"So was Dad!"

"That's as close as I've ever gotten to something like a religious emotion. I don't mean the bullshit that goes on with the people who are always talking about you. I mean… I actually believed that we might be able to make a better world."

"And you will."

"Yeah right. You're forgetting who's driving the big bus these days. Dubya and company never take a road that isn't marked 'straight to hell.'"

For a moment Jesus forgot that he had short hair. He seemed surprised when he tossed his head and nothing happened. "Oops," he said. "Listen, we'd better get a move on."

"Aren't we like saving that dude from here?"

"No Lyla, I got info that changed that. But it's good you were here. Can we go where there is a TV? We need to watch something at 9."

"Let's go to my house, if you don't mind hangin' with grandma. What's on?"

"Your favorite President is addressing the nation. And then the news will cover another disappearance."

"Another disappearance?"

"I've been busy."

As they turned and headed for the subway, the quiet of the Brooklyn Street gave no evidence of the chaos a couple hundred miles to the south.

CHAPTER 40

The news about the Joint Chiefs of Staff arrived at the White House three hours before the Presidential address. Karl Rove spewed, "It's not like things weren't bad enough already." Swinging his arm angrily he knocked his personally autographed photo of a pre-operative Ann Coulter to the floor. He grabbed it, dusting off the signature that said "To Karl, Love forever, Andrew."

He sat down at his computer to compose an email to his staff. An absurdly energetic man with a cherubic visage and a heart like hardened pepper spray, Rove preferred to communicate electronically rather than personally. He hated most people's faces.

"As you no doubt have already heard," he typed, "at 4:45 this afternoon, the entire Joint Chiefs of Staff disappeared. Attempts are being made as I write to untangle the pile of little medals and clips they left behind. There is preliminary confirmation that the disappearance includes all branches of service. The President will address the nation tonight at 9 o'clock and will mention these disappearances. He will also announce that until further notice Condoleeza Rice will be serving as Secretary of Defense *and* that she will also be the entire Joint Chiefs." Muttering, "She's man enough," Rove signed off on his email and hit *send*.

He picked up the phone and punched in a code. "Rupert, yeah, it's Karl. We need to spin this Joint Chiefs thing for George Junior's speech tonight.... No, he's just going read whatever we put in front of him. He'll stumble all over the place, but that's what makes him so loveable, right?... Get past the Condoleeza replacement thing as quickly as possible. There's been way too much in the press lately about her 'friendship' with the President.... Yeah, heh, heh, you're right. If they only knew! Heh, heh. He is one sick mufucker, I'll say that for the ol' Commander in Chief. If at first you don't succeed, try, try.... She must be a patient woman! Heh,

heh…. Yeah, well, keep all that shit out of the speech, just slide her in there sideways so people know everything is under control. We don't want more panic than we've already got…. Once he's delivered the speech—well, then it's a whole new ballgame. We haven't been able to add this much power to the executive since 9/11—and unlike that happy little event, we didn't even have to *plan* this one! Yeah, well it should be fun. And let me see the revised speech by seven, okay?" Rove hung up the phone. "Asshole," he said. "A talented asshole, but an asshole just the same."

He leaned back in his chair and folded his hands behind his head. Self-satisfaction of that degree is rarely bestowed upon a living human being. Perfect wheels had been set in motion and soon the entire nation would know it.

CHAPTER 41

Chandra was frantic. "I can't reach them, Hogan," she said, tossing her cellphone on the table. "My mother never goes away, and with all that's happened, shed've called me to find out how I was. Now there's been no answer since yesterday."

"Is there someone else you can call to go check on them?"

"Nobody I know."

"Call the cops."

"I don't want to draw attention…"

"I think you'd better." He handed her the phone.

CHAPTER 42

The President's speech was promoted all day. By nine o'clock Eastern time the nation was watching. Leaders in China, Russia, Japan, Europe, Africa, Canada, Australia, Central and South America were watching as well.

Because there would be no questions from the press, and because only one video feed was going to be allowed from the White House, Karl Rove decided that the address would come from the Oval Office. In order to make it clear that whatever the President was about to say was within his God-ordained right, Rove had a copy of the U.S. Constitution enlarged and hung over the windows directly behind the President's desk. The Constitution was flanked by 100 American flags. A huge Bible lay on the President's desk, propped up so the gold-embossed title was clearly visible.

At 8:30, the President was summoned to the office and given a print-out of the speech he would read off teleprompters at 9:00. The President's tutor arrived and read the speech out loud making sure that George knew what the words were. The *meaning* of the words was irrelevant, but it was important that Dubya could at least read each word in succession. Emphasis marks and phonetic spellings were placed on the paper copy, so they could be included on the teleprompters as well. The speech timed at just five minutes plus a surprise. The President had gotten through it once by 8:50.

Erin Tory, the President's make-up artist dusted him with dark tan powder and scruffled his hair. Erin had come on board after the famous "attack of the killer pretzel" incident, and was adept at covering cuts, bruises and eruptions on the Commander's face. She never asked questions, never seemed to smell alcohol on his breath, and could remove white powder from his nostrils faster than either of the two "first daughters" could swallow a jello shot. Her job was secure.

At 8:57 the President was seated behind his desk. While final adjustments were made to lighting and the three cameramen finalized their white balance and focus, the Commander in Chief made funny faces, did his "look how many obscene gestures I can make with my fingers" routine, and complained about his dry septum.

Karl Rove feigned amusement with the boyish pranks, but at 8:59, he said, "Okay George, the feed is beginning."

President G.W. Bush suddenly looked serious, although vacant, and stared directly into the camera ahead of him waiting for his first words to appear on the teleprompter.

At 9 PM the telecast began:

"My fellow Amer-cuns. For the past several days we have seen unprecedented turist attacks on the citizens of our great country."

Bush remained oblivious that his unique mispronunciation of "terrorist" was killing the travel industry as tourists considered themselves the presumed enemy.

"The attacks have taken from us some of our greatest citizens, including our beloved Vice-President Dick Cheney; all of our Joint Chiefs of Staff; one of our most beloved men of God, Reverend Teddy Dobbin and over 1,500 of his staff; my dear and trusted friend Governor Duke Wexler of Texas; hundreds of brokers from the American Stock Exchange; my personal friend Donald Rumsfeld; and many faithful God-fearing men and women from various locations around the country."

Karl Rove had carefully vetted the speech and removed the reference to Rumsfeld's suicide, choosing instead to lump him in with the disappeared. He also removed reference to the thousands of missing prisoners and CO's from America's prisons, and the astonishing fact that in every case the remaining prisoners had stepped in and gracefully taken over the administration of the facilities. There had been no riots or escapes. This fact was eliminated, for several reasons. One, it was bad publicity for the President's get tough on crime message; two, very few people cared what happened to prisoners; and three, Rove wanted to make sure that in case it was convenient to spin the disappearances as the Divine Rapture, he had not included any facts that would complicate the message.

The Condoleeza Rice announcement was indeed handled adroitly. The President continued to hold his "I've got a rock in my shoe" expression and said, "While Condi Rice is gonna cover all the missin' people's jobs, I still have grief in my heart at this very moment, because not only have I lost those that I love who are real close to me, I am havin' to realize that the turists have sunk to a new level of horror in their pursuit of showing that they hate our love of democracy, freedom, and… God Almighty. We are a nation founded on Christian principles, a nation which treasures each and every life—born and unborn—and which believes that every single individual in this beautiful, God-blessed country has the right to the pursuit of life, liberty and the pursuit of happiness."

Marie, Lyla and Jesus were sitting in Marie's living room eating popcorn and commenting while the President spoke.

"See? That's what I hate," Jesus said, putting a little more salt on his popcorn. "That guy is always saying that this country was founded on Christian principles! Hello? The people who came here in the first place were trying to get *away* from a lot of what was being called 'Christian principles.' I resent this more than you can imagine. The founding fathers, including the guy who wrote the Constitution believed that it was okay to own slaves! And listen! How does this guy get off saying that he believes everyone should have 'life, liberty, and the pursuit of happiness?' He's got millions of people relying on private soup kitchens, they've got no health care, millions of them have got no place to live."

"He didn't say they *should have* those things. You've got to listen carefully to this guy." Marie never took her eyes off the screen. "He said he believed they have the right to the *pursuit*. You've got to listen to every word they write for him, sneaky bastards. I never thought I'd actually say this, but Jesus, you're talking to much. We've got to listen."

"Sorry, he's just makin' me so mad."

"Join the club."

The President continued with a list of platitudes about the benefits of being an Amer-cun. He commiserated with the Japanese people who had lost their brokers. He praised all branches of the military. He turned to look at a camera stationed to his right, signaling a change in the mood of his talk.

"I am speaking to you tonight, because you have a right to know everything that's going on in your government."

That brought a shriek of laughter from Marie.

Jesus pointed at the screen. "Right to know? Has there ever been an administration that gave people *less* knowledge about what it was doing? I mean he sent young people to Iraq under the assumption that they were going to be finding atomic bombs under every rock. And the whole time he was planning his 14 permanent bases for absolute control over the world's remaining oil. Oh, and hoping the Christian crazies would vote for him because he was helping to bring Armageddon a little closer."

Dubya leaned further onto his elbows and stared into the camera. "Due to the extraordinary effectiveness of these turist attacks, and by the power given to me under Patriot Act III, I have declared Posse Comitatus and the Insurrection Act null and void. I have instructed the Pentagon, the Department of Homeland Security, the National Guard, the nation's regional police forces, the CIA, NSA, and FBI to merge into a single preparedness force, and I have declared martial law.

"Damn him." Jesus was pointing at the TV. "Dad warned me he might do this. He said if he did this, my job was going to be a thousand times harder. But he assured me that I'd be able to finish my mission. Right now I wish I was more the way I was when I was here as Jael."

"Jael?"

"Remember? I saved the Children of Israel by putting a nail through the head of a Philistine."

"Oh please. Shh. Listen!" Marie was tired of interruptions.

Dubya had taken a moment to let his announcement sink in. "I am calling this merging of the nation's defense forces, *Operation Divine Shield*. I am calling upon our God for guidance and protection at this time. In keeping with that, beginning tomorrow night I am ordering a 10 PM curfew throughout the nation. Anyone not in a home or shelter after that time will immediately be detained and considered an enemy combatant. Those persons designated as enemy combatants will be held indefinitely without charges being filed, will not be allowed to seek counsel, and will be removed to appropriate centers of detention."

"In addition to ordering protective military operations, martial law, civilian curfews, and immediate detention of all turists who defy the law of the land, I am also calling for a suspension of Presidential elections during this national emergency."

A coffee cup crashed to the floor in a room far below the White House. Tim Michaeljohn stood dumbstruck in the middle of his "war room."

"That son of a bitch, that evil son of a bitch! He can't do that! He can't suspend elections! He's got no right. That would be up to Congress, right?"

"Actually," Elizabeth Garvin shook her head. "It's no longer up to Congress. What he's doing is based on that study the Rand Corporation did for Nixon when he wanted to suspend elections. He got stopped, but

Bush just incorporated it into Patriot Act III. I always thought of it as the 'dynasty protection plan.' Sort of a giant condom for the Bush family."

Michaeljohn shouted, "He's not going to get away with this!"

"Tim. He already has."

CHAPTER 43
SUMMERWOOD, CO—6:05 PM MST

Chandra dropped her phone. It hit the floor and ricocheted into a corner as she slumped to the floor.

Adam, his eyes on the TV, slammed his hand against his wheelchair. "I told you! I told you! Halliburton got those $385 million in contracts to build 'detention centers' that Bush said was in case of a sudden influx of immigrants. Hell no! They are concentration camps that have been built for American citizens, and they are gonna use them." When Chandra didn't answer he turned and saw her. "Chandra! Hogan! Hogan, come quick!"

Hogan, who'd gone into the kitchen to get more coffee came running. "Bush just said there were going to be detention centers—those Halliburton things—and the next thing I know I see her like this." Adam was holding Chandra's limp hand. "At first I thought she was just mad at Bush."

"Chandra, it's me, Hogan." He stroked her head. Chandra opened her eyes.

"They've got the children," she whispered.

CHAPTER 44

The President was now addressing the camera to his left. "We pray to almighty God for his protection of our people, and for the fast recovery of those who have seemingly disappeared. Because the attacks have been so massive and so targeted at Godly people…"

Jesus cupped a hand over his mouth. "I'm going to vomit."

Bush continued, "therefore, exercising my powers as *The Decider*, I have created a new cabinet post, and have determined that our first Czar of Spiritual Life of the newly formed National Protestant Evangelical Church, shall be the Reverend Robinson Patrick."

At that moment, the video feed switched to a door in the Oval Office and in walked the grinning, bobbing and nodding clergyman Bush had just mentioned. His piggish little eyes were already assuming their squishy prayer position. His shoulders were stooped forward in an attempt to project humility. His mouth contorted from time to time—a sign to the faithful that he carried a message far too heavenly to adequately communicate. His suit was Armani, his tie pale blue in tribute to his President, and his shoes bright red Prada in homage to Pope Maximillian IV. In his right hand he carried a King James translation of the *Holy Bible*. In his left hand he carried a *Q'ran*. A *Watchtower* magazine protruded from his breast pocket. Following him was Pearl Millicent, the woman who appeared regularly with her hair on *The 144,000 Club*. She was carrying a silver platter on which lay a *Book of Mormon*, a small brass Buddha, a yarmulka, and a little blue monkey.

As Reverend Patrick approached, the President stood to greet him. The good pastor did not see the outstretched Bush hand, but seemed intent on displaying all the religious artifacts on the Presidential Desk.

Once Millicent had set down her tray, she seemed unsure of her duties, so she concentrated on smoothing down her rather elaborately patterned skirt even though it seemed in no immediately danger of lifting up and flying away.

The good Reverend saw the unfortunate President still holding out his hand as he had been instructed to do by the teleprompter, grabbed that hand and pumped it so hard and long one might have expected an abundant flow of water to issue from the Chief Executive's mouth.

The greeting completed, Bush said, "I have asked Reverend Patrick, who will preside over our national church, to bestow a blessing upon our nation."

Without hesitation the Reverend tipped his head back and spouted the words "Oh Jaesus!" at the ceiling. "Oh Jaesus, hear the cry of Thy humble, humble, humble servant as I take on the mantel of Spiritual Czar of Thy newest and most beloved church."

Marie threw a donut at the TV screen. "Can't you make that guy disappear?" she asked, hoping that she would see one of Jesus' miracles immediately.

"Unfortunately, can't yet," Jesus replied, taking another handful of popcorn. "This is all part of what Dad warned me about. Once it gets set in motion, I've got to let the thing play itself out. There are other things I can do, but this one… well, there's a reason it has to follow through."

Just then, Reverend Patrick let forth with another particularly powerful, "Jaesus!"

"Although, there are times I'm tempted to ignore Dad and just go with my own judgement. I did that once, you know, when I was here as John Brown. Obviously, it taught me a lesson. That's why when I was here as Sojourner Truth, I didn't make the same mistake."

Lyla looked at Jesus obviously feeling she'd found a fatal flaw. "John Brown and Sojourner Truth? They both lived at the same time—so how could you possibly be two people at once?"

"I'm a Gemini." Jesus broke into a charming smile and Lyla laughed.

Reverend Robinson Patrick's prayer was long and inclusive. He made it clear that the new National Protestant Evangelical Church of America was including everyone under the banner of Christ. Oblivious to the utter offensiveness of his every word, he intoned, "We are big-hearted. We even welcome into Christ's fold all of our Jewish person friends." He picked up the yarmulka and spun it on his finger like a Frizbee. His point made, he continued, "All the folk there from the Al Queda religion—with that Mohammed fella." He slapped the *Q'ran*. "Our little Buddhist friends with those pretty orange outfits." He patted the brass Buddha on the head, and then on impulse tickled his stomach. "We embrace all our Catholic brothers and sisters and want to invite everyone who has followed off after that Pope to know they are welcome back in our church anyway." He stuck out one of his red Prada shoes to emphasize his ecumenical spirit. "We got nothin' but love for you Mormon folk, and thank you even now for holdin' out against the Blacks for so long. That choir of yours sure does help us swalla all the rest of the stuff you preach." Infinitely pleased with himself, the little pastor pressed on. "We're delighted to have you *Watchtower* folk with us, whatever you call yourselves, and thank you for not using up our blood supply. And I don't want to forget for a minute our special little Hindu folk. I couldn't find the fella with eight arms or whatever, but I want you Hindu folk to know that this little blue monkey is just a token of my respect for you and all those things you've managed to believe."

Bush beamed approval as the new Czar rambled on.

Karl Rove was unhappy that Patrick was so far off script, however he found nothing offensive in his remarks. Meanwhile, air time was limited, so he signaled the Reverend to stop in order for the President to make his final announcement.

It took Reverend Patrick a while to wind down, since he was eager to include every possible aberrant aspect of religion in his new inclusive Jesus-driven fold. He had just apologized to the Santaria folks for not bringing a chicken when the President saw his teleprompter rolling.

"My fellow Amer-cuns," he began, interrupting the ongoing list of religions popping into Patrick's head. "Since it is my duty to protec' this one nation under God, I am making one final announcement. It is the establishment of the National Terrorist Wanted List. As many people are already informed of,…"

Marie was nearly spitting at the TV screen. "Speak English, George."

"Marie, don't interrupt."

"Okay, Jesus."

The President, unaware of that particular conversation, plowed forward. "I have ordered thorough investigations of people who were close to these disappearances, but who were left behind.

"This is a turist cell. The man behind the disappearances at the New York Stock Exchange identified himself as Jesus Christ." The President, who thought the last statement was a joke, stopped and looked around expecting laughter from the crowd. When there was dead silence, he forged ahead with his labored reading. "We have apprehended one of this ring and are holding him in an undisclosed location. His name is Jerrod Parker. We have been unable to provide a new photograph of him because part of his operation was to destroy the cameras that might identify him."

An old picture of Jerrod in the hospital wearing his elaborate stainless steel head apparatus flashed on the screen.

"But we've got him! There are, however, personages who we have reason to believe are directly involved in the disappearances. At first, they seemed to be victims, but now we now have credible evidence that they may have been perpetrators, not victims. Mr. Parker had an accomplice, a man who was attempting to help him escape from the Brooklyn Federal House of Detention today. This man."

And a photograph of Jesus in his Brooks Brothers suit and short hair flashed onto the screen.

"This man is believed to be linked to the mastermind who claims to be Jesus Christ. He should be considered extremely dangerous."

"I am to you," Jesus said, taking yet more popcorn.

The President wrapped up his speech saying the investigations were going to begin immediately. He gave an 800 number that could be called to report terrorist activity. He concluded with his usual, "Good night, and God bless America."

Jesus looked at Marie and Lyla who were clearly petrified. "Fasten your seat belts, ladies," he said, "it's going to be a bumpy night."

CHAPTER 45

Hogan installed Google Earth on Chandra's computer while the President's television address ground to an end. Adam stared at the screen in silence.

Chandra interrupted his thoughts. "What are we going to do? The President made us sound like suspects. I've got to get to California and find my kids!"

"That guy," Hogan said pointing at the TV, "the one they showed last."

"With the baldy and nice suit?"

"Yeah, him and the one who say's he's Jesus Christ. Don't they look familiar to you, Adam?"

Adam shook his head.

"I could swear I've seen them before."

"Don't say that if some Feds come asking questions."

Adam sounded downright cheerful. "Listen guys, now that you've got to get to California, I'm your man. No legs, but a high tech van! I'll hide you both in the back."

"Thanks Adam, but this still is the United States of America. I hardly think we have anything to be afraid of."

As Chandra was speaking, Army tanks rolled into Times Square in a gratuitous show of force. Breathless reporters covered the event, describing in extravagant detail the lengths to which the President was prepared to go to protect the American people.

CHAPTER 46

This is Charlie Nedick, Entertainment Tonight. Well, we have an amazing story for you right now. ET's on-the-street cameras have caught what seems to be one of the craziest scenes ever right in the heart of New York City. Our highlight of the night, "Pimps and Hos — Where'd They Go?" coming up next. But first a word from our sponsor."

A commercial for Biznee, the entertainment giant, followed. Bizneeworld in Florida was billed as the "giggliest place on earth," and the ad promised that a family of four would have three days of congeniality and happiness for just $2,300. The ad, shot prior to the disappearances, made no mention that the CEO of Biznee was missing. It also failed to mention that missing with him was about $300 million in corporate funds. The ad concluded with a video of fireworks reaching the stars over the trademark fantasy fortress of Bizneeworld.

"Okay, this is Charlie Nedick back with our highlight of the night. Check this out!"

A video began to roll showing New York City police standing in Times Square. Looking puzzled, one of them was actually scratching his head.

"Damndest thing," he said as the camera came in on a tight shot of his face. "It started about 5 AM. They just started wandering around calling out the guys' names."

Charlie Nedick was back on camera.

What the officer is referring to is large bands of prostitutes roaming the city calling out the names of their boyfriends. Local precincts have been flooded with missing persons reports of guys well known to the police as pimps.

A tall brunette in hot pants and a halter top hobbled towards the camera on six-inch platform shoes.

"Can't find him," she said, apparently not knowing whether to cry or celebrate. "I mean, who do I give my money to? What am I s'posed to do?

Keep it? I mean, this is crazy shit. An' other sisters here can't find their men neither. What we s'posed to do? Pocket the cash?" And with that profound question on her lips, the brunette tucked a money roll into her bosom, flashed a momentary smile, and staggered away.

Nedick, whose on-camera style resembled a college freshman on steroids and angel dust, seemed to think that the report merited high-energy amusement.

"Yes, these hos to go have got no place to go. And we're getting viral video from across the country showing that the same thing is happening in nearly every major city. Go figure folks. You can't make this stuff up!"

Nedick furrowed his brow.

"On a more serious note. Teen pop star, L'il Queen Roxie, broke down in tears yesterday when her toy poodle got tangled in one of Ms. Roxie's wigs. Firemen called to the scene at the Roxie mansion in Beverly Hills report that the dog is in fine shape, but that Ms. Roxie had to cancel a concert due to over medication."

CHAPTER 47

Marie was puzzled by Jesus' "bumpy night" quote. "What do you mean?" she asked.

Jesus turned to Lyla. "You've seen *All About Eve*," haven't you?"

"Yeah, I think so."

"If you had, you'd *know* so."

"Bette Davis, right?"

"Right. So you've seen it. Okay. What happened right after you found out your parents had disappeared?'

"I called Grandma."

"Then what?"

"Then this detective named Darcy O'Neil came and asked a million questions."

"Darcy O'Neil?"

"Yeah, why? You know him?"

"I sort of met him. We've got to get you out of this neighborhood. It's going to be crawling with cops and Feds."

"What would they want with us?"

Marie broke in. "Lyla, listen to me honey. I lived through the red scare and the blacklisting. They can do whatever they want. I'm with you Jesus, what do you want?"

"Do you know anyone who could hide us for a while?"

Marie shook her head. "My friends are the kind of people they'll go to immediately. Just a bunch of old lefties who show up at every demonstration, rally, leafleting and seminar. Gray ponytails and lots of anti-war buttons. You can spot them a mile away."

"What about you, Lyla?"

"Uh, I don't think you'd really be too cool about my friends. I mean, they'd hide us, but it's like…"

"Yeah?"

"Well, they're like a little weird."

"Weird how?"

"Weird like, y'know goth, tattoos, body mod, that kind of thing."

"Actually, her friends are adorable, Jesus. I've met some of them and they're good kids. They just don't want to look like the rulers of the empire."

Jesus had already raised his hands above his head and upon lowering them was dressed in black boots, a long, sleeveless black coat, both of his arms had heavily tattooed sleeves and there was a spectacular gold ring through the septum of his nose. His locks were pulled high and wrapped, creating something not unlike a fountain on top of his head.

"Will this get us in?"

"Awesome. How'd you know what to do?"

"Dad used to let me hang out with Black Sabbath and Marilyn Manson. I think we'd better get a move on. Oh, Marie. Take off the 'Impeach Bush' button. It'd be a dead giveaway."

"But *your* T-Shirt says 'Fuck the System.'"

"Okay, keep the button."

Marie pointed to the corner. "Subway's up there. We've got to get to Spanish Harlem. We'll take the Staten Island Ferry, then switch to the 6 when we're in NYC."

The ferry was full, so mingling with the crowd wasn't difficult. Once they reached Manhattan, they headed to East River Drive.

"We've got to hurry. Maybe we should take a cab." Jesus raised his arm and instantly a gypsy cab pulled to the curb.

"Holy shit. Did you see that, Grandma?"

The driver was Muslim. "Assalaamu Alaikum," Jesus said as he got in.

"Alaikum Assalaam," the driver returned.

"Manhattan, 127th and 3rd," Lyla said, slamming the door.

The cabbie took off at a rapid pace. Marie could see him repeatedly looking at Jesus in the rear-view mirror. Finally he spoke.

"You are the man on TV, right? Jesus?"

"I am." Jesus had a moment of uncertainty about the usefulness of his disguise.

"But you honored Islam just now with your greeting. You know the Q'ran?"

"Of course. It's another one of the books Dad helped to get published."

"What?"

"It's a long story, but yes, I honor Islam."

"Mr. President George called you a bad man."

"Yes."

"I say 'spit in his eye and spray him with camel's piss.' You like that saying?"

"Let the punishment fit the crime."

"Why do you wear coat like Greek Orthodox priest?"

Jesus smiled. The similarity between goth and Orthodox hadn't struck him before. "I'm going with my friends to a sort of costume party. I want to fit in."

"You OK with me, Mr. Jesus."

Touched, Jesus sighed. "I try. I try."

"Why does Mr. President George want to kill all Muslims?"

"Because he wants to control the entire world. And to control something, you've either got to understand it or destroy it. The President hasn't got the capacity or the humanity to understand anything that isn't his. Of course he wants what lies beneath your ground—the oil. But he's seeking world rule."

"Why? Why cannot we live as brothers in peace?"

"It's the thirst for power—a disease as old as time. Dad threw one of his sons out of the house because he wanted power without regard for the universe."

"His own son?"

"My twin, Beelzebub."

"And where is he, your brother, now?"

"In one form or another, we've just been talking about him."

"You mean?"

"I believe we need to make a right turn at the corner."

They drove in silence for some blocks, then the cabbie spoke again.

"Mr. Jesus?"

"Yes."

"What is Beelzebub?"

"Anything or anyone who is not good for the people of the earth. I've tried to explain this many times. I usually fail. The 'anti' forces are very great."

"We are here—127th and 3rd. God is good to send you to my car."

"May I make you a promise?"

The driver nodded. "Of course, my friend."

Jesus reached through the partition with his right hand and placed it on the driver's shoulder. "I promise that you will be left behind."

Marie handed some bills to a greatly puzzled Arab man who watched his three passengers hurry away.

"Go ahead," Jesus called after the others. "I'll join you inside." He headed up the block and disappeared in the darkness.

CHAPTER 48

"Son of a bitch suspended elections without even contacting me." Tim Michaeljohn slammed his fist on the table so hard his Jack Daniels shot out of the glass. Following the President's press conference, Michaeljohn and his advisors left Helen by the TV, and went into the secure room to discuss Tim's next move.

"I play his game, go along with all the shit he brings down on this country—even support his ungodly wars—and this is the thanks I get? He doesn't even say he's *sorry* he has to suspend elections! He had that usual smirk on his ugly puss and he just announces it like it's nothing."

"It was planned all along. Bush is just the little shadow of the Big Thing, you know." Grant Millican was sitting at his computer writing a speech for Michaeljohn to deliver. "So do you want this to support the President or do you want to commit political suicide?"

"I have to think about it."

"For Chrissake, what's there to think about, Tim? This bastard and his minions have decided to do a takeover. They're using the disappearances just the way they used 9/11. I mean, what do you expect? Nothing just *happens* with them. Remember back in 1997, *The Project for the New American Century?* Jeb Bush, Richard Perle, Paul Wolfowitz, Donald Rumsfeld, Dick Cheney and others, were saying that there would have to be a 'New Pearl Harbor' to get the American people behind an invasion of Iraq. Well, they engineered their New Pearl Harbor on 9/11 and were ready to seize the moment. It's no different now."

"So what should I do, Grant? Just sit here and say 'Okay, Dubya, it's your call,' and give him total support when I go on TV? Or do I say what I really think?"

"You're in a funny position to say that you oppose him on anything now. You've backed him on everything and everybody knows it. You'll end up looking like John Kerry or Hillary Clinton—voting for a war then trying to condemn it. You'll be a laughing stock."

"Maybe…"

"Look, man. Why don't you talk to Helen? She has stuck around loving you as person and hating everything you stand for, right? So why don't you go talk to her?"

"I know what she'll say."

"So don't talk to her… just decide if you want to take her advice."

"How do I know what her advice would be?"

"You just said… oh God you drive me crazy. I'm stopping work on this speech. You can either go talk to your wife and make up your own mind about what you're going to do, in which case I'll write the speech you want; or, you can keep up this indecision and just go on TV and wing it. Your choice. I'll be in my cubicle." He left the room and shut the door a little too hard.

Helen Michaeljohn entered. "I've got some coffee for you. What's with Grant?"

"I wish I knew."

"He seemed really mad."

"I can't make up my mind about something."

"Want to talk?" Helen, for all her disgust with Tim's choices, was still the person who loved him the most. Even now with so much going wrong, she had a gentle tone and sincerely wanted to help. She would have been lying if she had said in addition to "helping" she wouldn't like to *influence*.

"Look," Tim said staring into the coffee mug like it was a seer's tool, "In the beginning I thought I had Bush and his crowd all figured out. I knew they wanted enormous power and wanted to shift lots of money to their friends through military contracts, prisons, tax cuts—you name it. But I didn't think they'd actually go through with…"

"With what?"

"With what they've set in motion now."

"Do you hear yourself?" There was a tough edge to Helen's voice. "You talk like your hands are relatively clean! You've been right there in the bloody hog slop with him. How are we going to keep a war going for a hundred years if we don't invent things to fight?"

"He didn't even consult me."

"Be glad. At least you won't have more lives on your conscience." Helen turned to leave.

"Wait. Helen. I do want to know what you think."

"I don't think you possibly could."

"But I do. I'm afraid."

"Play with wolves, get eaten."

"I know you hate who I've become."

"Look, Tim, it's a little late for this. It's a little late for *us*." She walked across the room and sat in an overstuffed chair. "Come here and sit," she pointed at the chair's twin. "I'll talk."

"He's moving into the final chapter. He's doing it without me." Michaeljohn settled into the chair.

"You think he never intended for you to be the next President, is that what you're saying?"

"Yes, but…"

"And you want me to believe that your great moral compass would have had you quit cooperating with them if they hadn't pushed you out?"

"To get where I am—to get us out of that endless defeat with the unions and the losers—I had to agree to certain things. Helen, there are things I *know.* And if I'm being pushed out, those things could become very, very dangerous."

"Why are you telling me this? I mean we've had years to reconsider the direction you're going. There've been countless times when you could have opened up to me and asked my opinion and really wanted something different."

"I see that you're still here—in this nice house, with your nice car and your nice circle of friends. Indoor plumbing."

Helen looked down at her hands. "If you want me to say that I've gone along and sold out… I have."

"There was never a time you said 'I'm leaving you,' that I had the slightest worry that you meant it."

"So what are you going to do?"

Michaeljohn hesitated. "I'll contact the few people on my staff that I trust."

"And keep the campaign going—advance your current platform?"

"The suspension isn't temporary. He's been looking to do this for a long time. I just didn't think he could."

"Could what? You *knew* he was going to declare martial law?"

"I knew he wanted a pretext and that when he got it, it wouldn't be temporary. Helen, he's just made himself president indefinitely."

"Oh my God. But that's impossible." Helen stood and faced her husband.

"It may not be. Not if…"

"What aren't you telling me?"

There was a knock at the door. It was Grant Millican. "Tim, the President's on the phone for you."

Tim looked at Helen.

"Well, Tim, what are you waiting for? Your connection to power is on the line."

Tim signaled Helen to be quiet and answered. "Hello Mr. President."

"Timmy Boy, listen, I don't know if you were just watchin' the TV…"

"I was, Mr. President," the candidate tried to hide his fury.

"Well listen, me and Karl—well, y'know Karl *unofficially*—we're real sorry that we hadda sorta blindside you. You know how goes sometimes. Just hadda do it that way. You're not sore, right?"

"I'm fine, Mr. President."

"Look, Timmy Boy, these things happen. We've got a helluv a sichation right now. Hadda move fast. Y'know."

"Right."

"Well, I jest wanted to check up on ya and see how ya were doin'."

"Thank you."

"So, bayh for now… . oh, jest one other thing. You do remember that your knowledge of shall we say 'events' is all classified, don't you? I wouldn't want you forgetting that in all the upset about the sichations out here."

"Events?"

"Don't fuck with me asshole." The President's genial tone disappeared as fast as Dick Cheney.

"*Sichation* is under control."

"Don't mess, cocksucker."

"Thank you for calling, Mr. President."

The "aw shucks" returned. "Just call me George."

CHAPTER 49

"I've got to get the children!" Chandra cried, trying to get up.

Hogan helped her stand. "Do you know where they took them?"

"They wouldn't tell me."

"*Who* wouldn't tell you?" Adam's normally calm disposition had disappeared. "What kind of animals…"

"Homeland Security. I called the police in Van Nuys and they transferred my call. Someone came on and said the children were at a juvenile detention center. They've taken my mom and Felice somewhere else. They're not with the children." Chandra broke for the front door.

Hogan chased her. "Where are you going?"

"To get them."

"Chandra, you can't. They're watching us. For all we know there's an arrest warrant for you. And where would you go?"

"I don't know. But I've got to find them."

"We'll come with you. Right Adam?"

"Right." Adam was already rolling towards the door.

"Let's do a little detective work first. Chandra, have you ever used Google Earth?"

CHAPTER 50

The news of the President's address didn't reach the residents of Gitmo. Locked in chain link cages that resembled a neglected dog pound, hundreds of men sat on concrete floors in various degrees of restraint. Some were able to get up and count off six feet each direction in their cage. Others were fastened by an arm or leg to the fencing. And still others were bound by two chains—one to a wrist and one to the opposite ankle—linked to steel rings in the floor. Like distraught circus elephants, these men rocked back and forth, stopped each time by the tensioning of chain.

Some more fortunate were in the outdoor facility covered by a metal sun roof. The others, those doomed to long conversations with interrogators, were inside. Rarely had a single English word been able to evoke such terror, such submission, such resignation as the word "inside" spoken at Gitmo. "They're taking you *inside*," was enough to reduce a strong, healthy man to a quaking organism. But it was *inside* that Jerrod Parker found himself. Jesus had assured him that no one had heard their conversation, no one knew Jerrod had had a visitor. But now Jerrod had doubts. Just fifteen minutes after Jesus vanished, two uniformed soldiers—a man and a woman—unlocked the door of his cage.

"You're going *inside*," they said. They placed a black capture hood over his head. The heat intensified. Jerrod felt his panic return as he struggled to breathe.

"Take off your jumpsuit."

Jerrod obeyed, removing his orange jumpsuit. He stood in his thin undershorts waiting.

The woman handcuffed his wrists behind his back. The man placed shackles on his ankles connected by a solid steel bar. Then Jerrod was prodded to walk. In order to walk the shackles had to rotate on his ankles, and since they were tight, each step tore his skin. He begged for the shackles to be loosened, but his requests provoked nothing but contemptuous laughter.

He heard a door open and through a change in sound and echo could tell he was indoors.

"Keep walking," his female captor said again and again. "Captain thinks it's not good you're always alone. He said you should meet some of your friends, spend a little time with them. *Play* with them."

Jerrod felt his undershorts being pulled back and then heard a slicing sound as a knife ripped into them. In moments they were stripped away.

"Get down," it was the female voice again.

"Down?" Jerrod was afraid of incorrectly following the order.

"What don't you understand about down?" A foot hit him squarely in the back. He tried to keep his balance, but the shackles made it impossible for his feet to move and he crashed forward to the cement floor. He could hear more laughter. He also thought he heard a low moaning sound.

The impact on the floor had broken something—just what he wasn't sure—but he imagined that weak points from his old injuries were again detached. The pain was intense.

"Good news, shithead," it was the female again. "We're removing your leggings. Don't be a dick and do anything. Just say thank you."

Jerrod's response was immediate. "Thank you."

There was relief and pain at once as the shackles were jerked from his legs.

"Now more good news, prickface. We're going to remove your hand-cuffs. One false move and we won't be so nice."

The handcuffs were removed.

"Now say hello to your hot shit friends." As she spoke she pulled the hood off Jerrod's head.

The rapid removal of the hood jarred the injured bones in Jerrod's face and he felt like screaming. Instead he took in a breath and held it. Sweat and tears burned his eyes, but he could tell that he was in a lighted room. Then the sounds came to him. They seemed to come from all around him. They were unearthly sounds. Human, and yet not human. They emanated from something beyond conscious expression. They were the sounds of souls searching for compassion and finding none.

A boot connected with his ribs. "Open your fucking eyes you worthless asshole. Say hello to your friends, your partners, your buddies." It was the male this time.

Jerrod forced his eyes to focus. He imagined that he was hallucinating.

Perhaps he was back in the hospital and the morphine was in control but ineffective against pain. Everywhere he could see there were contorted, naked bodies. Immediately in front of him, perhaps two feet from his face, was a tangled human pyramid. Arms, legs, heads, torsos, pelvises and genitalia intertwined into a writhing mass. Jerrod had been to Vigeland Park in Norway and seen the Monolith sculpture of struggling humanity. But what was in front of him was not stone, it was alive, and it smelled of putrefying flesh and sweat and the excretions of terror.

The boot connected again forcing Jerrod to his other side. He first saw the man's eyes. They were larger than human eyes should be. They did not blink. They were in a permanent expression of horror. The clamps holding them that way tore at tender tissues. There were electric wires extending from the clamps to somewhere. Jerrod couldn't tell where. And then there was the sound—the buzzing, crackling sound. And then Jerrod couldn't look because the man's eyes were smoking again.

The boot hit his ribs again and again, but Jerrod couldn't respond. He had lost consciousness. When he came to he was lying on the pile of living bodies too weak to move. But then the bodies moved, and little by little freed themselves from one another. In time he was lying on the floor.

He searched the room with small motions of his head so painful he feared he would collapse again. The soldiers were gone. He and fifteen or twenty men were alone. That's when it happened.

The man next to him addressed him in perfect English, but his mouth was moving as though he was in a dubbed movie.

"My name is Siraj," he said. "I saw them bring you in. You are an American, no?"

"I am Jerrod. Yes, I'm an American."

"Ah, you speak Arabic. I am surprised."

"No, I am speaking English."

"It is Arabic I am hearing. Allah be praised."

Jerrod, stunned and unbelieving continued, "I was arrested in New York City. I have been brought here. Is this Guantanamo?"

"You are in an American concentration camp. We do not know where we are. It is hot, but we are not at home. I am not a terrorist."

"Neither am I," Jerrod replied. "I am a stock broker."

"Terror comes in many forms," the man said simply, waiting for Jerrod's reaction. There was none. "I am not a terrorist either. I am a barber by trade. They came to my shop one day and arrested everyone. I do not know why. We have not been told."

"How long have you been here?"

"I believe it is four years. I sometimes lose days. They have placed drugs in my body."

To Jerrod, the oddest thing about the conversation was not that he and a stranger were lying on the floor in an unknown prison speaking in one language and understanding in another, but that they were speaking at all. All around them lay naked men who had endured torture and humiliation and who awaited their fate silently. Jerrod understood their submissiveness because he too was afraid. He wondered if he could tell this man about the visit he had received earlier. He wondered if there were questions he should be asking. He wondered what it was that he was supposed to be finding out. He wasn't going to have to wait long.

CHAPTER 51

It was the pink golf shirt that seemed most incongruous to Chandra Boolean. Of course she had seen many photographs of Tiger Woods in bright colors, but there was something disquieting about this particular outfit—the cut off jeans, the headband, the Roman sandals. Then again she thought maybe it wasn't the outfit, but rather that it was being worn by a very large Black man who suddenly had turned the threesome in her study into a foursome.

Adam and Hogan stared blankly, too shocked to move.

"Hi. Sorry to intrude. I'm Jesus. I need to talk to you."

"Where did you…"

"We don't have a lot of time. Sorry I didn't knock."

"Did I leave the gate open?" Chandra glanced at her security monitors.

"I didn't come that way. Don't worry, I'm a friend."

Suddenly Hogan was pointing at Jesus. "Now I remember you! You're the guy they just showed on TV and, and . . ," he seemed nearly overcome, "and you were in the Jesus Dome just before. . . *Oh my God!*"

"No, that's my Dad," Jesus said, misunderstanding Hogan's exclamation.

"You were there! And then everybody just disappeared. I was the only one left. You were gone too. What are you going to do to us?"

"I'm not going to do anything to you. I've come to ask you a favor. It's not exactly a favor for *me*, it's Dad's plan, and well, you're an important part of it."

"You've kidnaped or killed everyone I know and you want a favor?" Hogan's gentle nature was pushed to the limit.

Jesus stepped forward and looked at Chandra's computer. "Hmm. Google Earth. You're looking for your children, right?"

"You know about *Google Earth?*

"Of course."

"You know about the children?"

"Yes."

"Will you help us find them"?"

"Yes. But you'll need to be patient. I know it's late and I don't want to take up a lot of your time."

Chandra managed a weak smile. "Are you really who you say you are?"

"I am. I'm sorry. I know this is all very fast and you've all been through a lot. You too, Adam. I'm sorry about your injuries."

Adam advanced his wheelchair. "How did you know . . ?"

"Uh, I can see you don't have any legs."

"But you knew my name."

"We've actually met. You just don't remember it. I was the Imam who dragged you to safety the day you were hit by the roadside bomb."

"You were the Imam—the guy who showed up from nowhere?"

"I keep coming in various forms hoping that I can get someone to actually hear what I'm saying. But I've been a terrible failure. I just talk until I'm blue in the face, and then predictably, someone wants to make a religion out of what they think I've said and we're just in a bigger mess than before."

Chandra broke in. "Wait! You said you know about my children. Where are they?"

"They're in a detention center up in California's Angeles Forest. They are safe for now, and they'll be fine just so long as we do everything right."

Hogan shot in, "*We?*"

"Yes. I need you. Like I said I keep doing this, but nobody really listens."

"You keep coming back?"

"Yeah. Sometimes I'm more successful than others. The best one from my standpoint was when I came as Buddha. I got to eat whatever I wanted and was able to laugh and be happy. At least that time nobody hated me or tried to kill me. But they still started a religion…"

Hogan suddenly stiffened. "So you admit you're the guy from the Jesus Dome!"

"Right, Hogan. That's right."

"What did you do there? What did you do with everyone. Oh!" Hogan could feel the hot air moving in his brain. "Fuck you lousy shit! Forgive me Jesus."

"No problem, Hogan. No offense taken. But you really don't have to be so upset." Jesus put his hand on Hogan's shoulder and immediately the good man relaxed.

"I felt the hot air again in my head. But I don't know why I say those terrible things"

"We can talk about that later. There's a lot you're angry with—and you happen to be right. You just need to know what those things are."

"You're really the guy who saved me?" Adam couldn't imagine how anyone could know about the Imam who'd appeared and pulled him out of harm's way. Nothing about him was included in any reports.

"I'm the one."

"Wow. Thank you."

"You're welcome. Now we'd better get down to business, because I left some people in New York who are going to need me real soon. Chandra, what can I do to have you more comfortable with my being here?"

"Just tell me that I'll see my children. I'm a little jumpy."

"You'll be with your children soon, but I need you to cooperate with a plan."

"I'll listen, but…"

"How can I reassure you?" Jesus seemed honestly concerned.

"Tell Hogan what you did with all the people in the Jesus Dome."

"Oh that. Yes, well, it's part of the reason I'm here. Dad feels that things are getting out of hand."

"Dad? You keep saying 'Dad.'"

"Sorry. A lot of people call him God, Yahweh, Allah, Vishnu. We're close, so I call him Dad."

"You're saying that God is a person."

"In a manner of speaking, yes. He's a person, a thing,… everything. Have you ever looked up at the stars at night and just felt like talking to them? Kids do it all the time saying 'Star light, star bright, first star I see tonight.' Well, it's like that."

"Can you see Him?"

"If you're traveling fast enough. We tried to explain it to Einstein. He got close with his theory of relativity. But then he got off on E=MC^2. I did everything I could to warn him what he was playing with. Hmm," Jesus seemed far away for a moment. "He lived to regret the day he didn't listen. Now look what a mess there is. But that's what happens. I get involved with someone, or actually appear, can't make myself understood, and things are worse off than if I'd never tried. I'm hoping that this time—for once—I'll get it right."

Hogan was impatient. "So you were going to tell us about the Jesus Dome. Was it part of the Divine Rapture?"

"Not exactly. It's a kind of Rapture, but different from what all the crazies have been predicting."

"Crazies?"

"People who believe what's in that series of shoddy *Left Behind* books, you know."

"Oh, those."

"Well, you see, the universe is out of whack. So much has gone on here, so many of the wrong people have gotten power, so many ideas have gotten twisted around, that Dad feels disgusted and bored with the human race. He thought maybe things should just play themselves out and then it would all be over—completely over—and he wouldn't have to deal with this planet any more. We had a lot of arguments about it. I tried everything. I pleaded with him. I do that from time to time. Sometimes it works, sometimes it doesn't. This time I was getting absolutely nowhere."

"So what happened?"

"I pulled out my ace."

Chandra couldn't hide her surprise. "You play cards?"

"When things get completely down to the mat and I feel that no matter what argument I bring up Dad just isn't going to listen because he's totally had it—and when he's totally had it, he is usually thinking about destruction of some type—I use my ace argument which is that destruction is exactly what my brother would want."

"Beelzebub, you mean?"

"Exactly. He's taken more forms, come back in more ways than you can imagine. He's always wanted to rule everything. He's a sociopath. He doesn't care what he causes, just so long as he's ruling."

"So there really is a Satan and. . ."

"See? That's where I have to be so careful. I'm trying to explain this, but you're in danger of trying to turn it into something religious. It isn't. It's like plus and minus in math. That's the only way I can explain it. Plus goes to infinity in positives, minus goes to infinity in negatives. Do you understand?"

"I'll feel better if you'd just say what happened at the Jesus Dome."

Hogan nodded. "I need to know too. I liked some of those people and they are just gone."

"I wish I could have warned you before it happened but there are some things that work better as a surprise." Jesus pulled his locks back over his shoulder and leaned forward. "Here's the deal," he said. "Dad finally listened and said there was something I could do—if I wanted to risk it—that would set things back on track."

"If you could risk it?"

"They've killed me more than once."

"Right."

"Okay. Dad was angry and fed up with a lot of people. So he said I should come and start removing the people who have derailed things. He thinks they're boring."

"Boring?"

"Yeah, well, they never think of anything new. They just keep pulling the same tricks and causing the same problems. They *are* boring."

"You killed them?"

"No! I wouldn't do that. See, all those people like to be exclusively with their 'own kind.' And so I've just moved them to another resonance where they can be troubled by nothing but their own kind. It had to be a part of reality which doesn't impact the other parts—that was tricky—but we found a resonance where they could just carry on, preach, fight, do whatever it is they are going to do and affect nobody but themselves."

Hogan stood up and walked over to Jesus. "Let me get this straight. You just *moved* over fifteen hundred people to another *resonance?*"

"Right. Same thing with Winslow Boolean—you were never really in danger by the way, Chandra—and the stock brokers and even, heh, heh, Dick Cheney. Did you read about that one? I was not expecting that thong. I thought of making it disappear, but I reconsidered. I figured it would be good for people to know that little detail, just in case someone wanted to start eulogizing him as a great man. Bush tried tonight, but if you could have heard the laughter around the world, it would've warmed your heart."

"So the people you don't take—the people left behind—*aren't* the damned?"

"Heavens no! I was afraid people would think that. No. By the time I get finished, the people 'left behind' are going to be the people who will take care of this planet and get along. I don't mind that phrase, 'get along' by the way. I told Rodney King to use it, but seeing as how the media in this country is run by some of the people Dad is maddest at, it got laughed at. Now before I get off on a tirade about the corporate media in this country, I think we'd better get to the point I came for. You feeling reassured Chandra?" Jesus gave such an earnest look, Chandra relaxed slightly.

"I'm doing the best I can," she said. "Just tell me again that my children are all right and that I can see them."

"I assure you, Santee and Vertaine are well and safe. But listen very carefully to what I'm going to tell you. I really need to have you come through. I've planned this in detail, but you're going to have to cooperate. I'm only contacting a few people—you're three of them—and you're essential to the plan. Are you in?"

Chandra, Hogan, and Adam nodded.

Jesus smiled, leaning forward and resting his elbows on his knees. "Good. Now here's what I'm going to need you to do."

CHAPTER 52

ABC ANNOUNCER: *We interrupt our regular programming to bring you this special ABC Breaking News.*

CHARLES GIBSON: *Good evening. This is Charles Gibson reporting from New York. In an apparent about face, the Bush Administration today acknowledged the widespread severity of the disappearances that have swept the country. No longer saying the occurrences are "random" and "unrelated," President Bush made an unscheduled appearance in the Rose Garden and established the cause of this growing tragedy.*

PRESIDENT GEORGE W. BUSH: *Please be seated. Due to faulty intelligence from branches of the FBI, earlier assessments of the scope of the persons missing in areas of this nation have been somewhat underreported. More importantly, the cause of these events was erroneously interpreted as unrelated. However, new intelligence has established with absolute certainty that these are terrorist actions, perpetrated by fanatical people who have no regard for the sanctity of life, the preciousness of every human being.*

Here, the President paused for a moment, his eyes searching the room for approving recognition that he'd used so many big words without stumbling—particularly the word "terrorist."

I have therefore given the order that anyone suspected of participating in these disappearances, anyone who has given refuge to the terrorists, or who is perceived as having lied about the circumstances of these criminal acts, shall be shot and killed on sight. We cannot allow these inhuman barbarians—many of whom are suspected of being aligned with the liberal Democratic Party and other leftist organizations—to breathe another breath. This is one nation under God and we will crush, maim, kill and utterly destroy anyone who wants to interrupt our Christian freedoms.

CHARLES GIBSON: *The President went on to make clear that these terrorists will be hunted down. Those already in custody at civilian detention centers will be afforded no refuge and will be presumed guilty until they prove conclusively otherwise. Stay tuned to this ABC station for more breaking news, and to ABC Evening News tonight when we will be bringing you coverage of the ongoing scandal unfolding in Quincy, Massachusetts where Angelina Jolie is attempting a building variance to construct a home large enough to shelter her growing family. We will also be following latest developments on the filming of the new* Batman V. *For ABC News this is Charles Gibson.*

CHAPTER 53

"This is it." Lyla pointed at a nondescript building with bricked-up windows. The entrance was unmarked. She led the way into a small foyer. There was a black door on the left. Directly ahead there was what looked like a ticket booth with a two-way mirror so the teller couldn't be seen.

"Is Deemon here? Tell him it's Lyla and it's important."

"Okay," came a voice from the other side.

"And in a little while another friend of mine is coming. Tall, goth with locks—he'll use my name. Let him in to, 'K?" Lyla turned to her grandmother. "They'll buzz us in, give them a second."

The lock on the black door buzzed and Lyla pushed. A long, dark corridor lay ahead, lighted only by small red globes. The walls, floor and ceiling were painted black. In the distance came the sound of pounding techno house music. At the end of the corridor a narrow stairway led up to the right.

"Is this where you usually come, Dear?" Marie, for all her liberality was somewhat uncomfortable.

"Yeah. Well, this is where we meet. Then we… Hi Deemon." Lyla stopped abruptly on the stairway. A man wearing only a red leather thong-like waist apparatus and knee-high red boots was looming ahead. He was at least six and a half feet tall, with deep chocolate skin and powerful muscles. At first Marie thought that he had a Mohawk haircut, but then she realized that the man's head was shaved. What she thought to be hair was actually a row of thin metal spikes protruding through the skin of the man's scalp.

The man, standing a step higher than Lyla bent down and kissed her, then took her by the hand and led her upstairs. Marie followed.

At the top of the stairs he opened the door and the music became deafeningly loud. He waited until Lyla and Marie were in and then pulled the door closed. They were standing in a room one hundred feet long and fifty feet wide painted entirely in red and black. About two hundred dancers were on the floor.

"Grandma, this is Deemon. He's in charge here."

Deemon nodded. "I'm sorry I can't hang. The show is about to start."

"But I need to talk to you, Deemon."

"Right after the show, okay. You know you guys've got the run of the place. Have a good time." He skirted the sides of the room to avoid the crowd.

Near them was a large bar. Behind the bar were three girls in skimpy leather outfits revealing full-body tattoos. A fourth girl, with a shaved head, wearing a bustier and garters, was tattooed from the top of her head to every visible point. Half of her face was ornately tattooed, the other side painted brilliant white.

"That's Gina," Lyla said pointing to the fourth girl. "She's like my soul mate."

"What did you say, dear?" Marie was struggling to bear the level of sound.

"I want you to meet someone!" Lyla took Marie by the hand and led her to the bar. "Gina," she shouted. "Gina, this is my grandma, Marie. And guess what? We're with Jesus Christ!"

"Right," Gina said, obviously thinking she was in on a good joke. "You fall in love too fast."

"Haven't you heard the news tonight?"

"News? Are you kidding? Does it look like I'm here trying to get depressed?"

"This Jesus guy is the *real deal*. He's going to be here any minute. He's like on Bush's most wanted list—and he's cute!"

"Then I'll put him on my most wanted list any day." Gina winked.

"I'm serious. Look, we need a place to hide. The Feds may be after all three of us."

Gina stepped back, "You buggin'?"

"I'm dead serious. Turn on any TV."

"You tell Deemon?"

"Didn't have a chance. He said to wait until after the show."

"You might as well, I don't think the Feds'll be looking for you here." She laughed. "We're not exactly their type, y'know what I'm sayin'? We can probably get you over to Snagg's later."

"Snagg?" Marie was trying to follow the conversation.

"Later, Grandma. Gina, you got anything we can put on so we don't stand out like Jersey tourists?"

"Sure. I'll go get something while you watch the show."

Gina went to another room while Lyla and Marie moved through the crowd towards a low stage. There a group of young men were arranging sterile instrument packs on a large white sheet.

One kid sat on the edge of the stage. He had already pushed about a hundred needles through his forearms and biceps, and was now pinching the skin on his forehead and forcing needles through the ridges. Around him were the discarded blue and white sterile needle packs. Watching him was an attractive young woman with rainbowed hair wearing the top of a white wedding dress and white tights. Little pink bows were attached to the backs of her legs by needles pierced through her skin. She occasionally stuck out her tongue which had been surgically bifurcated, so that she was able to curl the ends around like two snakes engaged in lovemaking.

A few minutes later, Gina returned and handed Marie a red neglige with a frilly lace collar, and Timberland boots. Lyla got spike heels and a leather bikini. They went to the bathroom to change. When they returned, Gina was waiting for them.

"I feel ridiculous," Marie shouted. "It's like bordello meets mountain goat."

"It will work fine. We're safe here for the moment."

Just then, Deemon jumped onto the stage holding a microphone. The music lowered slightly and he screamed, "Showtime!"

Two shirtless men, both covered in ornate tattoo "jackets" climbed on stage and kneeled on the white sheet with their backs to the audience.

"You may or may not want to watch, Marie," Gina said, resting her arm lightly across Marie's shoulders. You going to be okay?"

"After all that's happened, I think I'm up to anything."

Marie was wrong.

CHAPTER 54

Santee and Vertaine Boolean were not spoiled children—not in the sense the word is customarily used. They were used to good food, comfortable surroundings, and respectful treatment, but they were not demanding or obnoxious. Still, lying as they were on two hard cots next to one another in a very strange place, they couldn't help but comment on their surroundings.

"I don't like it here, Santee," Vertaine said, his voice at the point of breaking. "I don't like it here at all." Try as he might to be brave, the little fellow was having a hard time remaining calm. He wanted to convince his sister that there was nothing to worry about, but the hot tears that kept coming to his eyes seemed to betray him.

"I don't like it here either, Vertaine. Do you think mommy knows where we are?"

The question tore at the little boy's heart. He didn't want to frighten his sister, but he didn't want to lie. "I'm not sure," he said. "But I know she's trying to get here. I just know it."

"Where are we?"

"I don't know. Don't cry, Santee."

"I can't help it. I'm so scared."

Vertaine took his sister's hand. "Look around," he said, using his other hand to point. "Look at all the children in this room. None of them know where their mommies and daddies are—none of them really know where this place is. But we'll be okay. I just know we will."

Santee was looking at a man by the door wearing a dark jacket. "What does it say on that man's jacket?"

"Blackwater."

"Why does he have a gun?"

"Santee, I don't know, I don't know."

Vertaine was right. There were *many* children together under one roof at the Halliburton-constructed juvenile detention center on Mt. Potrero. 7,208 children to be exact. Most were picked up as they wandered the streets looking for their disappeared parents. Some, like Santee and Vertaine were captured in the night during raids on their homes.

The man in the dark jacket was walking toward Santee. "He's coming here, Vertaine."

"Don't be afraid. He's not going to hurt us." Vertaine prayed he was telling his sister the truth.

"I'm only going to tell you once," the man in the jacket said. "I tell you once and that's it. You've got red markers. That means that you're potential trouble or that you have got terrorist ties in your family. So I've got my eye on you. Don't try anything. Don't say anything. Don't ask anything. You got that?"

The children were speechless.

"Answer me when I talk."

"Where's my mommy?" It was Santee who spoke first.

"What did I just tell you?"

"I really, really need to know."

The man grabbed Santee's arm and yanked her to her feet. "Maybe if you can't plot with your brother you won't be so much trouble." And with that he dragged Santee out of the room. Vertaine tried to stop him, desperately tried to reach his sister, but it was no use. The man knocked him away and slammed the door.

"Oh my God!" Marie covered her eyes and felt her knees giving way as Deemon bunched up skin above the shoulder blade of one of the kneeling men and forced a large stainless steel hook in one side and out the other— exactly corresponding to four marks he'd placed on the man's back. The man grimaced in pain but remained on his knees.

Marie turned to Lyla who was watching the familiar procedure. "Honey, I think I might faint."

"Oh Gee, Grandma. Don't do that. Just sit here on the edge of the stage. Wait, let me just wipe this blood off there." Lyla grabbed a rag and cleared the spot of some droplets. "They're going to do a basic suspension and then a two-man tug. They do it all the time."

"You've seen this before?"

"Grandma, I *did* it once."

The music, the view, and the news about her granddaughter were quickly humbling Marie's notion that she was up to anything.

"You'll be fine, Grandma. Don't watch if you don't want to. But it's really going to be okay. These are my friends. You'll meet them all. They'll take care of us."

The fourth hook had been inserted through the man's skin, and Deemon helped him up and walked him to the edge of the stage. There, from a huge pulley in the ceiling hung a rope that terminated in a kind of wooden bracket with four rope hoops. Deemon quickly fed the hoops through the eyes of the hooks in the man's back. He gave a signal and slowly four men began pulling the other end of the rope. The skin on the man's back began to stretch.

Marie, who was still watching, gagged.

When his skin had stretched about four inches away from his body he began to sway. Little by little, his feet left the ground and he swung freely off the stage and over the crowd. Hands gently touched his legs and pushed him in a large circular arc. He extended his arms like he was flying. He didn't seem to be in great pain. Marie thought he was actually smiling. This wasn't going to be so bad.

As before, Marie was premature in assessing her stamina.

The man who was flying was slowly lowered to the ground and stood directly under the pulley.

The other man who had been patiently kneeling all this time was being prepared by Deemon. That man had tattooing everywhere on his body, so as the hooks were inserted in his back, various creatures, mostly female, were being skewered. With his hooks in place, the man walked to the center of the room where a similar wooden bracket was attached to the far end of the rope. That was attached to the hooks, and under Deemon's direction, the man began to walk forward. When the rope grew taught, he leaned forward and used all his strength to move. Several men took hold of his arms and pushed him forward. The skin on his back stretched at least five inches from him, and rivulets of blood trickled down his back. But he kept moving. At the other end, the first man began to rise from the ground—lifted solely by the hooks placed through the second man's skin. As the music pounded, the crowd roared its approval.

Marie was surprised by her limberness. Feeling faint, she easily placed her head between her knees—a position she would have said was impossible. She felt a hand on her back.

"You okay?"

"Yeah, Lyla. I just felt a little…" She looked up. It was Jesus. "Oh, sorry, I thought you were Lyla. I couldn't bear to watch this. It's so horrible to see these kids doing this to themselves."

"Reminds me of something I went through once," Jesus said softly.

"I didn't mean to offend you."

"Not at all. But don't worry too much about these kids. One of these days this won't be necessary. Right now, well when you feel that everything has been ripped out of your control and someone else is doing a lousy job with the only world you've got to live in… you do things to release that pressure. These are good kids. They're not out blowing people up. And you notice that they haven't disappeared."

"How did you get so cool?"

Jesus smiled. "It comes with age," he said.

Deemon was the final performer. He laid down on the edge of the stage with his knees pulled up. An assistant brought two huge stainless steel hooks and with experienced hands shoved their sharp points through the skin just above Deemon's kneecaps. The wooden frame was quickly attached and Deemon was hoisted in the air, hanging from the skin over his knees. That skin stretched much farther than the skin on the other men's backs, and Marie was sure that it was going to rip.

"I am going to be sick after all," she shouted in Jesus' ear.

"Hang on just a minute longer, Marie. I think it's just about over."

And he was right. Deemon was lowered to the floor, the crowd applauded, and within seconds were back to dancing. When Jesus reached him, Deemon was pouring alcohol on his knees.

"So what did you think?" he asked.

"About the show?"

"Yeah. Did you like it?"

Jesus smiled. "It brought back memories… so *liking* it? I'm not sure that's the right word. But the fact you're doing it by choice is a plus."

Deemon stood. "So what do you guys need? Lyla looked scared."

"She's got reason." Jesus leaned in to keep the conversation private. "We have a problem with the Feds. We need a place to hide, but also a place where we can get messages out, start organizing something. You know of a place like that?"

"Hold on." Deemon went to the bar, got Gina and brought her back. "Lyla, her grandma and *Jesus* need a place to hang where the Feds won't find them, but where they can still get messages out and stuff. You think Snagg could help?"

"I already figured he was the right person."

Marie, feeling steadier on her feet joined them.

Lyla dove in. "There's so much shit going on, guys. It totally sucks. You probably haven't heard, but there are thousands of people disappearing— and stupid Bush is saying it's terrorists. My parents are some of the people who 'disappeared.' I mean, they actually did! One minute they are downstairs bellowing shit to *Jaesus*—not this one, he's totally cool, but the one in their twisted heads—and the next minute they're gone. And then these cops come to the house and are checking out everything. Then *this* Jesus shows up at our house—but he's not the fascist idiot my parents were praying to. And then we see on the news that Dickwad Bush is starting investigations on people close to the disappearances. He's saying *this* Jesus is terrorist #1."

Deemon was taking it in. "So he can arrest you, hold you without charges for indefinite periods of time and deny you a lawyer, right? Motherfucker! Oh, sorry Jesus."

"No problem, Deemon. Sometimes you've gotta use the right word."

Marie joined in. "Halliburton just finished those civilian detention centers. They got hundreds of millions to build them, then had 'cost overruns' and finished 'em for just over $2 billion. I bet that's where we end up."

"Not bad for Cheney's little friends. You did hear that Cheney is one of the people who disappeared didn't you?" Lyla was still shocked when people didn't keep up with the news.

"Naw, I don't listen to that shit on the TV." Deemon was honest. "They just tell you what they want you to believe anyway. But Cheney's gone, huh. Cool."

"Nothing left but his metal parts and a *thong*."

Gina and Deemon both laughed at that.

"Look, Jesus is right," Lyla said. "We don't have a lot of time. You said something about getting us to Snagg. Can you do it? Bush announced he's starting a 10 PM curfew tomorrow night. We can't be out running around in daylight—it's got to be tonight."

"You're serious, aren't you? I mean you're really scared, and you really believe you're with Jesus, right?"

"Deemon, ya know I love you, but right about now I'd like to punch you out! Of course I really believe. Do you have *any* idea what it's like out there?"

"No. That's why I'm in here. This is sanity. Out there is crazy."

Marie saw the irony of the statement, Lyla went right past it.

"Deemon, hundreds, maybe thousands of people have disappeared. Jesus has got to do with it—uh, in like a good way—I mean, my *parents* are gone. While Bush is saying it's terrorists, the Christians are saying it's the Rapture. The whole world is going fuckin' crazy. So *please*—get us to Snagg right now."

"Gina, get Lord Xilla and tell him he'll have to close up the club."

"Okay, where is he?"

"He's in back doing an acid burn on that girl."

Gina said "Good bye," and headed off.

Deemon took a deep breath and said, "Well, are you ready to meet the Lord of the Underground? Give me a minute to get into some street clothes, and we'll go."

It was 3 AM. Even for New York they were a strange sight as they made their way up Third Avenue—a six foot six giant of a man wearing a black cape with knee-high red boots and steel spikes sticking out of his head, a 19 year old goth girl in a leather bikini and spike heels and black trenchcoat, a grandmotherly woman in a red nightie, Timberlands and a flowered parka, and a tall tattooed Black man in a sleeveless black coat, with a spectacular gold ring through the septum of his nose. What lay ahead of them was stranger than their appearance.

DAY FIVE

Sunday

November 2, 2008

CHAPTER 56

Cardinal Vonsecco was awakened by the telephone in his room.

"Hello?"

There was no answer, just a tapping sound.

"Hello?"

The same. Then he knew. The call was coming from inside the Vatican on a proprietary line. It could be only one person. The Cardinal dressed and quietly walked to the Papal suite. Two Swiss Guards stood watch.

"I have been summoned by the Pope," Vonsecco said, bowing to the unsmiling guards. They stepped aside and he knocked on the door. Moments later he heard the lock turn and Giuseppe Fognolio greeted him. He took Vonsecco's hand and pulled him inside, locked the door and walked quickly to the papal desk, passing the Cardinal a hand written note.

The Cardinal read quickly and then signed, "So it is as I thought."

Fognolio nodded sadly.

"I will do as you have asked," Vonsecco replied, his hands duplicating his words. "There is one person I know we can trust. I will summon him." He reached for the phone. Fognolio grabbed his hand and strongly shook his head.

"They are listening to everything," he signed.

"Then I will go to him at once." The Cardinal produced a small black object from his pocket. "Take this," he signed, handing it to Fognolio. When I am at your door it will flash so you will know I am here. Until then, bar your door. He folded Fognolio's note into a pocket and left quietly. Fognolio locked the door behind him. All he could do now was wait.

CHAPTER 57

Another taxi conveniently appeared. Deemon, Lyla, Maria got in the back seat. Jesus rode shotgun. "Hunt's Point," Deemon said.

The driver shook his head. "I don't go there at night."

"You'll be fine." Jesus produced a $100 bill and handed it to the man. "We are in need of your assistance and in return you'll have my protection."

The bill spoke louder to the driver than a promise of protection from a man with a gold nose ring. He headed up the FDR and took the turnoff to the Willis Avenue Bridge.

"Tiffany and Viele, four blocks past Spofford," Deemon directed, referring to Spofford, a prison in New York's Department of Juvenile Justice.

It wasn't hard to see why the driver had been reluctant to drive into the area. Residential streets gave way to warehouses, car glass shops, and wrecking yards. Young women in skimpy outfits stood on corners, in doorways, and paced by vacant lots. Men in darkened cars drove slowly past the women, occasionally stopping to talk and pick one up. In the distance, there was the roar of drag racing.

"Are you sure where you're taking us, Deemon?" Marie, for all her feeling that she'd been around the block, had never seen anything to match this. To her left, looking like a mental hospital from a 1950's horror movie, was Spofford Juvenile Detention Facility. Marie couldn't help feeling like crying for the children inside.

Deemon leaned forward. "Stay on Tiffany. Let us off two blocks up."

The cabbie obliged stopping just short of a deserted corner. As the four got out, Marie scouted the scene. Straight ahead she could see the outline of a pier and what looked like moonlight reflected on water. To the right, a few houses. To the left, a junk yard and a small brick garage.

"This way." Deemon didn't wait to see if he was followed. He walked swiftly in spite of the enormous boots on his feet. Lyla and Marie took Jesus' outstretched hands and walked as quickly as they could.

Deemon disappeared behind the brick garage. He looked back around the corner and motioned for his charges to hurry. He seemed displeased at their pace.

When they reached him, he was fumbling with a keypad hidden under a rusty bucket that was cleverly hinged to the side of the building. The proper numbers entered, they heard a "click" and Deemon reached down and lifted a metal basement door.

"Oh my God, it's like in a movie." Lyla was looking down a stairway lighted by a single bulb. She couldn't see the bottom.

"Go ahead." Deemon pointed down the stairs. "Watch your head—the ceiling is low for a while. And hold onto the side rails. You don't want to fall. It would be a long way down. Once you're in, I'll close the door."

Jesus led the way, followed by Lyla and Marie.

"What is this place, Deemon?" Marie wasn't thrilled about the current safety route.

"It was part of the original water tunnel system of New York. It goes down over 800 feet here. Uh, we're not going that far, don't worry. We'll stop at around 300 feet."

"And this is where Snagg hangs?"

"Yeah. But stop asking questions. We've just got to get there."

Each time it would get too dark to see anything, another bulb overhead would light the way.

Marie was counting steps. She was at 582 when Deemon said, "Stop." He passed them and felt along the wall. There was a small flap, disguised as a brick. He lifted it and found another keypad. He tapped in a code and a light came on revealing a small alcove.

"Come over here one by one," he said. Just face forward and wait until you hear a click, then move over and let the next person stand here. Just like this." He demonstrated. There was an audible click. "Lyla, go next." When they finished, there was another click and a door opened at the end of the alcove. The light from inside was bright, blinding them for a moment. Deemon moved ahead. "Cummon," he said, motioning for them to move quickly.

Once they were inside, the door closed.

"Deemon!" The voice was friendly and warm. "I've been expecting you and your guests."

Emerging from the shadows Marie could see someone moving. As her eyes adjusted and as the person got closer, she took a breath of such obvious shock that she was embarrassed.

"It's okay, young lady," she heard the man say. "I surprise a lot of people. I'm Snagg. Glad you're here. I've heard you're in a bit of a bind."

Standing three feet in front of her was a man of indistinct age wearing denim shorts and sandals and whose head, his face, chest, arms and legs were completely covered with tattooed green scales. Along his arms, he had round protrusions beginning large and getting smaller as they approached his wrists. There were similar but smaller protrusions on the crown of his head. And most strangely, a distinct three-dimensional cross on his chest. Marie stared helplessly.

"The cross," Snagg said, "you've already noticed it." He grabbed the edges of the shape with his fingers and pulled outward, stretching skin with it a full three inches in front of his body. "I've always believed in you," he said, nodding at Jesus. He released the shape and it snapped back against his body. "It's an implant," he said smiling at Marie. "Teflon coated nylon. Nothing more. It just sits in there and waits for me to give it a tug from time to time. Same as the bumps on my arms and head."

"How did you know we were in trouble and that we were coming here?"

"Gina. Sent an encrypted email. Simple. Nothing weird."

Deemon, acting as the host, put his hand on Snagg's shoulder. "Snagg, you remember Lyla. This is Lyla's grandmoms Marie, and, like you figured already, this here's Jesus. And guys, this is Snagg, the original slithery lizard man of the underground. He's another kind of savior, which you'll soon find out."

"Come on in," Snagg turned and led the group into the next chamber. "This used to be a valve chamber for the water tunnel that runs through upper Manhattan, into Queens and Brooklyn. This part was abandoned a long time ago when the tunnel underneath partially collapsed. They figured out a way to get around the mess so I guess they're still drinking water in Brooklyn. There are fifteen rooms here—but this is the biggest."

They were standing in a hexagonal room some thirty feet in diameter with a vaulted ceiling and doors on all six sides. Along one wall was a bank of computers, screens and keyboards. Along another, television monitors, some displaying the stairway they had just descended.

"This used to be the control center, so it seems fitting that now it's our control center," Snagg said.

"Aren't you cold?" Lyla blurted the question, pulling her trenchcoat tighter around her.

"Naw. I'm down here so much—and besides, as a reptile I have a naturally low body temperature." Snagg laughed.

"I'm sorry, I didn't mean to…"

"No problem. Ask anything you like."

Marie, always interested, joined in. "Are those green scales on your eyes makeup?"

"No, even my eyelids are tattooed. I won't get graphic, but everything is. I'm thorough. It's my modus operandi, as you'll soon discover."

"Snagg has lived down here for seven years," Deemon said, dropping into a comfortable chair. "He kinda monitors everything—I mean everything—for, uh, alternative people."

"Had to do it, man. Look, when Bush came in, it was clear he had one thing in mind—total takeover of everything. Somebody had to start figuring out how we were going to get through it. Right, Jesus?"

Jesus smiled and nodded. "I look forward to a long conversation," he said. "You're definitely onto the main story of the age."

CHAPTER 58

"Well, come on in and meet the others. I doubt you'll get this good a welcome anywhere else." Snagg was walking as he talked, leading the way into another room nearly the size of the first. "Everybody's been tripping that you're actually coming here—I mean you, Jesus. And with the disappearances and everything, we've all got questions."

As Jesus reached the doorway about eighteen people began to applaud. Even in the dim light provided by hundreds of candles, Marie could tell that she was in unusual company. The applause continued until Snagg gave a signal to quiet down.

"Well, they're here," he gestured at his guests. "And Numero Uno is Jesus himself. My take is that he's authentic from what I heard from Gina. And he's cool with us, right Jesus?"

"Of course. If only the rest of the world was as welcoming of me as you are. They only want the myth."

"Can we get you something to eat?" It was a young woman in a fairy outfit. Marie thought she looked very normal, until she turned around and revealed beginning wings protruding under her skin. "You must be awfully hungry. It's all vegan, so you should be okay with it, right?"

The three guests nodded. Jesus seemed particularly pleased.

"I'm Tinkerbelle. I'll be right back." The fairy skipped out of the room.

"Listen, please be comfortable. Sit where you like. But let's not waste any time. We've been really excited that you're coming. What is going on up there?" Snagg had moved a couple of chairs while he spoke, pushing one towards Jesus. "We're all interested in that. I mean maybe we aren't the model American citizens, but it matters to us what happens. They've been fucking this country over so long, but now… you can't even live up there."

Jesus gave a knowing look. "Where should I begin?"

Pappa Wazzo, a heavily pierced and tattooed young man with no arms spoke first. "The disappearances, is that the Rapture like those crazy preachers are saying? I grew up with Pentecostal parents and they were constantly talking about this. I always figured I'd be left behind, but I would'a never put money on the people it seems you're Rapturing."

Jesus was obviously pleased by the questioning. "You don't know how good it is to be asked questions rather than having some nut with a *Bible* trying to shout me down and telling me he knows what I said 2000 years ago. And you can relax about the disappearances. Dad's just got me doing some housecleaning."

Tinkerbelle entered with a tray of cold vegetables, some humus and pita chips. "I hope you like these." She smiled, curtsied, and then waved a little wand over the food. "They're blessed now, go ahead and eat."

Jesus immediately dipped a pita chip in the humus. As he did so he smiled. "See? I've been telling Lyla and Marie, I never meant to start a *religion*. I mean, some of what people call my 'disciples' were really nice guys, but by the time they got around to writing down their experiences with me, myth had completely overtaken reality. I think with some of them, it was ego. Definitely ego. They just wanted to look important and act like they had been part of some big supernatural shindig. By the way, I never called them 'disciples.' They were just my friends—but that got changed too. Then there's the stuff so-called religious leaders have made up since! Have you seen what they do in churches? They pass out wafers and tell people that they are going to say a prayer that'll turn 'em into my body? Do you honestly think I would tell people that in order to go to 'heaven' that they had to become *cannibals*? How crazy do they think I am? But that's what they've done. They have made a religious ceremony out of cannibalism and claimed that I started it! How bizarre is that?"

"But didn't you say, 'Take, eat, this is my body?'" The voice came from a dark area of the room.

"No! Look, we were all sitting around the night before they killed me and I was wanting to share some nice things with the guys because I knew they were going to go through a lot and so I'd made some of my favorite Passover recipes. I'd just made the best baba ganoush of my life. I'd added a little fresh basil—incredible—and I wanted them to have some. Now maybe I didn't talk loud enough and maybe I had had a little too much wine and slurred my words, but honest to Dad, what I said was, 'Take, eat, this is my baba.' What's more Jewish than that? We're always saying, 'Take, eat.' But do they listen? Fifty years later when they got around to writing about that night, they'd changed it and are telling everyone I said, 'Take, eat, this is my body.' It was my *baba*! They turned some eggplant into a cannibalistic affair because it made them look more mysterious and important." Jesus was pretty intense.

"But what about the wine? You said it was your blood."

"It *was* red wine. I was serving baba ganoush and red wine. I said the wine looked like the blood I was going to shed. But I never, and I mean *never*, said that it *was* my blood, or that they should drink *my blood*. It doesn't seem I can ever manage to communicate right. People are always turning what I say into something it isn't. Drinking blood? Really?"

The person from the voice in the darkness stepped forward. He was about eighteen and wore all black. His canine teeth had been lengthened to make him look like Bela Lugosi in the Dracula movies. "It wouldn't make me sick: I drink blood all the time."

"But it's your choice. It's not like someone told you that you had to do it—every week—in order to get into heaven."

"No, but I sort of figured that if people were doing it in church and it was actually your blood, then drinking it out here from…"

Jesus gave a compassionate smile. It wasn't condescending, it was genuine. "I understand," he said. "There's a lot of stuff happening up there that is confusing, alienating, deeply disturbing. It can make us want to do all sorts of things. A lot of people up there are doing what they call communion arising from the same frustrations that may have had you want to be part of a vampire family. I understand. Just protect yourself. I don't want you getting sick."

The young man seemed satisfied with the answer for the moment.

An older woman with no immediately apparent unique appearance asked, "What about the disappearances though? They don't make any sense. I mean Dick Cheney and Reverend Teddy Dobbin? Who is getting Raptured or whatever?"

"Let me make something clear first," Jesus said suppressing a laugh. "Dad and I never have said anything about a Rapture. That's just pure baloney. It seems to be selling a lot of books, but it's absolute hogwash. Why would Dad take people to heaven and then stay away from earth for seven years and have the place go crazy and then come back down here and have peace for a thousand years? A thousand years? If he's going to all that trouble, then it would be a billion or two. No, there is nothing to the 'Rapture.' But the people who are pushing the idea sure are eager to make money. Seems like a lot of work if the world is about to end. But I won't go into that.

"See? What Matthew wrote in his 'gospel' was another misquote. He was always too eager to make everything supernatural and centered around the *religion* thing. I was talking about the fact that there are going to be prophets, seers, teachers that are important—sometimes it's me in one form or another, sometimes it's just somebody who sees things that are true. And you never know when they are going to come. So I was saying that two people would be working together and if one of them didn't keep his eyes open, didn't work to understand things, then they would be gullible and would be caught unawares. I said he would be *taken*. Like 'taken in by a scammer.' It's so simple. I didn't mean some big thing by it. I just meant that people ought to stay on their toes.

"Another thing people are still in the dark about is the whole thing about Noah, the flood and creation. Early people knew the truth, but that got changed over time because you know people don't want to think in big terms, big numbers. They want everything little and manageable and under their control. So, instead of talking about the billions of years it took the world to develop, they decided to make it all tidy. That's where Moses comes in. For all the good he did, Dad and I are pretty mad at Moses. He knew a lot and it's true that Dad did appear to him once. But Moses had a huge ego. Instead of recording what Dad told him, he decided to write a script that he was more comfortable with and which protected his power. Dad told him the real history of the world, the magnificent story of evolution of species and the ascension of man. But Moses—like some other people you've still been burdened with down here—decided that billions of years of natural progress didn't put him in a position of power. Dad told Moses that he should write about the whole sweep of history, the amazing way that one thing led to another and developed in such a beautiful and awe inspiring way that if you know about it, you can't go around destroying things. The big polluters of the world now cling to the creation myth because it doesn't engender much wonder. They want to feel they were some personal, special creation that makes them superior. They think they have the inside story. Well, that's the way Moses was thinking. He decided that what would put him in power was if he wrote down some laws and made up a history that put him back in the driver's seat. That's what he did. He's the one who made up that fantastic story about Adam and Eve and how Dad 'created' everything in seven literal days and how he made a woman out of Adam's rib. Nice story, but how stupid do you think my Dad is? Do you really think he's such a bigot that he'd set up a situation that was going to have women subservient for thousands of years? And, do you think he's so stupid that he'd rush and try to do something like creation on a *schedule*? Do you have any idea how many mistakes he would have made trying to design a world in seven days? Do you really think if Dad had anything to do with creating the world that he'd have made sure to include mosquitos, fleas, bed bugs, and Dick Cheney? Give me a break.

"But see, by making the world's history finite, Moses got himself a lot of power. So he started giving everyone orders and saying they were from my Dad. He went up on a mountain, stayed there a long time—and then came back with two stones with lots of rules all written in *his handwriting*. He told people my Dad wrote them with his finger. Uh, Dad doesn't write on rocks with his fingers. But that's another story. Truth is, Moses stole ideas that came from West Africa that he'd learned training in Pharaoh's schools and wrote them down as "Dad's original recipe" called the Ten Commandments. Please. They were plagiarized from Hammurabi as far as Dad and I are concerned. The power went to his head. He started adding about a million rules about everything from sex and eating to bathing and capital punishment by stoning. Do you really think that Dad would spend his time making up rules about how to have two separate kitchens so you never mixed meat with dairy? My Dad isn't itsy bitsy. Do you think he'd tell people to stone women who have an affair? No!" Jesus was getting a little hot just talking about it.

"Anyway, one night Moses and his brother Joshua were sitting around drinking and Joshua got Moses loosened up and Moses copped to the fact that he'd made up the Adam and Eve stuff, and that he'd stolen the ten rules from his Egyptian school days. But he never would tell Joshua what Dad had actually said to him up on the mountain. Joshua was really angry and went to the heads of the tribes and they voted to keep Moses from following them because they already didn't like the rules he'd made up and they figured if he went with them he would make life totally miserable. So they told him he was out. He was so mad at what they said that with his high blood pressure and all, he had a stroke and died. Now Joshua was nice. He didn't want to make Moses look bad, so he wrote some stuff about his going up on top of the mountain and looking over into the Promised Land and then dying. That was pretty good writing, but it was fiction. Moses got what he deserved because he cheated people out of thousands of years of decent knowledge. You stayed in the dark until Darwin stumbled on facts that began to get things back on track.

"Dad and I just watched the whole thing down here evolve. It was fascinating. Surprised Dad no end. He'd keep calling me and saying, 'Look at that! Those little fish in that pool are trying to get up on land.' And then about a hundred thousand years later he would call me and say, 'Will you look at that? They wanted out so bad, they have grown some little stumps that let them crawl out of the water!' He pestered me like that for about a billion years. Not that I minded. It was interesting. Time doesn't mean much to either of us."

"So then the 'Intelligent Design' people are right!" Jesus couldn't see who said it, but he didn't like it.

"No! We didn't interfere in any of this. We didn't start it, we didn't help it, and we didn't hinder it. We just let it happen. It was slow but it was interesting. In fact, since you asked, we haven't interfered with anything until now. I've come here a lot of times in different forms trying to give pointers on how to survive on the planet and I've essentially failed. But Dad and I haven't done anything to directly interfere. Now things are so bad that it's interfere or the whole thing will be gone. It's too interesting a place for that to happen."

Someone else asked, "What about earthquakes? Are you saying God didn't cause them?"

"What are you talking about? Why would he cause earthquakes? It wouldn't make sense. We like this planet. It's not as advanced as some others. There have been a lot more mistakes made here than on some others. But it's *interesting*. Dad wants it to stay that way. So now he's letting me make a move. That's it."

Tinkerbelle returned carrying a tray with steaming bowls of bean soup. Jesus waited for Lyla and Marie to help themselves, then took a bowl and continued.

"But now I'm getting away from your question about the disappearances. I said something earlier about housecleaning. Dad's just angry with some people, sick of others and totally bored with a bunch more. He wants to get rid of them so earth can get back to normal. He said I should come and do some selective weed picking. Cheney and Dobbin, both of them, *weeds*. They were both about twisting facts to honor the bottom line. They both were creating forms of destruction, and in Dobbin's case, like that guy Robinson Patrick, he was one of the people who made you think that if you were going to love my Dad, you had to be a warmonger, a lover of everything military and someone who thought that financial success was the ultimate sign of Dad's blessing. Those sick bastards. Dad encouraged Frank Baum to write

The Wizard of Oz just to warn people against these phony guys."

"I thought you guys didn't interfere in anything down here." Deemon was worried there was a flaw.

"We never interfered directly. We did give people ideas. We never forced or did anything 'supernatural.' For instance, Dad had me encourage Anatole France to write *Revolt of the Angels* to try and undo some of the damage that was being done by religion. But like with everything else, we essentially failed to help you guys out." Jesus looked angry. "I'm sorry," he said, "I think I need to concentrate for a moment here and release some of this steam." He stopped for a minute and was very still. Then he opened his eyes and sighed. "That's better."

"What just happened?" Someone asked.

"Oh, a little more housecleaning. I just removed a whole lot of people at General Electric, Westinghouse, General Dynamics, Honeywell and Dow Chemical. Can you imagine that they have made millions planning how to destroy people? They call themselves 'defense contractors'—when really, they will sell that stuff to both sides of a conflict. That's not defense. There's nothing noble about it. They're *offense* contractors. So they had to go."

Snagg was enjoying every moment. "So you've sent them all to hell?"

"Hell no." Jesus stopped to relish his joke. "There is no hell. I'm just sending all these people who interfere with the world working right—the people who drain it of goodness and interest—I'm just sending them to an alternate space where they can be together and run things the way they want, but where they can't reproduce, where they can't do anything but affect one another."

Snagg wasn't finished. "And George Bush. Why's he still here? Why didn't you get him over to that alternate reality the fastest of anyone?"

"Oh that," Jesus said shaking his head, "that would have been a very foolish thing to do."

"Why?"

"He may have low approval ratings, but take him now and he'd become a hero. He'd be like Ronald Reagan—someone who was responsible for the deaths of hundreds of thousands of people, began to dismantle the United States Constitution, and who was the driving force behind enriching the top 1% of America's most wealthy at the expense of everyone else. Then he got old and doddy. So the powerful people played on everyone's heartstrings and made him both pathetic and heroic—and now most people have forgotten the evil truth about him and turned him into an American hero. Same thing with George W. Take him off the planet now, and everyone would be going 'boo hoo.' Except my Dad, of course. He wouldn't mind if that guy was completely off the face of the earth yesterday. But removing him prematurely would backfire. So we have to let something play out first. It's not going to take long. Everything is in place. I just hope I time things right so it doesn't go all the way."

The room was quiet for a while. There was the occasional snap of a pita chip, but no one was talking.

Lyla was deeply pensive. She'd wanted to ask Jesus a question from the beginning but had been afraid. Now she knew she had to.

"Jesus," she said. "I don't want to make you mad or anything, but can I ask something?"

"Of course."

"Well, neither Grandma or I believed in you, in fact I cursed you out every chance I got because I thought my parents were so fucked up *because* of you. So why is it that you showed up at our door and have gone to all this trouble to protect us, when we haven't even been friendly to what you're about?"

"That's the best question of the night."

Lyla winced. "Are you like being sarcastic?"

"No, I mean it. It's the best question of the night, because it's got the whole story wrapped up in it. Look, your question deserves a thorough answer. Can we hold it for a minute? There's some place I've got to be. You're safe here, just stay and relax. Snagg's a good man and he'll make sure you're okay. As soon as I'm back, I promise, we'll sit back down and I'll explain this whole thing. Deal? In the meantime, maybe someone here would like to tell their story. I think it may have everyone understand just why you've *all* been left behind."

With that Jesus got up, started to walk towards the door and just disappeared.

They were sitting on damp cement, the light from the candles the only illusion of warmth in the vast underground cavern. Lyla and Marie were drinking coffee. An older man came in and sat near Deemon and Snagg. He was new to the underground. He was hungry so Tinkerbelle gave him soup and a chunk of bread.

The conversation meandered—cops, shelters, drugs, football. No one had volunteered to tell a story. They did find out that the new guy's name was Torque. "Used to drive pretty hot cars," he explained. "I was always sayin' some dumb stuff about 'this has really got torque,' and it stuck, I guess."

Inevitably Marie asked a question about where he was from and how he ended up in the tunnels. At first, Torque bristled. He wasn't interested in telling his life's story. "I've got enough to do dealing with it myself, let alone telling it." But then he seemed to warm to the idea. And so, in the lamplight, a lonely old man opened his heart to strangers.

"My real name is Tom Keller. Came from Pittsburgh, Pennsylvania. My daddy worked the mills 'til the mills stopped working. Then he left and went somewhere. My mother had four kids to raise. I was the oldest so I dropped out of school—I think I was in about grade seven then—and did what I could. I can't say it wasn't rough, 'cause it was. I was blessed though, 'cause my mother wanted to hold us together and 'cause she didn't want us to hate my daddy. I think that saved me. You'll see what I mean.

"There was this fellow I'd been in school with—Pete Rawly was his name—who figures pretty big in this whole thing too. Just remember that name for a little while.

"So my mom and I raised up them three kids—two sisters and a brother. They did okay. My little brother, Kenny, is somewhere in Kansas now. Got hisself a wife and some kids too. Ain't seen him in years, but heard some time back that he's okay. My sister Doris is up in Massachusetts. She got married too. Fellow she married has got hisself a garage and fixes cars. He's good at it and treats her good. Her and me is real close. I spoke to her a couple of years ago—that's how I know about my brother too.

"My other sister—her name was Bess but we called her Sissy—she's dead. Died the same year my mom died. Can't go into that too deep. Got herself a boyfriend—no good son of a bitch that…. See, she missed my daddy and was always lookin' for someone to take care of her. So when this guy comes along and talks all sweet and sugary and tells her how beautiful she is and everything—she's gone in a minute. Mom couldn't stop her, neither could I. She already knew Mom was sick. We couldn't afford to be going to doctors and things, so Mom was taking Milk of Magnesia and stuff for her stomach pains. Didn't know it was cancer. She just wasted away. Big, powerful woman always. She could knock our heads pretty good. But we sure did love her."

Here he stopped. The lines in his face were accentuated by grime of the streets. Years of sidewalks and benches had taken their toll. He didn't cry. He couldn't cry much any more. But something happened sometimes in his throat—a strange, aching feeling that tightened everything and made it hard to swallow. At those times he would simply stop what he was doing and wait—wait until some of the pictures in his mind had gone away, wait until he didn't feel the pressure behind his eyes, wait until he didn't want to lie down and never get up.

"Are you all right?" Marie asked quietly, leaning forward and looking into the man's face.

"Suppose so," he said. "I just have to stop sometimes when there's too much in here." He touched his heart. "I'm okay. Just don't like remembering some things on the way to what I'm telling you."

Marie wanted to make it right. "You don't have to."

"I do," he said, shifting his weight and leaning back on one elbow. "I do. See, my sister, Bess, she knew Mom was sick but she didn't know how bad. Can't fault her. She thought she was in love and that she'd be helping the family moving on. But then the cancer got Mom—and Bess, well she didn't want to trouble me so she didn't let me know her man was beating her. Poor little thing, he killed her for crying about Mom. They caught him and took him to court. He stood up and said how he had to show her who was boss because her cryin' was keepin' him up at nights—two nights in a row. *Two nights* and he beats her to death. That was my little sister. Lost her and my Mom two weeks apart.

"About that time I met Pete Rawly again. He's the one I told you about. I was about twenty as I recall. He'd finished high school and got hisself a pretty good job and all. I saw him a few times at the Silver Leaf bar where I used to go. He always sat in the same place at the end of the bar and carried on with his stories and jokes. Lively fellow. Always into something. He'd tell about it too. He'd have some scrape with a guy and punch him out, or he'd get pulled over by the cops and have his car searched or something. Not a bad man, not at all. Just too full of life and vinegar—like my Mom used to say about our neighbor boy.

"So then one day we hear that Pete's been arrested. We figured he'd got caught driving home from the bar or something. But turns out all that time he was in trouble for money, kids were hurtin', wife trying to hold things together, and they were fallin' farther and farther behind. Him and this other guy hatch some sort of plan to fix things. They tried to pull a robbery at a liquor store two towns over. Things went bad. Cops came. He's got this stupid shotgun—turns out it would've killed him if he fired it 'cause it's this old thing that's got a shell stuck in the barrel. I mean that's how much this guy didn't want to hurt nobody. He was just desperate and got out of his mind. His friend has got a bag in his hands that he planned to put the money in, he turns around when the cops come in—they say they thought he had a gun and they shot him. Dead man. Dead. He was this guy who was kinda slow and a friend of Pete's. He used to come into the bar all the time too. We called him Dingo. I never really knew his real name until it was all over the papers: Rodney Lattimer. Isn't that something? Rodney Lattimer. The guy was a nice guy, man. He wasn't some violent criminal. They just both had their backs to the wall. So when they shoot Rodney, Pete turns around with the shotgun in his hands, and the cops blow off his right knee, charge him with armed robbery. He got fifteen years.

"All this time I just know the guy from school and then from the bar. But I hear that he's got a wife and three kids. Now they're left alone, and people see them in town lookin' pretty run down. Always clean, but you know, torn clothes and things. Heard once they were getting teased at school and it got me. Just got me. I knew what that was like, y'know? So I go back to the bar and we take up a collection for the wife and kids. And everybody says I should take it over to 'em. So I do. We're all in the neighborhood, so it was easy to find the place. One of those little row houses there with the steps in front. Pete'd been away for about nine months at that time and the place was lookin' kind of run down. So I knock at the door and his wife answers. I'm not ashamed to tell you, I took one look at her and I fell in love. It wasn't the way it would happen in the bar where I just wanted to get into someone's panties. It wasn't like that. I look at this woman and she's got these eyes that are so strong and a face that has got so much pain that she is holding back. I didn't dare show nothin', so I just held out the money and said that it was from the guys over at the Silver Leaf. She took the money. She just stood there lookin' blank and sort of starin' at me. I didn't have a clue what to say to her, so I just said, 'Your house could use some paint.' 'Yes,' she said back. So that's how it started. I went and got some paint and tried to spruce the place up a little. Kids liked to watch me—Kate, Johnny, and Ralph."

He stopped again. Same feeling in his throat and eyes. He waited until it passed. This time no one said anything.

"You know how it is. One thing leads to another. First it was paint, then it was a leaking pipe, and then the plaster in the bedroom was startin' to crack. I'd finish work—I was stocking shelves at the grocery store nearby—and go right over to Sarah's place and look for something to fix. She was grateful. That was it. Nothing going on between us—not on the outside. I just tried to keep things together. Since I was always over there after work, I started bringing some groceries. Couldn't stand to see the kids eating the way they were—cheap stuff that most of the kids in Pittsburgh have to eat.

"All this while Sarah is writing to Pete. If she had a little extra money she would try to get him the things he needed—a pair of sneakers, white undershorts, some shaving things—whatever little items he wrote about. She'd get it and bundle it up and visiting day take it to him. It took her all day on a Saturday once a month. I started watching the kids for her so she could take the three buses that got her to where he was. She'd get there and be all smiles and tell him about how good the kids was doin', how proud they was of him, and how they knew he wasn't bad. Everyone falls down sometimes, but the measure of a man is how he gets back up. That's what the kids thought about him. And he shouldn't worry, the time was going to fly by and he'd be back home with 'em and they would be fine again.

"Then she'd come home from being so brave, and she'd try to tell the kids about their daddy and how handsome he looked in his jumpsuit, and how strong he was because he was lifting weights, and how happy he was with the present they had sent. And then the kids would go to bed and we would sit in the living room and she would cry until she fell asleep. I'd cover her up and go home.

"One night she couldn't fall asleep. I put the blanket over her while she was still awake and while I was trying to straighten it out, she took ahold of my hand. It wasn't something cheap or lewd or nothin' like that. It was just one soul trying to reach out ta get a'hold of something in another that he couldn't show.

"I never left after that night. I was the kids' father. Sarah was my wife. I did my very best for them. I took extra jobs and every third Saturday of the month Sarah went off with a bundle for Pete. We made sure he got the things he needed because he sure as hell wasn't gettin' them inside.

"I took good care of the kids. Loved 'em like my own. I made sure they did their studies in school—two of 'em were already in school--and that the little one was looked after good. And I loved Sarah with my whole heart. She was a woman who was good to the center. Aw, we'd fight. We'd have times that things wasn't perfect, but I loved her—and I loved the kids—and I wanted to make everything right.

"We never talked about Pete in that way. I mean we talked about him and what he needed in the joint and all that. But we never talked about him as her man. He wasn't there. I was.

"Years went by real quick. Kids were all in school—oldest was in junior high, littlest was about in his third year. One night we was havin' dinner together and there was a knock at the door. Sarah got up to answer it, opened the door and fainted dead away. It was Pete. He'd served seven years. There was some thing where a bunch of politicians decided they had to clear the jails because they were too crowded, so they just turned about a hundred men loose. No notice, no parole hearings. Just turned 'em loose and sent 'em home. They got freed, sent home with instructions to check in with their parole officers. So there stood Pete, his wife passed out on the floor and me getting up from the dinner table.

"'Hello, Torque,' he said to me. We both went to pick up Sarah. I was just reaching for her when he said, 'I'll do it.' He picked her up gentle and carried her into the living room. His kids was cryin' and runnin' after him, and when he set her down he was huggin' them and cryin'. She come to. I brought in some water and we all sat there kinda stupefied just lookin' at one another.

"I sat in a straight chair and watched 'em. He was holding his wife with his one arm, wrestling the boys with his other and kissing his Kate on the head. From time to time he looked up at me knowin' in his heart why I was there. I slept on the couch that night while he went upstairs with my children, with my wife and while he took her to my bed. From the moment he came to the door, Sarah had never looked at me.

"He woke me the next morning. 'We have to talk,' he said. I knew we did, so I got up. We made coffee in the kitchen. I knew where everything was so I got it together. We sat down to drink it, but it seemed too strange. 'Let's walk,' he said.

"We went out. I remember the morning. It was beautiful, crisp, sunny. I don't do so good on mornings like that anymore. I guess that's why. We didn't say anything for a long time. We just walked along the street—him looking at everything he hadn't seen for all those years, me looking at everything that was tied to my heart so deep.

"'I thought about it all night,' he said finally. 'About you and Sarah.' He stopped and ran his fingers across the bark on a tree that grew near the sidewalk. See? I remember things like that. I think there's nothing I don't remember from that morning.

"'I thought about it all night,' he repeated. 'I know'd the instant I seen you at the table. Sarah, she never let on for a minute all these years.'

"'We didn't want you to have that on your mind,' I said. It sounded so stupid as it came out, but it was honest. It wasn't that we were sneakin' behind his back, it was that we didn't want him suffering where he couldn't do anything.

"'I know,' he said. 'While I was in there all I could think about was me. I wasn't tryin' to let her down—do you understand me?'

"I remember I shook my head. I didn't know what he meant. I'd never been locked up. Couldn't imagine what it was like.

"Pete kept talking. 'I had to shut everything out. I couldn't let myself think about her, the kids, anything. I would've gone crazy. When she'd come to see me were the hardest times. I couldn't tell her not to come, it would've broken her heart, but seeing her, having her so near and then leaving, it was worse than being lost. I just had to shut it all out. I'd take the package, say thanks and go away. She tell you that?'

"'No,' I said. 'She always told me stories about how good you looked, how strong you were mentally—how you were handling all the pressure real good and keeping things together for her and the kids.' It was true. That's what she would always tell me. She never said that he took the package and pulled away without asking how she was or how the kids were.

"'When I saw you there with her and the kids, I had it in my heart to kill you.'

"He said that so simple it just sounded like a regular thing one guy says to another on the phone during some kind of business. But he said it straight and looked me in the eye while he did.

"He says, 'I knew that I could find a way to take you out and be done with you. And that's how I was thinking when we went upstairs last night. That's what I was thinking while I was trying to get up the courage to hold Sarah next to me and couldn't—while I laid there as alone as I was in jail. I wanted to kill you for doing what you done.'

"We walked for a long while without saying nothin'. We were by the playground where I'd take the kids every day. We sort of walked around and then he sat in one of the kid's swings and started to move back and forth. Don't laugh at this, but I sat down in the swing next to him and just listened. There we were, two big guys sitting in these kid's swings—you know the kind with the canvas seat hanging from two chains? We were just goin' back and forth a little—sort of tryin' to get the tension out or something. He was lookin' down at the ground. I could see that. I felt scared—maybe he was gonna try to kill me. I didn't know, but I didn't think so. Then he looks up and he's got tears coming down his cheeks. His face is all scrunched up and he's got to kinda grit his teeth to talk. I turned and looked him in the eye.

"'I thought all night. I hated you. I *hated* you. I got up, thinking maybe there was a knife and I could slit your throat. But then I saw Sarah, peaceful there in our bed. I saw the plaster was fixed on the ceiling, and then I walked past the kid's rooms and they was healthy and sleepin' and happy I was home. And I started askin' myself what should I do? And I just stopped on the stairs and I looked up and said the first prayer I've said in seven years. I said, "Thank you for that man that saved my wife and kids, Lord."'

"He stuck out his hand. I took it.

"'You saved my wife and kids. You made it possible for Sarah to bring me the stuff I needed to survive in that hell. So you helped to save me too. I have gratitude to you, Sir.'

"We sat there in those swings—two men with our rough old hands together—lookin' at each other and wondering how life could do this. It was right there on a cold, sunny morning that I knew my job was done. I went home, told Sarah and the kids that I was glad their Daddy was back home and that I had to go and try to find mine. Sarah understood. I hugged the kids. I kissed Sarah on the cheek and I left.

"Life hasn't gone so good after that. Jobs fell through, I started drinkin', got burned out once, ended up without a home just sleepin' on the streets beggin' change, in and out of the system one way or the other. But I got one thing to be proud of in my life forever. One thing to be proud of forever."

Snagg had fallen asleep and his light snoring was the only sound above the constant rumble in the tunnels. Marie got up. "Thanks," she said. She touched Torque's shoulder, then headed into the darkness, followed by Lyla and Deemon. The old man pulled his blanket around his shoulders and took another tunnel to his new home.

CHAPTER 60

Overnight, dire reports flooded network newsrooms. Most of the Saudi royal family was missing; the Queen of England couldn't find her husband; hundreds of Nigerians were missing, seriously affecting the flow of email notifications about Americans inheriting $25 million; a cadre of Monsanto chemists and biologists were missing along with the world's entire supply of genetically modified seed; areas of Africa were littered with high-powered rifles left behind by vanished big game hunters; thousands upon thousands had disappeared from bull fighting rings in Spain and Mexico; also missing were the entire Russian Mafia and huge numbers of sex trade entrepreneurs. The official disappearance count reached 450 million. People from every nation around the globe were missing. So it was not surprising that the NBC Morning News began:

"Good morning. This is Brian Williams. An astonishing rescue today has captured the imagination of millions. Tinkerbelle, a Turkish Van cat somehow managed to get caught 35 feet up a sycamore tree. Tinkerbelle's owner, 12 year old Tommy Regent, tried to rescue his cat, but got stranded some twelve feet below her. Local firefighters in Rahway, NJ were called to the scene and rescued both the cat and her owner. Tommy' mother, Georgina Regent praised the fire department for its heroic work."

There followed four minutes of eyewitness accounts, and a touching montage of photographs of the little boy being reunited with his cat, accompanied by Barry Manilow's, "I Made It Through the Rain."

The broadcast moved on to a bill working its way through the Senate that would cut funding for research on genetically altered watermelons. There were claims that melons in excess of 100 pounds were not selling well.

It was not until 22 minutes into the broadcast that the disappearances were mentioned and that mention was limited to reports from unnamed government sources implicating persons close to the disappeared as terrorists.

CHAPTER 61

Santee wasn't sure how long the lady had been sitting there. In fact, it wasn't until the lady stroked her forehead that she really woke up.

"Hello," she said, thinking that the lady had very kind eyes.

"Hello, dear. I'm sorry to bother you."

"It's okay. Have you seen my brother? Have you seen Vertaine?"

The lady smiled nicely. "Yes I have," she said. "And that's why I'm here. You shouldn't be by yourself. I've arranged everything for you to be back together."

"The man who brought me here, he's very, very mean."

"Yes, I know. He won't be mean to you any more. I promise you."

Santee searched the lady's face. "Are you sure?"

"I'm sure. It seems he just disappeared." The lady winked. "Maybe I helped that just a little bit. Now everything is ready for you to go back with your brother. You take these papers—they show that you and he belong together—and you just walk down that hall right behind this door…"

"It's locked and I can't get out."

"You'll see, it's unlocked and nobody will bother you. Go now. You'll find your brother in the big room at the end of the hallway."

"Come with me?"

"I can't. I have some other work to do. But you'll see me again."

Santee walked to the door. Just as the lady said, it opened easily. Santee turned to thank her, but she was gone.

CHAPTER 62

Dr. Biff Hendrick, George W. Bush's personal physician was administering an experimental dose of Dynorphin to the President, hoping to rouse him from his cocaine-induced stupor. It was important to have the Commander in Chief appear functional since the Prime Minister of Israel was arriving that afternoon.

The Israeli meeting was top secret. Deprived of Dick Cheney, Donald Rumsfeld and his joint chiefs of staff, Bush's brain trust was down to Condoleeza Rice and Karl Rove. Rove was squirreled away somewhere beneath the White House and was talking to Hendrick through an earpiece.

Dubya was not responding quickly. His nose was bleeding, his body stunk and he drooled uncontrollably. Dr. Hendrick slapped him several times hoping that the combination of the drug and the physical pain would return him to his normal partially lucid state.

The only response from the presidential lump was, "Condi?"

Hendrick shook his head. "I don't know, Karl. What time is this guy arriving from Israel?"

"Three o'clock. You've got to have him ready."

Hendrick applied an ice pack to the presidential nose hoping it would stop the bleeding. "Even if I get him roused, he'll be acting stupid."

"And?"

"Well, he'll make a fool of himself."

"And? Everyone's used to it. I'll be there, Biff. I've been invited as a non-official guest. But I'll be doing the talking. Instead of through Dubya's earpiece I'll be doing it in person. It's simple. You just get him up and going. Oh, and tell his dresser to make sure he wears the big stuffing, like the one he wore when he landed on the carrier. If he can't impress them with his brain…well…"

Rove signed off from the bowels of the White House.

"There's a message for you sir." Rove's secretary, Betty Allen, stood and handed him a note. Rove scanned it quickly.

"Get Bill Frist on the phone immediately," he barked. "I'll be in my office. Let me know as soon as he's connected."

Moments later Betty announced, "Senator Frist for you, Sir."

"Bill. Got your message."

"Look Karl, this thing is out of control. We've had civil war in Iraq for three years, Israel's occupation of Lebanon is a year old. We've got every Arab country dying to slaughter us. And I'm getting creamed in the polls. We've got to do something to have people think we know what we're doing."

"We do."

"What do you mean, 'we do?' We've been fucking up there since day one. Now we don't even have anyone to run the show—Rummy and Joint Chiefs gone—and Karl, you resigned. You're officially out of the loop."

"So I've been told. Meanwhile, it's all under control."

"Is Dubya going to start stumping for that Armageddon thing again? Pull the whole 'get Jesus to return' thing? It's not going to work again, Karl. You've got all the Christian crazies running around saying that the Rapture has already happened. You have this guy claiming he's Jesus Christ appearing and disappearing everywhere. And everything else is falling apart."

"I'm telling you, Bill, we have everything under control. You'll see. It won't be long now until you see."

Frist paused. He had long relied on Rove to spin Republican debacles into victories, but his faith in the pudgy little retired guy was growing thin.

"Look, Karl. If something big doesn't happen to turn this around in the next three days, I'm telling you…"

"What? That there are going to be riots in the street? We've got it covered. We've got a 10 PM curfew—and for the daytime, well, let's just say that people have seen enough footage of Gitmo and Abu Ghraib to know that they don't want to be guests of the government." Rove couldn't suppress a smile. His own brilliance was a source of constant delight. "Nobody is going to be doing a thing to oppose us. Got that? If they do, we have a wonderful solution: enemy combatant status."

"I hope you're right."

"Oh, I think you'll be singing my praises before the end of the week." Rove said a quick good bye and turned to his desk. There, bound in red leather, was the Master Plan. His was the only volume that collected all the individual chapters. Rove had always operated successfully on the idea that a plan is like a jig saw puzzle. Thousands of people each hold one piece of the total. Each does his or her job. The big job gets done. And nobody knows it was all part of the Master Plan. There is deniability for every one of the thousands of actions.

He poured a shot of Scotch and sank back into his leather recliner. Even 150 feet underground it was nice to be sitting on a comfortable chair that was about to be the world's catbird seat.

CHAPTER 63

Divine X Marcus wasn't expecting visitors. When the disappearances occurred, he'd done all he could to keep peace in Huntsville, but Superintendent Lester Merles had grown weary of having prisoners in charge. It wasn't that they weren't doing a good job. On the contrary, the prison was running better under their direction than it ever had. Even the food had improved. Same prepackaged stuff, but better preparation. There hadn't been a violent incident inside—not one. But Merles, still determined to find evidence of a prison break despite disappearances all over the country, was in no mood to commend anyone on a job well done. In the last seven hours he'd ordered a lockdown of the entire prison and ordered what he called the "leaders" on death row into the box, solitary confinement.

Huntsville's solitary was old school: a metal room 8' x 8' with a metal floor, a metal door with a slot for viewing the prisoner, and a 2" gap under the door to slide in a food tray. That slot was the only place light could enter the cell because there was no bulb inside. Divine X had been stripped and brought naked to the cell, shoved onto the cold and damp metal floor. He was given no explanation for the lockdown, no indication of how long it would last.

It is no wonder that he thought his mind had failed him when he sensed the presence of another person in the darkness and heard a voice.

"Assalamu Alaikum wa rahmatullahi wa barakatuhu. Peace unto you my brother X."

"Alaikum Assalaam." The response had fear. "Where are you?"

"I am here." And Divine X felt a strong hand on his shoulder.

"Who are you?"

"A friend. You have known me best as Muhammad."

"From over in 'OK Corral?'" he guessed, using a prison nickname for one of the blocks.

"You've known me through the Q'ran."

At that moment the big man, afraid of so little, began to shake. "Am I buggin'? I've been in here before, but am I buggin'?"

"No. It's me, and you're doing fine. I don't have much time. We must speak."

"How did you get in here?"

"I came to meet with you. I was there, but I needed to be here. And so I am here."

Divine X was not a man easily convinced. "How do I know it's you? How did you die?"

"I was coming home from the cemetery when I fell ill. I died three days later."

"Teacher, what do you need of me? I am far from the man you teach I should be."

"I have failed many times myself, my son. I have come again and again and tried to teach people how to live without launching another religion—but that's a long story. I know you and I know your heart. You're a good man and you have risen above much adversity. I feel I have been a success with you."

"How can you say that? I'm here in prison. I'm condemned to die."

"You were condemned for who you *were accused of being*. You aren't that person. You weren't then and you certainly aren't now. There were other lesser mistakes, but when a man changes in his center—he becomes greater than if he had never erred. Your center has changed."

Divine X continued the conversation, scarcely believing it was taking place. "Are you really Muhammad?"

"Yes."

" What do you need of me? I'll do what I can."

"There is going to be an enormous occurrence in the next few days. The entire Arab world will want to go to war, and so will all American Muslims. You must arrange a way to warn them not to react. If they stay quiet, if they refuse to engage in war—the world has a chance."

"I'm in solitary. How am I going to do what you're asking?"

"If you want to, you will."

To have Muhammad instruct him not to react, not to go to war, had Divine X seriously doubt that the man in his cell was the holy prophet. "You were a military man," Divine X began. "You did not refuse to fight.

Why should I believe that you are to be followed now when you're contradicting everything you did when you were here?"

"There is no contradiction. Both were to save the world. I know more now. I don't want anyone trying to make a religion out of what is going to happen next. Just follow your heart and take every opportunity. You do have your radio show."

"I just smuggle tapes out of the prison and people take it from there."

"You have your answer then. No matter what happens, don't let the Muslim world react. Don't be overwhelmed. Your message will get out. It will all become clear to you in time. You'll have help. I have to go now."

Divine X was suddenly alone to consider his possible madness.

<h1 style="text-align:center">CHAPTER 64</h1>

Within an hour of his conversation with the President, Tim Michaeljohn was escorted out of the White House sub-basement by armed guards. Left behind was his entire command center.

"You understand, Sir," Colonel Nelson Kopland said as they reached ground level. "It was highly unusual that you were allowed space in the White House—your being nothing but a candidate for the presidency. Our commander in chief couldn't take the risk that your presence down there was any kind of bending the rules."

"My computers, my records…" Michaeljohn began.

"With the election suspended, you won't be needing them," Kopland countered. "I think even *you* would agree that the space and the resources down there are much better used by Mr. Rove."

"Yeah, I'd hate for Bush to bend any rules." Michaeljohn oozed years of cynicism.

Kopland wasn't amused. "I suggest you stop talking and leave the premises," he said, pushing his mirrored sunglasses back up his nose.

Michaeljohn knew when to bow to authority. He nodded to Kopland, motioned for Helen and his chief of staff Elizabeth Garvin to follow him, and led the way to his limo.

"Headquarters," he told the driver.

It didn't take long to cross the Potomac and reach the official *Michaeljohn for President* headquarters in Arlington, Virginia.

"I dread telling everyone that they've got to go home," Tim said as they pulled to the curb.

"It doesn't look like you'll have to tell anyone." Elizabeth Garvin pointed to the "closed" sign on the front door. "I think the boys have already broken the news."

She was right. The office was completely deserted. The President's news had already been delivered.

From the beginning, Michaeljohn had been aware that the Arlington office was bugged, that the phones were tapped, and that no one could enter or leave without being taped by multiple cameras outside or photographed by agents in a van parked across the street. That wouldn't stop with the suspension of elections. No matter how angry or betrayed Michaeljohn felt, he knew that he had to proceed like a man with unchanged direction—complete allegiance to the Bush agenda. It was a matter of life and death. He knew with certainty that the state secrets he carried with him could easily cost him and his family their lives should he make a false move. And so his daily pattern needed to be as close to normal as possible. He had a little time since everyone would expect that a national campaign would take some weeks to shut down. He was aware that the world was about to undergo a sea change unless enormous forces were stopped. He also knew that he had been rendered essentially helpless under the current intense surveillance placed on him.

When it happened, Elizabeth and Helen were in the outer office making coffee and shredding files, and Michaeljohn, avoiding his computer, was writing his thoughts by hand to escape the reach of the CIA's Carnivore spying program.

"Hello Tim."

He didn't recognize the voice—certainly didn't expect to hear a male in the office. He swivelled his chair in the direction of the sound. There stood a very Ivy League WASP wearing a blue and white seersucker suit.

"How'd you… who the hell are you?" Tim wasn't amused. "Elizabeth know you're here?" He knew every door and window was locked except the front door where his wife and chief of staff were working.

"I'm your savior, Tim. At least I could be. And I mean savior with a small "S" just in case you want to start making a religion from my statement."

"What?"

"Seriously." The man outstretched his hand. Tim was about to grasp it tentatively when he noticed the immense scar in the palm.

"Oh shit."

The Irishman laughed. "I've been called worse."

"I didn't mean you. I meant… well, you're not… are you?"

"Try reading between the lines. I'm not Irish. You can count on that."

"You're?"

"Yes, I'm the very troublesome Jesus."

"Then you know…"

"Know what?"

"Everything that's about to happen."

"Actually I don't. That's why I'm here." Jesus pulled up a chair.

Michaeljohn scribbled on a pad and held it up. "The office is bugged. Don't say another word."

"Oh that. Don't worry about it. I may not know everything that's going on, but I know how to jam a bug. You can talk freely while I'm here."

"What do you expect me to say?"

"Expect? Nothing. I've watched you for a long time and know what kind of decisions you've made. So I don't come with expectations. At least not very high ones."

"That hurt."

"Truth does occasionally, Mr. Michaeljohn."

"Call me Tim."

"I think we should keep this formal."

"Okay, Mr. Jesus."

Jesus leaned back in his chair. "You know that kind of sarcasm's got you in the mess you're in. Maybe the word is cynicism. You always looked at the little picture and decided it was the whole picture. And then you gave up. Just like that. You gave up. And now you're here."

"Look, I'm sorry, okay? I did my time in the trenches and it was getting me no place. You blame me for looking around and seeing who was making it?"

"No. Like I said, I could be your savior."

"Savior?"

"I'm giving you another chance."

"Chance for what?"

"Redemption."

"Wait. I'm not even sure you are who you say you are, and I sure don't buy into all that 'salvation' and 'redemption' stuff."

"You don't have to buy into it. It is what it is. Opt out and you're still in."

Michaeljohn, a man used to giving orders, accustomed to praise, wasn't amused. "I think you'd better state your business and move on," he said. "I've had a few setbacks—I guess you know. Elections are suspended… indefinitely… and now we're going to go to hell with Bush."

"Let's talk turkey," Jesus said. "You were ready to be Bush's clone up until a few hours ago. You've played along with everything he was planning… until he dumped you. Right?"

"What's your point?"

"My point is that you didn't outwardly disagree with a damn thing until it interfered with your ambitions. Are you following me?"

"I'm hearing you."

"So to redeem yourself, and not just to be another in a long line of schmucks, you need to tell what you know publicly."

"That would be suicide."

"Dad's not against that sometimes."

Michaeljohn recoiled. Jesus continued, "There are times when speaking the truth may be suicide." He raised his palms to eye level and turned the palms towards Tim. "I think you know that I speak from experience."

Annoyed, Michaeljohn said, "Okay," as he turned his head away from the scars. "So what do you want me to tell?"

"I don't know. Dad didn't say. He just said that you knew things that needed to be told. Mr.… Tim… I'm asking you to give the world a chance. I know your heart was once in the right place."

"Lot of good that did me," was the surly reply.

"Depends how you look at it."

"You going to get cute?"

"No, just depends. Take Helen. She liked you better then."

"Like I predicted, you're going to be cute. Look, I wouldn't be next in line for President if I hadn't switched sides."

"You're not next in line for President even *though* you switched sides, and… you've lost all the great respect Helen had for you."

"Make your point."

"A lot of people would have succumbed the same way, Tim. In fact, most people. It's just that I was rooting for you."

"My own private celestial cheerleader," Michaeljohn quipped ruefully.

"Your choice," Jesus said with a slight shrug, "but after what you've told me, I'd say that you ought to do what I mentioned earlier so all that ugliness could be made public."

"Thanks for your opinion. You apparently wish me dead."

"I could make sure you wouldn't be."

"Time for your 'oh ye of little faith' speech, sandal fella. You're fairly convincing, but whatever I do, it will be my decision and I'll do it my way."

"Suit yourself. But I can only protect you if you decided to come on board all the way."

"Guess I'd rather swim." Michaeljohn tapped the table signaling that for him, the conversation was over.

There was an exquisite sadness in Jesus' eyes as he looked across the desk. "Life is short, isn't it Tim?"

"Could be. I'll take my chances."

"It could have been quite a life… At least it could have had a sunburst at the end."

Michaeljohn scowled. "Hallmark is in Kansas City," he said.

"Until next time," and Jesus faded from view.

CHAPTER 65

AUSTIN, TX—11 AM CST

Daisy-Ann Wexler, destined to take her husband's seat as governor of Texas, poured another gin and tonic. "It just don't make sense, Judy," she said to her chief of staff. "It just don't. He always tol' me he was absolutely sure. Absolutely. And now this." She rapped her knuckles against a pile of papers on what had been Duke Wexler's desk. "Ah don't care how you look at these, they don't add up to what he said they did."

Judy Seymour sighed. She had worked for Daisy-Ann nearly nine years. The realizations dawning on the wife of the dead governor had been obvious fact to her for at least eight years, but her employment depended on her seeming as unknowing as her boss. "Is that so," she said dryly.

"Ah even tolt that Babs woman 'bout this when she was here, Judy. Ah put my very trustin' soul on the line for Duke, and look at this. He's gone and skunked me again!"

"Skunked," was the proper word and "again" was the right adverb. Duke's history with Daisy-Ann was littered with "skunkings"—primarily of the female variety. But there was something far more sinister in the papers to which she presently referred.

After the Babs Waller interview, Daisy-Ann announced her intention to run for her husband's gubernatorial seat against acting Governor Harry "Crackerjack" Lowery. The move was met with a sniggering superiority in much of the press, but instant polls indicated that voters would support their first lady's bid to govern them. Naturally, the disappearances reduced the importance of her intentions to back-page status, but nevertheless, the plucky lady was determined to carry on.

Her candidacy announced, Daisy decided it was time to clear off Duke's desk. That is when the offending papers came to her attention. She might have missed them had she not remembered the name of the unfortunate soul whose name resided on the top paper. It was Willie Tookem, a reformed gang leader that Duke had sent to the electric chair. Mr. Tookem, who fully acknowledged the destructive lifestyle he had led when a young man, had long since changed his direction during his incarceration. The author of fourteen books for young people about the dangers of gangs, Mr. Tookem was a force in dissuading street violence.

But in 1975, over thirty years before, Mr. Tookem had been arrested, convicted and sentenced to death in the shooting of a liquor store owner. William Tookem maintained his innocence in the case during his entire incarceration, even while readily stating that he had participated in other crimes for which he had not been punished. Due to continued appeals, then governor George W. Bush was unable to execute the man even though he frequently expressed an eagerness to do so. It was not until Duke Wexler assumed the governorship that Mr. Tookem's appeal process ran out. Duke was as eager as Little George to terminate Tookem and made many public statements to that effect.

Daisy-Ann, as a devoted first lady, had no inclination to meddle in her husband's affairs. She felt it right that bad people be punished for their crimes and was offended by the time and money frequently invested in the ongoing appeals of death row inmates. On the night of Mr. Tookem's scheduled execution, Duke and Daisy-Ann were having a quiet dinner in their media room. Duke turned on the TV, as he frequently did during the hours he spent with his wife, to watch coverage from the Huntsville Death House. Hundreds of protesters had gathered to voice their opposition to Tookem's execution. It was a widely held opinion that the condemned was far more valuable alive than dead, that his actions during his incarceration had more than demonstrated his intention to have a good effect on young people, that his admission of the error of his early lifestyle and his positive actions showed a contrition and regret that was admirable, and that the continued controversy surrounding his conviction in the case — including the confession of guilt by another prisoner, a white supremacist named Aubrey Jacks — should at the very least warrant a stay of execution.

Duke laughed as fervent statements were made by people holding signs.

"Look at that fat one there, Daisy-Ann," he said, pointing at the screen. "I'll bet she's just another one of them hard-up women who'd just love to get a piece of that man afore he fries." He took an enormous slurp of his fourth beer. "I tell yew, them women out there, they's jest all hot 'n bothered on account of that nigger goin' to the chair."

"He says he didn't do it, Duke."

"Hell, ain't that what they all say? 'I didn't do it. I didn't do it.'" Duke wiped some grease from his mouth. "They're all so busy tryin' to lie their way into acquittal, it's a wonder they don't just grow wings and fly right into God's arms." He belched. "'Scuse me, Lovey Pie. Didn't mean to be rude there. Now, this here fella. Guilty as sin and still singin' innocence like he should be in the church choir. Well, I'm goin' to help him get into God's arms real fast. I'm gonna call it the 'Electric Ride'—and give him the trip to heaven on a 10,000 volt one way ticket."

"You're sure he did it then," Daisy-Ann was partially making conversation, and partially serious. "I mean, you checked it all out, right, Duke? And he deserves the ticket you signed off on, right?"

"Absolute-a-Tutely." And Duke picked up the remote and changed the channel to watch the fights.

William Tookem was executed at midnight and the crowds went home. Governor Duke Wexler disappeared four days later.

When Daisy-Ann began to go through the items Duke left behind, the first thing she found on his desk was a letter from Judge Hector Thomas, the presiding judge in Tookem's case, stating that on the day after the execution, he'd discovered an entire box of evidence which favored the condemned's innocence. It had been left in front of the door to his office with a hastily written note that said, "Suppressed."

The judge's letter went on to say that in the box was sworn testimony by four witnesses—persons never called to the stand during the trial—who clearly stated that the crime was committed by Aubrey Jacks. There was a videotape from a surveillance camera. On its case was written, "Videotape of the shooting by Aubrey Jacks." And there were fourteen black and white photographs of a man in the process of the robbery and shooting which was clearly not William Tookem.

The judge described his horror over the discovery in detail. And then he wrote, "Most horrifying of all, was the discovery of Duke Wexler's signature on each of the aforementioned items along with a note from the Governor that read, 'Suppress at all costs.' As the presiding judge in this matter, now aware that I have the blood of an innocent man on my conscience, I intend to bring this matter to the police and the State Senate for a full investigation. And if my current assumptions are correct, I will be first in line to seek impeachment and criminal charges against Duke Wexler."

Stapled to the letter was a news item from the *Houston Chronicle* reporting the untimely death of the same Judge Hector Thomas due to an embolism. Scribbled on the news item in Duke's hand was one word: "Gotcha."

Daisy-Ann spent the entire afternoon reading the documents in the stack on Duke's desk. Each of them dealt with the execution of a prisoner in Huntsville during Duke's Administration where there had been similar interference with justice. And in each case, there was a signature of approval from Duke. Apparently, the good governor had been preparing to place the stack of papers in his private safe when he most inconveniently disappeared.

Now, sitting at the desk with the incriminating papers, Daisy-Ann considered her future.

"Ah believed the Duke when he towld me that he knew every man was guilty afore he fried 'em," she said. "He said he had learned everything he knew from George W., who showed him the ropes. George fried 133 people in 5½ years. Duke did 154 in seven. But now I know they both killed innocent men, and they knew they were innocent when they did it. Why would anyone do that, Judy?"

As Chief of Staff, Judy Seymour was accustomed to questions that asked for a flattering answer. Now she felt Daisy-Ann really wanted the truth. "Maybe that's the way you climb the political ladder all the way to the White House. Maybe that's the way you grease the wheels. You help increase the power and prestige of 'law enforcement,' and get a reputation for being tough on crime. You get the people feeling real good about how you have the gift for nailing the right people. And you make sure that the people you nail are those that can't really defend themselves. You get votes, you get backing, and you get rid of the opposition."

"Now Governor Lowery is set to execute that Divine X fellow tomorrow. I don't supposed his case is much different, do you?"

"Not with the pattern you've seen."

"Why did I praise Duke the way I did to Babs Waller?"

"Because you loved him. Because you thought that's what it meant to be a good wife. And because you liked the power he brought to you."

The last insight was unexpected. It burned in Daisy-Ann's ears.

"Yew know why I love yew?" she drawled at last. "'Cause you're the only person I know who'd say somethin' like that to me. And you're right. So in a way I've got the blood of those people on me to."

"I didn't say that."

"No, *ah* did. And I've got to try to do somethin' about it."
"And if the world is really ending like they were saying on TV?"
"Then I wanna be ready."

CHAPTER 66

Following Jesus' directions, Chandra and Hogan were walking along the Jesus Dome Promenade, an outdoor parkway leading to the main shopping and worship center. Adam followed them in his wheelchair. The fountains were off, the buildings locked and deserted. Police had sealed the Dome itself as a crime scene, but the rest of the complex was simply abandoned. "Jesus said we're supposed to find out who actually bears title to this place," Chandra said, clearly daunted by the instruction. "How on earth do we learn that?"

Hogan's brow lowered. "Always troubled me. We had insurance papers in security showing it was all in the name of Dobbin's own holding company. Mysterious operation, y'know? But that doesn't matter much now."

"Why not?"

"Everyone who had anything to do with Dobbin—his wife, his brother, his cousin, his employees—they all disappeared. There is no holding company anymore."

"Then who's got the power?"

"Dobbin always said that the church belonged to his staff. That's how he'd put it. I thought that was funny because all the money came from the congregation and it all went right into the holding company. But he said it 'belongs to my staff.'"

"He ever put that in writing?"

"I don't know. I never thought about it."

"Where was his office?"

"Right in there—inside the Jesus Dome. It was up on the seventh floor— right behind the VIP worship boxes."

"I'm delighted by that image."

Hogan was squinting and looking up at the Dome. "His office is right behind those huge windows. See?"

"How do we get in there?" Chandra was accustomed to doing what she wanted. With a personal fortune valued at over $18 billion, Chandra and Winslow Boolean had lived a lifestyle inconceivable to most people. So the thought of getting into a building that the police and Homeland Security had sealed as a crime scene didn't seem difficult at all.

Hogan shook his head. "You *don't* get in there."

"Of course we do. Where's the easiest entrance?"

"There's one down in the parking garage under the building. Security was always complaining that the door to the fire stairs was being left open."

"What are we waiting for?"

Hogan led the way to the south side of the Dome where a long ramp led to underground parking areas. Yellow police tape cordoned off the area, but there was no other security.

"Adam, will you stay here where there's cell reception? If anyone comes this way, just call my phone. We'll have to trust that nobody will be coming in the other entrances." With that Chandra took Hogan's hand. "Let's have an adventure." She tugged his arm and headed down the ramp.

As Hogan had suspected, the lock to the stairwell door was broken and seconds later they were in. Chandra took the stairs quickly and arrived at the seventh floor exit a second before Hogan.

"Hogan! It's locked. I can't open it."

"Just a minute." Hogan held out a plastic card. "This doesn't work on external doors, but we all had one of these so that we didn't get locked in stairwells. Some only opened public area doors. But I had clearance for all areas. He swiped the card through a scanner as he spoke. The door unlocked.

"Perfect. Way to go, Hogan." Chandra's hand rested on his arm a moment longer than he would have expected. "Now where is Dobbin's office?"

Familiar as she was with luxury, Chandra was shocked at the opulence of the Jesus Dome's private suite. The reception area was replete with marble floors, elegant wood moldings, and exquisite lighting fixtures.

Hogan stopped in front of enormous double doors. "Heaven's Gate," he said, using the employees' term for Dobbin's entrance. Each door had a handle crafted in bronze that resembled one of the tablets of the Ten Commandments. Hogan pressed the one on the right and the door swung open. There before them was the office of the man who professed himself a humble servant of the Lord. An intricate floor of inlaid wood was visible where it was not covered with thick Persian carpets. The entire back wall was glass, shielded at the moment by rich velvet curtains. Dobbin's oddly shaped desk was entirely covered in gold leaf.

"It's supposed to be a replica of the lost Ark of the Covenant," Hogan explained, "just a hell of a lot bigger."

Chandra shook her head. "Even Winslow didn't manage to do quite this much with his money. And this guy had no taxes to pay, right?"

"None. The whole thing was in court. Even the retail space in the Savior's Mall was tax free because of the religious names. Dobbin claimed they were all part of the church outreach project. He even claimed that *No-Gap (Between Christ 'n Me) Jeans* and *John the Baptist Water Park* should be tax exempt because they were fundraising efforts of the church."

"Do you know where he kept his personal papers?"

Hogan nodded. I know because I used to have to come up here and check his office. His lawyer taught me the checklist. He and Dobbin always worked over there." He pointed to a corner alcove. "It looks a little like the rooms in bank vaults where you can go through your safe-deposit box. In fact, that's where Dobbin's vault is. But they didn't keep the papers in there. They kept them over here." Hogan reached the alcove and tugged on a wood panel that opened revealing extensive filing cabinets. "What are we looking for?"

"I'm not sure. Just anything that says the Jesus Dome belongs to Dobbin's staff."

Downstairs, a police van pulled into the Jesus Dome parking lot and headed for the parking ramp. Adam quickly dialed his cellphone. Chandra answered.

"Cops are coming. I'll hold them off as long as possible. Better get out of there ASAP."

"Be careful."

"Me? *You* be careful and get out. I'll be fine." Adam hung up and headed his wheelchair down the parking ramp. It was steeper than it looked, but Adam was skilled and brought the chair to a stop at the bottom. Moments later a cop was pointing a flashlight at him.

"You down there! What are you doing? Get out of there!"

Adam waved. "Hello. Boy, am I glad to see you!"

"This is a crime scene. I'm ordering you to leave immediately."

Adam thought the cop must be blind. "Sir," he called, "I need your help. I'm stuck down here."

"What the?" The cop started down the ramp, his other hand on his gun.

"I was just taking a look at the Jesus Dome—I'm a long-time supporter—and I guess I got too close to this ramp. Damn near killed myself rolling down here. I couldn't figure how I was ever going to get back up." Adam was glad he was wearing a bulky windbreaker that concealed his powerful arms. "I guess that should teach me a lesson."

The cop approached slowly. Adam looked towards the fire stairs door. Chandra and Hogan had left it slightly ajar and light was spilling out onto the cement block wall. He propelled his wheelchair forward, trying to look like he was straining at the slight incline.

"Whoa, that was one scary ride down."

"What are you doing down here?"

"I told you. I was up there," he pointed to the top of the ramp, "and just got too close and whoosh. Would you mind giving me a push?"

The cop shined his light in Adam's face, then surveyed the area. "You alone?"

"Sure am. I was afraid I was going to die that way too—starvation, y'know. Doesn't seem to be anybody around."

"You haven't heard?"

Adam's apparent detachment from reality worked and the cop lowered his light.

"I'll push you up the ramp. But I suggest you go home and turn on your TV."

The cop's partner appeared at the top of the ramp. "George, you okay down there?"

"Yeah, I'll be right up. Got a guy in a wheelchair stuck down here."

Adam thanked him when they reached the top of the ramp. The cops watched while Adam slowly rolled away, then laughed and got in their van. They had just pulled away when Chandra and Hogan stepped out of the stairway carrying two large manila folders.

CHAPTER 67

Lyla woke up to the smell of coffee and eggs. Snagg was cooking breakfast. "Hello, beautiful," he said without looking up.

"You even know who you're talking to, man?"

"Sure do. It's Miss *Missin' Mom and Dad.*"

"Yeah right."

"Want some eggs?"

"No thanks, I'll just take some coffee. How do you get all this shit down here anyway?"

"Drop by drop. Seen your grandma?"

"Naw. She's cool, but hey—she's about a million years old so she needs more rest than me."

"Oh yeah?" Marie stuck her head in the room and lifted her coffee mug. "Beat ya to it, sweetie. I'm on my second cup. Snagg makes some mean brew." She walked over and put her arm around the shirtless man with green scales. "You're okay," she said giving him a squeeze.

Snagg transferred the scrambled eggs to a serving plate and turned off the hotplate. "Can I ask you guys something for real?"

"Anything, kid." Marie was in a good mood.

"What do you make of this Jesus guy? I mean I was going along with it yesterday and he says great things, but who do you think he is?"

"Does it matter?"

"Yeah, sorta. I mean. Is he really the one making all those people disappear? I was on the web this morning. The whole Russian mafia has disappeared from Brooklyn. I mean there's hardly anybody left in some neighborhoods. They're saying that all they're finding is piles of clothes and guns. You think the guy sitting with us last night is actually doing all that?"

"You have a better answer?"

Snagg shook his head.

"I don't know, Grandma," Lyla took a thoughtful pull on her coffee. "When I asked him that question last night about why he chose us--he'd answered all the other questions--but then suddenly he has to go and can't answer that. I mean, look at us. This whole place is full of freaks. I don't think there's anyone here who is like into the *Bible* or anything. In fact, I'd say we're all about as far from it as possible. Unless…" She gave a playful pause, "unless *you* voted for George Bush, Snagg."

"I did, but the voting machine changed it to Chairman Mao."

"Case closed."

Marie shook her head. "I pretty much believe him. If you had to spend eternity or whatever with people—who'd you rather be with, your parents and their friends or the people down here with Snagg? And don't forget Torque. Isn't that the kind of person *you'd* choose?"

"Definitely with Snagg and Torque." The voice wasn't Lyla's. It was Jesus leaning in the doorway. "Sorry I had to be gone for so long. I had a list of things to take care of. Could we get everyone together? I want to answer Lyla's question."

It didn't take long to wake people up and get them back into the big room. Curiosity and coffee soon had the group ready for a conversation.

Jesus led off. "Last night, Lyla asked a very important question: Why her? Why Marie? Why you guys? Why have people like Teddy Dobbin, a major religious leader, some heavy hitter politicians and a lot of business-people—why have they disappeared, and why did I decide to be with you? Fair rephrasing of your question, Lyla?"

"For sure."

"The answer is pretty simple. Dad and I have been trying to get a message across down here for millions of years. We could see that somehow things just got started off wrong. The inhabitants of earth you call the Australopithecus—I'm talking about your earliest ancestors—what did they do? They bashed one another over the head to get food, women, even a certain piece of fruit. Just a lousy start to a planet. Dad would send me down—remember that was before anyone could walk or talk—and I had to try to communicate a message of peace and understanding just using my hands and grunting a lot. Needless to say, over the course of more than four million years, I got clubbed to death more than once. Cave men just wanted to be cave men."

There was laughter of recognition in the room.

"I'm serious. I came back all through the ages trying to communicate. I think I did a fair job with Hammurabi. I didn't like the fact that he made rules rather than educate people, but he tried. Dad liked him. I spent some time in his court and I liked him too. But the rules don't work. People don't go by rules. Rules don't change people or educate them. Pretty soon there were punishments for people who didn't follow the rules even though they didn't understand the principle *behind* the rules. I mean, that's what matters, right? If you don't understand the principles behind a rule, then what good is it? You just have to keep adding stupid rules to fit every situation. Could I have another cup of coffee? I didn't get any sleep."

Snagg rushed out and returned with a steaming cup.

"Thanks, man. You know, when this stuff evolved—I mean coffee beans—Dad got really excited. There was a fire once down here and the plants burned and when Dad smelled the aroma, it was like dance time in heaven. Everyone had to try it. Can you imagine *my Dad* on caffeine? Now that was crazy. So the evolution of coffee is a good thing, a great thing even. But, then of course, there had to be the people who decided there was a pile of money to be made from it and so they enslaved people to grow it and charge outrageous money for people to buy *mochfrappalatteloco.*"

Whispers of "Dude's is hilarious," and, "This dude is a'right," could be heard throughout the room.

"Speaking of enslavement. Now there's a subject. Dad and I were getting a little hopeful about people. They were learning a lot, doing mathematics, getting interested in the planets and developing language and writing—all good. And then they started having wars over territory! I mean there weren't very many people in the whole world and already they're fighting over territory. Duh? Some people just moved other places—or got driven other places. At least they got away. Others stayed and kept fighting one another.

"Now here's one for you. When the Egyptians captured the Israelites— and that did actually happen—they turned the Jews into slaves. I can't tell you how bad that pissed Dad off. He was livid. He didn't like seeing anyone put under the control of anyone else—I mean, that's why he hates those organized religions so much. They're just a modern way of enslaving people—and getting a lot of people to work for nothing while the big boys get fat and rich. Anyway, just about the time Dad decides that enough is enough, Moses comes along and manages to lead the Israelites out of slavery. He did a pretty good job. Dad even talked to him a couple of times. Moses was a good guy—but he was another one who was always wanting to turn everything into a religion. That's why he never made it into what he called "the Promised Land." Long story. But the people he was leading eventually got to a place that they could call home. But here's the weird thing. They started calling themselves the 'Chosen People.' Of course they were! They were downtrodden and held in bondage. That's what Dad meant when he talked to Moses about them being chosen. Dad particularly loves people who've been through the mill, who've had hard knocks, and who have been subjugated. I mean he *loves* people who've had to work for Wal-Mart, I can tell you that.

"But it's nearly driven him crazy that people he's cared about because they suffered, have gone and forgotten their bad times and have turned around and used it to do the same thing to other people. I can talk about this. Most people can't. I'm not running for political office or anything like that. I'm here to try and clean up this mess before the whole world just blows itself up. It's nothing against Jews. It's just that nobody should think that they are more *chosen* than anybody else. Where people have been treated unjustly, they're right to say that Dad loves them. But that's where it ends. It doesn't give anybody extra rights or say that it's now okay for them to turn the tables on other people. He didn't go through all that trouble just to have people standing by a wall crying and asking him to destroy all Arabs. But that's a whole other story.

"Meanwhile, as you're going to see in the next few days… well, something is going to happen that's going to snap everybody's attention to 100%, I can tell you that."

Lyla was still waiting for an answer to her question.

"I'll get to it, Lyla, I promise," Jesus said.

"Cool."

"So where does that bring us? I've tried, God knows I've tried." Jesus chuckled at his own joke. "So now we're just days away from the culmination of one of the most Machiavellian plots against humanity that has ever taken place. I learned a lot more about it last night.

"In the past, Pop has sent me here with messages. He wanted me to reason with people about using their heads and changing direction. But like I've said, every time… somebody sees what I say as a chance to have power and turn my ideas into a religion. Do you really think that I made Peter the head of a *church* and told him that he was God on Earth and that he had the power to forgive evil—if some rich people had enough money to *pay for it*? Give me a break. Peter was a good guy, but people have turned him into something he never was and that I never intended him to be. Meanwhile, you may be interested in keeping an eye on the Pope in the next few days.

"So Lyla, why did I show up at your house when you don't even believe in me? I'll tell you—and I said last night that the answer is simple. I came to your house because you have been trying to use a very good mind to see what's true about things. You had parents who were just off the deep end with their rules and regulations and rituals—and you wouldn't stand for it. So you've been through a hard growing up, you've made mistakes, but you've used your head and you're interesting. And then there's the other thing."

Lyla started to blush.

"I know something about you that most people don't." There was a kindness in his tone that made for no apprehension. "When you were sixteen, you gave a kidney to your cousin so he could live a normal life. Isn't that right, Lyla?"

The tears on Lyla's face said "yes" louder than she did.

"So I ask you, who would I rather be around? Someone who is willing to do something truly selfless for other people, who wants to see what is true about things and not just read a 'script' about life, or a bunch of people— and there were plenty in your house—who spent a lot of time screaming my name and making other people miserable? I think it's a no brainer.

"Dad doesn't like exploiters, he doesn't like boring people, and he can't stand people who want life to be like some stupid cookbook with them as the big chef. You know who Dad likes? He likes people who can hold their heads up even when they've had it rough. Take Monica Lewinsky. Dad thinks the world of her. That kid went through a hell of a time. That Clinton guy—he paraded himself as such a man of the people that some started calling him the 'first Black president.' I heard that and I thought I was going to throw up—and I was in heaven and we don't even throw up there! Here's a guy who signed the most draconian anti-welfare bill in history that mortally wounded a lot of people, who bombed the hell out of Bosnia because it looked like the multinationals might need an oil pipeline through there to the Baltic Sea. That guy wanted to make sure the 'right' people were going to own it so he went to war. He was no liberal, as certain cretin neo-cons would like to paint him as being. He was a capitalist scarfer, just like the rest of them. And this same guy goes and hangs out with this girl—and trust me, Dad and I have got nothing against people having a good time together—but he goes and has a good time with her, and when it looks politically bad for him, he starts calling her 'that woman' and acting like he never knew her. She was a kid, for Dad's sake. She had a real heart. He tried to turn her into a national joke. How she got through it, I don't know. But she did. She held her head up and got it together. She's got a sweet soul. Here's an example: One night she went to a show that was done by a group of ex-cons. They hadn't been out of prison long, and they were doing a good thing to raise some money for a charity, okay? One of the guys does a poem about a girl he knew who died as a crack-addicted prostitute, asking how that could happen to such a wonderful child. And Monica Lewinsky has tears streaming down her face. She goes to all kinds of trouble to get the guy's addresses and writes them each a personal note to tell them that she truly appreciated what they had done, and to thank them for touching her emotions in such a deep way. You guys'll be meeting her before too much time has passed—she won't be disappearing any time soon."

Jesus was about to say something else, and then as an afterthought said, "Uh, about Clinton. Considering the President that followed him, he's even sorta missed by *Dad*."

"What's going to happen to Obama now that the election is suspended?"

Jesus smiled. "It's going to be tricky for a few days. But…"

"But he'll get in and change everything?"

"He'll get in and prove you don't become President of this country and still have a moral compass."

Marie nodded, "You mean he's like the Manchurian Candidate?"

"To this point it seems that there's always a soul sold for each political office. These guys are just puppets with the appearance of power."

Snagg quickly changed the subject. "You said something is going to be happening in the next few days that's a culmination. What are you referring to?"

"I have a job for you. It will have to be my answer for now. You have a blog, right?"

"Yeah, how'd you know? Uh, forget I asked that."

"I know you don't go under your own name or anything, but your blog has become influential. I respect your opinions and the way you question authority and the domination of the powerful over the increasingly weak. So far as I know, there are five blogs represented in this room, right?"

Five hands went up in recognition.

"Good. Something is going to happen. I need you to get the word out big time that when it happens, anarchists, socialists and all the other good people should just sit tight. There will be an attempt to draw you into violent protest. There's a time for that, but this isn't one of those times. You'll have to trust me on this. The next 24 hours are going to be crucial. I'll have to be gone a lot. Please, remember the things that we've talked about. If anything should go wrong—promise me you won't form a religion around the things I've said. Think for yourselves. Live for yourselves. Live for one another. That's the message. That's the whole message. What time is it?"

Marie looked at her watch. "Twelve twenty."

"Then I need to go. Protect one another, and get the word out as widely as you can. I don't expect you to do everything, you'll have help." And with that Jesus stood and vanished.

CHAPTER 68

Adam's van was waiting for them a block from the Jesus Dome. Chandra and Hogan, clutching the manila folders, climbed in and were greeted by their grinning chauffeur.

"So how'd you do? What'd you get?"

Chandra, pleased but nervous ducked below the window saying, "Let's get away from here before we do any talking. Hogan!"

Hogan slipped to the floor.

"And we're off." Adam adjusted the manual controls and began to drive. When they were at a safe distance, he asked, "What did you find?"

Hogan shook his head and got up. "We can't believe it ourselves. I knew where Dobbin kept stuff, but it turned out all the filing cabinets were locked. We were testing everything, trying to find anything that would help us out, but no luck. Then we got your call and knew we had to run."

"But right then," Chandra broke in, "one of the drawers just kind of slid open all by itself. And we got these!" She held up the folders. "Dobbin didn't own the Jesus Dome! His holding company didn't!"

"Then who did?" Adam watched the grinning pair in the back seat. "Who owns the Jesus Dome?"

Chandra pulled out an elaborate document and held it up. "It seems Dobbin was in serious financial trouble. In fact, he was being investigated by the FBI. They seemed to think there was a funnel running from his offering plates directly into his pants' pockets."

"So what happened?"

"Someone saved Dobbin's ass and bought the Jesus Dome—in a $435 million *cash* deal. All transactions were done through a bank in Antigua."

"A $435 million cash deal? Who could do that kind of thing?'

"Winslow Boolean. My husband."

"Then…"

"Yeah, I own the Jesus Dome."

CHAPTER 69

Daisy-Ann Wexler was sipping her morning tea and nibbling at a Texas-sized croissant. The house was empty and Daisy-Ann felt the lack of human company intensely. The weight of her discoveries about Duke coupled with the rush of Acting Governor Harry "Crackerjack" Lowery to execute Divine "X" Marcus had left her with a feeling of helplessness she'd never experienced. She was the first lady of Texas. Her opinions had always had influence in the state—until now. How could she stop the execution of a possibly innocent man when she had just been on national television praising her dear departed husband? She looked at her watch. It would be 12:20 in New York. She could try calling Babs Waller's office to see if she would be willing to do a second interview. That thought cheered her slightly. But then she remembered Waller's well-known right wing politics, and her hope faded.

She was reaching for her cellphone when she heard a slight noise in the kitchen. No staff was scheduled to arrive until noon.

"Hello?" Her voice had more than a touch of anxiety.

"Hallo," was the answer. It was a woman's voice with an odd accent.

The kitchen door swung open and there stood a small woman in a floor length black dress with a black bonnet. She appeared to be about sixty years old.

"Who are you? Why are you here?"

"I am very sorry to have startled you. I'm afraid I arrived in the wrong room."

The woman seemed to be of such a gentle nature that Daisy-Ann couldn't help but return a gracious smile. "Y'all might have knocked," was all the chiding she could muster.

"May I come in and sit down?"

"I suppose."

The woman sat across the table from the widow.

"Do ya mind tellin' me who y'are?"

"I'm sorry," the woman said removing her black bonnet and smoothing her gray hair and checking the tidy bun on the back of her head. "I'm Elise Amalie Tvede Waerenskjold."

"You're puttin' me on—'cause you're dead."

"No, I'm right here. But I'm glad you know of me."

"Of course I do, you're the abolitionist who came to Texas from Norway."

"The same."

"You died a hundred years ago."

"I suppose. But I'm here now and I need to talk to you."

Daisy-Ann looked at her coffee cup to see if it had telltale signs of drugs. Not finding any she returned to the conversation. "You're the little Norwegian lady who was fighting Texas slavery back in the early 1800's?"

"Yes."

What are yew doing here?"

"With all modesty, ma'am, you might say Jesus sent me."

"Am I gonna disappear?"

"No ma'am."

"I'm not good enough?"

"I'd say it's because you're too good." The woman leaned forward. "May I be very candid with you?"

"May I call you Elise? I cain't get my lips around that last name of yours."

"By all means."

"Well, Elise, go ahead with whatever it is you've got to say. These days are so odd, nothin' could really throw me. Ma husband has disappeared, Ah've discovered secrets y'all don't wanna know," Daisy-Ann leaned back, expecting some supernatural fireworks.

"I *do* know. That's why I'm here. I think we can help one another."

"What do yew know?"

"I know that Divine X Marcus is an innocent man and that he was being framed by your husband and Lieutenant Governor Harry Lowery."

"Gawd."

"And I know that we have to move quickly if we're going to succeed."

"Who are yew, really?"

The woman raised her arms above her head and slowly lowered them. As she did, she became a very large Black man with long locks and a cotton robe.

"Are yew . . ?"

"Yes, I'm Jesus. Seeing as how you've had some question as to how to see my people—particularly men—I thought I'd better come as someone you might not feel threatened by."

"Why her?"

"I haven't been able to work with too many people in Texas other'n Ann Richards. But I worked real well with Elise. She hated slavery and so I chose her."

Daisy-Ann knew Jesus was right about her anti-semitism. She felt terribly embarrassed. "I didn't know you were..."

"Anyone could have known—I'm a Sephardic Jew—I look more like Mos Def than Justin Timberlake."

Failing to recognize the names, Daisy-Ann just smiled and nodded and wondered what horrible fate awaited her.

"Daisy-Ann, may I call you Daisy-Ann?"

"Of course."

"I feel like I know you since I've been following your progress for so long."

"Oh Gawd."

"No, I'm technically his son. One of many prophets."

"What dew yew want with me?"

"I know that you've discovered that your husband was executing innocent men, just like the governor before him. Divine X is innocent of the charges against him. The bombing he's accused of, like the bombing Timothy McVeigh was part of, was carried out by a white supremacist militia with members in Idaho and Texas. The difference is that Divine X had *nothing* to do with the Austin attack. But your husband and Buck Lowery were members of that survivalist militia and *did* have to do with it. I can't go into detail now, but the whole thing which, as you know killed hundreds of people, was an elaborate plot to maintain power. It was a testing ground."

Daisy-Ann felt like she was going to faint. "Could yew tawk a little slower?" she asked. "Ah'm afraid I cain't take all this in at the speed it's comin' at me."

"I apologize for that, Daisy-Ann. But I'm in a terrible hurry. The next few days are going to determine the world's future. Will you help me?"

"Well, that depends on what yew want me to dew. I cain't break the law, ah'm gunna be runnin' for office."

"I'll make sure that whatever you do to help will not interfere with that. I would like to see you be governor of Texas."

"Oh!" The statement warmed Daisy-Ann's spirits considerably. Then she got suspicious again, "How dew I know yew are who you say yew are? Yew just walk in here and tell me this and that—of course yew are right about it all—but…"

Jesus held up his hands so Daisy-Ann could see his palms. "I could have come to see you as Abraham, Mohammed, Buddha, or a host of other people that I've been. I thought you would respond best to me just the way I've done it."

Daisy-Ann started to cry. "I'm so sorry," she whispered. "I should'a known it was yew."

"It's no problem," Jesus said touching her hand with his. "Just tell me that you'll help me save the life of Divine X Marcus. I have important work for him to do."

"I'll dew whatever yew tell me tew."

"You see, I can do a lot of things, but I have my limitations. Dad wanted me to go light on the miracles for fear that someone would start *another* religion after I was here this time. Here's what I need you to do."

There transpired a conversation between them that could possibly alter world history.

CHAPTER 70

Robinson Patrick's *The 144,000 Club* was expanded to a three-hour daily broadcast. The newly designated czar of the National Protestant Evangelical Church of America easily commandeered the additional airtime on Christ's Broadcast Network, but it took intimidation from the White House to get one hour of prime time each night from CNN and MSNBC. Of course, predictably, FOX network immediately ordered two hours of prime time on all its affiliates.

The good Reverend was in a difficult position. Certainly a champion of the idea of the Rapture, he was also a proponent of George Bush's rush to Armageddon, the final battle of the earth. The theological sticking point was that only those left behind in the Rapture—those not anointed and approved by Christ himself—would be present on earth for that cataclysmic battle, and Robinson Patrick had been *very* left behind. So he asked himself in his self preservational way: "If *I* have been left behind, if *I* have not achieved the level of righteousness required by divine law, if *I* have not been covered sufficiently by Christ's grace, then *I* am going to be one of the people that burns in the fires of Armageddon. How then can *I* go on TV and talk about the completion of God's work on earth and the coming destruction? If I do that, then I will be hastening my own suffering and death!"

Suffering was not something Robinson Patrick could tolerate. Imperfect coffee, a spot on silverware, and a blemish on his shoes—were the absolute limit of suffering he allowed. So facing the reality that he had been *left behind* when God Almighty collected his saints, that was suffering that exceeded his fragile tolerance. He prayed long and hard about his plight. His researchers were instructed to scour the *Bible* looking for texts that could be interpreted to explain how a man of God might be left behind to lead the world's reformation *after* the Rapture had taken place. Of course, he had not completely given up on the idea that he might disappear at any moment. That thought occasionally brightened his mood.

At the moment, there were no bright thoughts in the holy czar's mind. He was alone in his dressing room. Breaking news of further disappearances—Donald Trump and 26 other prominent real estate developers in New York—had further darkened his countenance. He was personally acquainted with many of the disappeared. "Lord," he prayed, "I know those men. I know their deeds. How can you have left your faithful servant behind in this vale of tears and taken *those* men? I have served you. I have covered for you. When people would raise questions asking 'how there could be a God when such and such happened,' I always had your back. I made up explanations that always had you look good. I never failed. But now, when I need you to take me, you have failed me. I am here with the ungodly, the communists, the liberals, the left behind. And you have taken those men—who are nothing but crooks and liars with awfully bad hair—to be with you. Oh Lord, I need answers. I have to go on television tonight and explain what is happening, and I have no idea! Your servant George W. has put me here in this position, but you know *he* doesn't have a clue as to what is happening… does he? If he does, he hasn't told me."

"Sir?" It was Swensen, Robinson's executive producer.

The troubled reverend interrupted his chat with God. "Yes?"

"I'm sorry to bother you, Sir, but Babs Waller is on the phone for you."

"*The* Babs Waller?" Robinson Patrick's mood brightened. He liked being seen as a major player and a call from Babs Waller—undoubtedly for the purpose of interviewing him, certainly qualified. "Tell her I'll be right with her."

"Yes sir."

Since he was already sitting in the leather shiatsu massage chair behind his desk, the Reverend had only to swivel slightly to the right to take the call.

"Yes?"

"Reverend Patrick, this is Babs Waller."

"Yes, hello Ms. Waller. I'm so glad that you called. I had somewhat expected it."

"Really?"

"Well, yes. There is naturally a very great deal to convey to the populace about the love of Christ, his coming kingdom, and his hatred of terrorists, anarchists, atheists and leftists…"

"Mr. Patrick, I am Jewish. My purpose in calling…"

"But we embrace you. You are welcome under the big umbrella of Christ."

"You are being offensive."

"No, no. I'm telling you the truth. I wouldn't kid about something so important. You are welcome to enter the embrace of our loving Lord Jesus Christ."

"Do you know his whereabouts?"

"He is everywhere. All you need to do is get down on your knees and say, 'Blessed Jesus, I accept you into my Jewish life.' It's that simple."

"Apparently *you* are. I asked you if you know his whereabouts."

"Well, we can certainly discuss that in the interview."

"Interview?"

"Yes, that's what you're calling about isn't it?"

"Reverend Patrick, I am calling to see if you know the whereabouts, the location, the hiding place of the so-called Jesus Christ who is wreaking terror on the American people."

"Oh. You're not calling about…"

"Do you or don't you? I just want a yes or no. Frankly, you have been so incredibly insulting already…"

"Then… yes I do know exactly where he is, but I won't tell you." And the little czar hung up the phone, his hand shaking in rage. He was triumphant until the moment he realized that he had just told an enormous lie, and that if Babs Waller was the vindictive kind—which apparently she was—she could report him to Homeland Security and say that he was harboring knowledge of someone on the most wanted list. He picked up the phone and dialed *69. He got nothing but a recording telling him that the number was unavailable to that service. He was about to ring for Swensen, when his door opened again.

"I'm sorry to trouble you again sir. It's the President. He needs to talk to you immediately."

Reverend Patrick answered the phone. His hand was shaking—the result of his fear that Babs Waller had already told the President that he was either harboring a fugitive or was lying. Either way his career would be in ruins.

"Robbie Boy, heck'uv a job you're doing there!"

"Thank you sir." The sigh of relief was audible.

"Listen, now that you're in charge of our national church and all, I'd really appreciate your doin' me a little favor."

What the Commander in Chief had in mind was not what Reverend Robinson Patrick had expected.

CHAPTER 71

Babs Waller was livid. She attacked the nearest target, her make up artist, Danny. "A whole day of searching, no sign of Jesus Christ, and an offer from that Goy prick Robinson Patrick to join his hot air Christian church!"

Danny flinched, expecting another smack from Bab's bony hand. "I could accessorize you with an adorable little cross that says 'shiksa bitch'!" Danny's notion of a bright idea.

"Can't you ever be serious?"

"Dear, if I was, I would say things about your career that would depress you."

"Where the fuck is Jesus?"

"Ooh, now you're quoting me! My mantra since I was a child. I mean with the state of the world and all—just where *is* he?"

"All my sources are drying up."

"Moisturizer?"

Babs whacked Danny on the butt. "All you do is joke around. I'm serious. I want to find Jesus!"

"But you curse out poor old Reverend Patrick when he offers you the chance to meet him."

"Right. Last thing he says is that he knows where Jesus is hiding, but won't tell. Lying son of a bitch."

"Call his bluff."

"What do you mean?"

"Go on TV and say that he told you himself that he knows where this guy is hiding, but that he's protecting him… apparently because he *believes* in him. That should shake a few eggs in the basket, eh?"

"Danny love, you just earned yourself a raise."

CHAPTER 72

Following Danny's advice, Babs Waller went on her talk show and announced, "In a disturbing conversation I had earlier with the Reverend Robinson Patrick, I learned that despite terror alerts for the man purportedly calling himself Jesus Christ, the television evangelist has taken it upon himself to *hide* the terrorist in a location he will not reveal.

"I find it troubling in the extreme that a prominent, albeit rather odd, clergyman of the gospel should defy the White House and the Department of Homeland Security in such an outrageous fashion. I'll be back in a moment with some fabulous cooking tips. Don't go away."

Babs' show was broadcast live. The commercial over, she was dipping pork chops in a cholesterol-laden batter when her producer signaled her. She didn't respond. The producer then walked directly onto the set, took Babs by the arm and said loudly, "The White House is on the phone."

Thinking that the White House was calling to thank her for protecting national security and that she was scoring another high point in her career, Babs announced, "We have the White House on the phone. Please patch it through so our audience can hear everything." She batted her eyes and said, "Hello, this is Babs Waller."

"Listen you Jew blabbermouth, leave my boy Robinson alone. You got that Miss Babsy?"

"Mr. President?"

"Yeah, what of it?"

"Uh, we're live on the air, Mr. President."

"And?"

"Well, everybody is hearing this on live TV!"

"Oh.… I was just rehearsing a little here, trying to work on my tough talk. Heh, heh. So, God bless you and God bless America. But leave Robbie alone." And the President hung up.

CHAPTER 73

News of the disappearance of the entire Saudi Royal Family would have shaken world markets if world markets still existed. Previous disappearances had so disrupted operations that trading had essentially come to a standstill internationally.

Arbet Portent, CEO of Exxon Mobil and hundreds of other oil executives were missing. Employees gracefully took over the daily operations of the major companies so the flow of crude and refined fuels was uninterrupted. In a breathtaking example of international cooperation, the employee-run companies agreed that it was economically viable to drop the price of gasoline from $10.35 to $1.50 a gallon.

In Africa, corrupt rulers in fifteen countries had disappeared and the liberation armies in each had been able to bloodlessly take control. The speed at which changes were taking place made interference from the superpowers impossible.

When Bill O'Reilly and Rush Limbaugh disappeared, there was near panic in certain parts of the White House. The President, however, seemed strangely calm. Some speculated he'd had a change in medication, but Karl Rove knew better. The Plan was in motion. George was about to make sure that his very own Messianic prophecy was fulfilled.

"You've outdone yourself this time, Turd Blossom," the President said offering his associate a toke.

Rove declined. "Gotta keep everything tick-tock up here," he said tapping his head. "Just wait until that idiot Robinson Patrick goes on the air. Then it will be bing bang BOOM."

The President chuckled. "I like booms," he said, then inhaled more of the relaxing herb. He coughed after he exhaled. "Good shit. Are you sure you. . ?"

"Look, you'd better start getting ready. You can't go on the air and introduce God's very own Czar of the American National Religion with a major buzz, now can you?"

"I don't know. I did the debates that way. Just so long as the little thing in my ear works—I'm OK. I just listen and repeat. I just do my 'deer in the headlight' look and memorize my next line." He took another hit.

"You'd better do a couple of lines of the white stuff before you come down to the Oval Office—I don't want you falling asleep during a speech from Jehovah's Messenger. The God-Suckers wouldn't like it." Pretense about belief in God and the *Bible* was Rove's favorite joke with the President. When the two of them were alone, vulgar euphemisms were in rich supply.

"I'll meet you in the East Room at 8:30. For Chrissake, George, don't be late."

"For *His* sake I'll be on time." The familiar smirk leaked across the President's face.

Downstairs, Rove met the nervous Reverend Robinson Patrick. "This isn't what I expected, Karl," he said, holding up the text of his speech. "I mean, when the President called and asked me to do this, I thought I was supposed to write something, but then I got the speech from your office and…"

"Do you object to doing this, Reverend Robbie?"

"No! On the contrary! I'm so honored that the President is putting so much faith in me. Why, why I'd have sold my soul to…"

"I was under the impression that you had."

"We mustn't joke about those things, Karl."

Rove shot a disapproving look at Patrick.

"I mean, we must cling to the truth that our salvation lies…"

Rove cut in, "Yes, we all cling to the truths of the Blessed Savior, Reverend."

"I've known it all along. I mean when people would say those awful things about the President, I always knew they were untrue. I knew that his support was from. . ."

"Mmm hmm," Rove's thoughts had drifted away from the Reverend's drone. "So just do a good job with the speech. Put your heart and soul into it, and try not to scrunch up your eyes so much when you're on the air. It makes you look like an idiot." He walked away leaving the Reverend somewhat less sure than he had been moments before.

Over two thousand miles away a man in a Correction Officer's uniform was fiddling with a stubborn lock and key.

CHAPTER 74

"Psst, X," Jesus tried to get the prisoner's attention. "You awake?"

"Yeah."

"Mohammed? Where'd you get that uniform? They'll kill you if…"

"Don't worry, they can't see me."

"I got you."

"Did you start getting the word out?"

"Definite! I taped a radio show and got it to the CO who smuggles them out. By now it should be going out across the country. It's just a message of peace that says no matter how much you are provoked, don't react. Our enemies want reaction."

"Perfect. I knew I could count on you. Now I need you to come with me."

"Get out!" Divine X used the phrase to register surprise.

"That's the idea: *get out*. I'm dead serious. I need you to come with me. You'll be able to walk out of here unobserved."

"Just let me get my *Q'ran*."

The man dressed as the Corrections Officer that Divine X recognized as Mohammed led him out of his solitary confinement cell, down a long corridor to a double set of electronically controlled gates. The CO in the control booth obviously could not see them, yet the first gate slid open. The two men stepped inside the holding area. The gate slid shut with a crash. The CO in the booth did not hear the noise. The second gate slid open, and the two men proceeded down a long corridor past prisoners and COs.

The process repeated itself as they reached the administration area and exited the front gate.

Seconds later Divine X was getting into a large black car.

"Daisy-Ann, this is Divine X," the mysterious CO said. "You know what to do."

Daisy-Ann Wexler was meeting a real prisoner for the first time in her life.

She'd been with her husband when he signed off on over a hundred executions, but she had never ventured inside so much as a county jail. Now, sitting next to her was a convicted murderer scheduled to die in the electric chair. To make matters more extraordinary for Ms. Wexler, the man in question was of a complexion she had studiously avoided all her life unless the person was a celebrity who could sing and dance. And even then her exposure was limited to a smile and an autograph.

But Daisy-Ann had never felt better in her life. Jesus said this man was innocent and needed help, and for once she was doing something just because it was right. At first she was afraid that she'd be caught "aiding and abetting," but Jesus said he'd changed Divine X's resonance, so he'd remain invisible to other people as they traveled. Waving good-bye to Jesus in his uniform and hoping the resonance thing was true, Daisy sped away and began a conversation.

"Well isn't this something?" she remarked with a nervous giggle.

"Thank you ma'am," X said softly.

"I'm happy t'do it, even though I don't know your story, Mr. Divine."

"Call me X."

"Mr. X, there is so much extraordinary happenin' around here that I have no problem believin' what Jesus tol' me about you."

"Mohammed."

"What?"

"It was Mohammed that brought me to the car."

"Is *that* why Jesus was dressed like that! Well, I never. You just don't know what he's going to do next, now do yew?" Daisy-Ann rambled on about her surprise at recent events and her visit from Elise Amalie Tvede Waerenskjold.

"And the lady said she was from Norway, and I jest 'bout fainted on a'cause she's been dead forever—and then she lifts her arms and there is Jesus sittin' right a'front of me."

Divine X was in more shock that Daisy-Ann. A short time ago he was locked in solitary confinement awaiting execution, and now he was sitting in a luxury car driven by a white lady. To top that off, Mohammed had appeared to him wearing a corrections officer's uniform and helped him escape from prison. And now the white lady was saying the man was Jesus.

"I think you gotta bring it way down, lady," he said finally. "I've been locked up for a long time. I've been facing death right up close. And now I'm out here with you thanks to someone I think is Mohammed and you think is

Jesus. You better just drive and not talk too much, if you don't mind."

"I don't mind at all, young man," Daisy-Ann said. "Why, when my own nephew was goin' away to college, I drove him all the way from Texas to Ohio. It was a fascinating trip. You couldn't imagine all that we saw. But he would always be afraid that I couldn't drive and talk at the same time. He kept saying, 'Auntie Daisy-Ann, you mind your business there behind the wheel. Yew don't have to talk all the time or entertain me or keep a conversation goin'. Yew can just study the road. I'll be okay.' Wasn't that the sweetest thing? And now you're worried for me the same way. I just think that's wonderful. But it's no strain, really. I can do both at once. I love to have conversations with new people and get to know everything about them."

Divine X couldn't suppress a smile. He'd read about people like Daisy-Ann, but he'd never figured them to take part in a jailbreak.

"D'yew mind if I ask yew a question?"

"Go ahead. Ask whatever you want. I still don't believe this is happening anyway." He figured he'd wake up and it would be time to go to the chair.

"Why, if yew didn't kill all those people didn't yew just say yew didn't?"

"Excuse me?"

"Well, I don't know about yew, but if it was me, I would just go in there and tell the judge I didn't dew it. And I'd write a letter to the governor tellin' him I didn't dew it. I mean, I'd stand up for myself."

"I've been doing that for seven years. Nobody listens. They all figure they've got their man."

"Tell me somethin' honest. Did ya write to Duke, the Governor?"

"I wrote to Duke Wexler, governor of Texas thirty-five times. My lawyer wrote to him. Three hundred people signed a petition asking him to have my case reopened. Ma'am, he never so much as answered saying 'No.' My lawyer presented evidence that had been suppressed by the DA. He had three eyewitnesses who had not been allowed to testify at my trial. None of that mattered to Duke Wexler. I was Black so I was guilty and he wanted me fried."

"He knew about all that?"

"Yes, ma'am. He did."

"Ah'm sorry Mr. Divine. You see he was my husband. Ah'm Daisy-Ann Wexler."

For a moment, Divine X felt a panic. But Daisy-Ann's admission had no rancor, no threat. "I'm sorry ma'am," was all he said.

"Only be sorry for the fact that I was married to him, not for what you just said. I'm the one who should be sorry. I was so comfortable in a way. It all seemed so black and white… uh, I didn't mean it that way. Ah'm sorry now. Ah just mean it all seemed so clear. There were the bad guys and the good guys. Duke and his people were the good guys and they were sure then they had the bad guys and they got rid of 'em. Now, well, now Ah know it wasn't that way. A lot of good people, innocent people, were executed by my husband, Mr. X. I think I've got their blood on my hands. I guess that makes *me* the killer in this car."

The miles passed without conversation. Divine X dozed off for a while. When he woke up, Daisy-Ann was pulling into a drive-through McDonalds.

"I thought we could use a little somethin' to eat. Do yew like hamburgers?"

"No ma'am. I'm vegetarian. But that's all right. You go right ahead."

"Yew wanna have one of those vegeburgers? They got 'em."

"That would be mighty nice."

"Anything else? A milkshake? Fries? An apple pie?"

It sounded too good to be true to X. He hadn't tasted ice cream in seven years, hadn't had a piece of apple pie in as long. "Don't mind if I do," he said. "I appreciate this."

"No problem." Daisy-Ann ordered a hamburger for herself, four vegeburgers, two milkshakes, fries, and five apple pies for her companion.

When she got to the drive-through window the cashier handed her the bags of food. "That's a lot of food for a little lady," he said.

"I think I'm hungrier right now than I've ever been in my life, I could eat enough for two." It reassured her that the owner of the major appetite in the car was invisible.

She pulled back onto the highway. She'd been driving four hours and figured there were eleven to go.

Little did she know that her destination would make her a permanent part of world history.

CHAPTER 75

At exactly 8:30, the President came downstairs. Some staffers remarked on how bright his eyes looked, while others joked how using *President* and *bright* in the same sentence was an oxymoron.

"Hello, Reverend," he said extending his hand. The hand and the rest of the President reeked of Fabrese, the fabric deodorizer used regularly to rid the Commander in Chief of telltale whiffs of 420.

"George, I just can't thank you enough for this opportunity," the odd little preacher effused. "I could never have written anything this comprehensive, this compliant with the Word of God, and never been able to reach so many souls…"

G.W. stopped him. "No, I don't supposed you could have, Reverend. Now why don't you just go and practice the speech some more and I'll get myself ready to do your introduction. Oh, and you can call me Mr. President."

The junior Bush brushed past the groveling, obsequious preacher and found Karl Rove. "Scrunchy Eyes is practically licking my feet for giving him this opportunity," he laughed. "He hasn't got a clue."

Rove's little chins shook when he nodded his head. "God works in mysterious ways, *our* wonders to perform," he said. "You clear enough to read?"

"No problem. You'll see."

The Washington press corp was assembled in the East Room. At 9 PM, the tech director and the President accompanied by Reverend Robinson Patrick walked down the red carpet stopping behind a central podium.

It was estimated that 80% of the population of the United States and an international audience of 1.5 billion was watching.

"My fellow Amercuns, and you there in the rest'a the world," the President launched into his familiar greeting, a few smirks, a duck and bob or two, and then on with his prepared message. "We are standin' at the threshold of some of the gravest times this country has ever faced. We've still got war takin' place in Af-gan-is-tan, I-rak, Seer-E-a, E-gypped, Leb-a-non, Ter-key, and a bunch of other countries run by Islamic Fascist folks. We've got Israel with its little back up against the wall. Turists are ruinin' the world. We've got one runnin' around right here in the USA claimin' that he's Jesus Christ and sayin' that he's makin' people disappear. I believe, as y'all know, in the one true Jesus Christ—the one we founded this free market nation on—and I'm not gonna let anybody ruin it. I believe that we may be facin' the very end of time. We may be headin' for what the *Bible* prophecies all pointed to—the final battle of Armageddon. I talked to God about this. I talk to Him a lot. And He talks to me. He told me to appoint a holy man to lead our nation's church—a holy man whose heart reflects the principles of Jesus. And I obeyed. And I chose, because I'm The Chooser." George was so inflated by that statement he blew his next line. "And so now I've got my *choosed* one here. I've asked the new Czar of our National Protestant Evangelical Church to say a few words, to lay out the plan that we as a Christian nation must follow in order to avert disaster for ourselves and to make sure that we are here followin' God's instructions for us as His people right here in His blessed United States of Amerca. The Very Reverend Czar Robinson Patrick."

The junior Bush stepped aside. A small hydraulic apparatus at the base of the podium activated, and by the time the little Reverend was in place, it seemed he was almost as tall as the Commander in Chief.

"Shall we pray?" And the man G.W. Bush proclaimed the nation's divinely appointed religious leader scrunched up his little eyes and let out a powerful, "Oh Jaesus!"

Reverend Robinson Patrick had never felt the spirit of the Lord just the way he was feeling it now. Perhaps it was the Lord's doing, perhaps it was the realization that over a billion people were witnessing his zeal, and maybe it was because just behind his right shoulder, the most powerful man in the entire world was beaming his uncomprehending approval.

"Jaesus!" The little Reverend loved the word. He loved the way the word sounded coming from his lips. He had practiced saying it so that with the right timing it could escape in such an unexpected way that it would make the complaisant in his congregation jump. At the moment, however, it merely made the audio meters jump and the technicians in the sound booth mutter, "Fucking loudmouth asshole." But that mattered nothing to Reverend Robinson Patrick who was about to deliver a slam-dunk for Dubya.

"My President, *Our* President and I have been talking to the Lord. We have been seeking his guidance in these very, very, very perilous times. We know that the terrorists are lurking everywhere. They are watching us. They are stalking us. We know that for thousands of years the righteous of the earth have been battling Satan. But brothers and sisters, my fellow American citizens, and you other people of the world, there is only *one* Satan. There are a lot of terrorists. There is a lesson there because like the President says, it's a whole lot harder to fight a whole bunch of enemies rather than just one."

Pondering the depth of the statement he'd just read, Reverend Robinson paused for a moment, then resumed with undiminished energy. "But tonight I come to you with a message of urgent importance to all of us, and with a call for all to come under the umbrella of Christ our Almighty Savior. You see, we live in troubled times. People are disappearing, different countries are fighting, and we're facing enemy terrorists around every single corner. But the question we must ask, just like our President always asks on account of the fact that he is someone who has such a burning desire to know and understand everything, is: *why*? Why are we having so much trouble? Why are there hurricanes and tornadoes and hail stones and maybe more five-legged frogs than there should be down in Florida? Why are we being punished with terror and more terror just like we were on 9/11?" Robinson Patrick turned to look at the President who, at the moment, was thinking about a particularly impressive swing he'd taken on the golf course two days ago. Reverend Patrick was looking for comprehension, assurance, and encouragement. He caught the President's eye. He stared with meaningful intensity.

The President shrugged. "What?" He was clearly annoyed.

The little holy man, deflated, returned to his designated speech.

"The question is *why! Why?* I'll tell you why. I'll tell you why God's vengeance is being visited upon our people. I'll tell you why the Lord of the Universe has turned his wrath upon us. It is because we have turned away from the straight and narrow. It is because we have welcomed *SIN* into our very midst! We have brought this upon our own heads because we have allowed the *homosexual* to be legitimized as a normal human being! We have allowed these people who welcome Satan's *perversions* of the divine principle to vote, to buy and sell, belong to churches, and in some very sick regions of this nation to *marry*! God did not intend to have Bobby and Bubba get married!"

Patrick turned to look at the President hoping to share a laugh, but the President was mired in a fantasy about two giant titties wearing wedding dresses. His little eyes, slightly crossed, were seeing nothing but nipples and white lace.

CHAPTER 76

Deep in the water tunnels beneath Hunts Point, Jesus walked into the big room where Snagg and crew were watching the Reverend's speech on TV. "It's a wonder Dad doesn't just strike them dead," he said.

Lyla instinctively got up and gave Jesus a hug. "Where've you been? I was worried about you."

"I had an errand to run. Everything's cool, but thanks for worrying."

Lyla pointed at the TV. "This dude is crazed."

"I know. Can you imagine? These people who scream my name and talk like they are my best little buddies—and all they can yap about is how much they hate gay people?"

On the screen, now muted, Robinson Patrick was mimicking an effeminate walk.

"You see that? What does that hate monger know? Wanna know how far off he is?" Jesus took a seat and continued. "Remember my disciple John? He's usually called 'John the Beloved.' You know why? He was the man I loved most in the world and he was gay. That Dan Brown novel a few years back tried to say that the person to my right in DaVinci's painting of "The Last Supper" was Mary Magdalene because it looked like a woman. DaVinci knew about my relationship with Mary, but he was smart enough to know she wasn't going to be at a Seder eating my babaganoush. But since DaVinci was gay, he *did* know about John and painted him authentically. John was the best, warmest, most understanding of all the guys with me. Why do you think I left him in charge of my mother when I was on the cross? Mom and he were always tight.

"And while I'm on the subject . . ," Jesus was appreciative of a friendly audience, "I'll tell you something else. You know that whole thing about how I raised Lazarus from the dead? Nobody who wrote about me wanted to deal with the real facts so they made up a miracle. The actual fact is that while I was away on one of my journeys, Lazarus confided to his sister Martha that he was gay. Martha had been indoctrinated with the Jewish belief that if a man is homosexual, he must be treated as dead. My beloved Mary Magdelene, one of the best people I've ever known, was caught up in the family drama and had the presence of mind to send a message for me to come home, which I did as swiftly as I could. But by the time I got there Mary and Martha were sitting shiva for Lazarus. He had been forced to leave town and was living with a friend in the desert. I was furious. I knew Mary and Martha were only doing what they had been taught by the people who claimed they had messages from Dad, but…" Jesus stopped for a moment and sighed. "Anyway, I explained that what they were doing was ridiculous, that Lazarus was every bit the same good person he was the day before they knew he was gay, and that they should bring him back and celebrate his life. So they did. Except that there was so much pressure from religious people, that when John finally got around to writing about it, he turned it into a miracle—a raising from the dead."

Marie shook her head. "Unbelievable. But why would John, of all people, change that?"

Jesus gave a wry smile. "Well, it was a little complicated for him because right after that is when he and Lazarus… got acquainted. They were together for the rest of their lives. If John had written the truth, both of them would have been stoned."

"Is that the same John that wrote the book of *Revelation?*" Lyla wanted to know who to blame because she had been disciplined so often with threats of punishment from beasts in that book.

The question made Jesus chuckle. "Definitely not," he said. "That was John of Patmos, and even Dad will say that's one of the places he, himself, made a huge mistake in judgment. Not as big as when he let Dick Cheney's parents get together… but a mistake nevertheless. No, *that* John was supposed to write a very inspiring book about how to save the planet. But then he discovered mushrooms."

"Mushrooms?"

"Mushrooms. They were so hallucinogenic he never really came down. I should have learned from what happened to him, but that's why Dad was so angry with me when I came and did the Timothy Leary thing. He kept saying, 'Didn't you learn anything from John? Hasn't *Revelation* been a big enough headache without you doing acid?' Well, I'm glad that part is over with. Unfortunately, the *Revelation* business is still going on, and it's about to get worse."

He pointed again to Robinson Patrick waving his arms on the TV screen. "And this two-bit huckster yapping on and on is as ignorant as the man behind him. Now maybe you'd better turn the sound back on. I get really worked up about this."

The astounding Reverend Patrick had moved on to the subject of stem cell research, which he neatly tied to abortion. "The Lord!" he screamed, "the Lord finds them abominable who take innocent life! He condemns them, he punishes them, and because those perverts and sinners dwell in our midst, we become collateral damage!"

Jesus slammed his fist. "Interesting to see this guy and George 'The Killer' Bush talking about collateral damage," he said through clenched teeth. "Bush is responsible for such a trail of death and suffering… but through what he claims as his belief in *me* he waits until people are *born* to start starving, alienating, torturing, and blowing them up. What a man! What a man!"

Snagg muted the TV again because everyone in the room wanted to hear what Jesus had to say.

"You know what Dad thinks about those little piles of cells in a petri dish? He thinks they are a little pile of cells that could have a thousand purposes. If they go one way, they attach to a form of immortal resonance. That boob in the cleric collar would call it a soul. It's not—it's a form of universal resonance. That's all any of us are. The cellular container—we call it a body—that develops here only lasts so long. But that's what it is, a container. I wish I could explain it to you better. But Dad's all for the container being improved, lasting longer, providing more protection and comfort to the universal resonance that spends time there. So he'd like those little piles of cells to be turned into replacement parts which could help further evolution. It'd be so nice if all the religious nuts who've tried to get power by co-opting everything I've said would do us a favor and drop dead!

"What about abortion, Jesus?" Marie had long wondered if the child she aborted could have been a better daughter than the one she raised.

"The resonance is what it is. If that 'container'—that particular body isn't coming into the world at the right time, the resonance waits. Nothing is lost. That child—that particular resonance—will be born, often into better circumstance."

Reverend Robinson Patrick was banging his little fists on the podium.

Jesus turned to watch and asked, "What's he saying now?"

Snagg restored the volume.

"Our beloved allies in Israel must be protected at all costs!" Robinson screamed. His face was red, his jowls shaking. "No matter what happens in this world—and we know that destruction could rain from the sky at any moment—whatever is happening, our friends, our allies, our beloved people of Israel must always be saved because only if Israel is saved can Jaesus return!"

Every eye in the underground room turned to see Jesus' reaction. He signaled Snagg to lower the volume again.

"It just gets better and better. The Most Honorable Reverend Robinson Patrick would be the first person to stick a stake through my Jewish heart," Jesus began with enough mirth that people in the room felt they could laugh, "Other than that, he is doing exactly what my Dad said he would."

There was a stir in the room. Clearly the particular subject made some people uneasy.

Finally a woman who had been quiet up to that point asked, "Are you implying that Israel doesn't have a right to exist?"

"Oh, not at all. It's just that it is hilarious to hear someone representing the Bush Administration talking about their passionate love of Israel."

Torque weighed in. "We've always been allies with Israel. Bush even backed them in 2006 when they invaded Lebanon and the rest of the world was objecting."

"Right. But Bush also says he cares about babies, about the environment, about *peace*! And what does it come to? It comes to the exact opposite. And it's the same with Israel."

"What do you mean?"

"Well, more will be seen in the next days, but I can tell you this. George W. Bush's grandfather, Prescott Bush—along with those other great defenders of democracy and the American way Henry Ford and Averill Harriman— was the biggest money launderer for Adolph Hitler during the 1930's and early 1940's. Bush, Ford and Harriman loved Hitler and were both staunch anti-Semites. They hated Jews and thought Hitler was a great guy. So they funneled millions of dollars into his coffers even after the start of WWII. They finally were stopped by the Federal government of the United States through the 'Trading With the Enemy Act' of 1941. If it hadn't been for that, they would have kept the money flowing openly. After that they had to do it in secret. Nobody in the Bush dynasty has expressed any remorse about their father's or their grandfather's actions. In fact, the Bush dynasty has pretty much operated in keeping with basic tenants of fascism—that is a government that's run by big business."

"But Bush says that the terrorists are 'Islamic fascists' and he hates them," Torque wasn't satisfied.

"Did you ever read George Orwell? The best way to use language against someone is to use his vocabulary and make it say the opposite of what it originally meant. But I'm talking too much. Let's hear the end of the speech."

The diminutive new leader of the National Protestant Evangelical Church of America had reached an apocalyptic frenzy, which seemed to have even gotten the attention of the Commander in Chief—at least to the extent he had it to give.

"The terrorists are rushing towards Armageddon," he screamed, "and the leftists and godless among us are greasing the wheels and plowing the great ship of America into the everlasting flames." The odd mixture of metaphors flowed past the President with pleasing speed.

"We have already seen the wages of their sins inflicted on us once," he cried. "We witnessed a moment when God turned his back on us because of the filth we have allowed in our midst! That, my brothers and sisters was the morning of September 11, 2001, when fire from the sky brought this message from God himself: allow abortion, homosexuality, false Arab religions, and communist ideas in your country at your own risk!"

Almost immediately after he was prompted to do so through his earpiece, George W. Bush began his applause and nodded his approval of something. He thought he was clapping for the end of the good reverend's speech, because with a slightly confused expression, he patted the little minister on the back.

Jesus stood up. "It's late," he said. "Even though Bush seems to think it's over, Robinson Patrick isn't done. He's still going to say that every loyal American must unquestioningly stand behind their President because he's following *me*. It boggles my senses." He looked around for a moment, appreciating the love in the room. "There is something I must take care of. But I would like to meet with you and any friends you trust tomorrow morning— say about 10 AM. There is something I need to explain." He got up and left the room. The main door never opened, but he was gone.

On the TV screen, Reverend Robinson Patrick plowed on.

CHAPTER 77

The little preacher, sensing a new stature far beyond his five foot two inch frame, wasn't finished. He had one more thing on his mind: his legacy. The President had assured him that it would be eternal, but the Reverend wasn't so sure. Something about George Bush's saying, "I've put it in God's hands," sounded vaguely obscene. So Patrick wrote a little finishing speech of his own.

He'd already blurted the "God bless you and God bless the United States of America" line that rolled by on the teleprompter. He was supposed to sit down, but he didn't. He shouted "Hallelujah," and then lowered his voice to something just above a whisper.

"My beloved friends," he began. And one might have thought he was speaking to an audience of two, not two billion. "My precious ones. I have been spoken to by the Almighty. And He has delivered unto me a final message for each and every one. He said to me, 'Robbie'—that's what He calls me—'Robbie, I wantcha to know exactly what is going on. You're doin' a heck'uv a job.'"

It struck millions of listeners as peculiar that the Divine One, the Master of the Universe, the Great Father God should reduce himself to a bad impression of George Bush. Apparently, the oddity was lost on Patrick.

"That's how He started, and then He says to me, 'Robbie, I know you have been spendin' time on your knees askin' me to tell you, so I will. You are in the *middle* of the Divine Rapture. Yes, the *middle*. I'm taking my beloveds home. I'm taking them to spend all of eternity in absolute joy with me in heaven. I know that you've been weepin' and wailin' down there thinkin' that I've left you behind. But ah, Robbie, nothing could be farther from the truth. I'm workin' on the *Big Rapture*, it's comin' just the way I need it to be. I'll be pickin' the sweet raisins out of the whole mess of sewage down there on earth.'"

At the mention of sewage, even the President seemed aware that the mighty Reverend had strayed from the script. The teleprompter was blinking "Shut up and sit down." The President was just blinking.

"'*You* Robbie, are my chosen messenger to help the world through this time. *You* are there to guide my little flock. One by one I will take them and bring them home. But *you*, Robbie, will be *the very last one taken.*'"

For a moment, the little minister countenanced supreme self-satisfaction. And perhaps he deserved that moment, for he had just delivered the ultimate justification for his being the world's religious leader, and—at the very same time—explained why he, of all people, had been left behind.

Finally acquiescing to the teleprompter's message, in one final surge of passionate discourse he shouted, "So I beseech each of you now to *follow exactly* the directives of your president and mine, the man who talks daily to God the Almighty and who is directly guided in his every move by our Lord and Savior Jesus Christ—the man of the hour, our righteous, but infinitely humble leader, George… Walker… Bush!"

It would have been a glorious end to his story, if it *had* been the end of his story.

CHAPTER 78

Even though the cement floor brought unrelieved pain to his arm, Jerrod Parker was too injured to move. He lay on his side, his breath coming in short, shallow bursts. His new acquaintance Siraj lay beside him at an odd angle. When their captors saw them speaking, they had both been dragged into solitary cells, beaten, then dragged back into the room with the filthy floor and groaning men.

Jerrod figured it had been about a day. When the soldiers left the room, a second door was sealed shut, and the light was turned off. They were in total blackness.

"God is good," Siraj said. "When it is dark, we can talk. We haven't much time. They will be back. But you must talk to someone here. You are from America. You must learn the truth."

Jerrod could sense some motion in the room. There were low moans. Whether the sounds were from current pain or to mask the sounds of movement he couldn't tell. Then Siraj's hand found his arm and traced down to his hand. A moment later he felt another hand in his.

"This is Shamsi Wahhaj," he said. "Try saying something to him."

Jerrod gripped the hand and said, "Hello my friend."

The other man responded in Arabic.

"The miracle does not happen with him," Siraj said sadly. "I will have to translate. But please, my dear American brother, listen carefully to what he tells you."

There in the darkness, in a room meant for torture, a young Saudi prince began to speak. He spoke softly and rapidly. When he paused, Siraj translated his words. And a shaken Jerrod understood why Jesus had left him in this place.

DAY SIX

MONDAY

NOVEMBER 3, 2008

CHAPTER 79

It was 6 AM in Rome. Giuseppe Fognolio, in full Papal dress, was waiting for a flash of light from the little transceiver Cardinal Vonsecco had given him. He'd pushed several heavy pieces of Papal furniture up against the door. Even though it was unlikely that Cardinal Marchese would burst in so early in the morning, he was taking no chances. Therefore, he was greatly surprised and quite frightened when he found a humble monk in a long brown robe and hemp rope belt sitting at the Papal desk. He was even more surprised to find that the monk was Black and had locks falling below his waist.

"Good morning," he signed.

The monk smiled and signed back, "Good morning. You have nothing to fear. I am a friend you have known for a long time."

Fognolio had no memory of knowing such a man, no recollection of a monk who knew sign language, and no knowledge of how he could have gotten into the apartment. But his sweet, trusting nature had him inclined to believe that the monk was telling the truth.

The monk smiled again, and signed, "I too am expecting that little light to flash letting us know Cardinal Vonsecco has arrived."

"How did you know?"

"I told you, I have been your friend for a long time."

"And you know of the third party?"

"Yes. He will arrive with the Cardinal and then we will go."

"No! We have work to do here."

"I have arranged for something else, something more effective. We will all need to go together. You have done magnificent work. I thank you."

Fognolio froze. What if the visitor was not a friend? What if spies in the Vatican knew of his discovery and planned to thwart him? How could he know for sure? When he looked up, the monk was searching his face kindly.

"I know you are worried," he signed, "but you have no need to be afraid of me. We have only to fear our enemies. It is for our mission that we must fear."

Fognolio was about to respond when the transceiver's light flashed.

"He's here," he signed moving towards the large furniture blocking the door. The monk moved to his aid, effortlessly shifting the heavy items. Fognolio opened the door slightly and looked out, then opened it wider and admitted two men. They stopped abruptly when they saw the monk. Fognolio quickly signed, "He is a friend." The men relaxed a little.

"Cardinal Vonsecco," the monk put out his hand. "I am glad you are here."

Puzzled, the Cardinal shook the monk's hand but said nothing.

"And Monsignor Popposi, I am honored."

The latter man would have shaken the monk's hand, but he was carrying a very large briefcase that required the use of both hands. He nodded and said, "Shall we begin?"

The monk shook his head. "No. It is not safe here. I have arranged something else."

Fognolio, not understanding what was being said looked apprehensive. The Monk signed so he would understand.

"Why?" Vonsecco asked.

"If we attempt the mission here, we will fail. Marchese is already on the way. You must follow me."

The thought of leaving the apartment masquerading as the Pope terrified Fognolio. He'd been willing to pose for some photographs in Papal robes to enhance the mission, but to walk through the halls of the Vatican? The thought was incomprehensible.

"You have nothing to fear," the monk signed. We will be invisible to all."

It was at that moment that the trust left three pairs of eyes. The men looked from one to the other, each supposing that they had been tricked.

"You mock us," Fognolio signed at last.

"No. I came to you in this way, because I knew if you accepted a lowly monk in your midst, you could be trusted under the difficult circumstances that are sure to come."

"You are not a monk?"

The monk raised his hands and as he lowered them, revealed himself as the Christ. This time, just to make sure he would be able to proceed quickly with the mission, he had arranged a circular glow above his head. He hated the extra show, but knew it would have a useful effect on his new compatriots.

In what seemed a single gesture, Fognolio, Vonsecco and Popposi all bowed low.

"Please rise." Jesus signed and spoke at the same time. "I will have time to explain everything to you eventually. But right now we need to leave the…"

As he spoke the door burst open and Marchese and three Swiss Guards entered in attack mode.

The three clergy drew back in terror.

"Follow me," Jesus said. "They can't see you or what you're carrying. They can't hear you. Fognolio, don't forget the Triple Crown over there. Move swiftly. Don't run into any of them, they could feel you."

It was clear that he was right. Marchese was furiously searching the room. He nearly ran into Vonsecco and a Swiss Guard came perilously close to Popposi.

Fognolio grabbed the Triple Crown. It vanished right before Marchese's eyes. He was astonished and screamed, "What the fuck?" The Swiss Guards stopped immediately and turned to him in disbelief. They had never heard such an outburst from the imperious Cardinal. Despite their years of training in stoicism, they started to laugh. Marchese glared at them.

"Repeat one word and you will rot in hell."

The poor guardsmen tried to regain their composure, giving Fognolio, Vonsecco, Popposi and Jesus ample time to exit the room.

"Where are we going?" Vonsecco asked, astonished at the ease of their escape.

"To the airport."

"But they'll stop us!"

Jesus shook his head. "Marchese cannot afford to have the faithful know that the Pope is missing and that he has been fooling the world with an imposter. He'll try to keep this completely quiet."

At Fiumicino Airport, Jesus bade his new friends goodbye. A short time later an Alitalia jet was on its way to the United States carrying the Pope, a Cardinal and a Monsignor in what appeared to be empty seats.

CHAPTER 80

Snagg and Lyla were finishing breakfast. Deemon and Marie were having coffee and a spirited conversation. Other people filtered in from the tunnels and began to eat. A young man named Pappo, who obviously had been seriously burned, came to the doorway. A tattoo artist had turned the rough, twisted portions of his face and neck into something that resembled a Van Gogh portrait. Bright colors filled the areas between the ridges. The result was nothing if not beautiful.

"Hey Snagg," he called. "Guess who's coming to breakfast?"

Snagg turned around just in time to see Jesus walking through the door. Pappo slung an arm around Jesus' shoulder in a friendly way and said, "Who'd a' ever thought?"

"Do you have any bagels?" Jesus was clearly hungry.

Snagg nodded and pointed to the table.

"Bagels and cream cheese! Perfect."

Marie turned back to Deemon. "If my daughter could have heard that Jesus likes bagels and cream cheese—I think she'd have gone a little easier on me!"

Bagels and bowls of cereal in hand, the group gathered around Jesus.

"What is it you're going to tell us?" Lyla was the first to ask.

"Most of you already know this," he said, flicking some toasted onion off his lap. "But it's worth putting the first part of the picture together. It hit me last night when Robinson Patrick was catwallering about September 11 and the terrorists, that some of the pieces might not be clear to everyone. I started telling you about Bush's ties to the Nazis. So you've got that. The Israel connection will get clearer in time. But for now, a quick look at September 11, 2001 is necessary, because the next days will test all of us. The more we know, the better we'll fare.

"In short, 9/11 was an inside job. Of course there was outside help, I'll get to that, but essentially it was the product of a cabal of neo conservatives who needed a big event to swing things their direction.

"In 1997, Jeb Bush, Donald Rumsfeld, Dick Cheney, Bill Kristol, John Bolton and 20 other men formed *The Project for the New American Century.* For all their patriotic posturing, they were really coming together to outline how the United States could maintain world supremacy through the application of fascist principles. Their goal is nothing less than imperial domination of the world, including its oil supplies. And, as you'll see, some of them have one objective beyond that. In 2000, they published a document called "Rebuilding America's Defenses." They said that the revolutionary change they were calling for would move slowly unless there was a "new Pearl Harbor." That refers to the Japanese Imperial Army's attack on U.S. forces in 1941, which marked the beginning of America's involvement in World War II. It is interesting that they chose that particular event, because it is well known that the President of the United States, Franklin Delano Roosevelt, knew of this attack in advance and did nothing to stop it. That attack changed public opinion and enabled him to declare war. The events of September 11 were orchestrated by persons in the United States government with the cooperation of foreign operatives to sway American opinion and have them back the takeover of the Middle East as proposed by The Project for the New American Century."

Marie raised her hand and Jesus acknowledged her. "What about Osama bin Laden? He *was* the mastermind, wasn't he?"

Jesus shook his head. "All part of the convenient picture," he said. "Osama bin Laden has been an operative of the U.S. government since the U.S. first invented the Muhajadeen as a force to draw the USSR into a Vietnam-like quagmire in Afghanistan. Bin Laden proved exceedingly cooperative. When the USSR was successfully repelled and the Muhajadeen morphed into the Taliban, the U.S. government continued its support. Without the protection of the USSR, the conditions of the Afghan people regressed by a century. Women were no longer able to get educations, were required to wear burkas, and the secular state was abolished. Death and mutilation became the standard punishments for disagreements with the state.

"While this was occurring, the United States, with its de facto emissary Donald Rumsfeld, was active in establishing the regime of Saddam Hussein in Iraq. It was during Rumsfeld's 1983 visit that Saddam secured the neurotoxins he would eventually use on the Kurds. The supplier? The United

States, with Ronald Reagan's blessings.

"The weapons used in Iraq's long war with Iran were largely provided by the United States. In exchange, U.S. contractors grew rich."

Marie was getting impatient. "And Bin Laden?" she asked again.

"Bin Laden was the 'ace up the sleeve' that the meticulous planners of the fascist takeover of American held until the perfect moment."

"So he was behind the 9/11 attacks?"

Jesus knew his next sentence was going to rattle even the most progressive people in the room, so he waited, and then spoke slowly. "He sincerely *thinks* he was."

"What do you mean?" The question came from several parts of the room.

"That will become clear in the next days," Jesus said.

Deemon wanted to know more. "But Bin Laden, he keeps making those videotapes threatening more attacks, keeps calling on all Muslims to join the jihad."

"I will tell you this," Jesus was choosing his words carefully. "Osama bin Laden *thinks* that he is a free man, *thinks* that the messages he is sending are in opposition to the United States, and *thinks* that he has successfully evaded the Bush Administration. He sincerely believes that. He is, however, as completely under the control of the neo-cons as he was on 9/11. The deal cut with the Saudi Royal family has guaranteed that the Bushites will jointly control the world's oil, and that Osama bin Laden will be the eternally elusive fall guy. When his usefulness has been depleted he will be "eliminated"—at least that is what people will be led to believe. However, his body will never be found.

"But I need to move to other topics. This will get clearer to you. It is best that you wait until you see the evidence before you."

Marie still wasn't satisfied. "Are you saying that Bush is…"

Jesus stopped her with an uncustomary sharpness. "I'm sorry, Marie, that is all I should say about a relatively minor player in that part of the story… at least for now. Please, I have very little time and need you all to be prepared."

Marie, unaccustomed to being stopped, nevertheless acquiesced.

Jesus got back to the timeline. "For a long time anyone believing that the attack on the World Trade Centers was an inside job was considered a 'conspiracy theory nut.' Just as they thought anyone who opposed the Iraq war was a 'traitor.' But time has proved otherwise.

"Everything pointed to by careful observers of 9/11 is true. It's common knowledge now that the planes that hit the Trade Centers didn't cause the towers to fall, but that they came down in a controlled demolition from nano-explosive paint installed months before 9/11. The Pentagon was not hit by an airplane, but rather by a missile. That is why there was only a small hole in the Pentagon's side, and no plane parts or bodies were ever found. And Flight 93 didn't crash during a struggle with the passengers. It was shot down by the military in order to protect the secrets of those in power. Don't forget that Donald Rumsfeld slipped during a Christmas speech in Iraq in 2005 and said the plane was 'shot down.'"

Deemon moved from the corner to sit closer to Jesus. "They'd do it again in a minute, wouldn't they?"

"I'm afraid so."

"What have they got in mind?"

Jesus looked at a small alarm clock on the bookshelf next to him. "I'm running short on time. I want you to have a brief outline so that you will understand what is going to be happening in the next few days. The same people are still at work trying to make sure that they maintain power. They could never maintain that power in a democracy, so they are doing it through tried and true fascist methods. The detention centers are just one example. That is all going to become vividly clear soon."

The room was quiet. Jesus was preaching to people who already questioned the government, but to hear the facts from him was a confirmation of their deepest suspicions.

"So Bush is behind this world takeover?" someone asked.

"Bush is a very willing participant, but he isn't smart enough or interested enough to craft the details. Behind his back the real powers call him the *doofus*. He just goes out and says whatever it is that they need him to say. Of course, he's not keen enough to do it right all the time, but he's completely their puppet. His reward is drugs, satisfaction of his very peculiar sexual tastes, and more vacations than any president in history."

Jesus looked at his watch. "I'm going to have to cut this short," he said. "It may be morning, but I haven't slept in two days, and I've got some big events coming up. Lyla, Marie, Deemon and Snagg, you will be taking a flight tomorrow. I'll explain everything when I wake up."

With that, Jesus left a room full of people who knew they were on the verge of something huge and undefined.

CHAPTER 81

For eight hours, Jerrod Parker moved from one position to another on the concrete floor, each time being introduced to another captive by Siraj. The pain in his face, the ache in his arms, the stench of tightly packed bodies—all was forgotten as an overwhelming picture came together in his mind, one piece of information at a time. If his mysterious visitor had not been so convincing, so utterly *human* in his presence and touch, Jerrod would have thought he was hallucinating. But now, as one wretched soul after another whispered to him, poured out eyewitness accounts that countered everything he had heard or read, he knew why Jesus had allowed him to remain in this horror.

With a crash, the door at the end of the room flew open bringing blinding light. It was coming from a single bulb, but to eyes accustomed to total darkness it was painful.

"Hey Towelheads! God you motherfuckers stink. Time to get your asses in the air for prayers. Get those butts in the air." A soldier armed with an automatic rifle stood in the doorway. His boot connected with someone unlucky enough to be near. Jerrod tried to look around. He could see about fifty naked men in front of him and figured there was room for another twenty behind him. They began to move, and despite their nakedness assumed a position of prayer. Jerrod joined them.

"Hey Sandbunnies. Get your faces down on the fucking floor." A boot came down on the back of a man's head, slamming him face-first onto the concrete. The tip of a rifle found its way between the man's buttocks. "You motherfuckers deaf? Pray to your fucking Allah. He likes it when you lick the floor. I wanna see those tongues out making love to the concrete. Let's go!"

The floor, smeared with feces, urine, sweat and vomit was the last place that Jerrod wanted to place his tongue. But the soldier, followed by others, was making the rounds of the room and coming dangerously near him.

"Jerrod." The voice was familiar. "Jerrod, get up."

Jerrod knew he couldn't stand even if ordered to by a man with a gun.

"I can't," he said. "My legs are shackled and numb and my wrists are tied."

"Yes you can."

"I can't," he repeated before realizing that he was standing already.

"Jerrod, it's me."

Terrified, Jerrod turned and looked into the face of Jesus.

"Get out of here!" He was trying to whisper, but he realized that his voice was uncontrollable and came out louder than it should. "They'll kill you."

"They can't see me. They can't hear us. Your ankles are no longer shackled, and see? Your wrists are free."

"Please, don't do this. They're going to kill me!"

"They can't see you either. Now just follow me."

"I can't. They'll shoot."

"Trust me, Jerrod. They cannot see you."

"I can't leave these men—look at them! Look what they are doing to them! All night they told me that…"

"I know." Jesus put his hand on Jerrod's shoulder. "You're going to have to trust me. Our mission is almost complete. Follow me. You're going to have to walk. I don't have the power to transport you. But if we hurry, you'll be on your way home."

"I can't leave these men like this, just walk away and do nothing."

"You're about to liberate them in a way you can't imagine. But it will be for nothing if you don't trust me and follow."

Jerrod turned to Siraj. The poor man had his tongue on the filthy floor and was openly weeping. "Good-bye my friend. I will honor your request. I will tell the story I have learned." It was clear that Siraj could neither see nor hear him.

"Let's go." Jesus pointed to the door. "Watch your step and don't bump the soldiers. They would feel you even though they can't see you. You are only a half resonance away from them."

Once out of the room, Jesus led Jerrod through a long corridor and out into the open air. In the distance a helicopter sat inside the razor wire perimeter. "You're getting on that copter," Jesus said, gently hurrying Jerrod along. "You will land in Florida. And then, this is what I need you to do…"

By the time Jerrod squeezed himself into a space in the cargo area of the helicopter, he had memorized everything he was supposed to do. He could see Jesus standing by the landing pad. The rotors began to turn the wind blowing Jesus's heavy locks out behind him—just before he disappeared.

CHAPTER 82

A Chyron on the studio monitor read:

"FOX BREAKING NEWS"

Then a voiceover began accompanied by footage of African Americans walking on the street.

"This is Dana Jeffries reporting from Washington. An unidentified source has confirmed that this afternoon the Department of Homeland Security will issue the following urgent warning: Based on studies conducted by four government agencies, it is incumbent on all Americans to be aware of a new threat to the homeland. It is believed that it is possible that there is a heightened degree of probability that Al Queda is targeting African Americans to recruit them to terrorist activity. Although these beliefs have not been substantiated, the populace should be aware that African Americans may be more susceptible to Al Queda propaganda than other races. If you hear an African American person speaking against the War in Iraq, Afghanistan, Iran, Turkey, or talking in negative terms about this nation's occupation of Columbia and Venezuela, please contact the Department of Homeland Security immediately on the Patriot's Hot Tips line. The study further indicates that there is some reason to believe that certain unnamed mosques may be encouraging young men NOT to enlist in the Armed Forces. If this should prove to be true, it lends credence to the heightened suspicion of African Americans.

"This is Dana Jeffries reminding you that FOX is your unbiased news source."

FADE TO BLACK

"And cut to commercial. Nice work, Karl." Etian Frank took off his headset and headed for Karl Rove who sat in the recording booth. "We morphed your voice perfectly."

"Thanks, Etian. Boy, this one is fun. I've been wanting to put darkies in the crosshairs for longer'n I can remember. Thank you Mr. Al Queda."

"Hey Karl!"

"Yeah?"

"Mr. Al Queda says, you're welcome."

There followed hearty laughter in the sub-basement of the White House.

CHAPTER 83

After her disastrous attempt to interview them, the last people Babs Waller expected to hear from were Chandra Boolean and Hogan Cafferty. But that is exactly who her secretary announced.

"Ms. Waller?" It was Chandra's voice.

"Yes."

"This is Chandra Boolean. I'm sorry that our interview was interrupted."

"Those things happen," Waller said curtly, not meaning to be conciliatory in any way. "What do you want?"

"Well, since you were kind enough to want me to tell my side of the story with Winslow's disappearance… even though we didn't get to tape it… I wanted you to be the first to know about something taking place."

"Yes?"

"Ms. Waller, if I tell you what I know, you have to keep it absolutely quiet or you will certainly not have an exclusive. In fact, you might not be able to get in."

"An exclusive about what where? I don't have time to play games."

Chandra paused. She was doing exactly what Jesus had instructed her to do in her Denver living room, but now it seemed terribly risky. She knew Babs Waller's reputation as a ruthless snake and was fearful that one mistake could put many people, including her children, in danger.

Hogan motioned to her, "Go ahead, Chandra." Adam, sitting in his wheelchair to her left seconded the motion.

"Are you there, Ms. Boolean?" Waller's voice achieved a razor edge.

"Yes," Chandra answered after a brief pause. "I want to be sure that I can really trust you."

"Ms. Boolean, I have built a career on trust. If I give you my word…"

"Yes, I know. I'm not questioning that," Chandra didn't like lying, but it was necessary at the moment. "It's just that there is something so big, and

I have to know that—in order to protect your own career—that what I'm about to tell you will remain absolutely between you and me."

"I am the consummate professional. Anyone can tell you that."

"Something of great importance is taking place at Denver's Jesus Dome tomorrow night. Should you decide to come to Denver, your crew can't know the real reason they're coming."

"Such cloak and daggers."

Chandra ignored the remark. "When you arrive, I will guarantee you the interview of your life. You will not only have an exclusive that brings you world attention, but you will also be asked to serve as host one of the most important events of all time."

"Oh please. What's happening? The Pope's wedding?"

"No."

"So get on with it. Explain. Frankly, Ms. Boolean, your disappearance and the failure of our interview did upset me. I think it was irresponsible of you to go running away just because…"

"I want you to have an exclusive interview with the man calling himself Jesus—before anyone else gets to him."

Babs Waller immediately pressed the record button on her monitoring device. This was the interview she had vowed to get and now it was within reach. "Go ahead," she said in a voice far more calm than she felt.

"You will have a sit down interview with Jesus prior to a major event at the Jesus Dome tomorrow night."

"Where is he?" Babs asked with more passion than she intended. She wanted to sound cool, slightly disinterested, but her question betrayed her.

"It sounds like you're excited about this, Ms. Waller."

"I am a professional. I've done thousands of interviews. They all excite me," the brittle woman replied.

"Then maybe it would be best for me to find someone else who would see it as the coup of a lifetime."

Hooked! The veiled threat got her.

"Where do you want me to be?"

"You are to be at the Jesus Dome in Denver at 4:15 PM tomorrow. The interview will be at 4:30 sharp. Is that enough time for your crew to set up?

"It will be no problem. We'll see you tomorrow. I can ask anything, right?"

"I suppose so. Apparently Jesus has some subjects he would like to address. I don't have to tell you that with an interview like this, you may not be entirely in charge."

Hooked! Second barb hit its mark.

"Ms. Boolean, I can assure you that I know how to conduct an interview, no matter *who* it is with."

"Very well, Ms. Waller. We'll see you here at the Jesus Dome tomorrow at 4:30. Oh, and Ms. Waller, Jesus has formally invited you to host the televised portion of the evening as well."

"What is the event going to be?"

"I have no more information than I've told you other than that by tomorrow night the whole world will be tuned in."

"I suppose I could oblige you with that." Babs Waller was shaking. She had vowed to find Jesus and report on him, but an exclusive was almost too good to bear. "Until tomorrow." Within minutes of hanging up, Babs had assembled a crew and was on her way to the airport.

"Way to go, Chandra!" Adam beamed. "Old Babsy Waller is on her way!" He did a wheelie and skidded to a stop. "Do you think she'll go through with the whole thing?"

Chandra shrugged. "I have no idea. I'm just a foot soldier—isn't that what they say? I just hope Jesus wasn't part of some reality show pulling a gag on us. He's been right so far. Remember how crazy it sounded when he said we were going to be having a huge meeting in the Jesus Dome?"

"And now you own it…" Adam was elated.

Hogan hugged her, "Oh ye of little faith," he said. "I think we had better get started on the security strategy."

On the East coast, another part of the story was unfolding.

CHAPTER 84
NEW YORK, NY—9:00 AM EST

While the 24 hour news channels continued their barrage of stories about celebrity break-ups, dog rescues and fashion tips, NPR and several Pacifica stations managed to squeeze in some hard news.

This is Democracy Now, the War and Peace Report, I'm Amy Goodman. Riot police and National Guard troops have quelled mass uprisings in Detroit, Los Angeles, Cleveland, Philadelphia, Atlanta, Houston, Newark, Chicago, and in Harlem. Demonstrators in each of the cities were protesting the suspension of presidential elections, demanding an end to war, and also demanding information about the mass disappearances. At least 40,000 arrests were made nationwide overnight. According to our sources, those arrested have been taken to local baseball and football stadiums that we have learned were all designed to serve as detention centers. The stadiums, reportedly, have been pressed into service since the Halliburton Detention Centers have already been filled to capacity. We are trying to confirm reports that many of those detention centers are filled exclusively with children under the age of sixteen. The children, most of them orphaned through the recent disappearances, have been arrested for curfew violations. Pacifica reporters are trying to verify these stories as quickly as possible, but their efforts are being hampered by the military. We will continue to monitor this… What are you doing? Get away from me! Leave those microphones alone! Ladies and gentlemen, police in riot gear have broken into our Firehouse Studio…"

Democracy Now disappeared from the air.

CHAPTER 85

Jesus had been specific in his instructions. Taking care of detail was something Chandra Boolean did well, so at exactly 1 PM she sent her private jet from Denver International Airport bound for Newark International Airport in New Jersey. Her pilot was aware that he was to pick up four passengers without questioning them no matter what their appearance. As soon as she saw her plane take off, Chandra hurried to follow Jesus' next instruction: to meet an important, unannounced guest arriving on Alitalia at 1:35 PM. Leaving her private hanger, she donned a light brunette wig, put on horn-rimmed dark glasses and ran to the central commercial terminal. Hogan was waiting for her when she arrived, breathless from the run.

"Who are we expecting?" Hogan asked when Chandra settled down next to him. "The arrival info says it's from Rome."

"You know as well as I do. All I know is that you and I are supposed to be here in Jeppesen Terminal near the fountain to meet three people on an Alitalia flight at 1:35. This is the right spot. That gate right there is where people come in from all three concourses. We should know what's happening in the next fifteen or twenty minutes. Did you talk to Adam?"

"Yeah, he's at the house waiting. I don't know what time the others are supposed to arrive, so it's good to know he's got that end covered. You think this is all for real?" Hogan couldn't shake his doubts.

"Cold feet, love?"

At the mention of love Hogan felt no cold. He blushed. "About last night," he finally stammered.

"Shhh. It was beautiful. Now I know why you didn't disappear with the others."

"If it was the Rapture…"

"It couldn't have been, because they didn't take you." Chandra reached for Hogan's hand and held it gently. "Hogan, whatever has brought us together is a lot bigger than anything I've experienced before. And our… connection… last night was just confirmation of that."

A sudden rush of security personnel past them broke the mood.

"They're heading towards arriving flights," Hogan was already on his feet.

"Do you think something has gone wrong?"

"I don't know. I don't want to get in the middle of anything. Someone could recognize us."

Uniformed officers and airline employees were swarming through and around the entrance. A crowd began to gather to watch what was happening.

There was another disturbance. Chandra and Hogan looked back towards the fountains and saw a group of Roman Catholic clergy hurrying in their direction led by the Archbishop of Denver, Jason Kaput. His flowing red robes with their familiar black piping made quite a show in the brightly lit, very modern airport.

The Archbishop was clearly in a rage as he approached the checkpoint. Spotting an Alitalia employee he shouted, "Why isn't there a bigger show of security? Why wasn't I given proper notice?"

The airline employee was polite but firm. "The pilot was under orders not to notify Denver authorities until thirty minutes ago."

"What right has he?"

"It was a direct order from the Pope himself," the employee said, not more than a little pleased to be able to hold her own with the Archbishop.

"The Pope!" Chandra, overhearing, sank into her chair. "Could that be who…"

"Well, we did speak to Jesus about this and he told us to meet someone arriving here at 1:35." Hogan was enjoying the event as much as the airline employee.

Security personnel began to emerge from the main gate, followed by Cardinal Vonsecco, Monsignor Popposi, and Giuseppe Fognolio in full Papal regalia. They were followed by a short white monk wearing a brown tunic.

The Archbishop and his attendants and a number of people in the crowd dropped to their knees in the presence of the perceived deity. They were signaled to rise by the Pope.

"Your Holiness," the Archbishop began.

Vonsecco stepped forward. "His Holiness has laryngitis," he began, "so has asked me to speak for him. Are our friends here?"

"Who?" The Archbishop rose to his feet, rather deflated at the lack of formal greeting.

"Our anticipated friends, are they here?"

The monk whispered to Vonsecco who made some discrete signs to Fognolio. The Pontiff then spotted two people who were standing towards the back of the crowd. He nodded to them.

"We should be on our way immediately," Vonsecco said, gesturing to Fognolio.

The Archbishop once again asserted his position, "I am the Archbishop of Denver. I have arranged the transportation for His Holiness."

"If you don't mind," Vonsecco replied, "the Holy Father has urgent business with certain people and wishes to travel with them. If you could just stand aside. Did you call for an electric car?"

"No, no, I just found out that…"

"Well, call one. Please."

Reduced to a position of servitude, the Archbishop moved to the ticket desk and asked that the employee send a golf cart for the Pope.

In his silent world, Fognolio was enjoying every minute of the ruse. It was clear that he had been right, Marchese was afraid to notify authorities. He decided that he would play his role to the hilt, so he began making motions of blessing towards the crowd that was increasing in size by the moment.

People, overwhelmed by their chance meeting with the Pope were pressing towards Fognolio, kneeling, and touching the hem of his robe.

With seeming casualness, Vonsecco led his company towards the spot where Chandra and Hogan were waiting. Chandra wasn't sure what to do upon meeting a Pope, so she bowed. Hogan, whose background in Protestantism was still painfully influential, just smiled. He had no more idea than Chandra that Fognolio was a Vatican-created impostor. All he knew was that Jesus had given explicit instructions for them to wait in Jeppesen to meet four individuals at 1:35.

An electric cart arrived and Vonsecco hurried Fognolio and Popposi in its direction. The monk urged Hogan to join Chandra in the front seat and then in the confusion, unobtrusively disappeared into the crowd.

The driver had to honk his horn frequently to part the hoards of onlookers now gathering for a sight of the Pope. By the time they reached the main exit, there were crowds of reporters waiting.

"Okay, Chandra. Now's the time to open and read the message Jesus gave you. He said that we'd be facing reporters after we picked up our guests and it looks like he was right again."

While Fognolio, Vonsecco and Popposi got into Chandra's waiting limousine, Chandra turned to face the cameras. She carefully opened the envelope Jesus had given her, took off her dark glasses and began to read—every word being captured by the national media assembled.

"That's Chandra Boolean," a reporter shouted. "Ms. Boolean. Ms. Boolean." But Chandra was undeterred.

"Ladies and Gentleman," she began. "I am very pleased that you are here to welcome the Holy Father to the United States. He is here on a matter of utmost importance and urgency. There are developments in the world—some of them taking place at this very moment—which demanded the Pontiff's presence. He will be in seclusion for the rest of the day, but will be making a major speech tomorrow night, here in Denver. You, the national and local press, will be able to cover that event. That will be tomorrow night at nine o'clock… at the Jesus Dome." Her message delivered, Chandra got into the limousine followed by Hogan.

Reporters were shouting questions to Chandra.

"Mrs. Boolean! Any news from your husband?"

"Mrs. Boolean, what do you think of the people who believe you were behind your husband's disappearance?"

"Mrs. Boolean, do you intend to keep your children? Are you glad they were left behind with you?"

The limousine had just pulled away from the stunned crowd of reporters when Archbishop Kaput ran out of the terminal, gasping for air. Apparently there had been no golf cart for him.

"Your Eminence," called a reporter, "what is the nature of the Pontiff's visit to Denver?"

Caught completely off guard, not having heard Chandra's announcement, the blushing and sweating Archbishop attempted to look in control of the situation. "I have invited the Holy Father to Denver… for a very special occasion that I will announce shortly," he said, trying to be as vague as possible without revealing the fact that he knew absolutely nothing.

"Would that be the speech that was just announced by Chandra Hogan that's taking place tomorrow night at the Jesus Dome?"

"Uh, yes, yes, that is the meeting that I am referring to," Kaput replied, wondering how in the world he was getting mixed up with the very controversial Chandra Hogan and the very Protestant, very Pentecostal and

Apocalyptic Jesus Dome.

"Is this visit about the disappearances at the Jesus Dome, Sir?"

Here, Kaput knew he had gotten himself into something that would be impossible to reverse if he went further. "I'm sorry," he said. "We must leave immediately."

"Are you going to be with the Pope?"

Not wanting to have his power undercut, Kaput snapped, "Of course!"

"Where was the Pope headed?"

Here, Kaput failed to exercise much judgment at all. His ego was so bruised by what he perceived as the Vatican's slight of him, that he wanted to soothe it at all costs. "He has gone to the Archdiocese, of course!" he said turning to get into a limousine that failed to materialize. "Get the car!" he hissed at a beleaguered attendant. "Get the car!"

"I sent the driver around the traffic circle, your Eminence, so we wouldn't have to pay these ridiculous parking fees."

"You idiot!" the chubby Archbishop screamed. Cameras clicked, video rolled, and printing presses went into high gear.

Within hours Denver was the focus of national headlines with photographs of Kaput screaming at his cowering aide with captions like, "Time for Archbishop's Confession," "Pope Arrives in Denver, Is Archbishop Kaput?" and "Will Holy Father Make Kaput Disappear at Jesus Dome?"

However, in the immediate wake of the Archbishop's gaffs, the rush of press, police, and politicos to the Archdiocese cleared the way for Chandra's limousine to have a traffic-free drive to her mansion.

With the Pope as her houseguest, Chandra was little prepared for her next arrivals.

CHAPTER 86

The President didn't like to have his schedule interrupted. His Texas vacation had already been postponed because of the disappearances. The aggregate number was approaching 35 million domestically and nearly half a billion internationally, but his department of Total Information had somehow managed to keep both numbers from being reported by media. A few independent outlets were giving accurate figures, but the networks and the big five newspapers were, so far, playing the Administration's game.

Jay Leno had inadvertently come the closest to telling the truth the night before in a joke that definitely bombed with the White House. "George Bush is a busy fella these days," the comedian said with his usual straight face before the punch line. "Yeah, he's just working his tail off. He's been running around the White House lawn looking under all the shrubs. He heard that there's about half a billion things missing, and he thought they were Weapons of Mass Destruction. I mean, the guy's got a right to find them at least *once!*" Kevin Eubanks laughed dutifully from the bandstand, but the audience sat in shocked silence. Apparently the number "half a billion" meant something to them.

Now the phone was ringing again. It was a private line, but when the private line rang, it had already gone through the White House operators and a private secretary. He had to take the call. He threw the $100 bill onto the desk, wiped his nose, and answered the phone.

"Yeah?"

It was his secretary, Madeline Fontaigne. "There's a call for you, Sir."

"Yeah, I guessed that since the phone was ringing. I told you I was busy for the next hour."

"It's been three hours, Sir."

"Well, I'm busy."

"I think this is a call you should take. It's from Sergei Vasillich."

Sergei Vasillich, the new director of the CIA, had been named by the President when a scandal involving the former director, Jorge Renta, forced his resignation. The President felt that reports concerning Renta's complicity in the sale of children's body parts—albeit in a country considered unimportant—would hurt contributions to the Republican party, so in a hastily arranged press conference he awarded Renta the Presidential Medal of Honor, announced that he'd done a "heckuva job," and pointed the disgraced ex-employee to obscurity with a large pension and bonus.

Vasillich was not lacking in baggage, but Total Information effectively erased his questionable past. Since he assumed his post during a congressional recess, there had been no confirmation process to date.

Even a message from the head of the CIA was an annoyance to George. Wasn't it enough that he made public appearances, got dressed for dinner and paddled off to the bedroom with Laura? He considered himself a simple man. "Give me some brush to clear, a gram of coke and I'm a happy cowboy," he'd often say to Karl Rove when he was sure the microphones were off.

But now the phone had interrupted his bliss, there was no brush to clear in Washington, and the bureaucracy expected him to be on call. Deciding to get the conversation over with quickly, he answered the blinking line.

"What do you want?" he demanded, forgoing the usual niceties associated with the presidency.

"Mr. President?"

"Who do you think this is? Some comic? Yeah, it's me. What, you don't like your job already or something? Heh, heh."

"I'm sorry to disturb you, Sir. I know that you have an impossibly heavy schedule."

George W.'s smirk got larger than usual. He bent over and picked up a dust bunny from beneath his desk and flicked it in the air. "It's heavy, all right," he said, trying to make sure he continued his brusk tone.

"Sir, we have a situation and it's going to require immediate action on your part."

"Talk to Karl."

"No sir, I would rather talk to you."

"Talk to Karl anyway. I'm feeling too good right now for some urgent business."

"Sir, I am talking about national security."

The phrase *national security* was on a list that Karl Rove had given George to memorize. They were phrases which, when he heard them, meant he was to look serious, cut the smirk, try not so say "heh, heh," and then shut up and listen— and *only* listen. He was not to make any off the cuff remarks when phrases on the list were mentioned. *National Security, alternative energy, freedom of the press,* and *graduate education* were on the list, as were phrases like *take a hit* and *doin' 420.* The list continued to grow. He was never again to discuss the books he read since he announced to the world that he had read "three Shakespeares" and that his reading list was "ekelectic." Now Vasillich had used one of the *high caution phrases* and George's deer in the headlights expression appeared for real.

"Mr. President?"

"I'm listening." That was the response Karl said was the safest.

"Mr. President, we have some very troubling news coming out of Denver." Vasillich's tone could have depressed Pollyanna.

"I hate Missouri, won't go there," George said, frowning at the thought of the mosquito infested swamps in the state where his brother was governor.

"Denver is in Colorado, Sir."

"I don't like the mosquitos there," he spurted. "Even if my brother is the governor, I won't go there."

"That was Florida, Sir."

"I'm listening." Lesson learned.

"You know that the Pope made an unscheduled appearance at the Denver airport this morning."

"He's Catholic!"

"Yes sir."

"Don't like 'em, never have. I went there to see him at his house in France and they made me bend over and kiss his ring and call him 'your holiness.' Damn worst thing I ever had to do—almost—and I hate those French people… whatever it is that they call 'em. Oh yeah, the 'Paris heathens.'"

"That's Parisians, Sir, and the Pope lives in Italy."

"Never been to that city. And I'm not goin' there any more than to this Denver place."

"Sir please, time is of the essence here. We have reason to believe that the announced appearance of the Pope tomorrow night at the Jesus Dome is linked in some way to the disappearances. The governor of Colorado wants you to send the National Guard to defend the Jesus Dome. There are over 37 million Americans missing, Sir. That news cannot be withheld effectively much longer. If the Pope knows the truth and makes reference to those numbers, if he has access to information about the cause of the disappearances, if this nation is under some form of terrorist attack either from another country or from alien abductors and the Pope in any way indicates that your Administration has been derelict in its duty… it could spark riots or a civil war. What do you think? Are you willing to take decisive action?"

"I'm listening." George was terribly confused at the moment. Vacillich was doing a lot of talking and using a lot of big words. It seemed like he was asking for something, but when he used the word *derelict*, George thought Vacillich was referring to him. *Derelict* was on one of the words on Karl's list that he wasn't supposed to get into.

"Mr. President?"

"I'm listening."

"Will you take action?"

"Call Karl." The bewildered commander in chief hung up and fumbled around his desk for his $100 bill and a razor blade. His good humor returned when, blade in hand, he remembered how worried his mother, Barbara, was when she had discovered a blade on his desk. "You'll cut yourself, George," she'd said. "You'll slice one of your pretty fingers. Use scissors—and don't run with them." His mother, bless her, always knew just the right thing to say. "Big Babs," he'd said to her one day, "you always know just what to say. When the whole country was shedding crocodile tears about all those welfare darkies down there in the state of New Orleans, and were all going 'boo hoo' about them gettin' to stay at that big convention center, you just cut through all the bull crap. You pointed out that all of 'em were comin' from nothin' so that our accommodations were workin' out well for 'em. Hell, most of 'em got on television, and I'll guarantee *that's* somethin' they would'a never got t'do without us!"

The phone was ringing again. "Gosh it to heck," he mumbled picking up the receiver. "What?" he practically screamed.

It was his secretary. "Sir, Mr. Vacillich is on the line again. He is demanding to talk to you and says that if you don't answer, he's taking this directly to the press."

"Left wing, liberal biased, communist leaning bunch of pinko liars is what *they* are."

"Who?"

"The people he's going to take his story to."

"Sir, take the call. I'm telling you, take the call."

"Is it okay with Karl? This guy was using some of the words on my list."

"For God's sake, Mr. President, this is the head of the CIA. He says it is urgent and a matter of national security!"

"That's why I got off the phone. *National Security* is on Karl's list." He heard a click and then Vasillich's voice.

"Mr. President?"

"Yeah, I'm listening."

"Mr. President, I don't want to have the Pope begin a national stampede tomorrow night. And sir, there is one more thing. I didn't want to be an alarmist until I was certain, but sir. . ."

"What? You keep calling. I'm getting confused. I've got lots of things on my mind—these next days I have to give a lot of talks and sign a lot of papers. We're about to make *Jesus* come back!"

"You know?"

"Know what?"

"About Jesus!"

"Of course I know about Jesus. I've been learnin' about him all my life. I've given speeches where I even say things about how I believe in his principles."

"What are you talking about?" Vasillich was far beyond the loss of patience.

"Jesus. You're the one who brought it up. We're about to make sure Armageddon happens so he can come back and take everybody to heaven."

"I'm not talking about Operation Omniscient Scepter."

"Then what *are* you talking about? You know what the Pope is coming here for?"

Vasillich screamed, "I'm not talking about the Pope right now. Everything there is on track. I'm talking about the guy who showed up at the stock exchange, made hundreds of people disappear, who said he was Jesus Christ, and who has just waved his fairy wand over 37 million people in the US alone!"

"I'm listening." George wasn't supposed to comment on any number higher than he could count on his fingers.

"I need you to mobilize the Army and the Marines in Denver. I need you to order a patrol around the entire city and particularly around the Jesus

Dome. We need to apprehend this Jesus fellow if he should actually appear, and we sure as hell need to prevent some all-out panic if people find out what's really been going on. Look what's been happening in the streets with the little information that's leaked out."

"What do you want from me?"

"Sir, I just told you. I need a full military callout to Denver."

"Well, if you talk to Karl tell him I said it was okay."

Fifteen minutes later, National Guard troops and six Army battalions were mobilized and heading towards the Jesus Dome in Denver. They had explicit instructions 1) to guard private property, and 2) to kill Jesus Christ on sight.

CHAPTER 87

During the drive from the airport, Cardinal Vonsecco alternately spoke for himself and interpreted Fognolio's sign language. There was no more astonished audience anywhere in the world than in that limousine as the story of the Pope's disappearance and the deception involving Fognolio unfolded. Chandra and Hogan were particularly struck by a vague reference to some information Fognolio had discovered and had been ordered by Jesus to make public at the Jesus Dome.

At first Chandra was in a near panic wondering what one serves a pope for dinner. But Fognolio, Vonsecco and Popposi were such excellent company that even before she knew that this Pontiff was an imposter, she had relaxed and decided what to thaw.

It was nothing but good fortune that Archbishop Kaput had drawn so much attention at the airport and, for ego reasons, given incorrect information about the Pope's destination. Hogan was able quickly to drive the limousine away from the airport and take back roads to Chandra's home. Once the electronic gates closed behind them, they were safe. Guests inside, Hogan parked the limo in the huge garage.

"Mr. Fognolio thinks you have a beautiful home," Vonsecco said, interpreting the weary Pontiff's signs.

Chandra smiled. "Thank you. It was a very nice place to live at one time. Now it's just our place to hide… until tomorrow."

Her cellphone rang. She answered and left the room as she began to speak to someone about security at the Jesus Dome.

"Let me show you your rooms," Adam said wheeling towards a hallway. There are a few steps, so I'll just get you that far and then you're on your own. You may want to change clothes or…"

"I'm afraid the vestments we are wearing are the only clothes we have," Vonsecco said. "Since we will need them tomorrow, perhaps there are clothes we could temporarily use?"

"Of course. Right down there—the huge closets in that room—they used to belong to… the master of the house." Adam pointed towards Winslow Boolean's enormous suite.

"Hogan!" It was Chandra. "Hogan!"

Hogan ran in from the garage wing. "What?"

"I think more of our guests are here." Chandra was watching a TV monitor. A car driven by a very blonde woman was pulling up to the front gates. Chandra recognized her—and as she stared a passenger slowly appeared next to the driver.

"Oh my God!" She pressed a button on the control panel to open the entry gates and the car made its way up the driveway. Moments later the doorbell rang and Chandra answered it.

"Hi y'all, I'm Daisy-Ann Wexler." The outstretched hand was eager and friendly. "An' this, this here… uh, this man here is Divine X… uh, my new friend that Jesus tol' me to bring to ya."

"All praise to the Beneficent One," Divine X responded.

"Cain we come in?" Daisy-Ann sounded sweet despite her obvious fatigue.

"Oh, I'm sorry. Of course. Come in. Come in." Chandra motioned in a sweeping gesture and watched as her two guests proceeded into the entry hall.

As though the situation hadn't been odd enough already, Chandra felt she was taking a giant leap into the odder. Crossing her threshold was a woman she had utterly despised and thought to be runner up as the most sickening creature in the country—right after Lynn Cheney, Sarah Palin and Laura Bush. And with her was a man she had learned was a cold-blooded killer who was about to be executed in Texas. Chandra abhorred capital punishment and had even signed a petition to spare the man's life, but until her meeting with Jesus, had not expected him to be a houseguest. The female was perfectly accustomed to the trappings of wealth around her. The male was shaken to his core.

"Just make yourselves at home," Chandra said, quickly glancing outside and closing the door. "By the way, where did you park?"

"Right there in your driveway."

"Can Hogan move your car into the garage—just in case they're looking for you?"

"Sure, no problem. But let me tell you, that Jesus has got everything covered. We was at a McDonalds, and the fella was starin' straight into the car and when I bought all the food for Divine here—he thought it was all for me 'cause he couldn't see him just like it was dark as midnight!"

Divine broke into a big smile.

"She's a nice lady. She's got some things to learn, but she's a nice lady. You guys can see me, right?"

"Clear as day," Hogan said laughing, as he went out to move the car.

"Do you know when I'm supposed to tell what I know?" Divine X was still looking around the room trying to place his new reality. "Mohammed said I was going to be able to tell the whole story to a lot of people."

"That will be tomorrow night," Chandra answered. "You saw Mohammed?"

"Well, he said he was Mohammed and he led me out of the prison. But Ms. Wexler here keeps saying it was Jesus."

"Hi," Adam rolled into the room and extended his hand to Divine X. "Am I glad to see you here!"

"Adam led demonstrations demanding a retrial for you," Chandra said, proud of her friend's efforts.

Divine grabbed Adam's hand with both of his and nodded towards the wheelchair. "Thank you," he said.

Daisy-Ann was stretched out on a large leather sofa. "Ah've been drivin' for over fifteen hours, and I'm pooped. If y'all don't mind I'm gonna take a little nap right here. Maybe you could wake me up 'bout dinner time." She waved at Divine X and dropped her head onto a pillow.

Chandra moved towards the kitchen and motioned Adam and Divine X to follow. "You want something to eat?" she asked.

"Thank you, ma'am."

"I'm Chandra."

"Okay… Chandra."

"We've got chicken and rice. Does that sound all right?"

"Sounds great."

"Coffee?"

"Thanks."

Chandra took a dish from the refrigerator, put it in the microwave and poured the coffee.

Adam wheeled over to the table and pulled out a chair for Divine. "Have a seat, man. You doing all right?"

"Yeah, but I'm still having trouble believing what's happening. And then there's…"

"There's. . ?"

"Well, could I ask the two of you something?"

"Sure."

Chandra put a steaming mug in front of Divine. "I'll bet you want some of this." She slid the sugar bowl to him.

"Just four teaspoons."

"Listen, Divine, we're all stunned about what's happening. I'd say you're in pretty understanding company," she said sitting down next to him.

There was a long pause. Divine spoke first.

"It's about that nice lady," he said. "Mohammed said there was going to be a time when I had to tell everything I know. He told me that when he appeared to me at Huntsville, y'know."

Adam leaned forward. "Nothing will surprise us anymore, man."

"It's not about that. It's that she's a really nice lady and I don't want to hurt her. I know some pretty terrible things about her husband. I was in prison for things that he did."

Chandra was up checking the chicken dish. "Did she tell you that she got a visit from Jesus?"

"Yeah, that's why she was waiting for me when Mohammed brought me out of prison. I just don't know if…"

"Divine," Chandra interrupted. "I've had to learn awful things about my husband too. Awful things. I think knowing is the best thing we can do. Mohammed wouldn't have told you to tell all if she couldn't take it."

"Duke Wexler helped George Bush and Dick Cheney prepare for 9/11." Divine slumped forward. "You think I'm crazy for saying that, don't you?"

"Not at all." It was Daisy-Ann. She was standing in the doorway. "I couldn't sleep. Thanks for bein' so kind in the way you think about me, but I gotta know everything. Nothin' about Duke's gonna shock me anymore. Jesus told me about some of this already. Particularly about his havin' to do with the bombin' you were in prison for."

Divine looked up. He spoke slowly. "He was behind Timothy McVeigh too. The Kansas City bombing was only a test to see what they could do controlling everything from the police to the media. I'm sorry I hadta tell you."

Daisy-Ann headed for the bar. "Ah need a drink."

Three thousand miles away at JFK airport in New York, Snagg was saying, "I need a drink," to Deemon as he settled into a seat on Chandra Boolean's private jet. The pilot, true to his orders had remained impassive as his unusual passengers boarded. He smiled a sincere smile at Marie who entered last.

"Well Snagg," Lyla said fastening her seatbelt, "Denver here we come."

"I'll drink to that!"

Marie was the first to spot the tiny bar at the rear of the plane. Soon all four passengers had their glasses raised in a toast to the success of their next adventure.

In Chandra Boolean's kitchen glasses were also raised in a toast to the success of the event at the Jesus Dome the following evening. There, in the midst of the toast, they turned to see three men in bathrobes entering the room. Giuseppe Fognolio no longer looked like a Pope. Expensive terrycloth engulfed the faux pontiff. Winslow Boolean had been a very large man and his robe seemed determined to make Fognolio disappear.

"You didn't have to take bathrobes!" Chandra felt embarrassed.

Cardinal Vonsecco laughed. "But they looked so comfortable! Please, if you don't mind, these were our first choice. We are accustomed to having to wear heavy vestments. These… these are like being hugged by a teddy bear!" He was signing while he spoke, and Fognolio and Popposi laughed out loud.

More wine was poured and the little group settled into comfortable conversation.

They would have only one more adjustment to make that night.

CHAPTER 88

Downtown Denver looked like a war zone. Troops, tanks, surveillance equipment, Homeland Security personnel were intermingled with network satellite dishes, cameramen and reporters. Television illumination in the area around the Jesus Dome gave an aura of broad daylight. Traffic blockades prevented most cars from entering what had become known as the "Hot Zone."

Video feeds from the area featured breathless reporters with perfect hair positively gushing that something very big and possibly terrible was about to happen. Vultures in full make-up and whitened teeth were poised to witness a kill.

High above the city, Blackhawk helicopters circled, carefully avoiding the six or seven TV news choppers. Radar, electronic telescopes, hi-def television, and eavesdropping technologies were trained on the Hot Zone.

"This is Bernard McKerick reporting from the Jesus Dome in Denver, Colorado. Today a city, the location of one of the most highly visible disappearance sites in the nation, waits in fearful anticipation as rumor points to a possibly extraordinary event here at the Jesus Dome tomorrow night. President Bush has placed the state of Colorado on the highest alert and has activated some 25,000 federal troops along with the National Guard to maintain order no matter what happens. Just twenty-four hours from now, we anticipate the appearance of Pope Maximilian IV before an audience of tens of thousands right here inside the Jesus Dome. Speculation abounds. Will the Pope bring an explanation of this nation's greatest mystery—the disappearance of over thirty mil... uh, thousands of people? Or, will the entire audience disappear? Stay tuned for updates throughout the evening and all day tomorrow. Of course we will be carrying live coverage of the event. Bernard McKerick, KCIC-TV News."

CHAPTER 89

Sergei Vasillich sat aboard a military jet transport reading his daily brief. Three days into *Operation Divine Shield,* hundreds of thousands of American citizens had been rounded up and put into the detention centers Halliburton built for the Bush Administration in 2006. "Curfew Violation" was stamped on all the paperwork, but a vast majority of the detainees had been abducted from their own homes in the middle of the night. Demographically the masses of terrified human beings did not reflect the general population. The white detainees were overwhelmingly Democrats, Socialists, Communists and Anarchists. The largest number were Black and Hispanic—regardless of party affiliation.

The demographics and numbers pleased Vasillich since one of the little facts that the Administration had managed to obfuscate about him was that he had openly advocated the genocide of Black people as a means of improving the nation's economy and lowering the national debt. George Bush found his ideas charming, but the party bosses insisted that all records of Vasillich's written and recorded ideas on the subject be destroyed and that a vigorous campaign be launched to restore his image as a heroic American before he was named head of the CIA.

Unfortunately for Vasillich, Black Americans' memories were not that easily erased, shredded, or otherwise destroyed. Black Americans remembered Vasillich and were actively reminding people who he was and what he stood for. That is they *were* until *Operation Divine Shield* and the convenient existence of George Bush's detention centers that could hold lots and lots of people Vasillich decided were "bad." Vasillich chuckled as he watched Black citizens being processed. "*They* didn't get raptured." It was a thought that added to his pleasure.

So, despite the fact that nearly 40 million Americans had simply disappeared, Sergei Vasillich was a rather happy man.

In an hour he would be in Denver, Colorado, to oversee CIA operations in and around the Jesus Dome. He was sure that before nightfall, the population of Colorado's detention centers would be greatly increased. He was also sure that if this Jesus Christ fellow was stupid enough to show his face anywhere in Colorado, he'd be blown to kingdom come. He relished knowing that Pope Maximillian IV was about to fulfill his part of *Operation Omniscient Scepter.*

Yes, Sergei Vasillich was a smugly pleased man. In fact, the self-satisfied smirk was still on what remained of his face when his badly charred body was recovered from the wreckage of the plane. The mystery of the crash was solved when rescue crews found nothing more of the pilot than his uniform, a St. Christopher's medal, underwear and shoes.

CHAPTER 90

The news of Vasillich's death upset the President for several minutes. A subsequent nosebleed upset him even more. He rang for his secretary.

"Madeline, get me Karl on the phone, will you?"

"Yes sir."

"And bring me some Kleenex!"

"Your nose again, Sir?"

"No, I cut my wrists because Al Sharpton is running again."

"You don't have to be sarcastic. I'll bring what you asked for as soon as I reach Karl."

George tipped his head back and pinched his nose. Why did the only thing he really enjoyed have to have such a miserable side effect?

Madeline entered with a full box of tissues.

"Those are Puffs. I asked for Kleenex," the President snapped.

"With the way your nose bleeds, Sir, you should be glad I didn't bring you Kotex! You really should see a doctor about that." With one deft sweep of her hand she brought a cascade of white powder off the desk and onto the floor.

"What the fu…?"

"It's for your own good. Pick up line three, it's Karl."

George grabbed the phone. "What do you want?"

"You called me, George. What do *you* want?"

"Oh right. Well, I want you to do something about this Vasillich thing. He was supposed to make sure that the Pope followed through tonight with that *Operation Ah'm Wishin' It Scepter* thing—damn it."

"That's *Omniscient* George."

"Whatever. Why didn't you let me know the old fart was coming to Amurica anyway? I thought he was going to do all his stuff from there at the Vatican in Paris."

"The Vatican's in Rome."

"They move it around? Never knew that. Anyway, how come you didn't tell me his Holy Fat Ass was coming to Denver?"

"I didn't know. I've been trying to reach the Vatican brass for two days. Nobody is willing to talk. They are clammed up but good. You'd think they would have wanted all kinds of security and promotion…"

"He *is* going to follow through, isn't he?"

Rove was the model of composure. "Of course. He's convinced if he does he'll be king of the world. I have to hand it to you George, you do follow instructions well. You had the old queen eating out of the palm of your hand."

"The Queen? I thought we were talking about the Pope? What's the queen got to do with it? Haven't heard from her since Tony got—well—*removed*."

"George, I'm swamped with work. I didn't expect the Pope to move so fast, so I have a lot to get in place by tonight. Was there anything else? Get to your point."

"Yes. Who's going to replace Vasillich? He was so good at keeping the Darkies under control and all. I really thought we were on a final roll to get rid of them, and then he goes an' gets on that plane…"

"He was traveling on your orders, Sir."

The President blanched. "What?"

"He was traveling on your orders."

"Heh, heh, you had me there! For a minute I thought you said on *my plane*, and that would really have ruined my day. I like that plane, y'know. They've got it now so I can get Cartoon Network and FOX News all at the same time!"

"Yes sir. As to your question."

"Did I ask one?"

"Yes. You want to know who's replacing Vasillich. We've named Condoleeza Rice to the position."

"But she's Secretary of State, Secretary of Defense, *and* head of the Joint Chiefs of Staff… in fact she's the *whole thing*!"

"That's why she's perfect for the CIA. She's running everything—just the way you will be soon, George."

"Now *that's* more like it."

"Right."

"I've got some pills you should take, Karl. You are just too up and down.

These would level you out so nice. They're the ones they had given me the morning of 9/11 so I could sit and listen to the whole goat story without acting all crazy when I heard our little plan had worked."

"Good bye, George."

"Bye Karl. Oh, and Karl…"

It was too late. Rove had already hung up, so the President sat for a long time trying to remember what he was supposed to do. He decided the first thing would be to send Vasillich's widow a funny card to cheer her up.

DAY SEVEN

TUESDAY

NOVEMBER 4, 2008

CHAPTER 91

Inside the Jesus Dome, private security hired by the Boolean Corporation at Chandra's orders were doing bomb and bug sweeps. Homeland Security demanded and got permission to enter for unspecified security reasons. The massive stage, where just days ago Reverend Teddy Dobbin held court as the nation's conservative religious guru, was now stripped of all the flags, bunting, and flying eagles, and had instead a simple blue cyclorama with many chairs and a modest podium. Chandra's security personnel had recommended a bullet-proof plexiglass shield around the entire stage, but she refused, saying that she was operating on very specific orders.

Chandra's private helicopter picked Hogan up at the house at 6 AM and flew him to the Dome to oversee preparations. Even though the copter was clearly marked and the pilot maintained appropriate radio contact, Hogan was met by Homeland Security as soon as they landed.

"Hello, Gentlemen," he called, ducking below the rotors. "May I help you?"

"Let us see your identification."

"Of course." Hogan produced his wallet. "I'm Hogan Cafferty, a representative of Ms. Chandra Boolean, the owner of this property."

The men studied his driver's license, then one walked away with it and began talking on his cellphone.

"I'm conducting important business for Ms. Boolean," Hogan volunteered. "You may have heard that there is a press conference being held here tonight."

The officer bristled. "Are you trying to be funny? We know everything already."

"Hmm. I suppose you do. So since you do, please give my identification back to me and let me get to my office."

The other officer returned. "Turner, this guy was one of Dobbin's people—the only one who didn't disappear."

"Is that a crime?" Hogan was growing impatient.

"We're watching everyone close to the situation."

Hogan smiled. "Good."

The first officer interrupted, "He's on the list Boolean sent as officials of the Dome. Let him in."

"Thank you gentlemen," Hogan said as he retrieved his wallet. "I'll do the best to make your day uneventful. By the way, Ms. Babs Waller will be arriving any moment with a television crew. Please make her feel welcome."

As the helicopter lifted from the pad, he turned and entered the Jesus Dome and headed for Teddy Dobbin's office. Once inside he closed the door and called Chandra.

"Everything quiet there?" he asked.

"Some helicopters circling, the phone is ringing, but I'm not picking up anything except your caller ID."

"The guests know all they need to know?"

"I think so. I'm just following directions and have outlined everything the way I was told. How is it there?"

"As expected. The place is crawling, but I got in."

"Any sign of…"

"I haven't seen him. I'm pretty sure he's not here."

"He said there would be one more person joining us tomorrow. Maybe they're coming together."

"Maybe. Chandra…"

"I know. I'm scared too."

If they knew the size of the force mounted against them at that very moment, "scared" would have been a mild word indeed.

CHAPTER 92

Jesus was exhausted. After appearing as a monk at the Vatican and again at the Denver airport, he went to Buckley Air Force Base outside of Denver to meet Jerrod Parker. He waited for three hours because the C43 transport plane carrying Parker was delayed due to mechanical problems. Now he and a somewhat dazed Jerrod—still invisible to those around them—hurried across the tarmac.

"There's a helicopter waiting for us," he said, grabbing Jerrod's arm to keep him moving.

Jerrod's ordeal had severely weakened him, but he did his best to place one foot after another.

Jesus pointed ahead. "It's right over there."

The rotors were already turning on Chandra's helicopter. Jesus momentarily made himself visible to the pilot who was expecting them. He waved and motioned for them to get in.

"Sorry we're late," Jesus said, settling into the seat.

"No problem. We've got plenty of time. Your interview isn't until 4:30."

"So Chandra got it arranged?"

"I've never seen anything that lady can't do. I just got word that Babs Waller has arrived. Her crew is setting up at the Jesus Dome."

"Good."

"By the way sir, it's nice to meet you and have you on board."

Fifteen minutes later they were hovering over the Jesus Dome's helipad. Jerrod was dozing and missed the moment that Jesus told the pilot they were going to disappear again. The pilot watched as the two men in the back seat simply faded away.

The helicopter was clearly marked with the MacroGent logo and was in full communication with the ground. Nevertheless the pilot could see marksmen with their ground to air missiles trained on him. He brought the copter down gently and opened the door. Jesus and Jerrod slipped out just as the armed Homeland Security troupers approached the plane.

"State your business."

Following Chandra's carefully detailed instructions, the pilot answered, "I'm picking up Mrs. Boolean."

"She's not in the building."

"No? Wow, sorry. I thought I was to pick her up here. In that case I'll be going." And he lifted the helicopter up and away, its passenger door still open.

CHAPTER 93

Jesus led Jerrod through the maze of hallways inside the Jesus Dome. They carefully avoided physical contact with the people rushing back and forth.

"Can't they see our clothes or anything?" Jerrod asked, his curiosity piqued beyond containment.

"Nothing. It's so simple to do—I don't know why the military hasn't discovered it—although I'm glad they haven't. I just alter your resonance a tiny bit—and that automatically includes everything that's touching you. If it was complicated, I could explain more, but when it's that simple, all I can do is say that's how it works. Same with our voices. The sound waves are just traveling a half resonance off, so the others can't hear."

Just then they came around a corner and saw Hogan. Jesus caught up with him and tapped him on the shoulder.

Hogan jumped, then looked around but saw nothing.

"Hogan, it's us." Jesus had altered his voice resonance making it audible.

"Aw, man, you scared me."

"Sorry."

"Get us to Babs Waller. We're going to stay invisible for a while. I want to know what she has in store for us."

"She's up in my office. Isn't that a laugh? *My* office? It was Dobbin's office before…" He was already walking down the hall to the elevator. "It's the one place in the building that's not crawling with military. That's why I put Babs in there." Upstairs, he opened the office door carefully so Jesus and Jerrod could enter unseen.

Inside, Babs Waller's crew was setting lights and doing soundchecks. She was very much in charge, barking orders at everyone.

"Jesus, if they can't hear us, why can we hear them—and why can that guy you call Hogan hear us?" Jerrod was curious again.

"Well that, that is a little more complicated, Jerrod. I'll explain it to you later, but right now I think we should try to learn a little of what Ms. Waller has in store for us."

"Us?"

"Yes, I want you with me. You're my 'preview of coming attractions' for tonight."

Jerrod laughed for the first time since his arrest. "You're a pitchman, Jesus. You're a pitchman."

Babs was holding her chin in an awkward position, trying to flaunt her best angle. "For the last time, goddam it, key light on my left, my LEFT. You'd think after all this time you'd…"

The key grip put the light down. "Babs, I know where the light goes. I had set it down because we needed another extension. You don't need to be nervous. You've done a million interviews."

"For a million years," Danny LaFogg chimed in.

Bobs shot him a dirty look.

"Mr. Key Grip man will learn his trade pretty soon," Danny purred.

The key grip leaned over to Danny and whispered, "If you really knew what you were doing, you'd be making up young models and not old ladies."

Jesus was amused. "No honor among thieves, eh, Jerrod?"

"No sir. There certainly isn't."

Babs saw Hogan and put out her hand. "Mr. Cafferty? Thank you for coming. I am assuming that everything is on track for the interview? Has my guest arrived?"

"I understand he's nearby and will appear on time." Hogan figured the truth couldn't hurt. He could see Jesus chuckling.

"Well he may be Jesus Christ, but I'm Babs Waller, and I expect promptness and cooperation."

"I can assure you, Ms. Waller, that your guest takes this interview with the utmost seriousness. But don't let me interfere with your preparations. I'm just going to be doing some work at my desk." Hogan nodded and moved to his new desk.

Waller turned around and whispered something to her cameraman. Hogan couldn't hear her, but gave an inquiring look towards Jesus who had heard every word. "She said that you're putty in her hands, and she's thoroughly prepared to have 'that Jesus nut' indict and convict himself. I guess I should be terribly afraid, eh?"

Hogan smiled. Jerrod didn't.

"Jesus, if she's determined to ambush us in some way, how'll I know what to say or not to say? I don't want to screw everything up."

"Don't worry, Jerrod. As soon as Ms. Waller starts the interview, I'll be saying some things that will have her speechless. At a certain point I'm going to say that tonight during the press conference inside the Dome, you are going to be telling what you learned recently while incarcerated on Guantanamo. All you need to do is nod."

"What if they try to kill us before tonight?"

"They won't be able to see any of us until showtime. I think the world is worth saving, and everyone will see that it only takes a little handful of people to do it. Let's see what else Ms. Babs has in mind… and then I think it will be time to welcome our friends."

CHAPTER 94

While Jesus Dome attendants helped get Adam's wheelchair out of the helicopter, and while Homeland Security, military and Blackwater personnel stared at Chandra Boolean as she disembarked, an invisible group of people—Lyla, Marie, Deemon, Snagg, Daisy-Ann, Divine X, Fognolio, Vonsecco, and Popposi wormed their way through the obstacles and then joined Chandra and Adam as they entered the building.

"Mr. Brigante is my guest for this evening—a military veteran who gave much for his country." Adam displayed his driver's license and security allowed him to pass.

The invisible group with him was careful to keep a distance from all military and government personnel. Chandra led them directly to Hogan's office and with great precision they all entered without causing notice or alarm.

Babs Waller was all gracious smiles when she saw Chandra. "Ms. Boolean, how nice that you could be here. You will, of course, be off camera, but you are welcome to take a seat over there." She pointed to a folding chair in a far corner.

"Thank you, Ms. Waller, but I prefer to sit at Hogan's desk, if you don't mind. I'm assuming that as owner of the Jesus Dome, I can pretty much sit where I want."

"Cheeky, aren't we?" Bab's Waller's response sent a tense ripple through the room.

"Don't worry, Ms. Waller, I want this interview to go well, and I have no intention of doing anything to interfere."

"I'm sure you won't, dear," Waller said casting a disgusted glance in the direction of her producer.

Jesus signaled Chandra to stay cool, and she obligingly joined Hogan at his desk. The nine other guests joined Jesus and Jerrod near the wall. Jesus made quick introductions. Jerrod was startled to see the Pope in the room, but quickly figured it was no stranger than anything else that had occurred.

At exactly 4:29, Chandra dialed her cellphone, spoke softly for a moment and then said, "They're here." She opened the door. As she did, Jesus and Jerrod slipped out before her. She stepped into the hall and closed the door. She waited a moment while Jesus and Jerrod became visible and then reentered with them. "Ms. Waller, I would like to introduce you to Jesus Christ and Jerrod Parker."

Babs Waller's stretched skin was always just a slight pull away from a smile, and now it tugged back a bit as she walked towards Jesus. "Thank you for coming," she said. "I know who Mr. Parker is. I'm surprised that he isn't in custody. Take a seat over there."

"We will need two chairs. Jerrod is joining me."

"No, I'm only interviewing *you*."

"Then I'll have to be on my way."

"What are you talking about? I have been promised an exclusive with you—no holds barred—and you think you're going to tell… . Where are you going?"

Jesus' hand was already turning the knob.

"Come back here. Danny, get another chair."

Danny let out a deep sigh and then moved another chair into place. "The lighting is gonna suck," he said. "No makeup and lousy light. This should win an Enema."

Jesus returned.

Bab's friendly manner was gone. "I guess you realize I'm committing a federal crime by meeting with you right now," she said. "You are considered a terrorist, *he* is supposed to be in a federal prison, and I'm risking everything for this interview."

"I'm sure you are, Ms. Waller. And you realize that I risk everything by being here with you."

"Granted. Shall we begin? I have no questions for Mr. Parker."

"He won't need any questions. When there is something for him to add, it will be obvious."

"I'll decide that."

"Perhaps." Jesus motioned for Jerrod to sit next to him. The lights were flattering and Jesus noticed that he looked very handsome in the monitors. He adjusted his locks to one side and brought them forward over his shoulder. He glanced over at his invisible audience by Hogan's desk. They smiled and nodded.

Babs Waller looked directly into camera one and began.

"This is Babs Waller. I am in a secret location to bring you an exclusive interview with the most wanted man in the world. He is the enigmatic individual who has appeared in various locations throughout the country in recent days identifying himself as Jesus Christ. President Bush has labeled him a terrorist and has implicated him as the person responsible for the disappearances of tens of millions of Americans and countless more victims around the world. It is a charge that this man now sitting across from me has not denied. With him is…" Babs checked her 3x5's in an obvious attempt to show that the second guest didn't matter, "Mr. Jerrod Parker—also a criminal on the FBI's most wanted list." She turned to Jesus. "You identify yourself as Jesus Christ, is that correct?"

Jesus was immediately in control of the interview. "Good evening, Ms. Waller. Thank you for providing time for me to address the nation."

"I asked you a question."

"If I wasn't Jesus Christ I wouldn't know what I'm about to tell you. So please listen well."

"But this is *my*. . ."

"Ms. Waller, you are doing the world an enormous service by allowing me to speak. Don't let your ego destroy the best thing you've been able to do in your entire life."

The diva's tongue stalled.

"Tonight, live from the Jesus Dome, the entire world will have dots connected… will have details provided… that will make sense of the last thirty-plus years of history. A conspiracy theory that many have subscribed to will be exploded, and the truth will be known. A major cause of world misery will be eliminated. The truth about recent disappearances will be revealed. The reason that some people remain on earth will become clear. The War on Terror will effectively be over."

There was a wild look in Babs Waller's eyes. Her usual ease in front of the camera had disappeared and now she showed signs of a frantic meltdown.

Jesus continued. "Mr. Jerrod Parker, the gentleman sitting next to me, will be appearing with the Pope. Mr. Parker recently returned from a difficult trip to Guantanamo, Cuba as a 'guest' of the American government. He will be able to shed valuable light on the situation there." He looked at

Jerrod. "Am I correct?"

Jerrod nodded.

Babs had asked only one question. It hadn't been answered. But she somehow felt that Jesus was right. This *was* the most important interview she'd ever done.

"Thank you. And now, Ms. Waller, wouldn't you like to tell people that you are going to be the moderator, the host as it were, of tonight's Jesus Dome conference?"

Babs stared at the camera. "Oh yes. I am. Thank you Mr. Jesus Christ for coming. I do want to remind my audience that they should stay tuned for the Pope's address from the Jesus Dome." She was momentarily distracted by gestures from her director. "What? Oh yes, after the Pope's address, don't forget to watch a special delayed edition of *Fright Encounter*. Tonight, participants will be eating live baby snakes while vying for a prize of over $50,000. Thank you and good night."

The cameras stopped.

"What was *that* about?" Waller screamed at her director. "Live baby snakes—following the Pope? Are you out of your mind? We're cutting that tripe for sure. Tape my extro over and don't you *dare* ambush me again!"

Cameras rolled and Babs Waller did a sign-off that Jesus suggested.

"I'm sure Ms. Boolean will be able to assist you in every way preparing for tonight," Jesus said, extending his hand to Babs. "I appreciate your cooperation, but now for obvious reasons, Mr. Parker and I need to leave. By the way, none of the video will be useable. But it was important that we meet and that you understood the gravity of tonight's event. Congratulations on being the featured host." He stood, motioned to Jerrod, and together they walked out the door. They turned into the corridor and disappeared. Chandra and Hogan stayed with the rather dazed Babs. The other guests, unseen, followed Jesus without a trace.

CHAPTER 95

The Jesus Dome was packed far beyond capacity. Busloads of nuns and priests were vying for seats. With much fanfare, Archbishop Kaput and his entourage arrived in five black limousines and were escorted to VIP seating in the vast auditorium.

Satellite dishes and news vans circled the Dome. Reporters ballyhooed the Pope's address throughout the day. Terrified American citizens were desperate to know what was happening to the world. Hardly a family internationally was untouched by the disappearances. Internet blogs were reporting total missing approaching 500 million people.

Since Reverend Robinson Patrick's impassioned announcement that the disappearances were definitely the Rapture, and since he made his stunning, if not self serving, televised confession revealing why he had been left behind, and since he had said that the only hope of survival and redemption was through a complete dedication to the National Protestant Evangelical Church, attendance was up 600%. Across the country, there were nightly prayer meetings, revival services and children's classes. One clever entrepreneur had, within a period of three days, begun to sell franchises for storefront churches in strip malls. Sales were brisk. Religion was the preeminent topic of conversation. The Pope was about to make an unexpected appearance in America. The entire world's eyes were on Denver, Colorado—and that most curious of places, The Jesus Dome.

In Washington, George W. chuckled to himself. When he first learned that the Pope was going to appear in Washington, he'd had a moment of fear. Why was the Pope acting on his own and not under the direction of Karl Rove? Was he going to undercut the President of the United States, one-up him or expose him? But then George thought it over and realized that even the Pope didn't have enough power to sway the masses in that way. No, the Pope would be forced to stick to the script of *Operation Omniscient*

Scepter. Anything else would be suicide. Yes, tonight the Pope was going to take to the podium of the Jesus Dome and announce that God had revealed to him that George W. Bush was divinely appointed to lead the world and that his unique "democracy" was going to be the basis for all future government. The Pope would conveniently leave out the fact that the "democracy" to which he referred was modeled on the work of Nazi propagandist, Joseph Goebbels.

Tired and frightened people worldwide would cheer the announcement and pledge allegiance to their new leader.

Next the Pope would outline *Operation Omniscient Scepter* in all its clever glory. Following Karl's orders he would address the world's population saying, "God has instructed all followers to uphold and revere his one true Catholic Church, to unite with the National Protestant Evangelical Church of the United States, and to pledge allegiance to US President George W. Bush. President Bush, Reverend Robinson Patrick and I are ordained by God as the New Trinity. What God has set in motion, let no mortal disrupt." And with that, the Pope would sit down.

Again, the masses would cheer. And finally, once that was completed, all that was left was to implement the "Israel Solution" and make sure the Pope was gotten out of the way. It was a simple plan, a brilliant plan, and Karl had it all in his head like a machine.

That's what he needed! He needed Karl's head. Eagerly George searched through the little Post-It notes on his desk, looking for Karl's phone number. Even though he dialed it many times a day, it was one of those long numbers ("It's got like eleven numbers," he'd complain to Laura) he couldn't remember. Finding it, he poked at the keypad and listened to the ring. There was no answer until a stark, "Leave a message," in Karl's voice.

The color drained from the President's face. Karl! Karl was the only person who had the whole plan in his brain. Yes, the orders were in motion, but Karl was the one who knew how everything was supposed to go, how to fix anything that went wrong, how to keep any opposition at bay.

George was not used to having trouble reaching Karl Rove. Feigning casualness he said, "Hey Turd Blossom, call me back. I need that stuff in your head."

Now he was rattled. He needed a snort, then two, then four. That done, he felt better even though his nose was threatening to bleed again.

Laura knocked at the door. "Geowrge," she pumped the Texas twang.

"Geowrge, yew in there?"

"Yeah."

Laura stepped into the room. "Yew going to watch the Pope on TV?"

"I guess I'd better. I can't reach Karl, and I probably will have to give a press conference once *Operation Ah'm Wishin' It Scepter* is out of the bag. I don't know why that Old Holy Fart couldn't have waited before flying here from that Vegegan place. Who knew Catholics didn't eat meat?"

"Vatican, Geowrge." Laura knew she was wasting words.

"The Pentagon said we only needed two more days. I wish Rummy was still around. He could'a sped things up. Hell, he'd 'a sent in what we've got there already and let 'em take the heat. They'd do all the damage we need even if they got a high body count. I never did care about how many of 'em got killed. They volunteered, they got a great deal and they got dead. So what? Do you see me missing any of 'em? Hell no. Tell me one person you know, Laura, *one person*, who ever lost a boy in any one of my wars—one person that we'd have dinner with, that is."

"I cain't think of anyone, Geowrge. Shouldn't you be puttin' on the TV? It's 7:45, and the Pope is supposed to be comin' on at 8."

"It was all goin' perfect until people started disappearin'."

"I know, Geowrge. You've worked so hard too. This is kinda one of those little steps assbackwards, huh?" Laura giggled at her cleverness.

The President scratched an inconvenient itch as he said, "I mean, if it's true that almost half a bazillion people are gone, that lowers my poll numbers, right?"

"Yew could look at it like that if yew wanna be all negative, Geowrge. But maybe there's a bright side. Maybe they're all good riddance. Maybe they were your enemies"

"No, Rummy and Dick and Sergei and the rest... they were good ol' boys."

Laura was quiet for a while. "The Lawrd moves in mysterious ways, Geowrge. Now turn on the TV."

The President struggled with a remote. A plasma TV on the opposite wall finally snapped on. The Colorado Catholic Youth Orchestra was performing. George shook his head.

"See? Somethin' is wrong. Sara Hill was supposed to be doin' country to introduce the Pope. Karl arranged the whole thing. Country music brings all the dumb nuts together under the flag. It gives you the *Bible* thumpers, gun totin' hillbillies, and idiot ladies with the cowboy hats and big tits. And what are they playing? Some dumb-ass classical long hair stuff like Yanni."

"That's the National Anthem, Geowrge. Everything's gonna be all right. I've been praying to Gawd all day that this'll go just the way you and Rummy and Dick planned. And I've also prayed for Condi's soul." She lowered her glasses and glared at her husband.

Actually catching the innuendo, George muttered, "Time to watch the TV."

The orchestra stopped. The First Lady and the President watched dumbfounded as Babs Waller walked onto the cavernous Jesus Dome stage and stood behind the podium.

"What the fuck?" the President screamed. "She's a *Jew*! What's she doin' there with *my Pope*?" He frantically grabbed for his secure phone and speed dialed Karl, only to realize there would be no answer.

If he had known what was about to transpire, he would have considered Babs Waller a bright spot.

CHAPTER 96

"Good evening ladies and gentlemen. I am Babs Waller, and I am pleased to welcome all of you here in the Jesus Dome and the billions of you watching via television and the Internet." The media diva was at her stunning best in a floor-length red gown that clung to her spindly body. Danny had outdone himself on her face and hair. She didn't look a day over 70. "It is my pleasure to host this extraordinary event—one which I know is going to bring both comfort and understanding to all of us who are living through this time of the Rapture."

Chandra, standing in the wings, smiled with satisfaction that the moment had arrived. She felt a hand on her shoulder. It was Jesus. "You've done well," he said.

For Reverend Robinson Patrick, squirreled away in the privacy of his study, the sight of a Jew on TV at the Jesus Dome was enough to make him drop a stack of photos of young children and quit masturbating. Deciding that a religious emergency was underway, he wiped his hands with a towel, picked up a pen, and began writing the first sentences of his next television broadcast: "I love the Jewish persons of that particular persuasion, and of course, I love all the Catholics who so foolishly and mistakenly believe that the Pope is some kind of divinity on earth, and of course the Mormons, Seventh-Day Adventists, Muslims and the Buddhists, and every other cracker-jack religion… I just love them all. But when Jews take front and center and start talking about the Rapture while introducing the Pope on national TV at the same time that some of the most Godly people who have ever lived—and I humbly include myself in that august company—are still sitting here on earth waiting to be called home to heaven by our one Lord and Savior Jesus Christ, well there is something terribly wrong. I am here to tell you that not until all the true believers—the notable Christians who *God* has rewarded with spiritual and material abundance—not until *they* have been taken to their reward will it be possible that some few of the other persuasions are able to talk about the Rapture and have any possibility of eternal life with the One, the Only, the One and Only Savior of mankind, the King of Kings, the Lord of Lords, the Intercessor, the very Protestant Deity, the One who gave his life for Democracy and Free Markets, My Lord, My Savior, My Best Friend, the Real and Only Jaesus! Jaesus! Jaesus!"

Patrick's long-suffering wife had been standing outside the door of her husband's study, puzzling over the strange gasps and moans that had been audible for the last twenty minutes. She noted that exactly two minutes after eight, those noises stopped, the good reverend loudly proclaimed his faith, denounced all other religions but his—with love of course—and then made a statement at high volume about the righteous, himself included, needing to be taken in the Rapture while shouting "Jaesus, Jaesus, Jaesus."

The police taking her report were impressed by the woman's detailed memory of the sounds that came through her husband's study door, and were particularly impressed by the facts that followed.

"He had just given the most beautiful and personal proclamation of Jesus Christ being his Lord, his Savior and his Best Friend, when I heard this peculiar little 'clunk' sound in there. It was odd enough that it impelled me to knock on the door—something I never do when Robinson is having his little private times—and say, 'Robinson, are you all right?'" Here the woman dabbed her eyes before continuing. "I didn't hear so much as a cockroach scuffling across the floor. I was truly frightened. So much so, that I opened the door and stepped inside. I believe that is when I took the Lord's name in vain. It is shameful that I should meet an instance of the Rapture with a curse, but I have to admit that one escaped my lips. I believe I was standing right here and I actually screamed the curse like this, 'Well, gosh darn!!!' And then I went over to where Robinson had been sitting but he wasn't there. And all I found were these pictures and… this." Her trembling hand shot forward, clapping into the palm of the inquiring policeman a very unwelcome and sticky tube of K-Y Jelly.

CHAPTER 97

Dubya snorted a "heh, heh, heh."

"What is it, Geowrge?"

"Just funny to be watchin' this and realizin' that the Pope is one smart fella. He's gonna snooker ever'body. He's doin' a heck'uv a job."

"How?"

"Well, look there who he's got as the 'host' of the evenin'. That Waller woman is a *Jew*. Won't the Heebs be surprised when they hear what ol' gold crown has got to say."

He stopped short to hear Babs Waller's further remarks. She wasn't missing a single opportunity for self-aggrandizement. George admired that inspite of her heritage.

"I am honored," she was saying, "to have been the single journalist in the entire world to be here, sharing the stage with His Holiness, the spiritual leader of the universe."

It was fortunate that Reverend Robinson Patrick had already disappeared because that statement alone would have killed him.

In Iraq, both Shiite and Sunni leaders would have given orders for there to be mass protests against the Pope and the blasphemous claim he was the spiritual leader of the world, were it not for a broadcast by American prisoner Divine X Marcus who cautioned all members of Islam to remain peaceful while Allah accomplished a great work on earth. Hundreds of millions of Muslims practiced their faith and trusted that the American prophet, Divine X did speak for Mohammed.

Buddhists were horrified as were Hindus.

But in a building in Silver Springs, Maryland, Elder Neville Dahlstrom, a former missionary, now a bureaucrat with the General Conference of Seventh-day Adventists, smiled with peculiar satisfaction at Waller's pronouncement. His church believed the Pope to be the "Beast of Revelation"—the single most feared person in all Biblical prophecy—the person who would bring about the final persecution of "God's little remnant flock." But now there was a miraculous turn of events, because an emissary of the President of the United States had called him—Nevell Dahlstrom—and given him a secret mission that opened the way for him to change all history. Having long felt like a tiny part in a small machine, Dahlstrom's ego was already feeding like a glutton at an epicurean banquet. Now all he had to do was wait.

In Denver, Babs Waller plowed on. "And so it is my great and distinguished honor, the crowning moment in my stellar career as a journalist, an overwhelmingly flattering personal triumph for me to be standing here introducing Pope Maximilian IV." With those words uttered, Babs Waller stepped out from behind the podium so the entire world could admire her gown, turned to her right and began to applaud. The crowd rose to its feet and began to chant, "Pappa, Pappa, Pappa!" The orchestra launched into another powerful number, this time "And I Will Shake," from Handel's *Messiah.* Strobe lights began to flash, runner lights went into high chase, pinpoint spots illuminated a gold door that had been erected stage right. Just when the din seemed more than the building could endure, the door swung open and Fognolio in regal Papal splendor strode onto the stage followed closely by Cardinal Vonsecco and Monsignor Popposi. Fognolio, heavily laden by his brocade robes and Triple Crown, repeatedly gave the sign of Papal blessing as he made his way to the podium.

Throughout the vast stadium, people from all faiths and many from none, were standing, crying, clapping, and hoping against hope that the Pontiff would be able to explain the wrenching occurrences of the last days, be able to tell them why some had been taken and some left behind.

It was a full ten minutes before the cacophony subsided and Fognolio and Vonsecco stepped behind the podium. Just when the audience expected to hear his voice, the Pope began to sign. Vonsecco translated every word.

"My dearly beloved, I have come here today with the most important truth to tell you. I must apologize for it seems that I have lost my voice. You will hear my words through my hands and through the mouth of my trusted brother, Cardinal Vonsecco."

The audience roared its approval of the arrangement.

"What I have to tell you tonight will bring peace to your hearts, for I will be explaining the recent disappearances."

Again long and loud response from the audience.

"In order to do this, to have you understand fully what is taking place, I have invited a number of friends who will begin to piece together this enormous puzzle of information."

The lights on George W. Bush's private phone were alight. He knew it would be the Pentagon, the NSA, the CIA, the FBI and the Secret Ops generals in charge of *Operation Omniscient Scepter.* The calls went unanswered because he couldn't explain what was happening. The Pope was supposed to walk out, describe *Omniscient Scepter* and cede all power to the President of the United States. Not one of the Pope's words thus far was from script.

"Geowrge, what is the matter? Why are you slamming that pretzel on your forehead?"

The apoplectic President couldn't answer that question either.

Fognolio continued, "There has been much speculation about the circumstances, the *affiliations* as it were, of the people who have disappeared. I know that many sincere people have proclaimed that this is *The Rapture,* and they are afraid for what is to come. We have all wondered 'Where did they go?' We have all asked, 'Why have I been left here, left behind?'"

The crowd inside the Jesus Dome had become unnaturally quiet.

"My dear children, while there are things that I must tell you and tell the world which are deeply troubling, I can assure you that by the end of this evening your burden of sorrow will be lifted.

"I have heard speculation in these last few days that the people still left on earth are the evildoers, the sloth, the detritus of the world. If so, I am happy to include myself in that number, for as you can see I am very much here."

If applause can signal relief, relief resounded throughout the room.

"Allow me first to introduce you to four friends of mine—people who, like me, have not disappeared: Lyla Edwards, Marie Cattel, Mr. Deemon and Mr. Snagg. Could you come out here and join me?"

To many people in the audience, it seemed that the four people materialized before their very eyes. Police, security and undercover officers scrambled to identify the persons now walking onto the stage—who, like the Pope himself—had somehow never passed through security.

When Lyla, Marie, Deemon and Snagg became visible, there were audible gasps throughout the audience. It seemed clear to many of the faithful why *those* people had been left behind by God himself—because they just didn't look the way the Almighty's children should look. Now the Pope was introducing these people as "friends."

"I have asked Miss Edwards to speak first." Fognolio bowed sweetly and Lyla went to the microphone.

Recent days had taken a toll on Lyla's appearance. There were light roots showing at the base of her jet black hair. Her clothes were rumpled, and the goth makeup she wore was heavier, scarier than ever.

"Hi," she began. "I don't know about you, but I just have this feeling that the world is really fucked up right now."

"Potty mouth!" someone shouted. There were isolated boos from audience members. "Shame!" shouted another.

"You can boo or whatever, but we're fucked up and it's our stupid ass-hole President and his friends that's gotten us there."

It was interesting that the few objectors were now shouted down by cries of "Let her speak! Let her speak!"

"I'm sick and fuckin' tired of hearing all this bullshit about 'freedom' and 'democracy' comin' from Dubya's stinkin' pie hole. I'm like with this great group of people who believe that the world should be totally at peace, that people should work together and share what they've got equally without corporations interfering. I believe people from every country could be cool if these imperialist governments disappeared. But instead of a world like that—a world I'd want to have kids in—we've got this frickin' nightmare with wars started by lies. Hundreds of thousands of people are dying and then this mutha'fucker dickhead Bush goes and turns the whole country into a prison camp! This Pope here is all right. He understands what's goin' on. He was like 'awesome' in a good way when I told him about how a bunch of us have been helping American GI's escape to Canada and Mexico. If I didn't do everything I could to help people escape this madness, work to bring down this sick-assed President, and try to stop war every way possible—I ought'a shoot myself. I'd just be another person sucking up air, drinking water and using food and doing the world no good. That's how I see it. I'd be like my *parents* who called themselves 'born again Christians' and made life miserable for everyone around them. They thought they were the only people in the world who knew anything about truth, and they shunned everyone else and thought everything and everyone else was evil. That's no way to live and it's no way treat other people. They disappeared. What does that tell you? I don't think it was because God wanted them living in *his* house. I'm not very good at talking, but that's what I wanted to say, and it's totally cool that the Pope wanted me to say it."

For a moment the audience remained silent. There were shocked, aghast, puzzled looks everywhere. But then from somewhere high in the stadium someone began to applaud loudly. Soon that person was joined by others and within seconds the sound was deafening.

Lyla went back to stand with her friends. Fognolio stepped forward and began to sign.

"Miss Edwards' grandmother is with us. She is someone I admire and want you to welcome warmly. Ms. Marie Cattel."

Marie came forward as Fognolio led the applause.

"Good evening. Oh, there's a funny delay in the sound. I'm hearing myself. Well, nevermind, I'll just keep talking. I'm grateful for the opportunity to be here tonight. I don't have much to say. I'm very proud of my granddaughter because she is a humanitarian. She *cares* about the state of the world. She wouldn't brag about herself, but her work with AWOL soldiers has been both arduous and dangerous. We're telling you about it tonight, because after tonight it will no longer be necessary."

Marie stopped for a moment. She wasn't supposed to say more on the last subject this early in the evening. She caught herself and changed subjects.

"Some of you may recognize me from protests and some of you have probably spent time in jail with me for opposing wars, objecting to corporate rule—and, oh yeah, for taking part in that glorious Battle of Seattle!"

Apparently she was right, because there were calls of "How you doing, Marie?"

She acknowledged the greetings and continued, "I agree with Lyla that we cannot legislate goodness. Violence and military might can never bring about peace. I've been a freedom fighter all my life. I carried anti-war signs when I was ten years old denouncing the Korean conflict. As a young woman I was a hippie working to stop the Vietnam War. It was hard, it was discouraging, but I'm here to tell you that it was a beautiful time. Do you know why? Because we truly believed that we could change the world. We were sure we could end racism and poverty. We had no doubt that 'peace and love would rule the planet' because it was our *will* that it happen. But there were forces at work in the background to make sure that anything but equality was achieved in the world, anything but peace. Those forces—all of them pro-capitalist, pro-corporate, pro-fascist enforcement of profit—took hold in a new way in 1980 with the election of Ronald Reagan, and they have been in high gear ever since. By the time Bush got selected—those of us who felt like a good world could be achieved… well, many of us just felt worn out and discouraged—disheartened. These have been horrible years.

"Why am I saying all this here in the *Jesus* Dome? In spite of the fact that there are some people booing here in this auditorium, I'm saying it because I'm finally sure we were right. The Age of Aquarius that we used to sing about is actually here. And the reason it's here and the reason it's going to win is because we're finally going to be able to see clearly what has been working against it. Thank you for listening."

Marie nodded, moved to Lyla's side, and then remembering something rushed back to the microphone. She leaned into and said with a big smile, "By the way, y'all notice, I was left behind!"

There was another round of laughter.

Fognolio was about to introduce Deemon and Snagg when there was a disturbance in the hall. A man was struggling with guards at an entrance about ten rows from the stage on the left. Breaking free for a moment he shouted, "I have a cease and desist order from the President of the United States!"

CHAPTER 98

"Pope" Fognolio, the humble janitor of the Sistine Chapel, didn't miss a beat. He began to sign. "Why would the President of the United States issue a cease and desist order against me when it was *he* who invited me here? I must ask that this man be removed. I want the military personnel in the room to be aware that imposters may try to foil tonight's very critical mission."

Laura Bush turned to her husband in astonishment. There in the plush surroundings of the White House, the raucous Denver event seemed very far away. "Geowrge," she began, "did y'all really send a cease and desist order there?"

"No. That must'a been Condi, or maybe Karl. Speakin' of Karl, where the hell is he?"

"Yew still don't know?"

"I've been sittin' right here all the time, how do you think I'd know somethin' and you didn't know that I knew it? Honestly, sometimes Pickles."

"Watch it, George." She knew the implication when George used her old nickname.

"Or what, you'll run into me with your car? Heh, heh."

Laura was tired of George's jokes about how, when she was 17, she'd plowed into her boyfriend with her car and killed him. She tired of his implication that she did it on purpose, and even more tired of his suggesting she might run him over… although the thought frequently entered her mind.

"Well what are yew gonna dew Geowrge?"

"What do you want me to do, Pickles? It's past eight o'clock at night. I'm sleepy. I miss Karl. Just let me watch the TV, OK? His Popeiness just said that he wasn't going to let anything stop tonight's 'critical mission.' That's *Operation Ah'm Wishin' It Scepter* to be sure. Now just relax. You worry too much."

"Sometimes it's a sign of intelligence."

"Well, I never worry, never think about the future or all those silly 'what if this happens, what if that happens?'--things that people are always and forever stressed about. I just make up my mind and that's that. I'm the Describer."

"That's *Decider*, George."

"Whatever. Whoo-Ee! Look! They've got about a hundred people dragging that fella out!"

"He's one of yours, Geowrge."

"Oh. Well, still, I'm glad that the Pope fella is gonna be able to set things straight. Sometimes Karl jumps the gun."

And with that, the leader of the ever-so-free Western world leaned back and munched another pretzel.

On the plasma screen, Dubya saw two young men who had just been introduced as "friends" by the Pope—one dressed in what could only be called a red devil outfit, and the other tattooed to look like a lizard. They told how, in the course of their lives, they had been disaffected from society, how they had felt hopeless about the future and how they had found community and acceptance with people who were called "fringe elements." Their discourse was brief, but even the drug-stupefied President felt their final words with unmistakable impact.

Deemon had his arm draped loosely around Snagg's shoulder, the latter being closest to the microphone. "I want you to know who I am," Snagg told the audience. And quickly, with Deemon's help, he removed his shirt. Under the penetrating glare of the spotlights, his green skin and trompe l'oeil scales and ridges were luminous—the effect startling. It was a full minute before he could continue speaking.

"Growing up—way before I got a single tattoo—I was an outcast 'cause I was gay. I didn't fit in. My parents were super-religious people and they preached about the love of God and Jesus. But trust me, I never saw any of it from them or from the people they hung out with. They preached about allegiance to this country right or wrong because it was supposed to be a place that just loved freedom and democracy. Well, that was a lie too. It didn't matter who you voted for or who you didn't want to bomb—the people in power just went ahead and did whatever they were gonna do. It was 'in the bag' like they say—and if you weren't playing their game, you were an outcast. I got real tired of being rejected for being me. And so I decided that rather than waiting to be rejected by all the good people of this God fearing country, I would make myself a reject. Then if someone cared about me, I would know it was for real, not some 'the *Bible* told me to care for you poor thing' shit that I was so used to. And believe me, I found people who truly accepted me. They haven't got homes, they live in tunnels and holes and have more problems than most of you out there have ever even thought of. But they are *real,* and they care about other people. Like me and Deemon, most of them have been left behind, and I'm damned glad to be with them. Thank you very much."

Deemon leaned into the microphone. "My buddy has said it all except for this. See? Snagg won't brag on himself, but he helps run the Hunt's Point Food Co-Op that feeds over 1,000 people a day. He's figured out a way to give a lot of people a place to live—maybe not fancy, but a real home. And, since he's like a computer genius, he's helped connect more good people than anyone I know. Our friends are useful. I write. I write about things like the fact that our health care system figures everything on cost and profit, not what a patient needs to live. Funny thing that it's in the same country where our military figures weapons on how many people they will successfully kill, with no regard for the cost. That's the kind of thing I write about. That's what I do. Other people we live with paint and make music and movies. I think that's how we can spread the message that we really can all live together and make things beautiful again… better than they've ever been.

That said, Snagg, Deemon, Lyla and Marie left the stage, passing Daisy-Ann and Divine X as they entered. Again, to careful observers, it seemed that the first group dematerialized as the incoming pair materialized. Some TV critics commented on the astonishing lighting effects.

CHAPTER 99

In Huntsville, Texas, Superintendent Lester Merles—like everyone else in the nation—was watching the broadcast. When he saw Divine X on the screen he tried to shout and point at the same time, spraying the contents of his coffee mug across his desk.

"Son of a bitch is there in Denver!" he bellowed. He was already dialing his phone.

"White House," a voice answered.

"Listen, this is Lester Merles, I've gotta speak to Karl. . . Karl Rove."

"I'm sorry, Sir. What did you say your name was?"

"Lester Merles, Lester Merles. I'm superintendent of Huntsville. I've gotta talk to Karl."

"Is Mr. Rove expecting your call?"

"Damn right he'd *better* be expecting my call."

"I'll be happy to put you through to his voice mail, Mr. Merles. One moment. . ."

"No! No voice mail. I've gotta talk to him right now. It's an emergency."

"I'm sorry, Sir, but Mr. Rove is not available at the moment. I'll connect you to his voice mail now." And the operator made good on her threat.

"This is Rove. Leave a message."

"Karl, Karl, this is Lester Merles at Huntsville. You've gotta call me right away. That fella we were supposed ta fry yesterday—he's in Denver—on TV! Well, he escaped, he's there and… oh God, he's gonna tell what he knows!"

The machine timed out.

"Damn! Merles slammed the receiver. He hit his intercom. "Druckle, get in here!"

Assistant Deputy Superintendent Harold Druckle, entered. As head of security he was taking as much heat as Merles for Divine X's escape.

"That nigger's on TV," Merles gestured at the tube.

"Huh?"

"Don't stand there like a cretin, look at the screen. Divine X is there on TV. He's in Denver with the *Pope*!"

"With the Pope?" Druckle strained to recognize faces. Everyone on stage looked tiny and pretty much alike. "Which one is he?"

"Which one do you think, you idiot? You think the Pope is a nigger, or do you think the nigger's got big tits? There's only four people there. Only one of them is a nigger. Holy crap! You be so stupid, no wonder we're up shit creek."

"I think I see him."

Just then a close up of Divine X came on the screen.

"Hey! That's Divine X Marcus! He's there in Denver!"

Merles sighed.

"What should we do?"

"I already called Rove. Only got his answering machine."

"We should call the FBI."

"Rove said never call them first about anything having to do with X. Always call him first. But I called the White House and he wasn't there."

"Call his cellphone. You've got that number, remember?"

"Shit! I forgot." Merles was reaching for his wallet. "He said never put it anywhere except on a piece of paper without his name. Ah, here it is." He quickly punched in the number. The phone began to ring.

A waitress in a Washington, DC steakhouse heard a phone ringing. It seemed to be coming from a booth at the back where another waitress said the customer had skipped without paying the check. The sound was coming from under the table. She got down on her hands and knees looking for it. There, its LED flashing, was a Blackberry lying between a man's suit, a pair of shoes, and a small black notebook. She reached for the phone but it stopped ringing. Picking up the Blackberry and the notebook she sat down in the booth. The Blackberry's screen said "Incoming Call—Huntsville CF, TX." She put down the phone and opened the black book. She laughed. It was nothing but a list of male escort services.

When Rove's answering message kicked in, Lester Merles turned bright red. "Well fuck you, Karl Rove, go to hell!" he yelled at the phone. But apparently, someone else was in charge and had the idea first.

CHAPTER 100

Daisy-Ann had never looked better. She'd never shied from the spotlight, but this was different. She was proud of why she was stepping into its glare. She was sure of herself. Taking Divine X's hand she led the way to the microphone. In spite of the bright lights shining in her eyes, she was aware that a phalanx of police was moving towards the stage. She looked towards the wing and saw Jesus nod, smile, and motion that she should go ahead, so she did.

"My name is Daisy-Ann Wexler." As she spoke, she saw the police draw their guns. But she continued speaking. "I am here tonight with a very dear friend—a new friend—but someone I'm so proud to be here with because as you'll see, he has courage way beyond most of us."

The police were now within twenty feet of the stage. One of them carried a bullhorn. "Freeze or we'll shoot." The threat was aimed directly at the two unarmed people in the spotlight.

People near the stage scrambled out of their seats to find safety. Once again the auditorium was filled with noise—screams, shouts, boos—the sounds of confusion. And then it stopped. As if they were a single body, the police simply relaxed where they stood. Their guns gently lowered and pointed at the ground. Then the attack force went to sleep. Their descent to the floor was gradual—just like children tired from too much play of war.

Jesus winked and Daisy-Ann continued. "Please take your seats. Everything is all right. I think you will understand in a minute why some people are trying to prevent us from speaking."

Daisy-Ann was far more understated than she realized. Outside the Jesus Dome, for a radius of twenty blocks, Army personnel carriers, tanks, jeeps and armored vehicles were stalled in the streets. Commanding officers slept at their posts. Blackwater officials snored. Helicopters circled the perimeter overhead, unable to get closer than five blocks from the Dome.

"Black Hawk to tower. We are attempting approach on Jesus Dome." Then a loud crashing noise. "Unable to approach. It's like there's a wall we hit. We've damaged a rotor, must set down." The same message from dozens of pilots was repeated over and over.

Unaware of the chaos outside, Daisy-Ann proceeded.

"As many of you know, I was married to Governor Duke Wexler of Texas. Some of you were mighty surprised that he wasn't Tim Michaeljohn's Vice-Presidential candidate. But you see, there's so much that we aren't allowed to know. And it's all stuff that we had *better* know or this planet is goin' to go to hell. That's why me and my friend are here tonight. He is Mr. Talib Ali Marcus, better known as Divine X Marcus."

Again, noise in the auditorium, but this time it was anticipatory as Divine X's name was recognized.

"As most of you know, Mr. Marcus was scheduled to be executed by the State of Texas yesterday. As a Governor's wife, I've lived those days from the other side. But I'm here because, on account 'o bein' on the other side, that's the *only* side I ever looked at. I took my husband at his word when he'd tell me that the reason he signed a death warrant or refused to grant clemency or a stay of execution because he knew for a 100 percent certainty that the condemned man not only was guilty, but *deserved to be murdered by us collectively.*

"I went along with ma husband becawse I didn't want to give any of my time to thinkin' about somebody else, somebody who's different from me. I thought that because Duke'd spend a whole fifteen minutes going over the convict's records—just the way George Bush used ta do—that he was bein' real thorough and knew what he was talkin' about. Pardon my French, but we were all bein' sold a total load of horse pucky."

Daisy-Ann had the audience's full attention. They were with her. Finally somebody from the inside track was talking like a human being and promising to tell some of what has been held back for so long.

"Y'all are goin' to be meetin' some people tonight who can tell you a whole lot more than I can about what's goin' on. That's fer sure. But in order for you to know that we're not layin' on a whole bunch of bull crap, and that we're not a nutty bunch of 'conspiracy nuts,' well, we gotta start some of this at the very beginnin'. So that's why it's gonna be important for y'all to listen real careful to what Divine X has to tell ya. I can jest say for myself that this man is innocent, and if he'd been executed yesterday, the real murderers, the real killers, the real *bad guys*—as some of the bozos runnin' this country call people they don't like—those real rats would've got away with their crimes. But they didn't, and a friend of ours made sure that they didn't. But right now I'd like you to give a real warm welcome to a very alive and very important friend of mine, Divine X Marcus."

Daisy-Ann stepped back and led the applause in the Dome. It thundered. It roared. And then it stopped so completely that Divine might not have needed a microphone to be heard.

"In the name of Allah, the beneficent, the merciful, we give Him praise and thanks for His goodness and His mercy. We thank him for Jesus and Muhammad. Peace be upon these servants of God," Divine X said as he began. "I greet all of you dear and wonderful brothers and sisters with the greeting words of peace. We say it in the Arabic language, Assalamu Alaikum."

The crowd, long schooled to hate Muslims and to consider them terrorists, was taken aback by the greeting. Still, there was a respectful silence in the great auditorium. And then from somewhere near the top of the farthest corner of the auditorium was heard, "Alaikum Assalaam." It reverberated alone, then was joined by other cries of "Alaikum Assalaam." Soon approving sounds and applause swept through the audience.

Then he smiled and said, "Hi. It's real good to be here. It's good to be alive."

More applause.

"I know that what I am about to tell you is going to sound impossible to some. It will be called treasonous by others. It will be called insane by more. And it will be denounced here and there. But my brothers and sisters, I have traveled too far, I have seen too much, I have been too close to death to do anything tonight but tell the truth. I praise Allah for his goodness to me. I praise the prophet Mohammed who has appeared to me. And I praise Daisy-Ann Wexler, who has shown me that even those who are caught in the trap of the Great Satan himself, can awaken, open themselves to truth and do mighty work for good."

By the time Divine X took the platform, the White House was in full-blown meltdown. Even though Laura was in the dark about most things, she did know something about Divine X Marcus. The prospect of his spilling his story on national television had prompted the First Lady to discard her perpetually stunned-on-Botox expression for something even more alarming. In short, she emulated her father-in-law. George, who was particularly sensitive to half-digested projectiles since his father's unfortunate dinner date in China, fled the room just in time to run into Condi Rice's private secretary.

"Mr. President, it's Paul Wolfowitz. It's urgent. He's calling from… wherever the hell he is. Pick up your inside line. *Please.*"

The news of an incoming call surprised the President because in his present condition, he truly believed that when he smashed his personal phone repeatedly on the floor, he was stopping other people from making incoming calls to the White House.

"Should I answer it?" he asked, just the way he normally asked Karl.

"Of course you should answer it! Condi says we're in meltdown and Wolfowitz is having a cow."

That last idiomatic expression was lost on the woefully high President who fully expected Wolfowitz's first sound to be *moo*. He headed for the Oval Office. There, the chairman of the Republican Party was waiting for him.

"Mr. President…"

"I can't talk to you. I have to take a call from Paul. He's in labor." The President picked up his phone. "Paul, are you all right? What were you doing fucking a cow?"

"Huh?"

"Well, that's your business. I can see a chicken or lamb—something like I did in college—but a *cow*?"

"Are you on drugs, George? Stupid question. Do you know that the whole thing is falling apart as we speak? What is wrong with you? Stop that shit in Denver. That Divine X guy is gonna be the break in the dam." Wolfowitz, speaking from the hiding place he'd used ever since the World Bank scandal, was seriously panicked.

Bush whimpered, "I miss Karl."

"Oh for heaven's sake. Miss him all you want. You're the Commander in Chief. Do something!" Wolfowitz slammed his receiver and the phone went dead.

"Can he talk to me like that?" Dubya was addressing no one. "I like what Karl and Paul and Condi and Dick do. They have good ideas. And I'm Top Dog. It feels good to be Top Dog. Karl worked it all out. They can't mess it up now. "

In Denver, soldiers were trying to enter the Jesus Dome to stop the proceedings, but it was as though an unseen hand held them back. Inside, just as Divine X completed his opening comments and got to the "meat" of his message, FOX News interrupted the broadcast.

CHAPTER 101

FOX BREAKING NEWS BULLETIN

"This is Max Sevillo with a FOX News special Breaking News Bulletin. FOX has just learned that troubled teen star Bisquit Slattern has checked herself out of the $50,000 a week rehab clinic in Boca Raton, where by court order she spent the last 24 hours following her hit and run arrest. Fortunately for Miss Slattern, the two victims—both deceased—were illegal aliens. Still, when our cameras caught up with her, Miss Slattern read the following prepared remarks:

Bisquit Slattern, dressed in her trademark minipants, knee boots, and halter-bra, stepped up to a phalanx of microphones.

"Hello," she said in her tiny grating voice. *"I'm so grateful to be here, a free woman. I just want to say that my addiction to drugs and alcohol is really truly over forever. I'm very, very grateful for that. But the way the judge went about sentencing me so harshly and making me be in this awful—expensive—place all night, that really, really hurt my feelings and everything. I was like awake all night because they claimed that they couldn't give me my sleeping pills on account of the judge. So I'm like sleep depraved…"*

Here, a lawyer standing behind the young star stepped forward and whispered in her ear.

"Deprived? Is that what I'm supposed to say? Okay. I'm deprived… sleep deprived, and that really doesn't seem right since even the terrorists in our jails are treated more better than that… probably. And the food! They made me eat it even though my doctor says my anorexia is a condition!"

Again the lawyer whispered something.

"I'm sorry. I'm just so stressed from this ordeal. What the doctor said was that my anorexia is a condition, and the judge didn't have a right to put me in a place where they <u>forced</u> me to eat. So I'm like going to sue them for that. But now I have to go. My band has like disappeared, and we have to start auditioning which is a real bummer on account of my being so tired because of not sleeping from the judge making me so stressed."

Her remarks concluded, Bisquit turned to go. Her lawyer intervened, whispering as he shoved her back to the microphones.

"Oh yeah, and I want like really heartfelt to say I'm sorry about those Mexicans who died on account of my car and all. I'm like really sorry that they won't be able to take jobs from loyal Americans—like 'God bless America'—and I just want to say that I'm really glad that at least I didn't hit anybody who counts. Okay, bye, and thank you very much!"

Pulling at the edges of her mini pants which had somehow inched upward to an alarming height, Bisquit Slattern walked away, turning several times to wave and wink over her shoulder. Max Sevillo returned in close up.

"This is an amazing turn of events. Bisquit Slattern, who only days ago was considered an out-of-control party girl, has just demonstrated her complete recovery from addiction and has given a most moving and sincere apology to the illegals. I'm touched myself. This is Max Sevillo reporting from Boca Raton, Florida. And now back to our coverage from the Jesus Dome there somewhere in the Midwest."

CHAPTER 102

Inside the Jesus Dome, Daisy-Ann smiled with pride as Divine X began to reveal historic truth.

"In 1993, the World Trade Center in New York was bombed. As you all know Sheikh Omar Abdel-Rahman was arrested and found guilty of planning the attack. His lawyer, Lynne Stewart, a translator Mohamed Yousry, and a paralegal, Ahmed Sattar, were later prosecuted and convicted of conspiring with a terrorist.

"In 1995 the Murrah Building in Kansas City was bombed, and Timothy McVeigh, a right-wing white supremacist was arrested, tried, and executed for the attack. His so-called co-conspirator is still in prison.

"In 2000, the Federal Building in Austin, Texas was bombed. The police immediately released the name and photograph of the person they said was the perpetrator. They arrested him, tried him, and sentenced him to die… yesterday.

"And then, on September 11, 2001, we are told that 19 men, under the leadership of one man sitting in a cave in Afghanistan, commandeered four commercial jetliners, crashed two of them into the World Trade Center towers, one into the Pentagon, and that the fourth crashed when heros on board attacked the terrorist pilots.

"I have just outlined the conspiracy theory for each of the four largest domestic terror attacks this country has endured. And I am here to tell you that in each case, the explanation—the so-called official explanation—is a fictional conspiracy theory of the worst sort.

"There are others who will be able to speak to some of these events. I will confine what I have to say to the case that came to involve me."

There was a loud crash, as a Colorado State Trooper, attempting to ambush Divine X from a catwalk behind the stage, fell over the railing. Hurtling down towards certain death in full view of everyone, just before he hit the floor, he simply disappeared.

When the crowd settled down, Divine X continued. "I was an active member of The Ubuntu Brotherhood—a group of brothers who joined together after the demise of the Black Panther Party, determined to carry out the original, noble vision of its founders. I was working at a food pantry in Austin and teaching martial arts to kids after school. We always knew the police hated us because we wouldn't accept disrespect from them in any way. In our neighborhoods, cops knew that they couldn't shoot an unarmed Black man and get away with it. That's because every one of us was armed— yes armed… with a digital camera or video camera, so that everything that happened in our neighborhood could be documented from many angles.

"I was at the pantry when the explosion at the Federal Building went off. Like everyone else, I was shaken by the sound of the blast and wondered what had happened. Since my wife and kids lived in the direction of the sound, I called 911 to find out what caused the noise and to see if my family was in danger. That was all I knew about the bombing until that night when my name and photograph appeared on TV as the "primary person of interest" in the case. I was arrested an hour later while serving some collard greens to a kid.

"I can't say much about my trial. I was barred from the courtroom because a judge said I was violent and posed an immediate risk to the jurors. Of course, they were allowed to hear that allegation. Many of you may have watched the proceedings—watched as videotape surveillance tapes emerged showing me buying materials for a bomb and finally exiting a van just before it exploded and brought down the Federal Building. You have seen all that. I was *shown* to be guilty on grainy surveillance videotape. When I was finally allowed in the courtroom, it was to hear my sentence of guilty and my penalty: death.

"But while I was being held in custody, I inadvertently learned what I am about to tell you tonight. I was sitting blindfolded in an interrogation room ten days after my arrest, when four Federal agents entered, accompanied by two people, one of whose voice I immediately recognized. After they had roughed me up a little, here's what they said."

Divine X took a drink of water. He needed to cool his throat. He was about to blow the fires of hell in the direction of the powers that be.

CHAPTER 103

Since his surprise meeting with Jesus, Tim Michaeljohn was a changed man. It can't be said that he was a man of clarity or undivided motivation. It can't be said that he was willing to accept advice. But it can be said that he was on a mission. Now, doing it his way, he was driving from the Denver airport towards the Jesus Dome. Traffic halted behind a police roadblock a half-mile ahead. Tim didn't have time to wait. He killed the ignition and leaving his keys behind, began to run towards the police blockade. His approach signaled danger to the very jumpy law enforcement officers. Rifles were raised and Tim saw red laser spots on his chest.

"Tim Michaeljohn," he cried. "Senator Tim Michaeljohn! I have to get to the Jesus Dome." He held his identification out on front of him. "I've come alone. No Secret Service. I'm unarmed. I must get to the Jesus Dome."

Still in the crosshairs of many rifles, Tim pushed forward and handed his wallet to a heavily protected officer.

"He's clear," the officer announced after inspecting the ID. "Let him through."

"Let me through? Provide me with transportation, you idiot! I've got to be at the Jesus Dome."

"Haven't you heard? Nothing is getting through. There's some kind of barrier."

"It won't stop me. Now get me in that jeep." Michaeljohn was already heading to a waiting vehicle.

"Suit yourself..." the officer said, adding softly, "asshole."

And so it was that Tim Michaeljohn, passing easily through what was thought to be an impenetrable barrier, arrived at the Jesus Dome. If he had known what Michaeljohn was about to do, Dick Cheney would have changed his resonance at that moment and ripped the former almost-President to shreds with his own false teeth.

CHAPTER 104

Inside the Jesus Dome, every eye was on Divine X. He was so sincere and vivid, and as he described what he had been through, much of earth's population relived the journey with him. They could *see* and *feel* it.

* * * *

Inside a secret bunker somewhere in Austin, Divine X came to. His jaw ached from repeated blows. It wasn't that they'd asked a question and he'd refused to answer. Instead, the blows came as a warning that he should "play ball" or suffer far worse. Someone had put thick pads under the blindfold, so even the faintest light not could get through. But they hadn't stopped his ears. Even though he heard a ringing sound as a result of the punches to his head, he could still hear the voices.

The first voice, which Divine X later realized belonged to Lester Merles, the prison superintendent, sounded like a bad Jimmy Cagney impression. "Don't worry boys," he said. "He'll soften up. They always do." Two blows followed.

Divine was used to pain. He'd grown up with pain. He smiled inwardly with the thought that his father used to hit him harder than these guys back when he was only twelve. *That* was pain. The fists would find their mark. The child always knew it wasn't punishment coming from love or a hope for him to learn, it was punishment arising from his father's hatred of the world and everyone in it including him. And so those gut slugs, those right hooks to the face hurt worse than anything his captors could do.

"Go ahead, ask him whatever you want." It was Merles again. "He knows he can either say 'yes' or we're gonna fry him like cheap bacon in grandma's pan."

He heard someone step forward. "Talib Ali Marcus?"

The voice. He recognized it, but he couldn't place it. He didn't answer.

The voice again. "Are you Talib Ali Marcus? I'm talkin' to you boy."

Again he didn't answer.

"Uh, nigger likes to be called Divine X, Sir. Won't answer to the name his bitch mamma gave him. Says God gave him the other one. And he don't like you to call it a name. You're supposed to call it a fuckin' 'attribute.' Don't that just rock your nuts?"

The familiar voice chuckled in a way that had Divine tighten his stomach muscles just in case there was a fist attached to the sound.

"So you like to be called Divine, huh, nigger?"

"I am Divine X," came the reply.

"Well, y'see boy, you're between a rock and a hot place." Again the chuckle. "I mean you either play the game the way we want it played, or we got a chair that'll turn you into fry cheese. Then we'll see how divine you are."

No answer.

"You hear me boy? We can turn ya into jack mack."

The voice was from someone on TV. He'd heard it on the news. Divine was angry he couldn't remember a face or name.

"I said, do ya hear me boy—stupid dumb-assed nigger!" And this time there was a fist that seemed to fly as fast as the sound. As it landed, slightly to the left of Divine's breast bone, he remembered. It was Governor Bush's attorney general, Duke Wexler! What was he doing in the interrogation room?

"Got your attention huh, you dumb fuck."

Divine nodded. Play along. Find out what they want.

"Good. So you realize your situation. We're in control, boy. There ain't no bleeding heart judge waitin' to see you in the courtroom. You're not even gonna *be* in the courtroom on account of we let everybody know they should be mighty afraid of you. So you're gonna rot in the box while one of Texas' most fair judges pronounces you guilty and sentences you to death. You got that, boy?"

Another nod.

"Good. But it would make us all feel real bad to watch you smokin' and shittin' your pants and all, so we're here to make you a little proposition. Are you listenin' good?"

A nod again.

"Good. So here's the drill. We're gonna bring a video camera into the box and set it up with some lights—just like on *60 Minutes*—I mean real star treatment for a garbage eatin' nigger like yerself. And then you're gonna look into the camera and you're gonna describe exactly how you went to Austin and blew up the Federal Building." He paused briefly. "Oh, and don't worry about what to say. We'll have it all written out for you so you'll be accurate and have all your facts right about how you did it."

"I didn't do it."

"Doesn't matter. Somebody did. And you're gonna get all the credit… or, should I say, *take* all the credit. I mean, you'll be a hero with lefty intellectuals and some trailer trash."

"I didn't do it."

"You a retard? I don't give a fuck what you didn't do. You're gonna *say* you did this. And then the newspapers are gonna report that you died accidentally in your cell right while the trial is going on—on account of your feeling so guilty and all. And then we're giving you a new name, a new identity, and sending you to a certain country so you can live out your life in peace. Capice?"

The fix was in. He knew it. Why the Attorney General? Had Governor Bush ordered this? Was it because of public pressure to get a perp? Political favor being returned? Something else? Divine whispered, "Why?"

"Why? You're stupider than I thought. Why? Because *you did it—* that's why."

"I didn't." He could picture video cameras capturing his words. He wasn't going to say anything damning.

"But everyone is going to hear you say that you did."

"I didn't."

"Do you know that at this very minute, in a private hearing, they are showing the judge video of you? Let's see. In one, you're meeting with a Muslim terrorist who's bartering with you for explosives. In another you're in a warehouse with your van picking up detonators, electronics and plastic explosives. And let's see—oh yeah, there's the one of you buying a ton of that fertilizer shit. And then the best one, the one of you running from the van that blows up and kills what?—a hundred and twenty-five people, including eight kids? Mm-Mm Mr. Divine, nope, I don't think you want to say you didn't do it."

"I didn't."

"Amazing how guilty a half million dollars of electronic wizardry can make someone. And you're that someone and you're fucked completely unless you play our game. You are going to play, aren't you, Mr. Divine?"

"I didn't do it."

"Your mother is Latisha Marcus, right? She has a rather weak heart, doesn't she."

"Leave my mother out of this."

"I don't suppose that a midnight raid of her house to find out how she cooperated with you in this terrorist attack—I don't suppose that would do her heart any good, now would it Mr. Divine? I mean they have to use concussion bombs to get inside and all that."

"You leave my mother alone!"

"You're hardly in a position to be barking at me, now are you dog? Now shut the fuck up and listen." Another fist.

"It's very important to the United States of America that you obtain your freedom in this manner, Mr. Divine. Like I said, if you don't, I'd say you're gonna be that bacon fryin' next to your mamma's eggs. Do you get my drift Mr. X?"

"I didn't do it."

He could hear Wexler back away. Apparently, thinking he was out of ear-shot, Wexler said, "This guy's a bigger piece of shit than that blond-haired, blue-eyed McVeigh. At least *he* stuck to his 'I did it alone' story to the end. Funny how he got the same offer, took the bait… but for some reason never got to collect on the new identity." And then, no longer softly, a laugh that chilled and grated. "Now he's another dead redneck."

Merles said something back, like he was joking around. He spoke too softly for Divine to hear. Then it was Wexler again. He'd moved farther away, but the words "Wolfowitz," "Cheney," "Bush" and "Rove" were unmistakable.

Wexler was back. "You ready to make a movie, son?"

"I didn't do it."

"You are one dumb fuck nigger," Wexler said. "You got no fat on you though—we're gonna have to feed you a lot to turn you into bacon."

Other people in the room seemed to think that was funny, and Divine counted four other voices.

Wexler retreated again. "He wants us to get him on tape. He's gonna be pissed as hell if we don't."

An unidentified voice chimed in, "We've already got him on tape, remember? But just so as not to make the conspiracy nuts go wild, before we show this guy on national TV, starve him a little. The body double in the video wasn't packing the kind of muscle this guy's got."

Another voice. "Cheney wants him to confess. It'll be cleaner."

Wexler's voice was the loudest and easiest to hear. "I don't know why they're so hard-assed about it anyway. Their little experiment has worked. People are clamoring for more laws to protect them. They're crying for revenge. Shit, this job was better than the '93 Trade Center thing. That one scared people, but they forgot it overnight. This one did the trick. Dick oughta realize that everything is ready."

CHAPTER 105

Divine X stopped his narrative for a moment and surveyed the crowd. Then he continued.

"And that's how it started, ladies and gentlemen. I heard it all that night and I've heard it repeated since. The Austin Federal Building bombing was an inside job. It was perpetrated by agents of the United States against the people of the United States just the way the '93 World Trade Center bombing and the Murrah Federal Building bombing were inside jobs. I was supposed to be the fall guy for Austin. I was supposed to die yesterday. But all praise to Allah and his prophet Mohammed, I was sent the bravest woman I know, Daisy-Ann Wexler, the widow of Governor Duke Wexler to save me. She rescued me even though it was her husband who was part of the design to have me executed.

"It's not for me to explain why our government sponsored those three attacks on its people, but I am here tonight to tell you that is what happened. There will be others who tell more of the story and explain what all this has to do with 9/11 and the recent disappearances. But for now, I just thank you for being here, thank you for your support, and thank this amazing lady. Good night."

As Divine X left the stage, a nun in the audience passed a note to a private security guard near the stage. It read, "Isn't the Holy Father going to celebrate the Eucharist?" When Fognolio began to introduce the next guest, the nun figured the answer was "no."

Fognolio's neck was getting tired from the weight of the Triple Crown, but as Divine X finished his address, he rose to his feet applauding. Cardinal Vonsecco moved back to the microphone and translated Fognolio's signs. "Please, my beloved friends, do not be afraid. We are approaching the final speakers—after whom you will understand what is happening and where we are in world history. We have heard of three attacks directed against the citizens of the United States by our own government. Now it is time to hear from a man who is going to help us make sense of the events of this nation's terrible day, September 11, 2001. He was rescued from "Gitmo" the US prison in Guantanamo Bay, Cuba, only yesterday. This gentleman was arrested without charges and put into the brutal hands of the CIA, NSA, and other inquisitors who formed part of Dick Cheney's private army. Ladies and gentlemen, here after a miraculous escape from his tormentors, I am proud to introduce Mr. Jerrod Parker."

FOX reporter Dirk Stillwater was again in high gear. "This is extraordinary!" he gushed. As you all remember, Jerrod Parker is the person who, five years ago, was nearly beaten to death with a baseball bat by his wife, Nancy Parker and her lover, cult follower Marcus DuChamps. And then—and this is so vivid to me I can almost taste it—he is the very person who helped the Jesus Christ imposter literally make hundreds of perfectly innocent people—and stock brokers—disappear off the face of the earth. I am a faithful Catholic, but I can tell you that for Pope Maximilian to show such approval of a person who is 1) obviously mentally ill, and 2) aligned with terrorist elements that seek to destroy us from within—well, it has me even more grateful that I'm a follower of our President George Bush, and of Reverend Robinson Patrick and the National Protestant Evangelical Church of the United States because they alone can be trusted to follow God's word and protect the United States of America." Stillwater stopped abruptly. "Uh, excuse me," he said listening for a moment to his earpiece. Then, with uncustomary humility he continued, "I've just learned that Reverend Patrick seems to be gone... somewhere... so I won't be *following* him right now. Uh, back to you in the studio."

The afore-named reverend was most definitely in no position to protect the United States. He was resonating harmlessly elsewhere.

Fognolio shook Jerrod's hand and gestured for him to step to the microphone.

"I can't begin to tell you how glad I am to be here tonight," he said. "The last four days have been the most incredible nightmare and the most astonishing awakening I have ever had. And I think many of you know I have lived through a previous nightmare and awakening." Jerrod looked to his right. "Thank you, Divine X, for presenting the events leading up to 9/11."

"As you may have read, I am, or was, a stock broker. It was my business to advance the causes of capitalistic enterprise to the best of my ability. I supported George Bush in 2000, I applauded the Supreme Court for over-riding the voting public and for installing Bush in the White House despite his loss in the election. I naturally supported Bush legislation that trans-ferred more wealth to the richest 1% of America's population and drained it from the poorest. And after 9/11, I believed and supported his so-called 'international war on terror.' I even supported the trillions of dollars of debt his Administration heaped on this country, rationalizing that it was a way to jump-start a sluggish economy. So you are not hearing what I'm about to tell from some long-term liberal who was always aghast at everything this President did in office.

"As you have been told tonight, our nation has been hijacked by men with a truly diabolical scheme. What I am about to tell you I have learned from the most reliable of sources—eyewitnesses. I'll probably be a little jumpy because I haven't slept during my torture at Guantanamo. But every-thing I tell you is true and can be checked out as thoroughly as you want." Jerrod briefly told about his arrest and how he was eventually thrown into a room full of naked prisoners. "Lying on the floor in total darkness at Guantanamo, with a stench that was beyond comprehension, I met Siraj, an Iraqi father of four who is being held captive without charges by our government. It was he who opened my eyes in the darkness.

Network coverage of Jerrod's speech was momentarily interrupted with a special news bulletin. Crowds of spectators were watching as Lynne Cheney, the woman Dick left behind, marched up a Denver street towards the Jesus Dome carrying one of Dick's assault rifles. Her private Halliburton helicop-ter sat near the Speer Bridge by the Platte River, its rotors still turning slowly. Spotting the cameras, she began to speak in the well-practiced demur voice Dick had always demanded.

"If we allow treason to be committed as we stand by, then we ourselves are guilty of treason," she began, holding the rifle high enough so that even a tight shot of her face would have to include part of the weapon. "My husband, the greatest American patriot ever to live, would have done what I am about to do. I am going to stop these treasonous actions the way Dick would have."

Someone in the crowd shouted, "Oh my God, she's going to go shoot one of her friends in the face!"

Lynne was not amused. She displayed a kind of dainty stoicism that Dick had found irresistible but others found brittle and arrogant. "Jerrod

Parker is a traitor and deserves to be shot between the eyes."

Another person in the crowd called out, "I didn't even know he was a friend of yours!"

Lynne began marching again. Members of the military and civilian police forces did nothing to stop her. They *hoped* she would be able to accomplish what they had not. A rugged woman who had learned to take the best punch Dick could throw, Lynne covered the half mile to the Jesus Dome with surprising speed. She lowered the AK-47 to firing position and forged ahead. And then, in full view of thousands of onlookers, she simply disappeared in the parking lot. It would later be reported that all she left behind was her rifle, an Ann Taylor dress, a rather cumbersome corset with metal stays, and one heavily lacquered wig.

Inside, Jerrod Parker was about to drop a bomb.

CHAPTER 106

Jerrod's face ached, and under the glare of the Jesus Dome spotlights, his eyes burned. But he had a story to tell.

"Siraj was a barber in Fallujah until the night American troops used a battering ram to knock down his front door. They used a concussion grenade that killed his three-month-old son. Then they shot and killed his wife and three other children in front of him. When we met there on the floor of that wretched room, he had been incarcerated at Guantanamo for three years. He may be the finest man I have ever met."

"In the darkness, Siraj introduced me to other prisoners, the first being Shamsi Wahhaj. There were men like Abdul Malik, Faisal Hamouda, Mazen Mokhtar, Nouman Ali Khan, Jamal Badawi, Ibrahim Negm, Amin Abdul Latif, and Azeem Khan. I will not name every remarkable person I met over the next 18 hours, nor will I be able to credit each person with the part of the story they gave me… but the story—the truth—is this. I begin with some background:

"A group of neo conservatives, the most extreme faction of the White House—Cheney, Rumsfeld, Wolfowitz, Perle and others including the President's brother Jeb Bush—published a paper in 1997 called *The Project for the New American Century*. It outlined their plan for the United States to complete its domination of the Middle East. They feared—and this you can look up on their own website—that it might be difficult to get popular support for an invasive war against Iraq and other Middle Eastern countries, unless there was a catastrophic event which they dubbed "a New Pearl Harbor." Bin Laden, their ace in the hole, was the means of providing that 'New Pearl Harbor'.

Conspirators with The Project for *The New American Century* and other people who had been called 'crazies' for years, patiently studied how to gain power. They learned that just as Hitler's propaganda minister, Joseph Goebbels taught, the greatest means of controlling the populace is through fear. The '92 World Trade Center, Kansas City and Austin bombings were practice runs to see what had the greatest psychological effect on the civilian population.

September 11, 2001 was the culmination—the fourth act of state conducted terrorism against the people of this country. And so, with a trademark 'shock and awe' beginning, airplanes were crashed into two towers, and somehow seven towers were brought to the ground. This was perpetrated by those who wanted to accomplish a coup in Washington, replacing our traditionally democratic government with a Nazi model. That is fact. The official government story is the real *conspiracy theory*.

"The local point men for the operation were New York's Governor, George Pataki, and that little tyrant who became known as America's Mayor, Rudy Giuliani. They cooperated with the genocidal plan in exchange for the promises from the White House that each would be the next Republican Presidential candidate. Of course neither of them knew the other had gotten the same promise. Obviously the promise wasn't kept—and we have Michaeljohn and Palin.

Pataki's recent, widely reported suicide, was… I'm sorry. I'm getting ahead of myself—and I have promised to stay with the account of what I have just learned first hand from the men at Guantanamo.

"I learned that most of the men who were accused of being the highjackers of the three airplanes are being held in US secret prisons. The aircraft of 9/11 were supposedly manned by 19 terrorists—men that Bush would have you believe were Iraqis—who, following some rudimentary flying lessons were able to maneuver 747's with pinpoint accuracy. But that is a lie.

"Three of the 19 men that Bush would have you believe were terrorists and who were 'miraculously' identified within hours after the attacks of 9/11 were nowhere near the United States that day and are still living in Afghanistan and Saudi Arabia. The other sixteen men who were identified as deceased in the attacks are very much alive and are being held in secret prisons. One of them is at Guantanamo. Shamsi Wahhaj introduced me to him in the dark. The United States government was willing to sacrifice the lives of all the passengers on board the planes, willing to sacrifice nearly 3,000 civilian lives on the ground, but it did not place the mission in the hands of amateur pilots. Hardly. Osama Bin Laden did give orders, but he was under the direct control of Dick Cheney's secret militia. Osama Bin Laden was *duped* into thinking he was operating independently, when he really was being used as an operative of the neo-con administration! Bin Laden gave his orders for suicide bombings, but there were no suicide bombers on those airplanes. The supposed video of the 'terrorists' boarding the flights was shot nearly six months before 9/11. The men in our secret prisons weren't suicide bombers. Those planes were remote controlled from the two headquarters of the 9/11 operation. The first was in Dick Cheney's 'undisclosed location'—the literal underground city in Virginia from which a shadow government has been running the United States for eight years. The second, which Faisal Hamouda described to me, was in Rudolph Giuliani's emergency bunker. Faisal was a security expert from Afghanistan who was brought to the United States by Giuliani to design an interception-proof communications system in the bunker. He thought his work was to protect the United States, not destroy it. He remains horrified to this day knowing that he contributed—albeit innocently—to the atrocity. Naturally, as soon as his work was completed, he was arrested without charge and has been held in secret prisons ever since.

"Giuliani's so-called bunker was on the 23rd floor of World Trade Center Building Number Seven. That is the building, as you may remember, that came down at 5:20 PM on 9/11, despite the fact that it had sustained little or no damage. It, like buildings one and two, were brought down by explosives installed by the military so there would be no evidence left behind. That's why, in a major blunder, the BBC reported at 5 PM that the building had collapsed—twenty minutes before it happened.

"Then there were the three airliners. There were no foreign hijackers on any of the three flights."

Someone in the audience shouted, "There were *four* planes!"

"No sir, there were three. I'll explain in a moment. Flight 93 was shot down by a US Stinger missile. The entire mission of Flight 93 was to have the American people believe that foreign terrorists wanted to attack the White House and kill the President and Vice-President. In a stroke of Orwellian brilliance, the greatest enemies of our nation were made to look like terrorist targets because of their 'patriotism.' But that wasn't the end of the horror.

"Again, I said there were three airplanes. The Pentagon was not hit by an airplane. The Pentagon was hit by a Navy Exocet missile. No matter how many lies White House officials spew out, the facts are the facts. The Pentagon was hit by a United States' missile. Ever wonder why so many Pentagon employees had been moved to the other side of the building before the attack? The official story is that there was construction going on so the building had to be evacuated at that time. Was it coincidence? Was it coincidence that hundreds of video surveillance cameras surrounding the Pentagon—the single most highly guarded building in the world—failed to operate at the precise moment of impact? I won't waste your time asking foolish questions. The empty airplane that supposedly hit that building was suddenly retired and then put back into service with a different paint job and serial numbers. For a step by step description of how it was done, look up Operation Northwoods, a plan drawn up by the joint chiefs of staff in 1962 wherein the United States planned to commit terrorist attacks on its own citizens and then blame them on Castro in Cuba.

"This is not the time to amass all the facts—I urge you to check them for yourselves. Some of you have already heard them. I am here to tell you that I have first-hand accounts. I voted for Bush, but there I was in Guantanamo, hearing what my government did against us—and I was hearing it from the very people who are being blamed. But it is not for what happened in the past that I am here. It is to warn you about what is taking place at this very minute."

Jerrod's words could not have been more timely. At the White House, the President—believed to be the least intelligent ever to have served the office—wiped the cocaine residue from his nose and said, "That's it."

As Jerrod continued to speak, an F-16 loaded with a tactical nuclear bunker buster blasted down the runway at Buckley Air Force base, the military communications nerve center twelve miles outside of Denver. It was operating under a directive from George W. Bush at the White House to eliminate the Jesus Dome.

CHAPTER 107

WASHINGTON, DC

Laura Bush was in the White House kitchen fixing chamomile tea with a little gin to settle her stomach. It was her practice to make her own remedies since she feared that the kitchen help—all of whom had foreign-sounding names and were considered by her as potential terrorists—would tell that her little tea cups contained 40% alcohol. At her request, a Secret Service agent always accompanied her to this part of the White House to make sure that she wasn't "abducted by the savages." She was about to make her way upstairs when she overheard the agent relaying the news that a tactical nuclear weapon was going to be dropped on the Jesus Dome. Immediately losing all of her usual soporific decorum, she stormed upstairs.

"You idiot!" she screamed at George who was in the arduous process of reading a bubble gum wrapper. "You big demented idiot!"

"What?" George looked up—caught halfway between a smirk and an "I dunno."

"You know perfectly well. Everybody in the House is talking about it. You're going to nuke Denver!"

"Oh that." George seemed to think there was something else more important.

"Georwge Walker Bush—don't you dare!"

George, once again straining to understand the complicated humor on the tiny wrapper, didn't respond.

"Geowrge! Look at me when I am speaking."

"I'm kinda busy right now. We've got ta change a whole lot of plans since the Pope is gonna blow up in five minutes."

"Geowrge! Stop! Listen to me!" Laura stamped her right foot—the very one which had been on the accelerator the fateful night of her lover's demise. "Geowrge!"

"Okay," he said. "I'm all ears." Any cartoonist could have told him that.

"Georwge. Do you realize that if you go and blow up that stupid Jesus Dome there in the middle of Denver, you'll likely destroy the library where I jest had 'em put a whole bunch of books from my readin' charity? How dare you! Those precious books about the sanctity of life before it starts, and those children's books about God's blessings on your endless war—they will all be blown to bits, and then who'll read 'em? You stop this madness right now, y'all hear? Darn it!"

Laura's face was all sweaty and beady, and her eyes—the ones that never quite pointed the same direction—seemed to rove with even more independence than usual.

"You've got a whole warehouse full of books, Tiger Tits."

"Oh! I'm going to tell Condi not to put out for you again—EVER!" And the First Lady turned on her heels and marched out the door.

CHAPTER 108

The F-16 was no match for whatever was guarding the Jesus Dome. The last communication from the pilot was a confirmation that the Jesus Dome was in his sights and that the missile was armed and ready to go. Then the communication stopped. When they found the plane in a Wal-Mart parking lot some time later, it looked like a Volkswagen that had been treated to a ride through a commercial garbage compactor. The pilot whose emergency seat had ejected successfully kept drooling and babbling about the "diamond bubble" around the Dome. EMS workers quickly proclaimed him certifiably mad and carted him away with a little bag of Thorazine dripping into an IV tube.

A visibly shaken FOX News reporter, Dirk Stillwater, stared into the camera and said: *"We have just received word that an F-16 jet fighter—apparently on patrol to protect the people of Denver from the collection of crazies that have overtaken the stage inside the Jesus Dome—has crashed into the parking lot of the Wal-Mart store just twelve blocks from here where there are always low prices always. The pilot safely ejected, but apparently suffers from post-traumatic stress syndrome. He has been transported to a military psychiatric unit for evaluation. Speaking of mental cases, we're now returning you to our live coverage of the Pope and the other very disturbed people at the Jesus Dome in Denver, Colorado. This is Dirk Stillwater reporting for FOX News where we give you fact without opinion."*

CHAPTER 109

The crowd inside the Jesus Dome had no idea that their end had been near. Jerrod Parker was concluding his remarks. "What I learned in Guantanamo is that if we change direction as a nation, if we end occupations, cease our aggressions, stop our persecution of Arab people, and recognize that we have no right to control the oil beneath another man's country, if we stop polluting the planet in defiance of other nations—if we do that, we have no need to fear an outside threat. In the words of my Iraqi friend Siraj, 'The US military has treated us so harshly, it has been easy for us to forget that the American people are not our enemy. I hope that very soon they will be our friends.' That is what I have come to tell you. Now Pope Maximillian will continue." Jerrod bowed quickly and left the stage. There was no sweeping applause—the audience was too stunned by what they had just heard.

Signing in a manner that showed great emotion, Fognolio said, "Children of the beloved flock, you remaining here on this earth, the one, the only great commandment that remains is to love one another. But, as you have just heard, there are those who have wanted war, suffering, and death. They stood to make vast fortunes selling tools of destruction. They have tried to pervert ancient writings—including the *Bible*—to justify themselves. Some have even claimed they were working to hasten the final world battle known as Armageddon. But these are false teachers and prophets, and they have left scars upon the earth. One of those scarred is our next guest who I am very proud to introduce: Mr. Adam Brigante."

Adam appeared in the doorway in his wheelchair and made his way center stage. The Pope lowered a microphone for him.

"Thank you, Mr. Pope," Adam began.

People in the Dome chuckled at the greeting. Fognolio laughed at Vonsecco's sign and returned to his seat.

To be on the stage of the Jesus Dome was overwhelming to the handsome young man in a wheelchair. Years of feeling voiceless were suddenly replaced with the knowledge that he was about to be heard by most of the world. He had an explosive secret to reveal. He took a moment and then spoke.

"I know that you are all impatient to understand why people have been disappearing, and that you wonder why so many of us are here telling what seem to be unrelated incidents. But I promise you that by the end of the night you'll understand why each piece of the story needed to be told. I'm proud to be here. I feel like I'm doing this to honor my legs. This gives me a chance to feel what happened to me was worth it because I can finally speak and be heard." Tears glistened on Adam's cheeks. He raised a massive arm to brush them away on a bicep.

"Your country has betrayed you. It has betrayed me. As most of you know, the Iraq War was based entirely on lies. A mood had been shaped in this country for more than twenty years preparing the way for that war to be supported. I was in the National Guard. After 9/11, like most of America, I believed that the United States was under threat of being attacked any day by the Arabs—it didn't matter which ones—they were all a blur to me. I believed that we needed to get rid of their weapons of mass destruction, and when we didn't find any, I believed that we'd gone to Iraq to get rid of a horrible dictator who was committing genocide against his own people, and when it became clear that Hussein had been a puppet of the US government obeying his orders to keep Iran in check, well, then I believed that we were in the Middle East to bring its people democracy and freedom. But when the civil war broke out I was told we should just stay the course and get the job done right. That's when I started asking questions.

"Did you know that we've built fourteen permanent bases in Iraq and also built the largest embassy in the world in Baghdad? Why? Cheney/Rumsfeld/Bush *always* planned a permanent occupation. Did it ever bother you that we didn't protect the Iraqi museums, but that American soldiers died protecting oil fields and pipelines and refineries? And did you know that the enslavement of the Iraqi people and their oil was only a tiny piece of a larger puzzle? Well, I've realized that I gave the use of my legs for that larger puzzle. If it was a good puzzle, if it would make the world better, my legs wouldn't matter. But it *isn't* a good puzzle. The people running this country don't care about us. I'm here because I want to tell you how

I lost my legs. But as I tell you that and the ugliness of people involved, I also I want you to see that good people made real sacrifices for what they believed. I hope that whatever you hear tonight, you'll remember that we soldiers ended up dead and crippled because someone lied to us. Maybe if our schools were better they couldn't have convinced us to join their stupid armies in the first place. I wasn't taught the truth about history in school. It was when I started questioning everything that I learned that there was a secret plan that could destroy the whole world. That's when I quit believing. I was just a soldier, but by chance I became part of trying to expose the biggest crime ever planned against this nation. I'll tell you about that in a…"

Adam was mid-sentence when a loud cry of "Get your hands off of me!" was heard from the wings as Senator Tim Michaeljohn struggled onto the stage, pulling with him a very tenacious military MP. Michaeljohn was about to strike the man when the MP's grip failed and he tumbled to the floor. Michaeljohn made his way center stage waving to the crowd.

It took a moment for Adam to recognize the Republican presidential candidate, but when the recognition hit, he was terrified. He relaxed a bit when Michaeljohn seemed intent on one thing only: getting to the microphone. He stepped past Adam without an "excuse me," sweeping the microphone into his hand. "Good evening! I'm Senator Tim Michaeljohn" he called, in his best pep-rally voice.

Adam looked to the wings. Jesus was still there, motioning that everything was okay, and that Adam should just stay where he was. It took all the faith the young man could muster.

Although the audience didn't reciprocate with a friendly "hello," Michaeljohn plowed on. "Until a couple of days ago, I was destined to be the next President of the United States of America. Destined because the same President who has now suspended elections and declared martial law, originally intended to have his buddies at Diebold make sure that 61% of the votes cast on their machines would be for me. But as you've seen, that didn't happen. He just went and screwed me over."

Michaeljohn seemed entirely unaware that his revelation was as condemnatory of himself as of Dubya.

"I'm here tonight because I've been working intimately with this Administration on a project which affects the future of every person on this planet. I'm hoping that by coming here and telling what I know—all of it top secret classified information—that I'll throw a little monkey wrench into Mr. Bush's plans and show him he'd better not fuck with me!"

He was gratified at the level of attention he commanded. Never mind that Jesus had asked him to appear as one of the invited guests in order to apologize for his treacherous role in history. What did that guy know? A presidential candidate wasn't just another guest. A presidential candidate would *never* apologize. On the contrary, it was time to commandeer the proceedings and get revenge by telling all—at least as much as served his purpose.

"In February of 2004, Bush was riding high in the polls, talking about his 'political capital.' Despite the high poll numbers, the Administration big boys were terrified that because of the President's botched job with Iraq, the economy and a host of other failures, the Republicans would lose control of Congress in 2006. They hatched a massive military contingency plan called *Operation Divine Shield*—a means of insuring that the Bush Doctrine, as it was called, would be continued and completed no matter who controlled Congress. I was in the US Senate and was asked to work with Cheney's office on *Divine Shield*. Of course, I didn't know at the time that the very plans I was working on would be used to destroy me."

Adam's gaze was fixed on the Senator. The genius of Jesus' plan was staggering. He knew he only had to wait for his moment.

Michaeljohn, summoning all of his massive self-congratulatory resources, continued. "I had no way of knowing that there was anything amiss with the Bush Doctrine." He paused. "I really shouldn't call it the *Bush* Doctrine. The man's too stupid, too ADHD, too devoid of curiosity or focus to devise any plan. I should call the plan the Cheney/Rumsfeld/Rove/Wofowitz/Perle Doctrine. Anyway, *they* call it the Bush Doctrine so I'll stay with that so we're all on the same page."

"*Operation Divine Shield* went into effect three days ago when George Bush imposed a curfew, declared martial law, suspended elections and established the National Protestant Evangelical Church. The detention centers built by Halliburton in 2006 have been activated. They are part of *Divine Shield*. In the last few days they have received hundreds of thousands of American citizens deemed by the Administration to be 'persons of interest' to one government agency or another. And all those new football and baseball stadiums you've supported? All were designed to be functioning prisons. Some of the people you think have 'disappeared' in recent days have become special renditions and are in these detention centers. These renditions are now completely legal under Patriot Act III, which you fools clamored for so you'd feel safe. There is no war on terror. We on the inside have known that from the beginning. There is only a war to *create* terror, because when you're scared, you'll submit to anything." Tim Michaeljohn's contempt for the masses was written in every line of his expression.

CHAPTER 110

The writers of ancient fables understood that one of the best ways to fool people and carry out nefarious plans is to "play dumb." The occupant of the White House, the Idiot-Boy President, knew that principle well. He'd played it better than anyone in history. Who could fully comprehend evil in someone who appeared so laughingly dull? He began crafting the image early, dropping the precise Connecticut pronunciation of words and substituting a backwoods drawl that mangled what was left of his English vocabulary. He practiced ticks—little shrugs and grimaces—that, when used at strategic times, seemed to be a cover for lack of comprehension. They were a kind of "Gee shucks" mask, honed and perfected by teams of his daddy's handlers into a caricature of a world leader with a deficient brain. It was not an accident, it was a triumph.

The belligerency of said world leader was not, however, part of the artificially created persona. The inability to change or admit mistakes was a genetic flaw that caused considerable tension in the Bush dynasty—neither parent wanting to consider the possibility that their family line had produced such a defect. Barbara Bush was particularly adamant that her son's obstinate nature could not have emanated from a source other than her husband's demonstrably defective loins. Hers was a world view far too pleasant for it to be troubled by the concept of familial imperfection. She was able to rest at nights free from the agonies that tormented her husband, because, unlike him she was sure that her contribution to the Bush dynasty's legacy was one of perfection. That the legacy was surely to be likened to Adolph Hitler's... well, that wasn't *her* fault. And besides, in her eyes, Adolph wasn't such a bad guy. Hadn't he found displeasure in the blights of society? Hadn't he taken bold steps to remove those blights, thus allowing people in nice society to enjoy a country free from the undesirable elements that drained away vital resources? Hadn't he devised ways to house, feed, and when necessary dispose of people whose usefulness to the larger good had either expired or been used up? Hadn't he gotten rid of a whole lot of Jews?

In moments of reflection—something the maternal progenitor of little George disliked but in which she occasionally dabbled—the warm reassurance of her family's sweeping goodness enveloped her. She had happy visions of "bad guys" being executed, inheritance taxes being cut, public education being reduced to its proper role as a charity service for the poor, New Orleans getting its skin lightened, and many, many other improvements made possible by her beneficent dynasty.

At that very moment in Washington, the aberrant son of this contented mother was standing alone, chasing away by sheer will the effects of the expensive white powder lining the mucous membranes of his nose. He gripped the edge of his desk to remain steady, never taking his eyes from the television screen.

"Bastard!" he whispered, directing the spittle in Michaeljohn's direction. "You think you are going to foil me? You think I have worked all my life to let a lousy little dick like you get in my way? You think that old Pope is going to protect you and hold back the fires of Armageddon? Hell no!" Even though George never liked talking to Israeli leaders, he knew what he had to do. Their accents always triggered memories of conversation around the family dining table where jokes about Jews were ubiquitous, and where Grandpa Prescott's albums of anti-Semitic cartoons from Germany were frequently circulated. In the midst of talking to an Israeli Prime Minister, George would get an uncontrollable desire to giggle. He'd found ways to blame the phone, blame a pretzel going down the wrong way, or say that the sound was coming from someone else in the room. But the overall situation was uncomfortable for him. Being the leader of the "free world" had always carried with it the drawback of having to act like he was fond of Jews. He wasn't. And he was tired of pretending.

The Commander in Chief smiled. "To think I have to thank another drug addict for dreaming up my perfect weapon, my ultimate threat: Armageddon. Thank you Johnny boy." And with that nod to St. John of Patmos, author of the *Bible's Book of Revelation*, George W. Bush reached for his secure line to the Pentagon. "Get me General Schravetz," he barked, flipping his Rolodex to his little crib file on the Israeli military chief. It was only a short wait. General Schravetz was on alert, expecting the President's call. Karl's instructions were always to begin the conversation saying, "How are your wife and two lovely daughters," whenever he called, but George found himself unable to fake pleasantries. "Do it," was all he said. He hung up the phone, confident that the history of Step Two would be written. He got up to do another line or two of his best friend.

Twelve minutes later, eight Israeli F-16 Fighting Falcons carrying nuclear warheads were on their way to Tehran. *Operation Omniscient Scepter* was underway.

CHAPTER 111

Michaeljohn had come to the part of his address that he imagined would stop George Bush in his tracks.

"While we were finalizing plans for *Divine Shield*, I heard of another plan—one called *Operation Omniscient Scepter*—which was so top secret that only the most highly placed of Cheney's insiders were allowed knowledge of it."

At the mention of *Operation Omniscient Scepter*, Adam nearly bolted from his wheelchair. Jesus signaled "Just wait."

"It is that part of the operation which I believe the President has ordered into action as we speak.

"If I am correct, and on matters of this nature I usually am, US troops at our fourteen permanent bases in Iraq have been put on high alert. The Israeli Air Force has been ordered to strike civilian targets within Iran—schools, hospitals, and such. I believe that could happen any minute. Bush expects the Iranians to strike back at Israel, providing him with the justification to order the Eisenhower Fleet—which is already stationed in the Straight of Hormuz—to attack Iran in a mission he will say was 'ordained by God.' Bush's handlers know that there will be massive U.S. casualties because Iranian Sunburn missiles travel twice the speed of sound and can vaporize a ship. The destruction of US air and naval resources will be enormous. But that's all part of the plan because Iran's retaliation will be the pretext for Bush to order that 'tactical' nuclear weapons be dropped on the Iranian civilian population. That is *Omniscient Scepter* phase one.

Tim stopped to admire the effect he was having, then continued, "There is a second phase to the operation that was the most highly guarded secret of the Administration. In 2005, I was informed by Cheney's office that a laptop computer which contained the details of *Operation Omniscient Scepter's Part Two* had been obtained by a rogue operative in Iraq, and that he was preparing to leak the information to the Israeli news media. As chairman of a covert operations unit, I was briefed on the entire plan, flown to Baghdad and assigned to oversee the recovery of the laptop and the elimination of the person carrying it. In what was made to look like a terrorist attack, this elimination was accomplished."

"Senator Michaeljohn," it was Adam. "I think you'd better let me speak."

Michaeljohn turned towards Adam intending to shut him up. But there was something that stopped him—a look in Adam's eye that said, "No more." And then there was the fact that his right hand seemed forced to pass the microphone to the young man.

"I was in Baghdad in 2005," Adam began. "I was ordered to my commander's office. You see, he was the true American patriot that Senator Michaeljohn just referred to as a 'rogue operative.' He told me that I was being assigned a special mission. Knowing that I had come to see the war as a crime against humanity, he entrusted me with the job of taking a laptop computer to the office of *Ha'aretz* in the Palestine Hotel. I never knew what was contained in that computer, but my commander did tell me that it was something called *Operation Omniscient Scepter Part Two*, and that the very survival of Israel depended on the success of my mission.

"When we got to the hotel, we were ambushed. My driver and my gunner were told to get out of the car. I was then instructed to hand over the laptop, get behind the wheel and drive. I tossed a different laptop out of the window and sped away. That's when the IED went off. I was left for dead. But I didn't die. An Iraqi cleric found me and got me to a hospital. I lost my legs, but I am very much alive. I believe, Senator Michaeljohn, I am the person you targeted for death."

Michaeljohn was staring dazedly at Adam. "You mean you're . . ?"

"Yes. I was carrying the laptop with the information that could have stopped the madness. You could have saved the world, instead you tried to have me killed."

"But now I've blown the whistle!" Michaeljohn appealed to the audience for support. "I have revealed what I know. You can't blame me for waiting!" He turned on Adam. "And *you* haven't told in all this time!" He looked around frantically as the audience began to boo. "He waited!" He pointed at Adam. "He waited until today!"

"You sorry schmuck." It was a five-star general striding towards Michaeljohn. "You sorry, sorry schmuck. You were in the position to have all this known and you did nothing. Adam only knew the name of the operation. You were ready to go along with anything no matter how horrifying so long as it advanced your dreams of power." The general winked subtly at Adam.

"Hold it!" Directly in front of Michaeljohn was a US Marine carrying a Bushmaster M4A3. "This is it, Michaeljohn. You're going to die for committing treason against the United States of America, for violating the Patriot Act III, section 42 USC. '141326. I am authorized to terminate you immediately!"

With that, the Marine pulled the trigger and a 5.56 mm bullet roared from the barrel and headed directly for the spot where Tim Michaeljohn's rather callous heart resided. Instant ultra-slow motion replays of the event showed the projectile reaching the Senator just a millisecond after he disappeared. A water glass behind him shattered and then there was silence.

CHAPTER 112
FOX BREAKING NEWS

A single call from a raving mad Laura Bush caused pandemonium at FOX News headquarters. "Get those Jesus Dome people off the air! They're ruining everything!" Ms. Laura, accustomed as she was to a steady diet of FOX, thought that a blackout of that network would effectively stop all news. FOX, ever ready to serve the Emporer's Wife, immediately shifted to "Breaking News."

"This is Marguelita Perez in Washington, DC. FOX has just learned that Senator Billy Ray Redden, Republican from Mississippi has recommended that the United States take direct military action against Hugo Chavez of Venezuela. Senator Redden, speaking on the floor of the Senate just moments ago had this to say:

Redden, a morbidly obese white man, had so many broken veins in his face that he appeared perpetually sunburned. Given to equally florid rhetoric, Redden was a great choice for "distraction of the moment." He was suffering from gout, and that added pain to his usual expression of fury. The overall visual result might have reminded a non-sympathetic observer of a red M&M candy with feet. At a volume not required for the nearly-empty Senate, Redden began his address:

"I have proposed today that the Senate of the United States condemn the actions of Venezuelan President Hugo Chavez in the strongest terms, and that our official policy towards the administration of that government be regime change! I make this proposal, with its request for military force, because the people of Venezuela can no longer exist under the brutal and inhuman rule of this terrorist dictator. I will not burden you with a list of his excesses, his eccentricities, nor even remind you that he has referred to our loving Christian President as the Devil. No! I will not take you back to those horrifying moments for even a moment!"

Redden was no orator, but his last sentence was so bad that even he stopped as though quizzing himself.

"I have only to inform you of his horrible misappropriation of his nation's natural resources to justify my call for the people of Venezuela to be rescued. It is this: Hugo Chavez, the terrorist dictator, is sending fuel oil to the people of the United States at rates far below market value! He is keeping people in Bronx, NY warm, while robbing the people of Venezuela of the kind of profit that we as Americans have come to expect from the oil industry. Can you imagine the economic agony that is being created in that continent over there?"

Here, Redden's lack of geographical insight was glaringly apparent. It was not, however, a lack that had hurt him in the eyes of the sitting President of the United States. In fact, when Redden once told George that the terrorists "down there in Canada" had to be wiped out, the Wise One replied, "Heckuv a job you're doin' there, Billy Ray, and added, "I always say, nothin' south of Texas can be trusted."

Redden was winding up for his finish. *"If that dictator can just <u>give away</u> the oil that belongs to the people of that Venezuela place, what can't he give away? See? We're so spoiled. Our oil companies don't give anything away. No, the profit from our oil stays right here."* Redden wanted to add, "with the American people," but even his brazenly deceitful logic wouldn't allow that. And in demanding another war, he thought it best not to name Exxon, Texaco, and Mobil as part of his rallying call.

Marguilita Perez was on camera again. *"That was the great Senator Billy Ray Redden speaking from the floor of the United States Senate in this FOX News exclusive Breaking News Break. Now back to the Jesus Dome where Senator Tim Michaeljohn—some of you may remember him—was speaking just before he disappeared. This is Marguilita Perez for FOX News, bringing you fact without opinion."*

CHAPTER 113

Inside the Jesus Dome, Adam and the five-star general were still standing on the stage. The crowd was straining to see where Michaeljohn had gone. The noise was overwhelming.

Adam leaned forward and said, "Now, to continue making sense of all this, it is my honor to present to you once again, His Holiness Pope Maximilian IV."

Spectators rose to their feet. At last the Pope would speak for himself. The applause for Adam, the general and the Pope continued—a concurrent cacophony of cheers, greetings, and weeping mingled together into a vast uncontrollable onslaught of sound.

The five-star general took hold of Adam's wheelchair and pushed it off-stage. Once offstage, he raised his arms and brought them down. He was Jesus again.

"That was awesome," was all Adam could say.

Snagg, who'd been waiting for him, hugged Adam. "You were amazing," he whispered.

Giuseppe Fognolio rose and came to the podium. Cardinal Vonsecco and Monsignor Popposi rose with him, standing to his right and left.

When the audio torrent died down at last, Fognolio's words were not those anyone expected to hear. There was no Papal benediction, no words of Latin, no pronouncements of blessing. Instead the world's Holy Father began carefully to sign his message, and Cardinal Vonsecco spoke his words.

"Brothers and sisters. Your attendance at this meeting here at the Jesus Dome and in every continent by satellite is so very welcome. It is also essential if the world is to survive."

A ripple of comment went through the crowd.

"I must first make a confession. I know that a Pope is supposed to be infallible and have no confession to make, but I have one nevertheless."

Some people apparently thought the Pope was making a joke and there was polite laughter.

"Listen to me carefully brothers and sisters. I am *not* Pope Maximilian IV. I am an imposter."

Although Fognolio continued to sign, the uproar in the Jesus Dome was so extreme that only the deaf reading sign language understood his next words. Fognolio, unaware that all hell had broken loose, continued his speech until Vonsecco tapped him on the shoulder and rapidly signed that he needed to stop and wait for some restoration of order in the room. Fognolio nodded and motioned for the audience to be quiet. Across the globe in bars, living rooms, airports, and on the street there was pandemonium. In Times Square, cordons of police had to contain the crowds watching giant TV screens.

In Rome, Cardinal Alberto Marchese quietly repaired to his quarters, placed a small pistol to his right eye and pulled the trigger. The bullet he fired erased what he thought was the only storehouse of secrets that existed. He was fortunately wrong. Another brain—Giuseppe Fognolio's—carried the same secrets, and they were about to be secret no more.

As much as individuals in the Jesus Dome would have liked to whisper to one another, shout their dismay, strike their foreheads and otherwise create the din known as "crowd noise," curiosity got the better of them. Soon loud "Shhh" sounds could be heard with "Quiet" called from every corner. When the decibels reached an acceptable level, Vonsecco nodded to Fognolio and he continued.

"My name is Giuseppe Fognolio. I am a janitor in the Sistine Chapel. And yet for reasons only now becoming clear, I was at birth given a face that is for all purposes identical to that of the man you have known as the Holy Father, Pope Maximilian IV."

Needless to say, there was another outburst of noise that had to be quieted before Fognolio could continue.

"When Cardinal Alberto Marchese, Prefect of the Congregation of the Doctrine of Faith of the Vatican discovered four days ago that the Pope had disappeared…"

Fognolio's signs and Vonsecco's translation were again lost. Attempting to cut through and finish the first part of his message, Fognolio began signing with grand gestures—indicating to Vonsecco that everything he did should be translated loudly. The result was unintentionally comic as the Pontiff waved his arms wildly, his body shifting awkwardly beneath the crushing weight of the Triple Crown, while his partner Vonsecco stood on tip toe screaming directly into the microphone at a pitch he could sustain only in short bursts. It was Laurel and Hardy on some kind of sanctified crack.

CHAPTER 114

President George W. Bush was distracted from the spectacle by a ring on his secure Pentagon line.

"Yeah," he said, annoyed to be bothered, but tingling with the expectation of reports of impending destruction.

"Baby," the voice was a cool purr, long practiced in soothing the savage beast.

"Condi?"

"Yes, Baby, it's me." The strain in the purr was lost on the President.

"Condi, where are ya? We should be watchin' TV together. Shit's about to hit the fan. I set the ball rollin' on our little *Ah'm Wishin' It Scepter*."

"Uh, Baby, it's *Omniscient,* and that's why I'm calling."

"Well, come on over and let's par-tee."

"Can't. I'm at the Pentagon."

"What? No cabs?" The President was overcome with his brilliant humor.

"Dubee, we got a problem."

At the sound of his favorite nickname, the President sobered—insofar as the chemicals coursing through his body allowed sobering. "What's the matter, L'il Rice Cakes?"

"Dubee, stop. I'm serious." There was a sudden edge to the purr. "We've got no pilots in Iraq."

"Don't mess with me Rice Cakes. I've had a tough day. I've ordered *Operation Ah'm Wishin' It Scepter* to commence—so whatever you're crying about really doesn't matter."

"That's what I'm talking about! I know you gave the order but—the Operation is on hold."

"On hold! What the fuck? On hold! I had 'em build fourteen bases—whatchacallit *permanent* ones—there in Iraq so that when I picked up the phone and said 'go shit all over them brown people,' there would always be someone to go shit."

"The Israeli mission failed. Its planes crashed and the rest of its air force has disappeared. We can't do anything because our bases in Iraq are nearly empty. Our troops have either deserted or…"

"Or what?"

"Or disappeared, Dubee."

"They what?"

"Now don't get angry. We just have to think this through. We can do it. We shut up Joe Wilson and Valerie Plame didn't we?"

"How many we got left?"

"None really. Reports I'm getting say that 80% have deserted and about 20% just disappeared. There are empty uniforms everywhere— in bathrooms, tarmacs, cockpits…"

"We don't need pilots for Plan B." The President's hands were shaking badly as he reached for a rolled hundred-dollar bill.

"But if you do that—if you send missiles to destroy both Iran and Israel…" Even *Condoleeza Rice* was troubled by the prospect of the Bush contingency plan.

"Do it, bitch." Bush slammed the phone, ruing the fact that he was bidding farewell to some of the best sex he'd ever enthusiastically attempted.

The phone rang again.

"Yeah?"

"You're premature, George." It was Condi again. "Just like in bed. I'm going to obey your directive, but you're a total idiot."

George started screaming into the phone. He wanted to say things that would hurt, but something was wrong. There was no response even though the background noise remained constant. "Condi?" he said at last.

The words fell on a red dress and spectacular red shoes. The rest of Condoleeza Rice had disappeared.

CHAPTER 115

Unaware that Condi Rice, the *Chief of Practically Everything* had just disappeared, Giuseppe Fognolio continued to sign his speech with Vonsecco brilliantly translating.

"Cardinal Marchese, did not wish to throw the entire Catholic world into turmoil. He did not wish to disrupt his very comfortable routine. And even more importantly he did not want George Bush to find out that the point man in his scheme for world domination had simply disappeared."

Fognolio was now accustomed to being drowned out by the crowd, so he took the current opportunity to have Vonsecco remove the Triple Crown. Vonsecco, not wanting to interrupt his translation, and quite overburdened by the weight of the crown, simply set it on the ground and prepared to resume his work.

A cry went up from the crowd seeing the holy object touch the floor. Ever mindful of the gentle sensibilities of the religiously fervent, Divine X rushed on stage and removed the object from its offending position. He was greeted with unexpected applause. He nodded to the crowd and disappeared into the wings.

Fognolio resumed his address. "So I stand here before you like each of the previous speakers, a simple servant of humanity. I preface my next remarks by saying that I commend you for your continued good sense in the face of what has seemed insurmountable evil. Recent polls show that President George W. Bush is reviled by 87% of the people of the United States. The thirteen percent of our population that may still have some allegiance to him falls into two groups: 1) the top 1.5% wealthiest Americans and 2) white people with less than a 5th grade education. The first group is operating from sheer greed, the second group has been scammed.

"I am about to detail some horrifying plans that this installed President has concocted and may enact in order to grab ultimate power.

"You know, when you are a lowly janitor, and when—like me—you cannot hear, some people act like you are invisible. They don't consider that you are clever enough to know what is going on, and so they are exceedingly careless around you. That was the case with a Papal tribunal that met in the Sistine Chapel, the same hall where the Cardinals meet to elect the Pope. Six months ago, they accidentally discarded papers they wished to have incinerated into a public waste basket intended for the used paper doilies and paper skirts given to improperly dressed tourists. When I emptied that receptacle, my eyes fell on some very troubling information about which I prayed daily, but saw no answers coming from on high.

"But then, four days ago, I was physically grabbed and rushed to the Holy Father's suite, dressed in his robes, crowned with his crown, and thrust onto his balcony to bless the crowd. I must admit that at the time I thought that I was going to be executed for having seen the documents I have mentioned. But instead, I found that I was to masquerade as the missing Pope.

"I determined to use the time to try to find the key to understanding the troubling documents I had discovered. And then, in a secret drawer in Maximillian's bedchamber, I found a document with the answers.

"As you know, there have been rumors, carefully dispelled by the church, that Maximilian IV is a Nazi who, in his youth, served in Hitler's army. When those reports emerged, he told the world that he served only by conscription and that he had no agreement with Naziism. Since we believed him to be God's emissary on earth, we had no reason to imagine his words to be anything but the truth. However, the documents I discovered on that fateful morning prove differently."

Here it was Fognolio who needed a moment to compose himself. He gave an apologetic gesture as he reached for a glass of water. From deep within the crowd the rich voice of a Black woman rang out, "You take your time, brother. You take your time. You're doing a'right, so you take your time."

Vonsecco quickly translated her words and Fognolio smiled. Heartened, he continued.

"Pope Maximilian IV had no disagreement with Adolph Hitler. He saw himself as divinely appointed to continue the Fuehrer's mission on earth. Sensing a philosophic kinship with the American president, Maximilian IV reached out across the great divide to his Washington counterpart and found his evil completion. The papers I discovered in that secret drawer were those of a clandestine agreement between the Vatican and the American President to establish a worldwide Nazi state under joint directorship of George W. Bush, Reverend Robinson Patrick and the Pontiff.

"As you know, Iraq, Turkey, Afghanistan, Syria, Saudi Arabia, Jordan, Pakistan, Lebanon and Palestinian Territories have all come under US occupation. Only Iran has remained independent. Throughout what Bush now refers to as 'The Crusades Against International Terrorism,' Israel has been a staunch ally, lending both airspace and air support.

"On the surface that has appeared credible, but even the most cursory look at history will raise serious questions about the Bush Dynasty's allegiance to the state of Israel." And here, Fognolio recounted the dark history of Prescott Bush, Averill Harriman and Henry Ford and their support of Hitler.

"So why would two Bush Presidents make such a show of being pals with Israel? Why would George W. Bush align himself with the Vatican if he liked Israel so much? Remember that the Vatican, under Pope Pius XII was complicit with Hitler in his plan to eliminate the Jews. What was the purpose? That is one of the questions that troubled me since seeing those first documents discarded in the Sistine Chapel.

"The agreement between Pope Maximilian IV and George W. Bush answers both questions. With the United States occupying and essentially controlling the entire oil-producing Middle East, and with the religious domination of the West provided by the amalgamation of Protestants and Catholics, the Bush Administration would accomplish one of its secondary goals: the elimination of its need for Israel."

There was silence in the Jesus Dome. Somewhere, in one of the sky boxes, a baby cried briefly—a sound audible to every person in the room.

"It has been a poorly kept secret within the military that the Bush Administration has always been intent on eliminating dependence on Israel. Eliminating the need to spend billions protecting and supporting Israel, has been an objective of right-wing forces within the United States for thirty years. This, despite the fact that some of the architects of the plan are Jewish. Commerce, it seems, trumps all loyalties."

Fognolio was nervous. He had been on stage of the Jesus Dome for well over an hour. During that time there had been no news from outside the dome. Now he was describing possibly cataclysmic events to a worldwide audience and assuring them that "forces" were on their side. Was he right?

He took another drink of water and looked towards the wings. There stood Jesus, smiling and nodding and gesturing for him to continue. Fognolio shrugged slightly to give indication of his unsureness. Jesus winked, smiled and nodded again. He did it so perfectly, that Fognolio's concerns vanished. He faced the audience and with renewed zeal continued his signed narration.

"There was another part to *Operation Omniscient Scepter*—a part that the Mossad, knew nothing about. It was called *Operation Omniscient Scepter: Armageddon*. That plan outlined how the US would authorize Israel to make massive attacks on Iranian civilians. Once the Israeli's strikes against Iran were completed, Pope Maximilian, as agreed, would condemn Israel in the strongest terms, calling upon all Catholics, all people, to consider Israel international war criminals and demanding an international boycott. The Bush Administration would not oppose the Pope's declaration, and would refuse to give Israel any further military backing. Using nuclear weapons, the United States then covertly bombs Israel out of existence, blames Iran, and uses massive nuclear strikes to destroy Iran once and for all. That is the Bush plan called *Armageddon*.

"George W. Bush plans to be the defacto leader of the Middle East, and also to have his 'Israel problem' out of the way." Under threat of attack, dictators in Africa and South America will place those countries under military/religious control. The neo-cons are certain that under threat, Russia will capitulate. Then, all that will remain is China. China will agree not to destroy the US economy by a mass selloff of US treasuries so long as Bush provides America's political prisoners as a slave work force."

In the time it had taken Giuseppe Fognolio to lay out the first two steps of *Operation Omniscient Scepter*, George Bush realized steps one and two of *Omniscient Scepter* had perhaps failed. It occurred to him that since Condoleeza Rice had never reported back to him, she might never have given the orders for the simultaneous missile strikes against Iran and Israel. This was a crisis for George. He would need to make a phone call. He picked up his secure line and called a number deep within the Pentagon. "Do plan B," he said and hung up. It seemed right, now that he had given his order, that he should take a nap. The Jesus Dome thing was boring—there were just speakers, no Powerpoint images—so George muted the TV, found his favorite coverlet and took to the couch.

He didn't know that as soon as he'd hung up the phone, the Pentagon went empty.

CHAPTER 116

At the Jesus Dome, Giuseppe Fognolio was concluding his remarks.

"That is what I have learned through the papers I discovered in Maximilian's desk. I am convinced that this horrific series of events will not be allowed to take place. I am convinced, because I have learned that for the first time in world history, an intervention is taking place. But in order to explain that, in order to have you know that the plans of the most insane person ever to arrive on the world stage and sit in a seat of power and to acquire the weapons to literally blow up this beautiful planet… in order for you to know that George W. Bush and his controllers will be unable to realize universal domination, I need to cede the stage. I need to have you hear from the one person who has the historical perspective and knowledge to make things clear. It is far beyond my honor to introduce to you the most misunderstood, misused, and underestimated person who has ever existed—the person known as Buddha, Mohammed, Isaiah, John Brown, Sojourner Truth and more. The person who is currently appearing to us in another form, the person labeled a 'terrorist' by the biggest terrorist of them all, the person George Bush has ordered to be shot and killed on sight by the many military personnel here in this auditorium. Ladies and gentleman, I present to you the man of the hour, Jesus."

It was an extraordinary moment. Jesus jogged onto the stage, his locks flowing behind him, and simultaneously throughout the audience, soldiers either dropped their weapons or disappeared altogether. The sound of clattering guns mingled with the cheers of the crowd.

"Hello!" Jesus pulled his locks back, twisting them up into a rakish bundle as he spoke. "Is everybody doing okay so far?"

There was a roar of approval. The surviving military personnel in the room had now all assembled in front of the stage and led the applause. Once the soldiers with guns disappeared, the crowd relaxed.

"There is only one piece for me to add to the puzzle," Jesus continued.

"The story might have ended right where Giuseppe Fognolio's concluded if George W. Bush was a different sort of man, but he isn't and it doesn't. The Dubya has never ever considered sharing power with the Pontiff. He hates Jews and he hates Catholics, so the idea of an allegiance with the head of the Catholic Church is laughable to him. The question for him: How is he going to remove the Pope from power without raising someone else to the same level? His solution is ingenious, and dispels any notion that the President is genetically stupid. It's dangerous to confuse evil with stupidity. Everything about the man is a studied attempt to slip selfishness and ruthless brutality past people who were more ready to laugh than seriously condemn."

Jesus was choosing his words carefully. He knew that what he had to tell would either end the cycle of earth's violence or incite more. What seemed to be a dramatic pause was actually a furious inventory of the people remaining on the planet. He recalled a few loose ends. Within seconds, there was an astonishing array of activity globally. Thousands of soldiers worldwide simply walked away from their weapons, others vanished. Rebel factions supported by the CIA in the Congo transmuted into a new resonance. Murderous thugs in Darfur left behind little more than machetes and American-made Jeeps. The entire staff of the Washington *Times*, the Republican National Committee, a percentage of Democrats, all stockholders in certain chemical and genetic food modification corporations traveled to their new resonance. The entire American Enterprise Institute and Manhattan Institute—headquarters and members—simply weren't there anymore. A laundry list of CEOs dematerialized in expensive restaurants, bordellos, limousines and mistresses' apartments. The Archbishop of New York, a particularly disagreeable and conservative cleric who thought far more of his involvement with the city's billionaire mayor Ari Barkin than with the good of his parishioners, seemingly evaporated leaving nothing more than a warm indentation in a mattress and a small, frightened, but very relieved young boy. In one instance, a wealthy businessman disappeared while being robbed at gunpoint. The thief—a man who felt he had nothing to lose—was so shocked by the experience he threw his gun away and returned to his wife and family. It will be left to history to marvel at the wisdom of those taken and those who were left behind.

Satisfied that he had rectified those oversights, Jesus proceeded.

"My Dad and I have watched many clever people operate on earth. Caligula and Pol Pot come to mind. But for sheer malign purpose, your President

and his handlers make them all look like relatively harmless domestic animals. Yes, he's been constrained by societal pressures, laws, and international
agreements, but he believes that *Operation Omniscient Scepter* will remove
every impediment.

"As Brother Fognolio explained, if everything had gone according to plan,
Pope Maximilian IV, Reverend Robinson Patrick and George W. Bush would
have shared a kind of ruling of the earth. This being unacceptable to George,
he had to find a means of ridding himself first of Patrick and then the Pope.
Patrick was going to commit the same kind of "suicide" as Vincent Foster.
The CIA would take care of that. For the Pope's demise, the solution was
masterful: find the person on earth who most saw the Pope as an enemy, a
person who was well shielded from public scrutiny because of his position
and also his relative obscurity. That person was discovered in a very willing
hit man: a prominent minister in the General Conference of Seventh-day
Adventists—a small, evangelical cult which preaches that the Pontiff is the
Beast of Revelation, the "666," the Antichrist. With the promise of sophis-
ticated weaponry and a CIA cover, the architects of *Omniscient Scepter* had
no trouble getting Elder Neville Dahlstrom to promise the timely demise
of Maximilian. But that plan was short-circuited. We have reason to believe
that George has tried to start phase one of *Operation Omniscient Scepter* and
failed. He has tried to initiate phase two and failed at that. I would imagine
that right about this moment George is considering something that would be
considered precipitous even for him."

Jesus' words were prophetic. Having awakened from his nap and realizing the Pentagon had failed him too, "Preemptive George" was at that very
moment entering the doomsday codes into his little black box. It seemed to
him that barring success of his dreams, Armageddon for everyone else was a
viable alternative. Glasses on, the President strained to press the right buttons
in the correct sequence. His tendency was to reverse numbers—not a form
a dyslexia, but a long-standing habit of changing facts and figures. He was
shaking and sweating. He wasn't nervous about what he was doing, he was
just craving some coke. Eventually the codes were entered, the sequence of
lights illuminated, and Junior George snorted four more lines to celebrate the
impending end of everything.

Apparently, Jesus wasn't ready to get blown to hell just yet.

CHAPTER 117

George's little prank started warning buzzers and flashing red lights in silos around the world. Jesus' Dad, as celestial observer, noted that the United States had nuclear weapons stashed away in places that even *he* had overlooked.

America's penchant for automation was well reflected in its weapons of mass destruction. No massive troop alerts were necessary, no technicians had to be scrambled or generals awakened from their slumbers in order to unleash the full fury of George's damaged Connecticut ego. Computer control insured that half the world's population would die in their sleep, and that the other half would die fully awake—but mercifully, both halves would be spared annoying warnings of annihilation.

The creak and groan of silo covers awakened or disturbed many a Midwestern corn farmer, Afghani poppy grower, Ukrainian caviar exporter, South American dictator, African oil executive, German munitions manufacturer, Iraqi political prisoner, New Jersey gentleman mobster, Panamanian lock operator, Japanese electronics CEO, South Korean rice farmer, and on and on. Each thought the experience an isolated anomaly. But with silos opened, thousands of missiles automatically slid into position. Clouds of hydrogen fuel and vapor mingled with the stale air surrounding long-entombed munitions.

If Jesus was aware that the world was about to disappear in a vast conflagration, he certainly didn't send any foreboding message to his audience. It is true that he'd announced that George was up to something precipitous even for him, but he said it in such a cheerful, "let not your hearts be troubled" way, that the spirit of the Dome was undampened. Instead of focusing on impending doom, Jesus was taking quite another direction.

"Folks, I know you've all been concerned about the disappearances that have been happening. I know a lot of good people have been pretty upset at the thought that they may have been 'left behind' by the Divine Rapture. And I know others have been in anguish thinking that some really hypocritical sons of bitches got to go to Heaven."

Jesus could tell from the reaction in the room that he was hitting very close to the bone.

"I don't want you to get any more pain from these situations. When Dad and I first started talking about intervening in this whole situation, we knew that in order to pull it off we were going to have to work 'under the radar' for a while. And we knew that if we did, some of you were going to be mighty confused and even hurt. Believe me, we're sorry for any problems this has caused. But we think that you'll exit this great arena into a much better world.

"What Dad and I have been doing is some big housecleaning. You've always had problems here. We know that. We've watched through billions of years while you developed. If you knew what you've come through to be here today, you'd be very proud. I wish each of you had been taught the truth about how this amazing world evolved. But for thousands of years there've been people who have told a lie to maintain power.

"Anyway, we keep having these people who rise to power and want to make Dad and me into some small minded yokels intent on vengeance. That gets us so mad. You don't know how many times Dad has just wanted to smack one of those guys. I manage to talk him out of it, but he's really had it. I want to make this very clear: *we have never intervened in your history*. We haven't done that. Your history is *completely* your history until the last seven days when Dad said, 'That's it, we're fixing this thing.'

"Then there's the guy in the White House now—who, by the way, is trying to blow up the world at this moment—who would like to burn books of real history, pillory honest teachers, and plow scientific research back into the Inquisition Age. You notice I didn't say Stone Age. That was actually a pretty good age because nobody had cooked up ideas about religion yet. It came soon after that, but the Stone Age was okay."

"I've told some of the friends I've made in the last days about my frustration. Why do you think I came back as Jesus? My mission was to tell people that they shouldn't be governed by sets of rules. They should forget all the stuff about hell and punishment and *religion*. But every time I come down here to try and do a little good and *undo* the damage religion is inflicting, there's always somebody around taking notes and turning everything I say into more rules, more religion, and more hatred. I've been exasperated for centuries, millennia. I hope that today—once and for all—that practice will stop. Well, I'm pretty sure it will because I think we've done a pretty good job of interfering this time."

The interference to which Jesus referred was much more than the disappearances taking place. Although the silos housing missiles armed with nuclear devices opened just the way they were supposed to around the world, nothing else happened. There were some puffs of vapor, some clicks and pops from the missile's innards, but nothing happened. The weapons just sat there. Other sites that were to launch airborne weaponry were silent. Submarines loaded with warheads rested peacefully on the bottom of the ocean. About 80% of their crews suddenly found themselves on land, with airline tickets for home in their hands. Of some 25,000 nuclear devices, not one detonated or left the ground.

TV networks began a lower-third crawl of news superimposed over the event from the Jesus Dome. "There has been a potentially catastrophic malfunction of our nation's offensive and defensive weapons systems," the crawl read. "We are receiving reports that there was a near-firing of 100% of America's nuclear devices. For some reason, equally unknown, none of those devices have become airborne or detonated in any way. An anonymous spokesman from the Pentagon said that tonight, the world narrowly escaped Armageddon. More on these news channels as information becomes available."

But everyone watching the broadcast remembered what Jesus had just said about the activities of George W. Bush and realized he had at last been stopped. Or so they thought.

CHAPTER 118

With his worldwide audience, Jesus was covering the bases. He was just finishing his appeal for the cessation of Christmas. "If you all choose to continue the holiday, take away Santa Claus, the star, the Wise Men, the Manger and all the religious connotation—because it's bogus. And then rename it *Winter Day Off*—and celebrate the end of having to waste a fortune on gifts you don't need in order to save capitalism through senseless spending. Can you imagine what I feel knowing that half of the world uses what they call my 'birthday' to go into debt from which they never recover?"

Surprisingly, this was one of the most enthusiastically received points he'd made thus far.

"Instead of exchanging gifts, exchange ideas, give thought to one another, study how to be kind and learn how to take care of the future. You don't have to be famous or rich or do spectacular things. You just have to do what I've said every time I'm here: think about how you'd like other people to treat you, and then treat them the same way. Think about what kind of world you'd like to live in, and then treat the world with the necessary care to have it that way. That's it. That's always been my message. Nothing more.

It was a remarkable fact that without help of translators, every viewer around the world was hearing the Jesus Dome broadcast in his or her own language. It was even more remarkable that those viewers were seeing the image of the person upon whom their religion of choice was based, decrying the existence of religion, calling upon his followers to think for themselves and to build a better world. Some viewers were seeing Mohammed, some Buddha, some Abraham, some Vishnu, and some Jesus.

"If anybody wants to add anything to that, or wants to go back to the books that have been written about my previous incarnations—whether it was as Abraham, Mohammed, Buddha or whoever—and try to shape rules and regulations and religions from what's been glommed onto my message every time, well, then you're heading the world back into the same mess it's been in.

"Keep it simple. See, the problem with turning everything into a religion is that it immediately stops thought. You go from thinking to memorizing. You go from figuring out individual situations and relationships to going through a list of do's and don'ts. It's voluntarily turning over your brain to someone else, rather than cherishing that organ that's been developed to this stage over millions of years. As soon as you do that, you stop progress. And trust me, watching what's gone on here for a few billion years, you don't want progress stopped. You've got a lot more progress to make."

As Jesus was speaking about the need for human progress, deep in a regressive wing of the White House, George was punching a pillow. A therapist told him long ago that punching was the cure he needed. It wasn't working. Feathers blew out of the poor object every time George's little fists pommeled it. Those feathers were getting soggy as venomous blasts of spray blew from his crooked mouth. No matter how many blows he landed, there was no release. At first, George was merely petulant. But as the magnitude of his failure dawned on him, he reached a point of horrifying rage usually reserved for Laura. In his defense, almost anyone would find it difficult to feel masterful proclaiming victory over the demise of a feather pillow when one's purpose was to destroy the entire earth in a radioactive fireball. But such was George's dilemma. Failure of that proportion was crowding out his usual trivial, pleasant, and exceedingly self-congratulatory thoughts.

A nasty symbol came into George's mind that frightened him. The trouble wasn't the little white passenger car rolling down the tracks. The horror was the big black choo choo train pushing and shoving the car toward a big cliff. In George's mind, that big black train represented the dawning realization that even though he had cooperated to the Nth degree with his handlers, even though he had been putty in the hands of the chosen few of the Illuminati— Skull and Bones, Knights Templar, Rosicrucians, Freemasons, Bilderburgs, Thules, Wolfe's Head and others—the promised vision of absolute power lay in ruins about him. Drugged as he was, the sham of his little white existence was clear. He was standing naked before the world as a fatuous, flabby Connecticut rich kid who was still trying to play the role of international cowboy with a Texas twang. His daddy was gone. His handlers were gone.

There was no one to pick up the pieces. Now the laughing would begin. He could hear it over the sound of the little white car as it was being propelled to destruction.

At that very moment in George's head a tiny red caboose appeared somewhere behind the big black choo choo. It was racing along the track rocking back and forth in the happiest way. It didn't look afraid. It looked determined and merry. And it rocked along the track straight towards the big black engine. And then like magic it hit the black engine and in one awful conflagration—made it disappear. Only the happy little red caboose and the white passenger car remained.

George knew what he had to do.

"Hon," it was the President calling down the hallway to the First Lady, "where is my special suit?"

Laura didn't answer. She had taken to bed with a sick headache. She had swallowed plenty of Oxycontin and Ambien so she wasn't saying boo.

George was weaving his way down the hall when he ran into his secretary Madeline Fontaigne who was exiting the Presidential bedroom. She stopped abruptly when she saw the very agitated and very medicated person careening towards her.

"Can't go in there," she said flatly.

"It's mah bedroom. Why not?" George was not in a mood for further humiliation.

"Because Laura is not feeling well and needs to sleep."

"So how the hell am ah supposed to get my suit?"

"Mr. President, your suits are not kept in the Presidential bedroom. Your suits are in the dressing chamber. What suit do you need?"

"Mah Victory Suit."

"Your Victory Suit?"

"Yeah, you know." George made an obscene gesture.

"Oh, *that* suit." Madelene Fontaigne looked disgusted. "It's in the basement."

"The basement?"

"Laura was embarrassed to have it in the closet. She had me take it down there."

"Well, get it!" George made another obscene gesture.

Madelene, her face grimaced in disgust, hurried off.

The suit in question was the green jumpsuit with the criss-cross belts and prominent genital pouch George wore the day he landed on the USS Abraham Lincoln to proclaim "Mission Accomplished."

By the time Jesus reached his concluding remarks, George had debarked from the Presidential helicopter at Andrews Air Force Base and was climbing into an F-16. He assumed the big bombs he saw under the plane were "nukulars." He took off and headed for Denver.

CHAPTER 119

Jesus was clearly relaxed. A person wouldn't have been wrong to feel that he was actually enjoying himself. Apart from the fact that the madman President was in an airplane with weapons he intended to use, everything was going according to plan.

"I'm feeling good tonight folks, because with about 10% of the world's population being moved to another resonance, this planet has a chance. Anyone here who still has any fear that they have been 'left behind' when I supposedly 'swept others up into Heaven' can totally take it easy. No such thing has happened. In fact, the idea of Heaven is just a myth. There are resonances, nothing else. People who were destroying the world, people who were causing misery, starvation, death, and wars have just been realigned so they won't cause your world further grief. They aren't being punished, they've just been removed. In their resonance there isn't the possibility of communication, physical contact or assembly. No sex, no meetings.

"Nearly everyone else—and I say *nearly* because there are still a few people to go—has shown the possibility of human warmth, kindness, or at least of obtaining it in time. You are being entrusted with the future of the world—without the interference of the impossibly greedy and cruel."

At that moment, as though he were answering the call of "greedy and cruel," a lone gunman appeared in the center aisle directly in front of Jesus. He shouted with almost superhuman volume, "Shut up Jesus, or I'll blast you to kingdom come."

Jesus was extraordinarily calm, considering that there was a 83mm SMAW MK153 Mod 0 rocket launcher pointed directly at him.

"Detective Darcy O'Neil," he said, nodding in recognition of the heavily armed man. "We meet again."

"Damned right we meet again, you frickin' prick." O'Neil was looking directly through the site as he spoke. "You're about to meet your maker."

"Been there, done that," Jesus said, finding some amusement at a peculiar time. "I think, Detective O'Neil, you've picked an unfortunate plan. I was actually hoping you'd come around. You had so many chances. You got to know Lyla and Marie at their house there on Staten Island. You got to meet Jerrod and me at the Stock Exchange. But I'd say that you have something of a learning disability."

"Shut up. I'm warning you."

"I have a few more things to say to these folks here, so I guess this is…" Jesus outstretched his hands towards O'Neil as the Detective triggered the spotting mechanism activating the rocket. An audible click was heard in the Dome as Jesus finished his sentence saying sweetly, "Good bye." And in full view of a world audience, an unsupported 83mm SMAW MK153 Mod 0 rocket launcher fell to the floor with a 16-pound thud. Detective O'Neil was gone.

There was a moment of silence, and then the applause in the Dome equaled earlier outpourings of approval.

Jesus/Mohammed/Buddha/Abraham/Vishnu waited for quiet to return. When it did he said, "I'll always be with you. My work on this trip is nearly finished. I've just got a few more things to do. The first of them is this." Jesus turned to his right. "Chandra Boolean, you might want to come to the stage." Jesus turned and watched as Chandra made her way towards him, then pointed to the back of the arena.

"Mommie, Mommie!" It was two small voices from the darkness. "Mommie!" Santee and Vertaine ran towards the stage holding the hands of their grandmother and their nanny, Felice.

The reunion of the courageous mother with her children was witnessed in person and on television by much of the world's remaining population. It brought most of that population to tears—that is, except in a certain house in Washington, DC.

CHAPTER 120

At the White House, Laura Bush, quite recovered from her headache, woke up. She rolled over and looked down at the floor where she let George sleep. He wasn't there. She checked the clock. It was way past her husband's bedtime. "He'd better not be at Condi's again," she whispered to herself as she staggered down the hall to Dubya's study, unaware that Condi was no longer a threat.

She pushed the study door open and felt an awful emptiness. George wasn't there. Had she thought to call Madeline Fontaigne, she would have learned that her husband left the White House in a helicopter wearing his famous jumpsuit. But Laura was in no state of mind to call anyone except the Secret Service. Shaking with fury she screamed into the phone, "Geowrge has run away again. Go to Condi's apartment and get him." And with that she slammed the receiver so hard that a pain shot through one of those hands so unaccustomed to practical use.

George Bush, desperately trying to pilot an F-16, managed to take off and had been airborne for ten minutes when both he and the plane vanished without a trace. The next morning, thirty thousand feet below, children arriving at Our Lady of Perpetual Admonition Elementary School near Pittsburgh, Pennsylvania were very excited to find a real Air Force helmet, a flight plan, a pair of boots, some gloves, and a green jumpsuit in their playground. They were puzzled though, when they found half a loaf of Wonder Bread stuffed into a protrusion directly behind the jumpsuit's zipper. A nun coming upon the scene wisely stopped little Jimmy Peterson from eating the rather misshapen staff of life saying, "It's been in a very bad place."

According to Dubya's flight plan, it appears that he believed the Liberty Bell was in Denver and that Denver was in New Jersey, and that the capitol of New Jersey was Philadelphia, and since the word Pittsburgh looked so much like the word Philadelphia, that's where he was when he tried to drop his bombs. But he disappeared instead.

Jesus was in swift cleanup mode. Laura Bush, owner of the throbbing hand, disappeared. Years of fashion speculation came to an end when it was discovered that all she left behind was her wedding ring and a lightweight plastic helmet encrusted with human hair. Mr. Blackwell had been right all along.

In Kennebunkport, Maine, George Herbert Walker Bush and Lady Macbeth Bush vanished while struggling over their part of a promotional ad for the conservative Hoover Institute. Disgusted by the false Christ on the television and enamored of yet another opportunity to extol the virtues of free markets and other wonders flowing on the great happy river of compassionate capitalism, George and Barbara Bush were trying to construct a sentence that praised wealthy American benefactors while stiffly condemning needy recipients of their charity. Babs was particularly concerned that nothing she authored could be construed as approval of what she called "sloth." The sentence, found on a scrap of paper lying between some unfashionable wing tips and a strand of enormous artificial pearls read, "Even though it may appear to you that these people are living in squalor, due to the largess of some of our friends and a number of their corporations, American indigents are really making out pretty well."

Jeb Bush left behind an incoherent Presidential Inaugural Address planned for 2012. It began, "I want to thank and praise the extraordinary wisdom of the members of the Supreme Court of these here United States…"

When Neil Bush's clothes were discovered the next morning, one arm of his shirt was stuck in the ATM of a savings and loan he was trying to rob.

Little needs to be said of the rest of the disappearances except, they worked.

In Denver, Jesus thanked everyone for coming and for watching on TV. "I said on one of my trips that I'd be with you until the end of the world. Well, I'm glad to say that together we've managed to push that a long way into the future. The people who were hurting you, ruining mankind and destroying the planet, are resonating differently now. You parents who have been missing loved ones, rejoice—the detention centers have been opened, your children, families and friends are safe, and each and every one of them will find their way back to you. All prisoners who've remained here have been released. None of them pose any threat to society, none of them will return to prison. Now I must go." And as quickly as he had appeared, he vanished.

The Jesus Dome spectacular was over. It was Day One on the new earth.

EPILOGUE

CHAPTER 121

Nine months later, Lyla Edwards, Marie Cattel, Snagg, Deemon, Chandra Boolean, Hogan Cafferty, Adam Brigante, Giuseppe Fognolio, Cardinal Vonsecco, Monsignor Popposi, Jerrod Parker and Helen Michaeljohn were sitting on the sand at Long Beach off the coast of Long Island. Nearby Santee and Vertaine were building a sand castle. In the middle of the group was a young man who looked enough like Chris Rock that several surfers called, "Hey Chris," as they ran past. He seemed pleased by the mistake.

"I tell you," he said. "That's so much better than everyone falling on their knees and starting to tell me their sins. That Chris Rock fellow has something going for him—and nobody is talking about starting a religion 'built upon his Rock.'"

Lyla, resting gently on Deemon's shoulder, laughed. "Jesus, you're a funny guy too."

"I have my moments. But don't write them down. Someone will want to put them into a book and make you memorize everything."

"Did George Bush really just go to another resonance like all the others?" For a moment, Lyla was hoping that the flames of Hell she'd heard about for so many years might be a reality.

Jesus blushed. "I was hoping you wouldn't ask that, Lyla. I guess now I'm the one with a confession to make," he said adjusting his dark glasses. "When it came to George, I took Dad aside and said, 'Look, you know that some people call you the *wrathful God.*' That made him laugh because it's so stupid. But I was hoping that He would be wrathful when it came to punishing Dubya. You see, there are some temptations even *I* can't resist, and messing with George is one of them."

"So did you switch his resonance?"

"In effect, yes. But switching him over didn't seem like punishment enough. I told Dad we needed to be creative, and He agreed."

"You mean like sending him to burn in Hell?"

"Uh, no, Lyla. There's no such place, never will be. Except…"

"Well?"

"I guess it depends on what the definition of Hell is."

"This is gettin' good. So what did you do?"

"Well, George *is* resonating differently, but there was one little addition. You see, he also… got *cloned*."

"You mean?"

"Yeah, he's literally going to have to live with himself forever. It was the worst thing we could come up with."

There was such a cheer from Jesus' friends that people up and down the beach turned to look.

"You know what's surprised me the most?" Marie was watching people walk by on the boardwalk. "You see all those people—and the billions of people all over the planet—in eight months, there isn't *one* who's said they miss someone who's disappeared. Not *one*! Not even the kids whose parents vanished."

Snagg agreed. "I thought about that. If someone was hurting the world, hurting the world's chances of survival, there's nothing to miss, right?"

"Right." Jesus tossed some bread to a hungry seagull. "The people who would have missed them, like that real estate developer's daughter who was always praising her daddy and who would have been all over the papers crying about his loss—those people disappeared too. She didn't really *love* her daddy, she loved what her daddy provided no matter how much he was hurting other people. You can't grieve the loss of someone who made the world ugly."

The newest member of the group, Helen Michaeljohn, traced her finger through the sand as she spoke. "You know what just amazes me? I mean, it shouldn't amaze me because I always was making jokes to the same effect, but it is astonishing that this government—the whole Washington, DC establishment—is functioning with only 12 Senators and 79 Representatives in the House! I start laughing every time I think of it. And Kucinich is Speaker of the House!"

"Back in the 60's," Marie said, "I thought the solution was just to get rid of everybody over 30. Your plan was a whole lot better, Jesus."

Jerrod, whose political education had been astoundingly swift, still wrestled with ideas that his stock broker self had taken for granted. "There's a few things I don't get, Jesus," he said. "I can understand things like Cheney being gone—pure evil, no contest. But we're hearing reports that confuse me. Like the fact that Castro is still in power in Cuba and has had an astonishing recovery healthwise? That's just plain weird to me. He was a totalitarian dictator."

"It's okay, Jerrod. You'll get all this in time." Jesus' wasn't the least bit condescending. "We had to look at the big picture. In terms of government and policy, who's been essentially right, who's been on the side of kindness, who's been on the side of fairness? Fidel Castro has been an amazing force for good. Naturally he's been demonized for years by some of the departed because he was anti-capitalist. That was, in the minds of the greedy power grabbers, the ultimate sin. But look at his legacy! Despite the embargos against Cuba he provided top-notch education and health care for the people of his country. The Cubans who hate him aren't the poor, they're the formerly super-rich who sided with the US-backed dictator, Fulgencio Batista. Same thing, by the way, with Hugo Chavez in Venezuela. I don't blame you for thinking that way, Jerrod, because you were fed such a load of lies by corporate media that it was virtually impossible for you to see clearly. Don't forget, I had the advantage of time and distance. I could see that the people lying about Castro and seizing on anything to claim he was a vicious dictator were equally blind when it came to seeing any fault with the real dictators who are responsible for the deaths and misery of millions, but who just happened to embrace capitalism."

Jerrod let out an astonished, "Wow."

"Enough with the politics," Jesus said with a mischievous grin. "Let's talk about some of the things that have *developed* since we were at the Jesus Dome. Anything you want to tell us, Hogan?"

Hogan blushed. "You know then?"

"Yes."

"Well everybody, since I've been put on the spot, I do have some very big news. Chandra and I have decided to get married."

"Congratulations, Hogan," "Way to go Hogan," echoed around the circle.

Chandra's smile was beautiful. "Like everything that's happened since November, it was meant to be," she said. "And when the children met Hogan, that was it. I think they would have wanted me to *disappear* if I hadn't said 'yes.'"

Hogan kissed Chandra and held her tightly. "I've never been so happy in my life. But… there is one thing I would like to know," he said, looking at Jesus. "I've tried and tried to figure it out and don't seem to be able to. Why, when Dobbin and the rest disappeared, why did I have the terrible feeling of hot air in my head, and why did it seem to help when I cursed? That's really troubled me."

"To be honest," Jesus said, not missing the humor of his saying it, "that was a little glitch in our system. You were present at the first mass disappearance, and you were the only person we left behind. The feeling in your head and the cursing to fix it came because with the huge release of negative energy as Dobbin and the others were shifted, you got side-swiped. That's the only way to explain it. It was no coincidence that you felt *hot air*. There'd been plenty of that released in that room by Dobbin! It took Dad and his team of experts nearly three hours to figure out what happened and get it fixed before the next mass disappearances. Sorry."

Jerrod couldn't help but smile. "I never thought I'd hear a confession from Jesus! That's pretty amazing."

"Nobody's perfect, but we try."

"Listen, that was a small price to pay for all the good that's come."

"Speaking of good," Jesus turned to Snagg. "I've got a feeling there's something you want to say too, right?"

"Adam, should we tell them?" Snagg was uncharacteristically shy.

"Sure."

Snagg put his arm around Adam's shoulder. "This has been really important time for us both—we've got more in common than we could have ever guessed. I think Adam's the most beautiful man I've ever met. And we've decided, uh, Jesus, if it's legal…"

"Of course it is."

"Well, Adam and I want to hook up—I mean get married—for the rest of our lives. I think we can be a hell of a team. Oh, sorry Jesus, I mean. . ."

Adam's tears trickled down to his huge smile. "This is beyond the best," was all he could say.

Jesus hugged them both. "You know you've got my blessing."

Jerrod Parker and Helen Michaeljohn were looking particularly joyous.

"What about you?" Jesus asked. "Don't tell me you're getting married too!"

Helen spoke first. "We think we may be able to give friendship a chance," she said. "After all we've been through, that's a big victory for us both."

"That should be a motto for this new earth, 'Give Friendship a Chance.' I like the sound of it." Jesus pretended to write in an imaginary notebook. As he did, he turned to look at Marie.

"What are you all staring at me for?" It was Marie sporting an impish grin. "Okay, look. Vonsecco and Popposi don't have to be celibate any more, Giuseppe doesn't either, so as I see it, maybe I can achieve a life's dream and become, y'know… an instructor!"

Lyla looked shocked. "Grandma!"

The men from the Vatican were the first to burst into laughter.

"It's a joke, sweety," Marie cried, enjoying turning tables and shocking Lyla. "I'm actually thinking of working with international groups finding homes for children orphaned during Bush's wars in Afghanistan and Iraq. And Fognolio, Vonsecco and Popposi here… well, tell us what you told me."

Fognolio, looking very much himself in casual clothes, was eager to answer. He signed and Vonsecco translated. "The three of us are returning to Rome. Since there won't be a Catholic Church as we know it, the Vatican will make a great museum—both a tribute to beauty, and also a huge warning for people about just how dangerous religion is. We have already been in contact with the Bishops and Cardinals who remain—they're all civilians now—and they are all in agreement. It will be wonderful to spend the rest of our lives telling people to use their good minds rather than obey someone else's instructions."

Deemon seemed as pleased by that news as anyone. "The Vatican!" he said, "I've always wanted to go there and see the Bernini pillars in St. Peter's. Maybe I'll get to do that now."

Marie, ever the proud grandmother, prodded Deemon to tell what he and Lyla were going to do.

"Well, now that it won't be necessary to get guys out of the country to escape the military, we're going to focus on finding housing for people. With all the disappearances, there is so much housing—a whole lot of it luxury housing—it shouldn't be too hard to get everybody a good home."

"And we're going to work on alternative energy," Lyla broke in. "Deemon has this great invention. Maybe now good ideas won't get blocked by the oil, nuke, and energy corporations."

"I can guarantee that," Jesus rejoined.

It was Snagg who turned the conversation back to recent events. "This whole thing with the disappearances and all—do you and your Dad really think it's going to work?"

"We hope so, Snagg," Jesus said running his hand over his shaved head. "So far it looks pretty good. All the people who thought profit should be the main thing in life have been given an alternate existence. The privately held wealth that people were fooled into thinking were governmental organizations like the World Bank, the International Monetary Fund, and the Federal Reserve have all effectively been destroyed because there is nobody left to run them. The secret societies that controlled the motion of currency and manipulated politicians like chess pieces—also gone. The criminal dynasty that has made itself available to the most malicious bidder is also gone. Can we have a moment of silence for the Bush Dynasty—that mom and pop and their litter of killers?

"It looks like the people now in charge of Washington want to make nice with Cuba, Venezuela, Chili, Nicaragua and other countries that think the people deserve something other than servitude. If the news was right this morning, North and South Korea are on the path of reconciliation. Iran, Iraq, Syria and Israel are discussing ways to coexist peacefully. The killers of Darfur are resonating differently. According to the papers, the US signed the Kyoto Agreement this morning."

"If everything is going to get better, then why did Obama win the election? He's already signaling that he'll just be Bush with a big smile. Isn't that going to wreck everything and start the whole mess over?"

"He was elected, we didn't have him disappear," Jesus said. "But you're right, he'll be a big disappointment. He'll do a little window dressing domestically, but he won't take advantage of his real opportunities. Dad and I just let him stay there as a sort of placeholder." Jesus stopped abruptly.

Marie looked disappointed. "Then who'll be the big turning point?"

"Now you want me to be a fortuneteller?" Jesus gave a funny little shrug. "It's going to take some time."

"Like in 2012, the end of the Mayan calendar," Snagg jumped in.

"It won't be the big change yet. Some other stuff will happen though. There will be some change in the magnetic poles and that will help clean up a lot of the pollution and will also stabilize earth's temperatures. That's a big change, but the biggest alteration of the United States and the rest of the world may take longer than that. You see, someone is going to emerge who is so honest, so charismatic, so forward thinking, so fair, that her election will be unanimous—and she is the one who will change America."

"Oh God."

"What Marie?"

"You don't mean Sarah Palin!"

"Hardly—in fact she got her own little altered resonation."

"What do you mean?"

Jesus seemed pleased to deliver the news to his friends, "Well, she sort of fell in the George Bush category so Dad said I could mess with her too."

"She got cloned?"

"No, in her resonance, only her voice was cloned. She's going to have to *listen* to herself 24/7."

Hogan slapped his knee. "Now *that* is what I call Hell."

"Sort of what I figured. Dad got a kick out of it."

"Back to the 'she' then—who is it?" It was Marie who pressed the issue.

"She's not on the national scene yet."

"But give us a hint. What is she doing now? Where is she?"

Jesus squinted into the sun in Chandra's direction. "I can't say more just now, but I'm pretty sure she's Black and that she'll want Chandra as a running mate. Now I've got a lot to do, but I don't want to waste these waves. Adam, you're coming in too. We're buddy surfing today, man."

Adam good-naturedly gave himself up to the arms of his friends, and together the hopeful future of the world ran towards the water. Jesus, his mission accomplished, reveled in his last day on earth… as a man.

CHAPTER 122

John Solomon, the cameraman who resigned from Babs Waller's *40/40* to voice his objection to that show's tolerance of racist speech, will be the cinematographer when the big screen feature of *Rapturous* goes into production.

THE END

ABOUT THE AUTHOR

Brent Buell is a theater director and producer.
He lives in New York City with his wife.

CREDITS

Cover Design: Putman Graphics
Back Cover Portrait: Basil-Malik
Stylist: Tianna Riley